July, 1956.

"Happy Landing", Monie dear,

Much love

from

Hattie

BELOVED

Books by Viña Delmar

BAD GIRL

LOOSE LADIES

KEPT WOMAN

WOMEN LIVE TOO LONG

THE MARRIAGE RACKET

ABOUT MRS. LESLIE

THE MARCABOTH WOMEN

THE LAUGHING STRANGER

BELOVED

Beloved

BY VIÑA DELMAR

Harcourt, Brace and Company
NEW YORK

With the exception of nameless people, no fictional characters have been used here. Everyone who bears a name bore it in actual life. However, no claim is made that this is a thoroughly factual account. Though authenticity has been held in high esteem throughout, invention and imagination, too, have played their parts in developing the life story of "the fascinating Benjamin."

LIBRARY OF CONGRESS CATALOG CARD NUMBER: 56-5336

PRINTED IN THE UNITED STATES OF AMERICA

One

THE STEPS OF THE CATHEDRAL

He looked at New Orleans with the eyes of one who would buy it if it pleased him. It had vitality, no denying that. True, it did not smell as sweet as Charleston. Its streets were filthy and the damp breath of the river carried the odor of mud and rot to every corner. It was a city that smelled of black sweat, of cargoes from all the world and of the roaring seamen who had brought them.

As he stood on the steps of the cathedral and watched the life of the city flow past him he was not insensitive to its fascination though he knew that New Orleans, like any experienced coquette, made a business of being charming. The well-dressed ladies in their carriages, the crisp cleanness of the slave women, the planters in town for that charming admixture of business with pleasure—he had seen all that before in another city. Here in New Orleans he was certain that the residents were very conscious of being picturesque and that their effects were arrived at after due consideration.

No ordinary errands had brought these people upon the streets. They were not on their way to market, office, or shop. This was not traffic. It was pageantry. This was the flower of New Orleans on daily parade. And none who witnessed could say it was not worth the viewing. The ladies were spectacularly gowned and quite unaware that Charleston would disapprove their bold display of bosom. They twisted their hair in complicated coiffures and wore satin and velvet as Carolinians wore

5

muslin. And he recognized that this elaborate show must be credited to the slaves. He gazed at the black women with interest. It was evident that among them were expert hairdressers and skillful guardians of fine materials. Here in this evil-smelling metropolis servants were trained as though for use by court ladies of France. It was wickedly extravagant and in an odd, unexplainable way it was exciting.

There was much that was exciting here: the swift, inquisitive glances of the young ladies; the cool, withdrawn look of the Creole men who walked with a grace of motion that would mark them anywhere as dancers and swordsmen. He let the young ladies see the frank admiration in his eyes but courteously avoided meeting the gaze of the men who called this city theirs. He could not afford to brew an antagonism. Tomorrow any one of these gentlemen might be his employer. If not one of these then some other, he thought comfortably. There was work to be had here. It was a great city, rich with opportunity and promise.

His mind turned to what he had seen in his first quick survey: the expensive residences, the busy shops, the theaters, even a theater in which English was spoken—a sure sign that Americans, though unwelcome, had come to stay. An invasion by barbarians was what the Creoles thought of their new neighbors. They did not seem to know that the face of the country was changing, that Americans were searching their land—exploring, settling, dying in the shadows of unnamed mountains and on the shores of distant lakes never before seen by light-eyed men. The expeditions moved ever west and faint indeed was the pulse that did not quicken at the thought of what lay beyond the safe and well-mapped places.

Why did I not choose adventure? Why did I never seriously consider exploration?

In his heart he knew that such was not for him. Victory over wind and wave or mountain held no allure. Neither forest or prairie called to him. Only a city offered the battle he wished to fight. Only a city offered the triumph he hoped to win.

And this shall be the city.

He was seventeen years old. His entire fortune added up to five dollars, but as he left the steps of St. Louis Cathedral he had made his decision.

I will make New Orleans mine.

He walked back to the house in which he had rented a room. It was an old house. The hallway and stairs were dark and airless and to pause there gave the effect of drowning in stagnant water. Someone on the Charleston schooner had recommended this house to him. A room could be had for almost nothing. And why not? All the foul smells of the city had doubtless also been urged to choose this address. The house itself breathed the odor of un-bathed generations and the walls remembered a thousand meals that had been eaten here. The courtyard cherished the memory of waste food that had rotted in the steaming heat of a Louisiana summer.

He had had no contact with the brand of poverty that leads to despair and filth. It was as unfamiliar to him as was a way of life that allowed for strong-backed Negresses to be wasted on dressing a lady's hair. He had known neither the rarefied heights of luxury nor the degradation that existed in this house. As he climbed the stairs he heard a baby wailing and he knew that it was a sick baby. It was certainly no house in which to expect a healthy one.

He entered his room and regarded with irritation the bags and bundles he had not unpacked. They awaited him in the corner where he had hastily thrown them in his anxiety to explore the city. Well, now he must put things away, create some kind of order if he was to live here.

Opening the wardrobe he remembered the landlady had called it an armoire. In French even unspeakably ugly objects assumed an elegance of name. Inside, a pair of boots confronted him. It startled him to see that they oozed with moisture and mold. He closed the door of the armoire, an unexpected fastidiousness seizing him at the thought of touching the boots. He walked to the bed and inspected the linen. It was clean enough, though limp and bodiless with damp.

There was a knock upon the door and the landlady pushed her way in. She was a woman with a coarse face and watery eyes. In her hand she held a newspaper-wrapped package.

"You requested me to bring sweet cakes from the market," she said.

"Yes, thank you. Put them upon the table if you please."

She did as he asked, removing for her own use the page of newspaper. "I think you will enjoy the cakes. They are made with brown sugar and grated pecans. Have you tasted such before?"

"No. I want to speak to you about—"

"Oh, and I wanted to speak to you. I did not write down your name and I have forgotten it."

"Judah Benjamin," he said.

She repeated the name and moved her finger foolishly as though making a memorandum upon the air.

"Madame, I wish you to fetch a broom and to tidy this room somewhat. Also, there are boots in the armoire that are not mine. Please take them when you go."

She crossed the room and opened the armoire door. Her watery gaze fixed itself upon the boots.

"Poor man," she said. "Poor man. It was the yellow fever, you know." She drew her shawl more closely about her. "It came last year again."

"He died here?"

She gave him a sour look. "Should I have placed him in the street to die? Of course he died here. What could I do? Even were I an unfeeling person I would have been afraid to have come near enough to dispossess him."

He looked at the hard face of the landlady and thought of the man who had died in this room. Who had brought him a sip of water or a cool cloth to ease the fever?

"It is the sickness of strangers," the landlady said. "They themselves bring it here."

He thought of the filth of the streets and he was silent.

"But the strangers keep coming," she said. "They pour into New Orleans as though living here was free. Especially the Americans. For years there has been nothing but the sound of ringing hammers as they build their mansions. And now we are giving them gaslight in public places and lamp posts in the street and water that can be drawn indoors in one's own home. With all that we provide, no wonder the Americans keep coming."

He smiled. "May I suggest, Madame, that the Americans already had these delightful innovations and have simply brought them here to share with you?"

"To hear them tell it one would think that was the truth. Braggards and liars and beasts, that is what I think of Americans."

"Indeed? And what did you think of the Spaniards?"

"The Spaniards are beasts, too, but—" and she raised her hand

as though to forestall interruption—"they are at least beasts whose
motives and thinking one undersands. Who understands Americans? Do you?"

"I think so."

"Really? And what is your nationality?"

"I am an American."

"Not so," she said and she stood eying with disbelief the blackness of his hair and eyes, the olive tones of his skin.

"I assure you that I am an American and, though it may be
shocking for you to contemplate, so are you."

She laughed derisively. "American! Twenty-five years ago when
Americans bought this soil my father said, 'They can make the
ground upon which this house stands anything they choose but I
remain French.' It was this very house, too, of which he spoke. He
had remained French through Spanish rule and I can tell you he
died a Frenchman."

"Very commendable. Will you get the broom?"

"And as for you—why do you say you are an American? I
promise you it will not further your prospects here."

"I say I am an American because it is the truth, but I wonder
why you do not believe me. Is my French so perfect, so fluently
spoken that—"

She laughed again, this time more loudly. "I wish to say that
though I doubt you are American I certainly do not suspect
you of being French. I think you are Turkish or Egyptian or Ara-
bic."

"I am from South Carolina."

"Your French—it is atrocious."

"I am crushed by your criticism."

"Perhaps you will find someone here who wishes to learn
English. You could make a trade with him of correcting each
other's errors."

" A valuable suggestion."

"But I will say this, Monsieur, you speak beautifully."

"You confound me. Did you not say I spoke atrociously?"

"I do not refer to accent now. I mean your voice. It is like a
bell."

"I thank you. Would you begin now to clean this room?"

She picked up the boots and set them outside the door. "I must
go downstairs and fetch a few articles with which to work."

"You are excused," he said.

But she did not go. She leaned against the doorjamb and fixed her weak eyes upon him thoughtfully.

"What delays you, Madame?"

"I am thinking about your mother."

"My mother?"

"Yes. Does she know where you are? Have you run away from home?"

"Are you mad? Those are odd questions from a sane woman."

"All the same I have been studying you. I judge you to be no more than sixteen years of age."

"Confine your efforts to your rooming house," he said coldly. "You have no gift for clairvoyance."

"As you say." She turned from him, implying with a deep sigh how extremely weary of lies she had become. "You are a man and you are an American. I will struggle to believe these things. Though perhaps they do not matter. Perhaps nothing matters in the end if only one is a good Christian."

He had been bent above the contents of his luggage. Now he straightened suddenly and faced her. "My regrets, Madame, for my inability to qualify. I am not a good Christian. In fact I am not a Christian at all. I am a Jew."

She cast a wild look about the room as though she expected the ceiling and walls to react to this disclosure. They remained intact, unmoved, and it may have been the first time in years that she had really looked at the room and seen that those walls and ceiling made up a most uninviting rental prospect.

"In all honesty these things are not my business," she said mildly.

"How true, Madame. I inform you of that which does not concern you only for my own comfort. It is hoped that you will thus be curbed from announcing—within my hearing—any opinions you may hold regarding those who are not Christians."

"I will get my broom," she said.

"A splendid idea."

He continued to unpack, surprised and annoyed to find how much he had brought. Books one must always have, of course, but he had not dreamed he possessed so many clothes. Carefully he handled the beautiful new shirts his mother and sister had made for him. He examined with pleasure the exquisite work that had been expended upon the tucks, the seams, the buttonholes. Where in this dim chamber could one lay such proud fellows? He opened a drawer, then closed it again and placed the shirts back in their white wrapping paper and returned them to his bag.

Could he hang his trousers in the armoire? Would they sprout fungus and mold? Who knew what could happen in this ghastly hole where men died of yellow fever and roaches crawled in bureau drawers?

But I am in New Orleans. What will happen here?

He wished the question had not occurred to him. He remembered that he had asked it of himself before. He had looked upon the face of another city and had asked the question. He did not consider the omen favorable.

Still, perhaps the question had no affinity for misfortune. It was possible that as a child he had asked it of his mother when their boat had docked on Charleston's shores.

And it is just as possible that I first asked it the day I was born. No doubt from my mother's bed I gazed with curiosity upon the Island of St. Thomas and asked the question: What will happen here?

There was a small growth of mildew in each corner of the room, so he stacked his books one upon the other beneath the table. His unpacking was completed. He was settled in this gloomy place, at least until his financial circumstances improved.

I will eat my cakes now, he thought, but he did not eat them. The ants had been more eager than he. They had been busily at work swarming up the slopes and into the sweet byways of their precious discovery. He did not disperse them. The cakes were lost to him but there was no reason to prevent their enjoyment by others. He drew his chair more closely to the table and watched the ants as they went about their business of living. It was interesting to observe, but a wave of drowsiness swept over him. After that it seemed to him that some of the ants wore velvet, that some had bright handkerchiefs around their heads, and that others walked with the haughty step of Creole aristocracy. The pageant differed little from that which he had viewed while standing on the steps of the cathedral.

Two

CHARLESTON

The West Indian island upon which he had been born was remembered only as a bright splash of color.

He remembered his mother's sisters, Penina and Sarah, and the heavy gold necklaces they wore. In dreams he sometimes revisited the homes in which his aunts lived and saw again the great, airy passageways and the sleeping chambers sweet with the scent of flowers and herbs. Always in his dreams the soft-footed servants belonged not to his aunts but to his mother.

His mother had no servants and no gold necklace. Still, upon her face was the same proud look of her sisters and she had a pair of gold earrings that flashed in the sun as she hung her washing out to dry.

That was what he remembered of the island. He was only five when they moved to Charleston. He knew it to be a fact that his father and mother had brought him, his sister, Rebecca, and his brother, Solomon, but in that first Charleston impression only the figure of his mother had a place.

An island-born child, Judah was not unfamiliar with the sights and sounds of shipping, but Charleston harbor was beyond belief, a spectacle to dazzle the eyes. Indigo, cotton, rice, nurtured by the black Carolina earth for the merchants of Europe. Sugar and coffee from the Indies waiting on the Charleston docks for transshipment to the great cities of the world. Sailors, slaves, planters, a riot of bustle and noise. Shouts and whistles and the rasping voice of the winches swinging the burlap-wrapped bales dangerously over the sapphire water but never failing to land them safely. The salt-encrusted ropes, the feel of the faraway, the wild desire to be part of such glorious activity. How could a small boy take time to sleep and eat in a city that had a harbor such as this?

Rebecca, his mother, answered the question. The harbor was not for him. Unless he was taken there by herself or his father he was to stay at home. Home was not like the harbor. It was dull, only a small wooden structure behind the store on King Street. But his mother's gold earrings were there and the fine china that had belonged to Grandmother Mendes.

"We must not fail here, Philip Benjamin," Rebecca said.

Philip looked at her with his dark, sad eyes. "My dearest, you fret yourself overmuch. We will sell our fruit. We will earn enough to live."

Judah and his brother slept in the small room off the kitchen and they heard the talk that passed between their parents.

"Philip, you must listen to me. Put the book away and listen."

"I am listening, Rebecca, only I was just now reading an inspiring message that George Washington wrote to the Jews of Charleston in 1790."

"George Washington's inspiring message will not support the children you have or the one who is soon to join them. I have a serious thing to say to you. We can keep our shop open but five days a week, do you realize that?"

"You have miscounted, my dear. We shall have six days. Only on the Sabbath will we close our doors."

"And I am telling you we have five days. Here you are not permitted to open your shop on Sunday. It is the law. If you sell your goods on Sunday you will be convicted of 'Profanation of the Lord's Day.' Only this week a glovemaker was convicted, so you see that we Jews have but five days to—in the name of God, Philip Benjamin, will you stop reading and listen to me?"

The world of the Benjamins was the fruit store and the house behind it. Judah went to school at the Hebrew Orphan Aid Society, which fortunately did not limit its enrollment to orphans.

In the spring the new child was born—a girl, and they named her Hannah.

"Rebecca, my love," Philip asked, "would you not like the child named for your mother?"

She shook her head. "My mother would want no namesake born behind a fruit store."

"But it is a good fruit store, Rebecca, and a wonderful child. Oh, Rebecca, soften your heart toward the life you live and the man you married. Let us give you what we have to give and do not hate us for having no more."

She turned her face into the pillow and wept.

"Philip, I do not hate you but you will not try, you will not try."

"I am only Philip Benjamin."

She swore there would be no more children, but the following year she was pregnant again. Her eyes were bitter as she scrubbed the store and sorted the fruit so that only the finest was offered for sale.

"Rest yourself, my dearest," Philip said.

"Rest myself! While you sit in the house reading?"

"There is a bell, Rebecca. It hangs over the apples, as you know. The customer rings, I hear, and in a trice I am there."

"Why don't you read in the store at least?"

"The passers-by distract me. Here in our home it is quiet."

All through the Sabbath he was busy at the Beth Elohim. He was an earnest churchman and a great adviser to those in the synagogue who suffered problems, a moderator in all theological disputes.

"I had a small controversy today with the rabbi."

"There is no such thing as a small controversy with a rabbi, Philip."

"Perhaps you are right. Perhaps I had what is simply the beginning of a very great controversy. I argued with him about the custom of Spanish being—after Hebrew of course—the language of our service."

She stared at him in bewilderment. "What then should be the language?"

"English, my dear. English! What is the language of this country? Is it Spanish?"

She sighed heavily. "Is the language of England Spanish? No, of course not, but in the synagogue of Bevis Marks in London we accepted Spanish without—"

He nodded impatiently. "Of course. Of course and why? Because no one dared ask questions. Why should Spanish be—"

"So that all will know who we are. We are Sephardim. Are we to speak German or Polish or Russian like the common Ashkanazim?"

"I mentioned English, if you remember, Rebecca."

"Very well then, English. If we use English who is to know that our people are as different from the rest of Jewry as a Scotsman is from a Scandinavian?"

"We are all Jews, Rebecca."

"Perhaps. But some are Sephardim and some are Ashkanazim. We were doctors, lawyers, statesmen when the Ashkanazim could not write their own names. My name was Mendes and I am Sephardic and when a synagogue no longer wishes to honor the great blood of Spain and Portugal then I will pray alone."

"Rebecca, almost all Jews in Charleston are Sephardic. You will not pray alone. My idea was as well received by the rabbi as by your dear self. But still my thoughts are held by others in different places. I shall continue to talk."

And as he continued to talk on the Sabbath to all who would listen Rebecca opened the store. She did a thriving business, for there was no competition. All the fruit stores of the neighborhood were owned by Jews and on Saturday no Jew but Rebecca Benjamin was at work.

When the last customer had gone she would walk across the little patch of grass to her house and fall sobbing upon the bed. Judah and Solomon would watch, not completely understanding, not completely sure she had a right to ask for forgiveness after what she had done.

She prayed aloud, pleading with a God whom she supposed was well aware of Philip's faults, a God who knew that money did not grow on trees, a God who above all else knew Himself addressed now by a Sephardic woman. She begged forgiveness for the sin of dealing in commerce on the Sabbath, for handling money, for having had no time for prayer.

"But where will the money come from if I do not open the store on Saturday? I am not a greedy, grasping woman as You know. I am a proud woman as my mother before me was a proud woman and I do not love money as some people do but I must have enough to feed my children."

The children grieved for her distress but they remained uncomprehending. They had not been hungry when the store was closed on Saturdays and—almost as important—they had not been obliged to apologize to their companions for Rebecca Benjamin's unorthodoxy.

God may or may not have forgiven her but Philip put an end to the Sabbath bartering.

"The store is mine," he said flatly. "There is no law by which any part of it is yours until I die. When you touch it or any object inside of it, it may be only with my permission. Open it once more upon the Sabbath and I will bring you into the courts and charge you with the crime of unlawful entry."

She looked into the face of her husband with wonderment. "Philip Benjamin, if you think for one moment—"

"I have thought for many a Sabbath, Rebecca. What I have just said is the result of that thinking."

After that the store remained closed on the Sabbath day and the children did not starve.

A daughter was born to Rebecca in the summer of that year— Judith.

"You have three daughters now, Philip. Have you thought how they will wish for laces and ribbons when they are older?"

"I have hopes they will wish for reverence and modesty, Rebecca."

She shook her head and the lamplight played upon the brightness of her earrings and they glittered richly in that plain, clean room.

Judah, at the table, making every effort to give full attention to his homework, was resentful of the gold earrings that caught his eye, resentful of the conversation that captured his interest. His parents, he realized, had long ago developed the comfortable belief that their children became unable to hear or understand the moment a subject unsuited to young ears was introduced.

"Philip, I do not know why a girl cannot have reverence and modesty along with some nice clothes and a few simple pieces of jewelry. I know of nothing that says position and wealth cannot go hand in hand with virtue."

"Granted, Rebecca, but I have a wish for the children that does not coincide with yours. I wish them first to worship their God and second to worship learning. If their minds are tenanted in this manner there will be no room for trivial desires."

She sighed. "God everyone must have. You have a way of

speaking that suggests that He is yours and yours alone. As for learning, my dear Philip, you are a learned man. Now tell me what it has brought you."

He got to his feet and walked slowly up and down the room. The scrubbed boards creaked even beneath the slim figure of Philip Benjamin. He walked to the window and stared out at the night without answering. Then he crossed the kitchen past the wooden tub in which clothes were soaking, past the iron stove and the rocking chair in which Rebecca sat.

He clasped his hands together and turned to her, answering at last. "What can I tell you, Rebecca? What can I tell you that will not insult you? You asked what my learning has brought. I may say to you now that my learning is very slight indeed, but for what it is I cherish it. I do not think you will understand if I tell you what it has brought me. It has been air and light and strength. I can only guess what it must be like to possess great learning. The very little I have has made me very hungry for more."

"You have not insulted me," she said, "but that is because you have not spoken all that is in your heart. You have not said that your books have brought you the only happiness you have ever known."

"I have not been a good husband to you, Rebecca, and you will notice that I have said 'to you.' By my thinking I have been a good husband. I am a religious man and I hope I have always been kind to you and the children. You have never understood that by my standards to clothe a family adequately, to feed it wholesomely, and to give of one's time and knowledge is to discharge one's duty thoroughly. But you—" he smiled thinly, "you were a Mendes and your sisters married wealthy planters."

She rose from the rocking chair and went to the tub. The clothes lying in their soapy water seemed to irritate her by their limp inaction. She plunged her arms into the midst of them rotating them violently, splashing suds upon her immaculate floor.

"The worship of God," she said, "we can leave out of this. I accept it as a necessity. After that I will take position and wealth as the natural goal. Learning is a splendid thing perhaps, but it should not fill a man's life so that he has no interest in making his way."

Philip Benjamin shook his head, not in argument but in despair.

"And, Philip, if you did not intend to seek success why did we ever leave London where we also had an unsuccessful business?"

"We left London for the same reason we left St. Thomas. I dreamed a foolish dream both times. I thought that in another place I would miraculously become the magnificent merchant prince you so desired. I will never dream that dream again, Rebecca. I am what I am. I accept it. Do you?"

Later, in the room off the kitchen, Judah lay on his cot and thought of what he had heard. In his ten-year-old mind he weighed the problem. His mother's materialism against his father's love of learning, and at last he slept, proud in the knowledge that he would scorn position and wealth if he were to be denied learning, shamed by the realization that learning without wealth and position would never be enough.

After that he thought often of the things that had been said that night. What exactly was position? He resolved to ask his mother. She was apparently an authority on the subject.

"How does one acquire position, Mama?"

She did not answer at once. She selected an overripe peach, split it, and after examining it carefully handed half of it to Judah.

"Position comes in many ways. Mainly through one's name."

"My name is Benjamin. Will that help me?"

She said, "Never forget that the family on your mother's side was named Mendes. Then of course position also comes from amassing wealth and handling it thoughtfully and charitably. If wealth is not inherited it comes from being better in one's chosen work than anyone else.

She bit deeply into the golden flesh of the peach and gave him time to consider all she had said.

"Were you wealthy when your name was Mendes?"

"Not wealthy but comfortable."

"Did you have slaves?"

She shook her head. "I lived in England. The English have no stomach for slavery. We had servants who were paid to wait on us. My father was successful enough." She touched an earring with her free hand. "My father gave me these. He gave my sisters the same but they do not wear them. They married money."

"Why didn't you marry money?"

"I was the youngest. My parents did not wish me to marry.

They wanted to keep me with them always. They did not write letters to friends and relatives all over the world describing my charms."

"That was fortunate for Papa."

"No. I was a bride who brought nothing. My parents were angry. Some girls of good families bring much money to the marriage."

"Could I have another peach, Mama?"

She said, "When I have just finished telling you that we are poor people?" She looked along the line of perfect fruit, chose one and gave it to him.

He munched it thoughtfully. "Money is very important, isn't it?"

She shrugged. "With it one can buy everything that is for sale. You see it has its limitations. Think well of those limitations. Remember it can only buy that which is for sale."

He lowered his eyes so that he could think more clearly. It was not easy to think while conscious of his mother's intense dark gaze upon him. Here was something to reflect upon carefully. In talking to his father she had not suggested that one could be wealthy and still unfulfilled. Why was that? Did a woman have two minds? One in which were brewed the thoughts that were to be served to her husband and the other in which her children's diet was prepared? Or did she disbelieve what she was telling him now? There were ways of discovering what lay beneath her words. Questions. There was nothing better than questions and if they were guilelessly presented one often penetrated layers of pretense and arrived at the truth.

He finished his peach and tossed the stone away. Careful now, the question must come as though it had little importance. It occurred to him that if he spoke of something else, drew her thoughts far afield and then returned to the main issue—

"Why doesn't the banana tree behind our house yield fruit which we can sell, Mama?"

"Charleston grows too cold to develop bananas properly, son."

"What is your favorite flower, Mama?"

"The japonica, I think."

"Do you think flowers are prettier than anything people can make?"

"Of course they're prettier."

"Would you rather have a bouquet of azaleas or a gold piece?"

She said, "What a boy you are for foolish questions. What would I do with a bouquet of azaleas?"

"And what would you do with the gold piece?"

"Spend it on something of course."

"Then you don't want the gold piece really. You just want what you can get with it."

"Naturally."

He pondered. "Then if *things* are important why did you send back to St. Thomas the gifts that came?"

Her mouth tightened. "I sent them back because I knew that they were packed for 'poor Rebecca.' I want nothing in the world so badly that I will accept it from those who give it to me pityingly. I am ready to say 'thank you' but never will I say it on my knees."

"Sister Rebecca wept for the blue silk you would not let her keep."

"I wept a little for the brown wool myself."

"I think you should have kept all four chests."

She shook her head. "I am not like that. I have pride and I can tell you that sometimes its taste is bitter but it never makes you sick."

He did not answer. He went out of the store to walk alone and to decide what among all the things that had been said was worth remembering.

As he walked down King Street people smiled and called a word to him. Abraham Moïse lounging in the doorway of his dry goods store said, "No school today, Judah?"

"I didn't have to attend the afternoon session, sir. They are studying English and history and I have completed those courses."

Mr. Moïse nodded approvingly. "That's fine. Fine."

Walking on the brick sidewalk with the Charleston sun shining, whistling a tune, skipping at times, running a little—life was wonderful. Only—only—please, dear God, no—but yes, it was happening. Mr. Moses Lopez, the revered founder and president of the Hebrew Orphan's Aid Society was calling his coachman to halt.

How can I speak properly with so esteemed a gentleman?

Should I bow? What shall I say? Will my tongue cleave to the roof of my mouth?

"Philip Benjamin's son, isn't it?"

"Yes, sir." His voice came but it trembled as he raised his eyes to the massive head and stern dark face that bent above him.

"Why are you not in school? Oh, do not bother. I think I know. They have no more to teach you, have they? You are now smarter than your teachers."

Judah managed a stammered reply. "No, sir. I—I would not dare to say that. It's—it's not likely that I'll ever be smarter than my teachers."

"Well said, though untruly. They are a hard-working pack of average-minded people. I heard you recite your lessons—" He paused and studied the small, upraised face. "Did you know I heard you?"

"Yes, sir."

"Tell me, boy, what will you do when you have completed this course? Your father has plans for you?"

"I have not asked him, sir."

"And you should not. He will tell you when he is ready to tell you." Mr. Lopez fell silent but he gave no signal to his coachman. Judah waited politely. It was not youth's prerogative to conclude a conversation. He stood attentively observing Mr. Lopez's elegant though rather outmoded clothes: the beautiful cascade of ruffles that fell from a snowy collar band, the embroidered vest, and expensive beaver hat.

"Pleasant holiday to you, young man."

"Thank you, sir."

"Oh, how do they call you?"

"Judah, sir."

"And you are ten years old?"

"Yes, sir."

"Well, ten-year-old Judah, you may tell your parents that Moses Lopez knows nothing in Charleston more promising than their son."

"Thank you, sir." Now should he bow?

The coach went on its way and he stood shivering in the sunlight. Had he been too forward? Come to think of it, what had he said? Perhaps he had conducted himself poorly and had shamed his parents. Would Mr. Lopez say at Beth Elohim, "The Benjamin boy has no manners"?

He walked on and the shivering subsided. There was so much to see in this wonderful, busy city. Even without a penny one could enjoy the sight of the vendors calling their delightful wares, everything from sugar candy to the succulent she-crabs. Pretty Mrs. daCosta in her spider-lace black shawl. Dr. De La Motta flashing up Beaufain Street to answer a call. The Seixas sisters in pink dimity admiring bonnets in a window on Princess Street.

"Judah, you're a man—" such flattery—"which bonnets would you like to see us in? The plumed ones or the others with the large, crushy bows?"

"I would prefer small bonnets for you so your faces may be seen."

"Spoken so gallantly that you must have a monkey-meat cake."

He went on his way chewing with contentment upon the cocoanut confection, so delicious to the taste despite its unappetizing name. Old Mrs. de Leon cautioned him that monkey meat would ruin his teeth and Mr. Cardoza said that eating between meals was a vice.

He walked so far that at last he met no people with whom greetings were exchanged. None of those whom he encountered now would be buried with services from Beth Elohim.

They looked upon him with kindly gray or blue glances. A little boy wandering harmlessly through the streets. No one hailed him with the sweet and heady wine reserved for such celebrities as ten-year-olds who had never given an imperfect recitation. No one knew that he had that very day conversed with Mr. Moses Lopez. And it came to him with sudden, awful shock that perhaps Mr. Lopez himself would not be at home here. He looked at the houses with their broad verandas and something within him responded to the serenity of the streets. He sat down beneath a catalpa tree and tried to remember all that his mother had said to him, but he could not think because there was a house across from where he sat, a house so palely blue that it seemed washed in moonlight. It was even lovelier than the soft coral shade of the one beside it, even lovelier than the delicate lemon hue of the corner mansion. The moonlit house was surrounded by wistaria and jessamine and the air was sweet with fragrance, and suddenly, for no reason that he could explain, he was aware of the living city of Charleston. For the first time it was not just the place where the store, the school, and the house stood. It was Charleston, South Carolina, and it was different from any other city, as one person is different from another.

I would know it by its looks, its smell, its sound, he thought with excitement. It's Charleston just as I am Judah.

It was made up of houses in soft, pale colors, of light-eyed people and of Mordecais and Avilas and Chumaceiros. It was dried fish roe and bene seeds and peach leather. It was flowers whose fragrance came straight from the gardens of Heaven. It was the most wonderful city in the world.

He walked home through the streets of the city that had just been discovered by Judah Benjamin, aged ten. His mother was bathing the newest baby, and he felt a pang of envy toward little Joseph, who all his life would be able to say "I was born in Charleston."

Philip came in from the store. "A melon the man wanted," he said in exasperation. "One melon, mind you, and for that I was interrupted in the midst of a most interesting conversation. I am glad you are here, Judah. You can listen with your mother. I was saying that the prayers should in some small way be altered."

"Altered?" Judah gasped. "The prayers?"

Rebecca nodded. "The prayers," she said. "Altered."

"But yes," Philip went on. "Why should we continue to refer to ourselves as a poor, miserable, homeless race full of woe and despair? Who could ask for a bettter country than America? A Jew who sits in an American synagogue and bemoans his lot is a base, ungrateful creature. I said to the rabbi—"

Rebecca groaned. "Not to the rabbi, Philip."

"Yes, to the rabbi. I said—"

"You will be expelled from the synagogue one of these days."

"Nonsense. I am for the survival of my religion and, mark my word, it will wither if it does not allow for new ideas and new lands."

Rebecca laid the infant on a towel and dried the chubby body carefully. "Philip, my American husband, the bell has just rung in the store. Another melon may be wanted."

"I heard. I heard." He moved toward the door, continuing

his conversation. "I shall be an American citizen one of these days, my dear. When I am, I shall be among the most fortunate men alive. I shall be an American Jew."

"When Papa is an American, shall I also be one?"

Rebecca nodded. "Will you like that?"

"Yes, very much." He noticed the troubled look upon his mother's face. "Don't you like America?"

She pinned a diaper in place and answered slowly. "America is well enough but England is home. Twice they have fought each other. How can I love them both?"

"I believe that you could—" He paused. "Papa is calling you."

She handed him the baby and left the room. "What is it, Philip?"

"Come, Rebecca, there is something I want you to hear."

Judah was aware of the strange note in his father's voice. Excitement, yes, but something else. It was as though the thing that he summoned his wife to hear would be unbelievable if merely repeated to her. She disappeared into the store and Judah, with his small brother in his arms, followed her quietly across the patch of grass and peered through the window. He could see three figures: his parents of course, and the third, when recognized, took his breath away—Mr. Moses Lopez. Then he had certainly given offense. If he could only remember what he had said as he trembled there beside the coach. In his nervousness it could have been anything and it had been enough to bring Mr. Lopez without much delay.

Softly Judah moved into the storeroom and picked his way between the baskets and boxes of fruit.

"Fayetteville," Mr. Lopez was saying. "Not a better institution for the purpose in the entire South. Christian clergymen are in charge but they do not seek to impress their religious opinions on others and they are very fine men."

"Fayetteville," Rebecca breathed. "How far away?"

"North Carolina, Madame. Very close by really. As I said, I realize your difficulties and it is my wish to finance this undertaking if you will permit. Perhaps by the time the preparatory phase is ended you will be in a position to proceed from there."

Judah hurried out of the storeroom. The baby had screwed his face into a very familiar expression. A wail was certain to follow. By the time the crisis had passed and Judah had returned the conversation had advanced.

"My choice is Yale," Mr. Lopez was saying, "but of course there's a great deal of time in which to think of that. Fayetteville first. Then Yale."

Yale? What was Yale? It was evident however that Mr. Lopez had not come to register a complaint. He was grateful that Mr. Lopez's visit had nothing whatsoever to do with him. Fayetteville. Yale. No matter. Words that doubtless his parents understood but which had no bearing on any matter of importance.

Three

NEW HAVEN

New Haven was not like Fayetteville, North Carolina. This was a northern city, strange and often incomprehensible. Voices and accents fell harshly upon the ear and the chilly reserve of New Englanders was dispiriting. His mother seemed to have been mistaken in her contention that good manners were identical in all spheres of culture. Here a cheery greeting offered to a passing stranger was more apt to bring a suspicious glance than a smiling return. The desire of the New England gentleman was obviously to have no bowing acquaintances whose antecedents were unknown to him. Proper introduction must of necessity precede even a remark upon the weather and introductions were not come by casually.

New Haven itself, tidy, prim New Haven pleased him. Its Puritan ancestry was apparent in every line and feature. It suggested a charming spinster, dressed in neat, gray clothes. No time for frivolity, no nonsense now. Earnest industry and unceasing piety, remember.

The strict theocracy of the city's beginnings were everywhere in evidence, and New Haven was almost—only almost—guilty of sin of pride, so great was her pleasure in the three churches she had recently built upon the green. The graceful construction of the new houses of worship spoke eloquently to a newcomer saying that New Haven, though properly occupied with honest endeavor, was not so stolid that she could not recognize architectural beauty when she saw it.

Judah, the fourteen-year-old freshman, viewed the New Haven churches and thought their simplicity a true expression of abiding faith. Was the architect a Congregationalist, an Episcopal, or only an artist?

The maple trees were the pagans of the city. They were beginning to flame scarlet and shimmer with gold, an incongruous note on a sedate New England landscape where even the sun dared not beam as brassily as upon the South.

It is appealing. I like it. What will happen here?

Yale itself was a world separate from the city of New Haven though not less stern of countenance. This was a temple of learning and he an ardent devotee bringing here his hopes and his ambitions.

Students lived in small, well-kept boardinghouses. His was owned and managed by a white-haired widow who was reputed to be a cook of amazing capabilities.

Six other young men lived in the house. On the second floor there were three in a large front chamber and two in the rear. The third floor had two small bedrooms—Judah in one and a tall, loose-jointed lad with surprisingly friendly eyes in the other.

His parents are also poor people. They can afford only a room such as mine. Shall I speak to him? Perhaps he feels as strange as I.

An hour later he was grateful that he had repressed the impulse. How ridiculous he would have appeared, for he discovered that his neighbor was a sophomore. Two others in the house were also sophomores but even the other freshmen knew each other and had an easy intimacy with the upperclassmen. They all had had the same preparatory schooling. They knew each other's families, and their conversation at the dinner table was of mutual friends and shared experiences.

The one with the friendly eyes was named Bacon. He nodded to Judah and kept him supplied with salt, bread, and condiments. It was well that he did for the boy felt such an intruder that he would not have asked a simple favor of any. None save Bacon had acknowledged his presence.

When the food had been passed by a waitress in neat blue cotton, the widow herself entered.

"Everything satisfactory, gentlemen?"

A buck-toothed young man spoke up. From the conversation

Judah had learned that this man's father and elder brother both were Yale graduates.

"I don't find it satisfactory," he said. "I'd like a word with you."

"Certainly."

He left the table and stood talking in low tones with the widow. She shook her head, shrugged, spread her hands, in short denied all responsibility for whatever defection it was with which he charged her. As she departed for the kitchen she said, "I take what I'm assigned. I have no choice. It's not my fault."

Bucktooth returned sulkily to the table. "It's a disgrace," he said. "I never expected such a thing to happen here."

Bacon leaned across the table and spoke to him sternly. "Don't be a child. You're a Yale man now."

"That's just the point. At Yale one would expect that—"

Bacon said, "You'll feel better about the whole thing when you've thought it over."

One of the others wheeled suddenly on Bacon. "Why do you live on the roof this year? Why don't you come downstairs with the crowd?"

Bacon smiled. "My room is fine, thank you."

Bucktooth spoke up again. "He has to live cheaply this year. His old man stuck a wad of money into—"

Bacon said, "Be quiet."

"Well, my old man's done the same thing. That's how I know."

"If you really know I'll thank you not to mention it just now."

"Oh, very well." It was clear that no one opposed Bacon very strongly.

When he had finished the large piece of pie that had been set before him, Judah left the table. He said no word as he departed. To excuse himself would have been absurd. He would not be missed.

He closed himself into his cubbyhole of a room and reflected, rationalizing the situation, preparing to accept whatever lay ahead. He was aware of his crime. He was guilty of being an outsider. He was not one with the others and they had not a Southerner's talent for quick friendships. It would take time. If only someone from Fayetteville Academy had matriculated at Yale then. He broke off his train of thought abruptly. What possessed him? For what reason had he entered Yale? To open social avenues for himself? Of course not. He looked about his small room.

armless nonentities, but they had been enlisted and drilled
young man with the buck teeth.
er the summer," Bucktooth said, "I'm going to train a
y to enter Yale next semester." He had finished his dinner
as in a mood for banter.
onkey?" someone prompted.
y not? It will not be hard on the little fellow. He will be
ck-skinned that he won't object to being where he is ob-
y not wanted. Certainly Yale will have no objections. They
verything. They take children and they take—" He leaned
the table and peered at Judah. "Do you know you ate
tonight?"
ry kind of you to have noticed."
always notice you, Benjamin. You interest me."
ere was laughter, the perfunctory laughter of people who
ipate the great amusement to come.
Vhy did you choose Yale, Benjamin?"
was recommended to me by one who admired the institution
eatly that he advised me to overlook the type of person
might be encountered here."
he young man with the buck teeth jumped to his feet. "You're
ng for a thrashing, you know. I can't punch a baby but I can
k one. How would you like to have your backside turned up
a strapping?"
dah felt a sickening wave of fear rise within him. For a
ment he did not recognize the sensation. It was new and it
awful, the dryness of the mouth, the icy prickling of his skin
desire to run.
Vhy did I answer him so impudently? Why did I not ignore
a or give him a soft answer? But if I had done so, would I now
happy? No, I would be ashamed instead of frightened, and
t is misery, too.
The dining room was swimming before him and he wa
mbling, but he rose from the table.
"If you wish to thrash me, come do it—if you can."
They stared at him, all six of them, and there was silence i
e room. He could hear the rapid thud of his heart and th
kening fear within him had not abated. There would be pai
en the strap fell upon his bare bottom and he prayed that h
uld not cry out for mercy.

It was as clean as any room in his mother's house. His trunk and
his possessions were here, a good fireplace in the corner of the
room, a chair, a table, a chest of drawers, a lamp. What more did
he need?

There was a sharp rap upon his door and there stood Bacon
with a pleasant smile.

"May I come in? My name is Francis Bacon."

"Oh, do come in, please. Yes, I know your name. I caught it in
conversation. I am Judah Benjamin. Sit down. Take the chair. I
will sit upon the bed."

They seated themselves but words did not come in a brisk interchange. There was a reticence, a slight discomfort evident in
Bacon's manner.

When he spoke it was hesitatingly. "I—I would not make a
point of this matter, Benjamin, except that it was raised at the
dinner table. I was able to control it then but it will be mentioned
again and if you know about it—well, you may be saved embarrassment.

Judah was puzzled. "I don't understand."

"Here in New England there has been a recent upsurge of—I
mean to say there are organizations being formed. They are new
but quite popular and most of our well-known people are putting
money into—Benjamin, it's a cause which will work for abolition."

"Abolition of what?"

Bacon stared in wide-eyed disbelief. "Abolition of slaves, Benjamin."

"Oh." Judah considered the matter. "I never heard of such a
thing. How does the organization function? What does it intend?
Abolition means to do away with, to destroy. Your father wouldn't
kill the poor creatures, would he?"

Bacon's eyes flashed but his voice was steady. "I said abolition of
slaves, Benjamin, not of Negroes."

"Your pardon. I see you thought me facetious. Truly I did
not understand. This is a new idea to me and one that seems
as practical as abolishing horses—your pardon again—I mean as
practical as abolishing the necessity for horses to work."

"People are not horses, Benjamin."

"This is incontestable. Actually I own no horses and no
slaves."

Bacon smiled his pleasure. "I congratulate you on having your conscience clear of such a weight. Of course my principles would permit you a horse."

They laughed together, Bacon sobering to remark, "I would not have you insulted in case you or yours were slaveholders."

"You are very kind, Bacon." There now, that was better. They had laughed together. Oh, it would take time but New England reserve would yield eventually and there would be conversation and cordiality. Already a pattern was beginning to form. Bacon would be his friend and gradually the others would accept him, too. It required only patience. Even now he felt comfortable enough with his visitor to inquire into the strange incident that had occurred in the dining room.

"That young man whose father and brother are both Yale graduates—" he began.

Bacon said, "The same is true of myself, by the way."

"Really? I wanted to ask—what dissatisfied him at table? What was he scolding the landlady for?"

Bacon flushed hotly. "Benjamin, I entreat you to put the matter from your mind. He is immature and overtalkative. A good chap who has not yet come to terms with his deeper self."

Judah averted his eyes from Bacon's unhappy, red face. "This is more distressing to you than to me, I know, but since I have so awkwardly blundered into this we must complete it. His displeasure was caused by my presence, I see. Is it that I am not a Christian?"

"He will forget by tomorrow that he has even mentioned it."

"Will he?" Judah considered. "Tell me, Bacon, have you ever known a minister well enough to ask a question of him?"

"My brother is a minister."

"Then ask why it is that the men closest to God can accept and even respect those of another faith while the ordinary churchgoer, who professes to esteem the beliefs of his minister, will often be a narrow-minded bigot?"

"My brother cannot answer that question," Bacon said. "He has often asked it of himself and of my father."

After Bacon had gone Judah stretched out upon the bed and determinedly kept his mind upon the fact that after all he was where he had wanted to be. For four long years every deed, every thought had been directed toward this day. He was at Yale. That

much had been accomplished because had recognized the unimportant things he must do the same.

        •

He worked even harder at Yale than at year-old freshman held a position that To be an average student was insufficie unfalteringly demonstrate for faculty an quality of one's mind.

The Reverend Jeremiah Day, presiden to the study of his red brick house.

"I wanted to see you, young man. I' you."

President Day was a heavy-set, gray-l faultlessly-fitted black broadcloth. His voi pulpit inflections. His commanding manne thought President Day could easily foun garner a million converts if the fancy seized

"So you are from Charleston? A magni since I have had the pleasure of visiting it its beauty and charm. Tell me, young man, from us here in New Haven?"

Judah swallowed nervously. "Sir, I am taki

"Oh, I know your courses. It has, howev servation that Latin and logarithms fade fr college days are done. What are we teaching through later life? What are we giving y in building your character, that will accom long, weary years, giving you strength and cour

Judah raised his eyes to the comfortably rou dent Day. "Sir, I am learning how to bear my b

"Good. Good. Excellent."

The major burden was the young man wi Three times a day Judah sat at table with him wondering if the ordeal could be avoided.

Could I live without coming to the dining ro myself on bread and cake upstairs? What a di make to me if I never had to see him. The oth laughed at his jokes could be endured. In ther nothing, only garden variety sycophants. Alone

been h
by the

"Ov
monke
and w
"A
"W
so thi
vious
take
across
pork
"V
"I
Th
antic
"V
"I
so g
that
T
aski
spar
for
J
mo
was
the
V
hir
be
th

Bacon said, "This will make trouble for everyone. Seat yourselves, both of you."

"What? Let that little Jew bastard think I backed down? You
know I can turn him up across my knee if I want to, don't you?"
Bucktooth looked at each of his friends in turn. They nodded,
smiling a little at the intensity with which he asked the stupid
question. "And you know it, too, don't you, Benjamin?"

Now all I have to do is agree and the fear will go away. I can
stop trembling. If I only nod my head all will be well again. But
if I do I cannot live with him at all. I must do what I know to
be ridiculous so that I can survive in this place which is more
his than mine.

"Benjamin, I asked you a question. You know, don't you, that
I could break you in two if I wished? Say it, say that you know
it to be a fact."

Judah shook his head. "I do not know it to be a fact at all.
There was a little Jew bastard named David who slew a giant."

And now Bacon laughed and the other spectators followed his
lead and there were cries of "Sit down"—"Forget it" and the
white-haired widow came bustling in from the kitchen.

"I'll have no bad language, gentlemen. I heard a word which
I will not tolerate in my house."

And the moment of danger was gone. It will return, Judah
cautioned himself, it will return. Only next time I will be no
stranger to fear.

Bacon came to Judah's room again that night.

He said, "Benjamin, he's not really a bad fellow. He's only
high-spirited and light-minded."

Yes, and he comes from your school, Bacon, and will probably
marry a female relative of yours. Aloud Judah said nothing. He
stood regarding Bacon with solemn eyes.

"Benjamin, it's hard for you at this moment to believe it but
he is at heart a splendid chap."

Judah sighed. "Convince me, Bacon," he said. "Convince me."

The freshman year ended and Judah was fourth in his class.
He had always been first at Fayetteville Academy. He would have
to work harder, that was evident. He would have to discover what
demon of incompetence was interfering with his mental processes.
Fourth. A disgraceful report to carry home to Charleston.

He had made friends with two Ashkanazim cousins who lived in another building. They had introduced him to a group in which they had found acceptance. He could visit now and enjoy conversation and congeniality. He even found himself joining in mild pranks and feeling at times the giddy delights of being young and free. He longed to move from the white-haired widow's, but there was no space available other than that which had been reserved for him.

No longer did he dread the sophomore year that loomed ahead. He could live now at Yale, even in a house with hatred. Even there God had provided hope in the form of Francis Bacon.

The second year at Yale was pleasant enough if one was accustomed to slights, if one had anticipated being greeted at table with an insulting "So they let you come back again." Well, there was Bacon and there was the house of the Ashkanazim. Above all there were the lecture halls where one could sit in ecstasy, drinking deeply, seeking to satisfy the thirst for learning that was never completely quenched. There was the debating society to sharpen wits and tongue. And there was the prize that came unexpectedly, bringing profound pleasure—the copy of Berkeley's *Principles of Human Knowledge* inscribed by President Day in token of "excellence in scholarship."

The junior year was the one which he was to remember, the one, in truth, which he would never be able to forget.

"So you're back again, Benjamin? Strike me dead, I thought everyone would have had enough of you by now."

Judah did not even glance at his tormentor. Judah was sixteen now, taller and heavier than the boy who had feared a strapping.

Bacon said, "It is a very fine thing that Benjamin is back. Your class will be well remembered for having graduated with him."

The pale eyes of the ancient enemy came alive. "I hadn't thought of that. We graduate with Benjamin, don't we? What an honor that will be! If only I had trained that pet monkey our class could be the most diverse in history. It would be composed of gentlemen, monkeys, and Jews."

Bacon said, "Why do you persist in making yourself obnoxious? Has Benjamin done anything to you?"

There was a long silence and Judah watched the pale eyes cloud, brighten, and cloud again.

He is thinking. It is an effort for him but he is thinking. One can watch as he does it the way one can watch the moving lips of a man unfamiliar with reading. Yes, he is thinking and he is evolving something in that wooden head.

"Come now," Bacon urged. "Has Benjamin done anything to you?"

"Yes."

"What has he done?"

"I am not yet ready to say. You will know when I am ready."

Bacon smiled gently. "We have all done something to our fellow man, I suppose. Even unwittingly we offend. Benjamin's offense, if any, has been small and unintended, I am sure."

"Don't be so sure, Bacon. Even people like you can be mistaken."

Bacon's gentle smile did not vanish, but Judah had seen evidence that behind the pale eyes of the buck-toothed young man thought was laboriously shaping itself. Through the autumn months he was conscious of the new attitude of the second-floor men. They taunted him no longer. They ignored him and when their eyes met the glances were baleful rather than contemptuous.

In December he knew what it had all meant.

It was on a Saturday and he had been at the library. Three books for which he had long waited were now his for a time and he hurried home anxious to devour them. As he reached the second floor he was aware that the doors of both chambers were open and the rooms unoccupied. Yet he heard the voices of his housemates. They must be on the third floor. No doubt they were in Bacon's room. That was odd in itself, for Bacon's room was too small for entertaining. Still, it was not a matter of great interest. He climbed the next flight to the third floor. They were not in Bacon's room.

They were in his room, all six of them. Like locusts they had descended, crowding into the tiny space. The drawers of his chest were open, his belongings scattered, the corners of the rug turned back. One was searching beneath his bed, another behind the curtains, the others pawing through his possessions, while Bacon, the senior, stood frozen-faced and disapproving against the wall.

"What are you doing?" Judah demanded. "Get out of here. All of you."

Bacon said, "I entreat you to be calm, Benjamin. This is a search to recover stolen property. They think you—"

"We don't *think*. We know. Who else is responsible for the fact that all this semester things have been disappearing? We've lost watches, knives, money, jewelry of all descriptions. Only this morning I lost thirty-five dollars while I was absent from my room."

And as though seized with sudden inspiration Bucktooth grabbed Judah firmly and thrust his hand into the boy's pocket. When it emerged it held a small wad of bills.

The others gathered into a close knot as the money was counted. Thirty-five dollars.

"You had it in your hand all the time," Judah said. He looked at Bacon. "He had it clutched in his hand. Truly he did."

Bacon did not reply. His face had whitened and he stood staring at Judah, his eyes full of pain and disappointment.

The boy with the buck teeth grinned. "Do you believe me now, Bacon?"

And still Bacon did not answer.

"You are a pack of filthy rats," Judah cried. "I did not steal that money and I know nothing of your watches. It was simple to keep the money concealed in your hand and to—"

"All right then. Open your trunk if you dare. Let us see what's in there."

"Why don't you open it? You've had no compunctions about—"

"It's locked. You have the key, Benjamin."

Judah took a step toward his trunk and raised the lid.

"You see it is not locked."

They converged upon the trunk, leaning over it, their heads and shoulders disappearing as they searched through the garments for which there had been no room in the wardrobe.

"My watch!" somebody shouted.

"And mine!"

"Here's a pocket knife. Whose is it?"

Judah pushed forward and they stepped away from the trunk so that he might see for himself what they had turned up. Three gold watches, one with a diamond-studded fob, a pair of silver-backed brushes, two pocket knives, and a ring with a purple stone.

He looked away from the trunk and addressed himself to Bacon.

"The trunk though unlocked was not opened. Wouldn't it have been natural to open the trunk considering that no delicacy restrained these hyenas from searching the chest of drawers? Why wasn't the trunk opened? I will tell you. It was because they themselves had placed the supposedly stolen articles in my trunk and they wished to establish this as an impossibility and so they claim that it was locked."

"I thought it was locked. Just before you came I tried to open it and couldn't," Bucktooth said.

"Yet," said Judah, "it opened at a touch of my finger."

"Naturally it did. You have a trick with it, a secret combination."

"Of course," said Judah sardonically. "Bacon, do you believe this charge against me?"

Bacon turned slowly to face him. There was a film of moisture in his eyes, a trembling of the wide, pleasant mouth. "I must believe what I see," he said in a low voice.

"You cannot even consider that I have been the victim of a rotten conspiracy?"

"Benjamin, I cannot conceive of people plotting so despicable a scheme as you suggest. Especially not these chaps. I have known them always. I know their families."

Judah said, "Every villain is well known to someone, Bacon. Your friendship with them and their families scarcely renders them unable to perform a deviltry."

"But what would be the sense? It is too evil to be named a prank. It isn't an amusing game. Would you expect me to believe that it was done in pure malice by young men whose families are among the finest in New England?"

Judah looked hard at Bacon and then his eyes went to the others and he knew there was no more to say. For the more he looked the more he saw that they were alike. They bore upon their faces tribal characteristics as plain as a savage's bright paint. They were united and strong and no one from the outside could shatter the bond that held them. Only a crime against another member of the tribe could be recognized. A plaintiff from afar did well to save his breath.

"Will you go now?" Judah asked. "Will you take your watches and gimcracks and leave my room?"

Bacon soberly bowed his head and departed. The others made no such move.

"Leave, is it, Benjamin? Oh, no. We have a matter to discuss. Do you think we're going to permit a thief to roam Yale at will?"

So that was it. At last they had arrived at the point to which all their contriving had been directed.

"We don't want you expelled, Benjamin. We don't want to ruin your life. We just want you out of here. This matter is known only to us in this house and it will go no further providing that you leave Yale."

He made no sound though there was rising within him a hysterical need to shout or to weep.

"Just go, Benjamin. Go quietly, explaining that you're tired of Yale or anything you want to say. We'll never tell on you. Just clear out. That's all we ask."

"And leave behind the story that I am a thief!"

"We'll never tell a soul."

"Your magnanimous offer is more than I can accept."

And suddenly he was running down the two flights and out upon the winter streets of New Haven. Under the cheerless skies, past the bare trees and the mounds of grayish snow. He sobbed as he ran and had no consciousness of the stares of other students who saw him flying coatless down the street. He never stopped running until he reached the red brick house of President Jeremiah Day. The maid who opened the door was brushed aside once she had parted with the information that the President was indeed at home. Blindly Judah forced his way past her and into the study where sat the Reverend Jeremiah Day and three faculty members all placidly sipping tea.

"Upon my soul, what's this?"

"Judah Benjamin, sir."

"Yes, yes. I know who you are. What are you doing here? You burst into this room, young man—"

The tea things tinkled a reproachful obbligato to the complaint of the maid who spoke from the doorway.

"He pushed me, sir. I told him he had no right—"

President Day's face darkened. "You may go, girl. Now then, Benjamin, what impudence is this? How dare you force your way in here?"

"I have been accused of stealing, sir. The men in my house

placed their own belongings in my trunk and pretended that I robbed them."

President Day set his tea cup upon its saucer and leaned back in his chair. Judah was aware of the bright blaze of the fire, the dark woodwork, the faculty members who sat motionless and silent. Most of all he was aware that President Day, who should have risen in avenging wrath, seemed not to appreciate the outrage. He was not responding in righteous anger to the terrible injustice brought to his attention.

"This is a dreadful thing of which I am accused, sir."

"Do you know that you have broken into my house?" President Day asked at length.

"Your pardon, sir. I am not thinking very clearly. I have been accused of stealing. I—"

"That will be considered on Monday, Benjamin. Just now—"

"Monday! It must be considered now."

President Day leaned forward, a frown of displeasure on his face, his gaze cold. "Must? A strange word to use to me, don't you think?"

"But this is an extraordinary thing which has occurred, a monstrous thing that—"

"And do not address me in that tone. Lower your voice and show respect for me and the other members of the faculty here present."

The gentlemen mentioned stirred slightly in their chairs as though to prove their presence or to acknowledge gratitude for being noticed.

"I intend no disrespect but, before God, I am not a thief and only you can help me."

"Without facts I cannot help you. I will have those facts on Monday."

"It cannot wait till Monday. I am accused of thievery. Can you understand what that means?"

President Day said, "I may tell you that I like your manner not at all. I am, at the moment, not considering this thing that troubles you. I am considering something that troubles me. What shall I do with a student who forcibly enters my house and my study and speaks to me in a manner that—"

"Forgive me, sir. I can only say again that I am so troubled by what has occurred that I am scarcely responsible."

President Day said, "You are responsible, Benjamin. If you are
not, then you have no business being at Yale. I will tell you what
I think. I think you are dramatizing that which is nothing more
than an acute case of injured feelings."

"Indeed, sir, an acute case of injured feelings. I have been
accused of thievery."

"You have already told us that. Who are these base characters
who have accused you?"

As he recited their names Judah was conscious of the weakness
of his position. How could President Day judge them any differently than Bacon had done? How could President Day know
what these boys and their buck-toothed ringleader were like
when they were not in the august presence of their masters?

After a moment of silence, a sip of tea, a polite clearing of the
throat, President Day spoke. "I think," he said, "that this is a
prank that went sadly astray. Somehow it got out of hand. Surely
it was never intended to be a serious threat to your security or
welfare."

"Sir, they told me to leave Yale. They told me—"

"Are you sure you understood the intent correctly? Have you
somehow missed the point of what was only a practical joke?"
Judah did not reply and President Day continued in his rich,
booming voice. "It is my guess that you have small understanding
of those who indulge in simple foolishment. I assure you that
standing aloof has its faults and student merriment its virtues."

And Judah found himself suddenly cold with anger.

"No doubt you are quite correct," he said. "I have missed the
point of a practical joke. Now let us see if you can perceive its
subtleties. For more than two years simple foolishment has revealed itself in discourtesy and insult. Today Francis Bacon, who
befriended me, has been deceived and thinks me a common thief.
Student merriment reached its climax indeed in its attempt to
deny me further education and to strip me of my good name."

"Benjamin, I'll not be shouted at. You may withdraw."

"This is not what I expected of you. In your exalted position
you should be understanding and merciful. You should be sensitive to a student's distress. You should be willing to call the others
here forthwith and thresh the matter out."

President Day rose to his feet. "The question of your guilt or
innocence is not at issue in what I have to say. Of insolence you

stand convicted on a dozen counts. You are hereby suspended,
Benjamin."

"You mean that I am expelled?"

"I mean that you are suspended. That is what I said, isn't it?"

"It is what you said."

"Then leave at once. I am being generous only because of your
extreme youth."

"To leave without a hearing will brand me as a thief."

"I think you are exaggerating the importance of that incident.
Your attitude is what disturbs me. Your singular manner of address to me and to the esteemed members of the faculty is a
matter of grave consideration." President Day raised his tea cup
and across it he looked at Judah. "Go now," he said. "I will
consider the matter. If you are reinstated you will receive a letter
in due course."

"Am I to return to my home in Charleston?"

"That would seem sensible, wouldn't it?"

"It would seem final," Judah said.

He walked back to the house not feeling the cold, not even
conscious that he was without his coat. The numbness within him
bore no relation to the winter day. He was finished with Yale.
That he knew with awful certainty. But sorrow would wait. There
would be time for that, a lifetime. Now he must assemble his
thoughts. He must try to understand how it had happened. It
shouldn't have ended this way. Right was on his side and President Day was not a harsh, unreasonable man. Carefully he rehearsed all that had happened in the minutes he had left behind
him there in the oak-paneled study.

I began hysterically. That was a mistake. Then I shouted. Why
wouldn't a shouting, hysterical person seem imaginative and unreliable? That was a great disservice I did myself. I must never do
it again. I must never raise my voice if I wish to sound convincing.

Yes, but why didn't President Day make allowance for my
distress? Why didn't he realize that I was loud and uncontrolled
only because of the shock I had suffered?

And the answer to that came, too, when he had thought
enough. He had placed President Day in a very difficult position.
A sifting of the plot against him could have resulted in the expulsion of five of New England's highborn sons. President Day
was no fool. He had been sensitive of the danger. But President

Day was no monster either. He would not have invented a cause for ridding Yale of Judah Benjamin. Judah Benjamin had richly provided the cause. He had forced his way into the house. He had shown disrespect and anger. He had behaved in a manner that justified grave punishment. He had done everything that was needed to save his tormentors from expulsion, to extricate President Day from his difficulties, and to leave behind himself a name that Yale would forever dishonor.

He thought with horror of returning to Charleston, rejected and disgraced. What would he say to his parents and to Mr. Lopez?

"When a man graduates from Yale the world is open to him. There is nothing that a man who has that proud distinction cannot do."

Philip, his father had said that. His father who had wept with joy because he had a son who studied Greek and Euclid.

No one said good-by to Judah when he left the home of the white-haired widow. He stood irresolute for a full minute before the closed door of Francis Bacon's room. There were things he would have said to Bacon.

I thank you for your never-failing kindness and I understand a man's believing his friends instead of a stranger. Only I would like to say again that it was all a cunning trick, Bacon. I am not a thief.

In the end he did not knock on Bacon's door. It remained closed and when it came to him that there was a sorry symbolism in the sight of it, the tears that he had intended to delay flowed freely.

And that was the way he left Yale.

They reacted in characteristic ways. His mother could think only of the outrage, the shame of having the word "thief" attached to the name of a boy who was Solomon Mendes's grandson.

"How dare they?" she demanded. "How dare they?" And she trembled with fury and her face, as she asked her futile question, flamed red.

His father suffered for what had been lost—the chance to acquire complete education, the graduation, the diploma.

"My poor Judah, to have had all this within your grasp. My

unfortunate child. God help you to bear the disappointment."

Moses Lopez quarreled with the injustice, the cruel indignity which he accepted as an affront to his entire race.

Judah called upon him the first morning after his return to Charleston. They sat in the front parlor. It was a high-ceilinged room which despite its large pieces of furniture seemed bare. There was a curiously institutional look about the room, as though it had been furnished and was maintained by the very people who managed the Hebrew Orphan's Aid Society. The tall, narrow doors, the straight-backed chairs, the plain curtains somehow overpowered the excellent painting above the mantel and the rich carpet that covered the floor.

Mr. Lopez paced the room, his huge head bowed, his hands clasped behind his back.

"It would not have happened to a Gentile," he said. "Somehow this matter must be made public."

"Please, sir, do not consider that, I beg of you."

"And why not?"

"I answer your question with another. I ask who would like me better if I whined and complained and tried to explain?"

"But Yale should be exposed for—"

"Yale did nothing to me, sir. A handful of mean-souled idiots is not Yale."

"But as a Jewish boy who was unfairly dealt with you should—"

"I have thought much of the matter. I am determined not to begin life weighted down with a bag of self-pity. I will not believe the Gentiles hate me. I will not believe that to be a Jew limits one's opportunities." Judah paused remembering a story his father had often told.

Moses Lopez was too alert, too sensitive to be unaware of even the smallest change of expression.

"You smile to yourself, Judah. What is amusing?"

The smile broadened. "I was thinking, sir, of an old man who swept the synagogue in London. The man was an ignorant, uncouth wretch given a few shillings a month only to save him from starving. He could scarcely phrase a sentence or write his name. Yet he applied for a position as a clerk in a countinghouse and when refused, preserved his self-esteem by saying that his rejection was only to be expected considering that he was a Jew."

A cold, dry smile appeared on Mr. Lopez's face. "Yes," he agreed, "there is much of that, Judah. Too much. And yet—no, I will not say what was in my mind."

"I do not believe a Gentile boy would have been pardoned for behavior such as mine. I try to be honest with you and with myself. My manner toward the Reverend Jeremiah Day was most objectionable."

"I cannot believe that, Judah."

"I pushed my way into his house."

"You were perturbed."

"I shouted at him."

"You were beside yourself with anguish."

"Had you seen me you would have been ashamed to know me."

Mr. Lopez shook his head. "You could not have acted in an unmannerly way, my boy. I know how you were reared. I know your parents and your background too well to entertain such an idea for a moment. A boy of your breeding conducts himself always with a propriety that would bring pride to his family and friends."

And Judah sat there staring at Mr. Moses Lopez, who could be every bit as biased as the Reverend Jeremiah Day.

I am to him as those fellows are to Reverend Day, of course. If I had killed one of them he would not hesitate to call it an accident but, ah, if one of them had killed me it would be different.

"So, Judah, you do not want to make an issue of the matter. Very well then. What was the other possibility—the mention of reinstatement?"

"I mentioned it only so that you might be acquainted with all that passed. Actually there is no smallest chance—"

"Let me think a moment." Mr. Lopez resumed his pacing. "I believe you should write a letter to President Day, a good letter, Judah, apologizing—if you choose—for your slight offenses against good manners. Request in straightforward, manly language to be readmitted to Yale."

Judah said, "If it is your wish, sir."

"It is. Naturally I appreciate that you cannot be expected to live again among those scoundrels who persecuted you. I will see to it that you are accommodated elsewhere. Now hurry home, boy, and write your letter to Reverend Jeremiah Day."

Judah went home and wrote the letter. He wrote it because

Moses Lopez had asked him to write it. He knew even as he wrote that it would be as well to post it in Charleston harbor for all the effect it would have on the President of Yale.

To do other than write the letter would be a denial of Moses Lopez's importance in the community, an act of rebellion, almost an insult. And yet he knew now that Moses Lopez himself was not worthy of leadership. He was only a middle-aged man with more learning than most, a more authoritative bearing and a more arresting voice—another Jeremiah Day.

There were changes in Judah's home. Rebecca, the oldest sister, was married and gone from the house behind the fruit store. Philip had been naturalized. Through him they were all Americans. The new baby sister born within the month came into the world an American. She was named Penina for one of the West Indian aunts.

"Why, Mama? You never loved Aunt Penina."

"I love her more than your father's sister Hannah and I have named a child for her."

"There is no logic to that answer, Mama."

"Maybe not but the explanation satisfies me."

The house was changed in other ways. The fine china that had belonged to Grandmother Mendes was gone.

"I donated it to Yale," his mother said bitterly.

"You sold it! Oh, Mama, why did you? Mr. Lopez told you that if it was ever difficult he would—"

"I know. I know. We had an idea, your father and I, that we ourselves would like to pay your way through college. He, poor man, had no more to sell. He had already sold his books."

Judah stood in silence thinking of the young man with the buck teeth.

I could do murder. Before God, at this moment I could do murder.

He went rarely to stroll the streets of Charleston. It was no pleasure any more to encounter the pretty Seixas sisters or old Mr. Moïse. They asked questions, the interested questions of people who truly care. What could he say to them? Could he list there in a Charleston street all the miserable details?

"Judah, what happened? Why are you home?"

He could not bring himself to help in the store. There were

questions there also. Moreover, he was not needed. Solomon was a demon of energy and the small fruit business scarcely tested his need for activity.

In the kitchen his mother sewed. Hannah sewed, too. What were they making that needed such careful stitching? Again and again he would hear his mother's soft rebukes.

"Rip it, my child. It isn't fit to be seen as you have worked it."

His father asked, "What will you do, Judah?"

"I don't know yet." He knew but he would not say. There would be a family council, perhaps even Mr. Lopez would be asked to comment, to advise, and he was no longer willing to submit to the decisions of the elders. He knew what he would do. He knew what he must do. He dreaded the thought that they would oppose him and that he would be forced to embarrass them by exercising his own will against theirs.

"You have not heard from Yale, Judah?"

"No, Papa. I will not hear from Yale."

He held the baby, Penina, in his arms and was saddened by the thought that she might be as old as Hannah before they met again.

He borrowed money from his new brother-in-law and bought a ticket on a New Orleans-bound schooner. When this was done he told his parents of his plans.

His mother nodded. "It is good that you did not go sooner. We have just completed the shirts for your journey, haven't we, Hannah? You see them, Judah? They will not shame you no matter where you go. The child does exquisite work."

"Louisiana is a fine place I have heard," Philip said. "Only admitted to the Union a few years ago and already they are building a synagogue."

But it was the St. Louis Cathedral that he found that first day in New Orleans. It was from its steps that he saw and recognized the strength, the promise of the river city. It was from St. Louis Cathedral that he walked back to the dirty little room where ants boldly devoured a stranger's pecan cakes and where a man had died of yellow fever.

Four

NEW ORLEANS

The city never slept. The rhythm of the bamboula throbbed in its veins. It danced, it dueled, it laughed and held a poor opinion of those who wept. Grief was a shabby, ill-bred creature with whom New Orleans had no acquaintance. Death was not a solemn, black-garbed angel but a sniveling wretch not worthy of respect. When the fever came it was only a matter for wagering who would perish, who would survive. An exciting gamble rather like the turn of the wheel at John Davis's Palace of Chance or perhaps more like placing a bet at the race track since fever was a seasonal affair.

Nowhere was the search for pleasure so highly regarded, nowhere but in New Orleans could one find frivolity and extravagance honestly, wholeheartedly accepted as major graces. Nowhere was the temper that flamed in murderous passion so admiringly marked as a cultural achievement. The streets were often muddy quagmires, but there were fashions from Paris to be seen on those streets. Dogs, sometimes even horses, died and lay neglected there for days, but dinner tables were decked in priceless lace and the food that was served was not only fit for a king but for an Orleanian who could appreciate delicate flavor. No mansion was without its legion of fat, scampering rats, but the great Seignoret himself had carved the woodwork behind which they lived.

This was New Orleans—the New Orleans that existed for those who could afford it. There was another New Orleans. In charac-

47

ter it varied little from the glittering city inhabited by the rich.
No duels were fought by the poor, the dinners were simpler, the
fashions were not from Paris—but anyone could dance, anyone
could laugh. Love could be had for a kind word. True love
came higher.

Without a picayune one could have a glorious time, for one
always had friends. In New Orleans someone always had a bottle
of wine to share, a Congri simmering on the stove, or a chair
at the coffeehouse to offer. On Sundays one might go to Congo
Square and observe the holiday dancing of the slaves and marvel
at the savage beauty of their performance, the originality of their
curious minds. If one was not too distracted by the flash of their
cheap ornaments or by the jungle grace of their bodies, one could
listen to the words they sang. One who understood the patois
of the slave gave attention to the verses that were chanted between the oft-recurrent chorus.

> *Danse Calinda, bou-djoumb! Bou-djoumb!*
> *Danse Calinda, bou-djoumb!*

There was always a story told in the little verse. An innocent
animal story perhaps—the black cat owned by a man who thought
her a white kitten; the vixen who whelped in the forest and returned to her old fox claiming she had found an abandoned pup
—simple songs that the slaves always insisted had no meaning
other than the obvious. Yet often the singing of them ended in
terrible whippings. Those with something to hide dreaded Sunday afternoons in Congo Square and the sly reprisals of those who
all week long were helpless.

Or one could walk down St. Peter Street and be beckoned
by an acquaintance into a house where a party was in progress.
There was sure to be wine, good food, and a wonderful story.
Every Orleanian was a storyteller born. One might choose to hear
a thrilling tale of Spanish rule. If so, drop in on the old man who
has the bookstore. He will show his scars—but so entertainingly.
A story of romance? Ask the lady who dozes in the sunlight of
the Toulouse Street courtyard. It was she, in scarlet satin, who
rode to the dueling oaks and watched her lover die. Of course
the lady is insane and her story is not true. But does it matter?

A man could have conventional employment. He could even
be deplorably industrious and still somehow make friends, be at

home from Esplanade to Canal Street. It was impossible to live in New Orleans and not be of it.

Judah worked as a clerk for Mr. Greenbury Stringer, who was a notary. The position had come easily on his first day of seeking.

"You look intelligent."

"Thank you, sir."

"How much education have you had?"

"Three years at Fayetteville Academy in North Carolina."

"Any college training? No, of course not. You're too young."

It was there again, the sharp pain that never failed to cut cruelly with each remembrance of Yale. He looked at the round-bellied man who was questioning him, at the sharp, gray eyes and easy smile. Mr. Greenbury Stringer.

"Well, Benjamin, we can try each other, can't we? You write a good hand."

Judah sat on a high stool and wrote all day long. He never knew a moment's boredom, for from the beginning he was captivated by the documents that passed over his desk.

"Mr. Stringer, may I ask a question?"

Mr. Stringer grinned and ran a hand through his thinning hair. "I'm getting pretty tired of your questions, boy. Besides, they're embarrassing. I don't know the answers to half of them."

That was not the truth. Mr. Stringer knew the answer to any legal question a boy could ask.

"You were a lawyer, weren't you, sir?"

"For your information, young man, I *am* a lawyer, only I am too smart to come to grips with this mob. Christ Almighty, Louisiana breeds legal brains as easily as she breeds mosquitoes."

"Would you explain the wording in this will? It is unusual and I know it has a purpose but—"

Mr. Stringer always explained and at the end of his explanation he would say, "Anyhow that's the way I see it. Ask some of those smart lawyers who come in here. Those fellows will answer all your questions. You ask them."

Judah asked them and he remembered their answers and tucked them away in his mind with Mr. Stringer's answers. The Louisiana lawyers did not always agree with Mr. Stringer or for that matter with each other. The difference of opinion was worth pondering and the documents took on vivid personalities of their own as he came to understand the words and phrases he wrote so neatly upon them.

Life was very busy, for there were the Spanish lessons he was receiving and the English lessons he was giving and the girl with the yellow hair who lived in the room next to his.

When he wrote home he filled his letters with detail, for he knew his parents were interested in all that interested him, but he wrote no word of the yellow-haired girl nor for that matter of the blue-eyed enchantress in Exchange Alley.

You will note that I have moved. I am in a room now that has crisp, white curtains at the window and a floor so clean that even you, Mama, could find no fault with it. The house is owned by a Free Woman of Color and this, I have found, is the only kind of landlady in all New Orleans who takes pride in renting spotless rooms.

I am paying for my Spanish lessons but that will only be a matter of another few weeks. After that I will have sufficient grasp upon the language to use it as I do my French, exchanging with some Spanish speaking contacts my knowledge of English for their Spanish. Incidentally I now have two French pupils who are paying me for English lessons. I continue however to accept correction in my French when they offer it. My aim is to speak three languages perfectly.

Mr. Stringer had arranged for the paying pupils.

"Judah, you're a fool. They can afford to pay, so why shouldn't they? You don't need any more help with your French. Hell, it's better than mine right now."

Judah had repressed a smile. In his opinion almost anyone's French was better than Mr. Stringer's.

Sometimes they talked quietly, secretly behind New Orleans's back.

"Sir, how is it you made friends so easily and built a business when Americans were hated even more than they are now? Is there a secret?"

Greenbury Stringer nodded. "Yes, and it's a funny thing. Most Americans never get wise to it, most of them never even stumble upon it by accident."

"Would you tell me your secret?"

"Gladly, my boy. I'd like to tell it to all Americans but they wouldn't listen. It's simply this: When you come into a place that's full of people whose language, customs, and manners are different from yours, you have two choices. Number one, you can study hard and make a pretty good show of imitating them. You can speak and act like they do and make yourself one of them. They like that just fine because it's human to like being imitated. It's flattering."

Judah nodded. "Yes. And the other choice, sir?"

"Well, it's the one I took. I wasn't built for imitating elegant manners and Creole-ing myself all up—so I remained American."

"Many Americans do, Mr. Stringer, and I assure you it adds nothing to their popularity."

"Ah, that's where the secret comes in. Here it is, boy: Be as American as you like. Do things your way but never forget for a minute to respect their ways. You understand? Stick to your tastes but don't laugh at theirs. Make up your mind that they're different and have a right to be different. Above all never say your way is better. There's a chance that it isn't, you know."

"Thank you for sharing the secret, Mr. Stringer. It will be remembered forever and will be helpful to me, I am sure."

Mr. Stringer said, "You'll remember it all right. I don't think you ever forgot anything, boy. I picture that mind of yours looking like my mother's attic—all full of things she kept dragging up there for years. Say, you want another paying pupil?"

"I could use another, sir."

"Well, there's a man coming in today. He has a daughter who wants to learn English. I mentioned you. Seems like a good prospect."

"Thank you, Mr. Stringer."

The prospect was a Creole gentleman of chilling dignity. Judah slid from his stool and bowed as the presentation was made. It was always a presentation when a highborn Creole was involved. Introductions were for Americans.

"Fine boy, this Benjamin," Mr. Stringer said. "His English is remarkably pure and I doubt you will find an imperfection in his French."

The gentleman nodded briefly and indicated that he wished to speak privately with Mr. Stringer. The two men walked into the inner office and Judah climbed back upon his stool. There was a sudden weight upon the contented heart he had carried for more than a year. In New Orleans he had almost forgotten that there were times when it was an unhandy thing to be a Jew. Now here was a reminder. The gentleman had not even cared to test his qualifications for teaching but had turned away from him in disfavor.

From where he sat he could hear the conversation.

"This is the young man you expect me to hire as a tutor for my daughter?"

"Yes, sir, and a very good tutor he is."

"For that I will take your word but I would not hire him if he were the only tutor in Louisiana."

"Why not?"

"How can you ask? Is he a suitable companion for an impressionable young girl? The boy is far too handsome. A father who has already selected his future son-in-law would indeed be encouraging mutiny if he introduced your clerk into his household."

Judah laid his pen down and sat silently hating himself. So for all his fine words to Mr. Lopez he was still like the old man in the London synagogue who believed that no one judged him on any ground save that of being Jewish.

If you are that kind of a Jew, Benjamin, if you are going to jump to mean conclusions whenever you are rejected, then there is no use learning French and Spanish. There is no use learning anything for you are too stupid to make much of your life.

Mr. Stringer and the Creole gentleman emerged from the office. Formal adieus were exchanged and there was a nod for the boy on the high stool. Mr. Stringer saw his visitor out and returned to Judah.

"Well," he laughed, "you just prettied yourself out of a pupil. Get rid of that curly black hair and those romantic dark eyes, boy, if you want to instruct young ladies. That is if you want to instruct them in languages."

"Thank you, sir, for having tried to get me another pupil."

"Oh, that's nothing. I like to help people. I like to help you in particular, Judah. I consider you a very worthwhile lad." He stood beside the high counter at which Judah worked, one elbow resting upon it, his sharp eyes peering inquiringly at his clerk. "What's your aim, boy? What are you working toward?"

This was the moment then. For weeks he had wondered how to word his request, how to approach Mr. Stringer and describe

to him the devouring ambition that scarcely gave him a minute
of peace. Here it was—the opportunity to say what he wanted
above all else and the moment had come without his forcing it.

"Mr. Stringer, I want to be a lawyer. Will you let me read
law with you? Will you teach me?"

Greenbury Stringer's eyes glowed and he flung his fat arms
exultantly about Judah. "God damn it, boy," he said. "I thought
you'd never ask!"

To be admitted to the bar of Louisiana, this was his goal. Later
there would be other goals, he knew. Later there would be the
desire for recognition and success and the restless striving to know
all there was to know of law. For now there was only the need to
be admitted to the bar.

He worked as he had never worked before, studying into the
pale hours of morning, falling exhausted upon his bed and rising
after a few hours sleep to return to the high stool in Mr. Stringer's
office. He loved the office with its ugly oak furniture and its smell
of ink and leather-bound law books. Here were the answers to his
questions. Here was the doorway to a world whose rewards were
as great as a man's ability.

He was thrilled by the sight of the great lions of the New Orleans legal world. They came often to Mr. Stringer's office.
Sometimes it was business that brought them. Sometimes they
came to chat with an American who thought their traditions
neither outmoded nor amusing.

"You must meet my boy—Benjamin." Mr. Stringer never missed
a chance to present Judah to a man who might one day be of
assistance.

Judah met them all: Mazureau, the greatest of the Creole
lawyers; Roselius, famed for his honesty; Soulé, the spellbinder;
Grymes, who had defended Laffite, the pirate; John Slidell, tall
and handsome, a New Yorker more determinedly Creole than
Mazureau himself. Judah's awe for these greats of his chosen
profession was boundless.

"You must work very hard," they told him. "Law is not for a
man who likes leisure."

Even words as homely and trite as these seemed weighty when
a Roselius spoke them.

No one, however, needed to spur him on. He was dedicated to

the field which he had chosen. New Orleans herself and the titian-haired milliner's apprentice who lived on St. Ann Street could but rarely lure him from his books.

"You're making progress," Mr. Stringer said. "Don't worry. You're making progress. Take a night off, boy. You'll be better for it tomorrow."

"But there is so much I do not know."

Mr. Stringer looked at him gravely. "That will be a fact when you are sixty, Benjamin."

It was a sobering thought. It meant that one must work harder if one were to scratch even the outside surface of knowledge.

"I'm not going to let you take your bar examination till you're twenty-one, so you're not in any real hurry."

"Would you give me the papers on the harbor case to study, sir? I thought that during the evening I might—"

"No. School's out for a week."

Judah smiled. Mr. Stringer could not regulate the hours he spent reading and rereading in his room. Studying law books written in French and Spanish served a double purpose and improved one's powers of concentration.

Mr. Stringer came to him one day with a letter in his hand. "You remember the gentleman who was here about a year ago— the one who thought you were too fascinating to trust around his daughter?"

Judah said, "You are referring to the unfortunate man who could not see well?"

"He could see. You're a damn good-looking boy, Benjamin. But, be that as it may, he evidently mentioned your tutoring abilities to someone else—to a Mr. St. Martin—who also has a daughter who would enjoy learning English." He consulted the letter again. "Mr. St. Martin is apparently not afraid of your charms, or else he hasn't heard about them."

Judah considered. He could always use extra money. Paying his debt to his brother-in-law had kept him very short of funds and he was hoping to make the sending of small sums to his mother a regular occurrence.

"I don't really think of this as hard work for you, Judah. As a matter of fact it might keep you from going stale on your studies. Would you like to look the letter over?"

Judah took the letter from Mr. Stringer and read it carefully:

If the young man whom you once recommended to the above-mentioned gentleman is still in your employ, and if he is still giving English instruction, I would appreciate his coming any afternoon to 123 Condé Street.

It was signed Auguste St. Martin. Creoles of course. If they were friends of the "above-mentioned gentleman" they were Creoles. He had had no entree to a family such as this and he had long wondered if there existed in these groups phrases unknown to him—Creole idioms, well-bred catch phrases such as a Mazureau would know.

At five-thirty he presented himself at the door of 123 Condé Street. It was a pleasant house with the ironwork intricately and imaginatively wrought. A Negro man opened the door. As was so frequently the case, the man had no English and his French was of the variety that puzzled an outlander. However, Judah was somehow understood and led into the front parlor where Madame St. Martin received him.

"You have come in response to the letter. How kind of you, Mr. Benjamin. Be seated please."

There was an air of deep sadness about her, a tragic calm that was in no way mitigated by the fact that she was still very young. She was dressed in unrelieved mourning and she wore it with an air that made the somber black almost scandalously becoming.

"Mr. Benjamin, my daughter Natalie wishes to learn to speak English."

"Your daughter, Madame? Surely she is not of an age to have such a task placed upon her."

Madame St. Martin neither smiled nor colored. She said, "Perhaps the light has deceived you, Mr. Benjamin. Natalie is not a child. She is almost sixteen."

He said nothing. He sat quietly surveying the parlor, waiting for Madame to speak again. The room was almost perfectly square and it was painted a soft, creamy shade. Like all Creole parlors it possessed a dazzling chandelier of prismatic glass tears, and fine brocade upon rosewood chairs. On errands for Mr. Stringer he had seen many parlors before but none had had such large and glittering mirrors, such silky carpets. And yet here there was also warmth, and he thought it a tribute to Madame's artistic taste that a stranger could feel so comfortable in this Creole parlor.

"Of course you would not be here if you were not interested in my husband's letter."

"I am interested, Madame. I have some free time."

"The lessons will be at your convenience, Mr. Benjamin."

"The usual fee, Madame—"

"I am not greatly concerned with fees. I want Natalie to learn English." She leaned toward him, her sad eyes regarding him with candor. "You are very good looking," she said, "and your voice is the most beautiful I have ever heard. I will tell you now something of Natalie's studies. I am afraid she is not a very diligent scholar. Recently she has lived for some months with a kinswoman of my husband's in La Fourche Parish. There were, because of many young relatives and friends on the plantation, resident instructors." Madame paused sorrowfully and sighed. "The classes have been terminated, the instructors dismissed, because lessons were not taken seriously by the young people."

"A pity, Madame."

"Indeed. When Natalie returned to me I sent her to the convent to learn from the good sisters, but that has not been successful. She does wish to learn English, and my husband and I believe private instruction is the most sensible way to proceed." She reached a languid white hand behind her and tugged on the bell cord. To the black woman who responded she gave an order in the absurd patois that had never before sounded charming to his ears. "I have sent for my daughter."

It was strange and rather embarrassing that in the minutes that followed no small conversation came to his mind with which to break the silence. Not a word could he offer and he felt that he was indeed presenting a sorry spectacle, a thick-skulled lout with no conversation to dispel the awkward lull. He sat with his eyes fixed upon the door through which the black woman had vanished. He sat waiting for Natalie and it surprised him to find that he waited with impatience as though she were late for an appointment that had been made long ago.

Outside the parlor door a soft voice murmured unintelligible words to the slave. There was a rustle of silk, a breath of perfume, and Judah rose to his feet and took an eager step forward.

"Mr. Benjamin, my daughter, Natalie."

She was slim and as tall as he. She wore the fashion of the

day, the high-waisted gown with the clinging skirt that outlined her long, graceful limbs as she moved into the room. Scarlet ribbons crossed stylishly beneath the fullness of her bosom were not needed to draw a man's attention. She smiled at him and her eyes were yellow as a cat's and filled with secret amusement. Did she know that he had been overly preoccupied with the scarlet ribbons?

"Sit down, Mr. Benjamin—Natalie," Madame said. "We shall have a little wine and some small conversation."

The conversation was all Madame's. Her family, it developed, were refugees from the black horror of Santo Domingo. Judah had spoken to many such in Mr. Stringer's office and elsewhere. New Orleans had no dearth of those who were familiar with the terrible slave uprising, and the tales were all alike. Always the narrator's family had lived in a marble-terraced plantation home. Always had there been flight with bloodthirsty blacks in pursuit. Always a hiding place in the jungle, a few faithful slaves, and in the end, just as the violence-maddened savages were closing in, the white sails of an English vessel appearing by the mercy of God.

"So much tragedy. So much death. Life is very sad, Mr. Benjamin. My poor mama, she is dead, and my sister's blessed infant was taken by the angels only five years ago this time. I am never out of mourning." Madame sighed heavily and touched her eyes with a black-bordered handkerchief.

Judah made appropriate remarks and sipped his wine. Natalie said nothing. He wanted her to speak, he wanted to hear her voice and to know what she thought, what she felt, what she was.

"So it is your wish to learn English, Madamoiselle?"

He watched the play of light on her blue-black hair and the gleam of her long fingernails as she toyed with a lace fan.

"Yes," she said. "It is my wish to learn English. Will you teach me?"

"It would be a very great pleasure. Do you know any English at all?"

"Not a word."

"Are you deceiving me? Are you afraid to try?"

Natalie smiled. "Monsieur," she said, "I am afraid of nothing."

Madame laid her black-bordered handkerchief aside and sighing deeply once more brought her mind back to the present.

"When could you begin the lessons, Mr. Benjamin? Would to-morrow suit you?"

"Tomorrow. Now I will say good night and thank you."

"No, no, do not go, Mr. Benjamin. My husband will be but a moment longer now. Please remain. Perhaps you will dine with us."

"I am so regretful, Madame, but I cannot accept."

"Why not?"

He was startled by her kind persistence and he had not armed himself with a plausible excuse.

"Why, it would be an imposition, Madame. I came only to be considered for employment and perhaps—"

"You shall remain."

He glanced at Natalie. Was she pleased that he would dine with them? He could not guess, for the yellow eyes were unreadable. He had risen to leave but now he was staying. It certainly would not seem strange if he did not return to the chair he had been occupying. Casually he crossed the silky carpet and seated himself on the sofa at Natalie's side. The fragrance of her perfume instantly enveloped him, the simple nearness of her stirred desire.

Come now, Benjamin, remember she is the same as the lovely articles you see in shop windows. You may look but that is all. She is only another exquisite creation beyond your reach.

Madame St. Martin said, "I am overwhelmed by your French, sir. I had heard it was excellent but I was not prepared to hear an American speak in such accents."

He smiled. "I wonder how overwhelming it is, Madame, since you had no trouble in recognizing me for an American."

"Oh, we knew that, Mr. Benjamin. Our inquiries concerning you were quite thorough."

"I see." It was no light thing then, this engaging a tutor for Natalie. What inquiries would be made, what standards would be demanded of a man who would be Natalie's husband! "Speaking of languages, Madame, I am anxious to learn something of the charming one you use to communicate with your servants."

"I am pleased that you find it charming. But it is only French as it sounded to the Negroes when they first heard it, French spiced with a few Africanisms and adapted to their sense of euphony. Natalie, my dear, tell Mr. Benjamin the little animal story about Bouki and the macaques."

Natalie laughed. "Oh, Mother!"

"Please," Judah begged.

"Well—" She settled herself prettily and turning to him began.

"Bouki mette di fé en bas so léquipage et fait bouilli dolo ladans pendant eine haire. Quand dolo là té bien chaud Bouki sorti déyors et li commencé batte tambour et hélé macaques yé."

The moment she had abandoned proper French her personality had somehow changed. The yellow eyes were dreamy, her posture, so correctly rigid, had relaxed and she bent toward him, her body seeming suddenly soft and lazy. The brittle, well-bred voice had taken on a tone that made him think of a darkened room and the last words of a woman just before she falls asleep. In his mind he spoke to Natalie St. Martin.

If you come closer, Madamoiselle, I will be finished with New Orleans forever, for I will take you in my arms and kiss that red, red mouth.

"Mo chuite, mo chuite. Ah oua, macaques yé prend gros couverti, et couvri pove Bouki et yé dit li—si so té chuite to sré pas héél."

"Charming," Judah said. "Delightful. You must teach me, Madamoiselle."

"I will, Monsieur. I promise. Oh, here is Papa." She jumped from the sofa and ran to the door. "Papa dear, hurry to meet Mr. Benjamin."

Auguste St. Martin was less than middle-aged but his hair was gray and he had what New Orleans called the look of the refugee.

"I understand you study law, Mr. Benjamin. Most admirable profession. I, too, once contemplated a legal career when a boy in France. But my papa decided to become a planter in Santo Domingo and removed our family there. Alas, for his plantation was lost in the most horrible manner imaginable."

"I told him, Auguste, of our family's catastrophe."

"You could not tell him of the things *I* saw with these eyes, my dearest. Mr. Benjamin, some time I will relate to you scenes that will wring your heart."

The hour came at last when his departure must be expected, even by such cordial hosts as these.

"I will see you tomorrow," he said to Natalie.

"Do not forget, Monsieur."

"No, Madamoiselle. You may depend upon it. I will not forget."

The doors dividing the two parlors were rolled back for the lessons. Madame St. Martin sewed quietly in the front parlor and the lessons were conducted in the other. Thus they were properly chaperoned but still had the necessary privacy conducive to learning.

"Tell me about you," Natalie said.

"Later, when you know some English. Now we must begin with very—"

"I want to know about you."

"I am terribly flattered but I prefer to acquaint you with a few simple nouns."

"First I would like you to tell me—"

"Permit me to speak, Madamoiselle, if you please. I am not being paid to tell my life's story." He cast a glance at Madame St. Martin forty feet away. "I shall be dismissed if you learn no simple nouns, you know."

"What is your first name?"

"Judah."

"Judah?" When she said it it became beautiful though he had never liked his name.

Say it again, Natalie. It sounds so wonderful when you say it.

"Yes, Judah," he said briskly. "Now, Madamoiselle—"

"You were named for someone no doubt. Who was he, this Judah?"

"A Biblical character."

"What did he do?"

"I regret to say, Madamoiselle, that I know little of him save that his tribe inherited the cities."

"How delightful! What cities?"

"Oh, places like Zanoah and Hazar-Gaddah and Beth-dagon."

"Oh, dear. Not Paris or the beautiful Rome or Venice?"

"No, Madamoiselle, only Kirjath-Sannah and Jezreel and En-Gannin. With their villages, by the way. I forgot to mention that."

The first lesson ended with Natalie still happily unacquainted with a single English noun. She went upstairs the moment the hour was over but Madame St. Martin delayed Judah's departure.

"I would like to ask if she appears interested, Mr. Benjamin."

Judah smiled. "Madame, she appears to be interested in everything except learning English. I believe she was purposely wasting time."

"In what way was she wasting time?"

"Asking questions about anything that came into her head. My name for instance and—"

"Well, the first lesson, I believe, is always a matter of teacher and pupil coming to know each other. It is better so." She set aside her embroidery and asked, "Tomorrow would you care to accompany us to mass and breakfast afterward?"

"Thank you but I do not go to mass, Madame."

"Of course. How stupid of me. You go to Shaarai Chessed, do you not? No matter. We will all have breakfast together tomorrow."

Always Natalie left the moment the lesson ended and always he was expected in the front parlor for a small exchange of conversation with her mother.

"She is beginning to learn a little English, isn't she?"

"Yes, Madame, a little."

"It has been strange for her but she will learn. She has a good mind."

He studied the silkiness of the carpet. How could he meet Madame's eyes at this moment? A good mind? Natalie?

Madame, I fear I love your daughter. I sleep and wake with the fear growing stronger every day. But her mind, Madame?

"It is fortunate for her, since she neglects to cultivate education, that she has been blessed with beauty. You do agree that my daughter is beautiful?"

"Yes, Madame. I agree."

Madame sighed sorrowfully and chose a skein of silk that was exactly the shade of Natalie's lips.

In all their meetings Madame sewed and spoke of her daughter. Frequently she wept for dead relatives and always there was a story of violence or heartbreak, but those were memories of the past. Natalie was her present.

"Here in New Orleans there is much dancing and gaiety but Natalie goes nowhere. Do you know why, Mr. Benjamin?"

"I confess to having wondered."

"The youth of the social world do not appeal to her. Often she has said to me, 'Mama, Creole boys are boresome.'"

He would leave Madame St. Martin and walk down Condé Street with his heart beating fast. He thought that it would be sensible to remove himself from the St. Martins before his love for Natalie became too deep, too painful. Was Madame purposely teasing him or did she use Natalie's tutor as she might use a hair-dresser or a seamstress, someone in whom to confide trivial matters? Certainly Madame must know that a man could not spend time with Natalie, could not sit near her without wanting her. But that was undoubtedly of no importance to Madame. The penniless tutor could not have Natalie, so what mattered his desire for her?

There was a day when their hands met—he and Natalie reaching for the same book. He gazed quickly toward the front parlor. Madame's head was bent above her sewing. Ideas circled crazily in his mind. There was time for a quick embrace. He laughed quietly to himself and handed the book to Natalie. This was becoming ridiculous and must be ended. When a man began thinking like a naughty child of swift kisses that would lead to nothing then it was time to walk away and not return.

I shall tell Madame that I am too busy to continue the lessons. I shall tell her today.

She raised her eyes to him as he entered the parlor.

"Sit down, dear Judah."

Judah? She had never before addressed him by his given name.

"I have so wanted the lesson over, Judah. I need your advice. Natalie has so many invitations and she will accept none. What shall I do? Certainly a young girl should have young companions."

"Why will she not accept, Madame?"

"It is the same old thing. She does not care for the company of the Creole gentlemen. When I beg her to attend a masked ball or one of their dances she says, 'Mama, these boys have nothing to offer but money and I do not care for money.' Of course I agree with her, Judah. Money means nothing."

A breeze roamed idly through the cream-colored parlor and the crystal pendants of the chandelier chimed a faint, sweet note. The trailing sleeve of Madame's deep mourning fluttered and sent forth a breath of fresh rosemary scent.

"And then I say to her, 'You must in time choose one of these gentlemen, daughter, for they are of your faith,' and she replies, 'God is with all good men. My husband need not be Catholic.' There, too, I understand and agree with her. But this is mother's talk and must bore you." She lowered her eyes and gave full attention to her embroidery. "If you wish you may leave, Judah. Perhaps you have your own problems which you would like to think about."

He went back to his room and thought. There was no need to search his mind for assurance that his love for Natalie was real. It was so real that he did not want her married off to a man her parents had selected even if the man was himself. Such things happened in Creole families. It must not happen that way for Natalie.

But why would her parents choose him? If the St. Martins arranged a marriage for their daughter, surely it would not be Judah Benjamin who would be the groom. Handsome, wealthy youths of fine family background abounded in Louisiana. From a father's standpoint nothing could be less desirable than giving his daughter in marriage to a poor man of a different faith. Then what? He could find only one answer and could scarcely credit the one he found. Natalie loved him. It was the only solution to the puzzle. Her parents, kind and indulgent, wanted Natalie to be happy. They would accept any man she chose, they would permit her marriage to anyone she named. That must be the truth. And he would not allow his mind to dwell on the thought that Natalie loved him. Not just yet. There was something else, something that must be approached soberly, with a clear head and an earnest heart. Madame had said that a difference of faith did not seriously concern her or Natalie. But did it concern him? He must think. He had not been a deeply religious Jew. Again and again he had violated the rules. Still, Judaism was his faith and for him there would never be another. It was a matter of no great importance perhaps to eat the proscribed foods, to handle money on the Sabbath, to remain away from synagogue—these were trivial sins and the penalty not very grave. But words had been spoken in Beth Elohim, words not easily forgotten, and they came to him now on this solemn occasion in which he searched his soul.

"Any person being married contrary to the Mosaical Law shall never be a recognized member of this congregation and should such person die he shall not be buried within the walls of Beth-Hiam."

Did it matter that all synagogues would stand with Beth Elohim and that he would be received into the councils of none? Did it matter? The synagogue was only the work of man. God had not built it. God had not issued any sweeping edicts. God had not said that His face was turned from the man who married a Gentile. Let them keep Beth Elohim to themselves if they wished. Let them refuse to recognize him. Let them—ah, but wait. Those are the thoughts of a young man. What will I think when I am old and death is near? Will I not then weep for what I have lost? Will it not then be heartbreak that I canot lie within the walls of Beth-Hiam? It will be too late then to cry out and plead for mercy. It will be too late, and how shall I feel then?

He brushed aside the theological and philosophical arguments that occurred to him. He found one question here. One only, and he presented it to himself bluntly.

It comes to this, Benjamin: Do you want to lie with Natalie in life or with the devout in death? What is your answer?

And after a time he walked over to Burgundy Street to Mr. Stringer's house.

"Fine to see you, boy. Come on in."

"Forgive me if I do not. I have an errand—that is if your answers are right I have an errand."

"My answers?" Mr. Stringer looked at him thoughtfully. "What is the matter with you? Are you sick?"

"No, sir, I—"

"Come in. It's pouring rain."

"Sorry, I had not noticed."

In the house where the décor remained defiantly Ohio, despite the constant brewing of Louisiana coffee, Mr. Stringer studied Judah's face.

"What is troubling you, boy?"

"Mr. Stringer, will I make a good lawyer?"

"What? You? Why, I am expecting to become famous just because I—"

"I am deadly serious, sir."

"So am I. You should be a great lawyer. Not thinking of giving it up, are you?"

"No, sir. Do you think I'll pass my bar examinations at first attempt?"

"With flying colors."

"Then, sir, will you do me the honor of attending me at my wedding?"

"I certainly will, son. It will be a pleasure. Hey, you mean soon? You mean right away?"

"I mean when I pass my examinations. I am going to ask her father now."

Mr. Stringer poured more coffee and gulped it hot and black. "Judah, have you thought well? It isn't one of—"

"No, Mr. Stringer. Her name is—"

Mr. Stringer grasped his arm and shook with laughter. "Don't tell me. I know. It's the girl you've been giving lessons to over on Condé Street, the St. Martin daughter, isn't it?"

"Yes, but what is amusing?"

"The man who recommended you to her father. The man who wouldn't have you for his own daughter. By Jesus, he was right."

All that autumn the city lay smothered in a pall of acrid black smoke. Tar and pitch burned on every corner and filled the air with nauseous fumes. The corpses lay unburied at the cemetery gates and a nightmare of horror had descended upon the city. One-sixth of the population was dead within half a month and another sixth dying. Nurses, doctors, gravediggers, coffins were all in short supply. Asiatic cholera had joined forces with the yellow fever, and panic lay upon New Orleans.

The pious had redoubled their fervor, the pleasure lovers their desperate gaiety. Drays and handcarts dragged the dead down the muddy streets or dumped them secretly in the dark of the night. A bride still in her wedding gown lay unburied at St. Louis Cemetery Number One. The weeping man who had carried her there lay dead beside her. The rich died unattended and the poor were not discovered for days but lay where the plague had found them.

Bodies stacked one upon the other were the gruesome burden of wagons that passed by, the drivers drunk and singing bawdy songs. Dead children were carried to the cemetery in the arms of their sorrowing parents, who were thankful if they happened to find a priest beside one of the swiftly dug trenches. The wet ground of New Orleans, never suitable for burial, compounded the horror, and the grief-stricken turned away from unspeakable sights.

The cannon that was thought to purify the atmosphere sounded hourly. It frightened the dying and had no other effect. The plague raged on, and the rats that fed handsomely in the city of horrors seemed destined to become the sole inhabitants of New Orleans.

Madame St. Martin in her lovely cream-colored parlor looked up from her embroidery to give a word of assurance to Judah.

"I know you could not stand it if the plague touched Natalie, my dear boy. It will not touch her. That is why I permitted her to go to mass with me this morning."

"She should not be outdoors. None of you must go out while—"

Madame silenced him with a wave of her hand. "I have no fear for myself or my loved ones and that includes you of course, my dear future son. None of us will die of the plague." She dropped her work and reached for her black-bordered handkerchief. "You know why we will not die, Judah?"

"No, Madame, I cannot guess why we are different from others."

"It is because my husband and I have suffered so much, so very much, that God will not ask us to endure any further trials. My heart tells me that we will not be visited again by tragedy. You must believe, Judah, that the plague will go without hurting us. Will it not, Natalie, my dearest?"

Natalie said, "I am quite certain that you are right, Mama."

"And now, Judah, are you satisfied that it is perfectly safe for Natalie to go outdoors?"

Before he could reply Natalie had seized her cloak from the chair where it lay. "Of course he knows it's perfectly safe. Tell him, Mama, that I must go."

Madame smiled faintly. "Well, Judah, Natalie is very anxious to take a short walk with you. I think my husband and I have found you a little home. Natalie and you will, of course, need a little home."

"Madame, I had intended to search for one when the plague abated somewhat."

"Yes, but something occurred this morning. At mass we met an old friend who is going to St. Bernard Parish to live with her son. The move has been planned for many months but he insists that she come now, at once. The plague, you know. She left the city directly after mass and she will not return." Madame reached into her sewing box and brought forth a key ring. "If the house appeals, you shall have it as a gift."

"You are very generous, Madame."

The keys jingled a small, pleasant tune as she handed them to him. "Go, dear children, and see if the house is to your taste."

He hesitated and Natalie looked at him, her yellow eyes filled with disappointment. "Judah, please do not refuse to take me."

"Very well. I will take you." He slipped the keys in his pocket and Natalie smiled again. "You know which house it is?"

"Of course. Let us be off."

Madame tugged at the bell rope and the black woman came as swiftly as though produced by a trick of magic.

Natalie and Judah walked out upon the dismal street, the servant keeping her correct distance behind them. The cannon sounded its melancholy boom and the smoke of the burning tar was a rasping rawness in the throat. Natalie held a perfumed handkerchief to her delicate nostrils.

"Keep your cloak tightly about you, my love."

She pouted. "And conceal my new cerise sash and a dress never before worn?"

"Few will notice it, I am afraid. The city is preoccupied with other things."

"Well, I am preoccupied with my new dress and our new house. I have seen the downstairs and it is attractive, in a way. Judah, are you thinking what fun it will be to see our own house?"

"I am thinking that you should be at home."

The house was small and charming and covered with a vine that was popularly known as flame. Spanish dagger and oleander flourished in the garden, more fortunate than the family next door who had all died within the week.

"I did not know the house was next to theirs," he said. "They were friends of Mr. Stringer."

"I knew them not at all," Natalie responded. "Let us go to the back first. I wish to see how she kept her servants. Give me the keys, Judah."

He handed over the keys and they walked to the slave quarters in the rear. Natalie opened the door and spoke to the black woman.

"Go in. Look around. If my Papa is generous to me perhaps you will be living here."

The servant obediently moved into the whitewashed interior, expressionless, silent. The moment she was inside, Natalie, with one swift motion, slammed and locked the door.

"There! She is out of the way. Now let us look at the house."

Judah stared at her in astonishment. "Natalie, you must let her out." A wail from within the slave quarters came piteously to his ears. "Listen to her. You can't leave her there."

Natalie's eyes were soft and pleading. "I do so want to see our house this way. Just Natalie and Judah together and alone."

He melted. What harm if she had her sentimental little wish? The woman locked in the slave quarters was sobbing as though calamity had befallen her. It struck him as a strangely emotional outburst for a well-trained servant. After all, to be confined for a short time in a clean room where there was even a cot to rest upon could not be a very painful experience. The woman was calling now to Natalie and her voice was sad and entreating.

"Will she be punished for letting you outwit her this way?"

"Punished? By whom? We are angels to our servants. Besides she won't dare tell. Come, let us look at the house."

It was very dim inside. The draperies were drawn and it was almost impossible to believe that the house had been inhabited that morning. An air of desertion and loneliness had already taken hold. The parlor, he thought, looked rather like the inside of a lady's handbag, all clutter and fussy, useless objects.

"It could be changed," Natalie said. "Let us see upstairs."

"I have scarcely seen downstairs."

"We will look again later, but I have always been anxious to see the sleeping chambers of this house." She darted ahead of him up the stairs, the dark cape flying behind her, the silver buckles on her velvet shoes flashing in the semidark. "Here, this must have been Madame's room."

It was large and it could be sunny, he thought, if the sun was ever again visible in New Orleans. As he walked toward the window he noticed a fine bureau with a pink marble top, a large canopied bed, and a wardrobe heavily carved in what seemed an interesting pattern. That could be examined later. Now the draperies were the problem. Would they be parted by hand or dare one tug upon this silver rope?

"If I succeed in opening these curtains—"

"Leave them closed," Natalie said.

"But I thought—" He turned toward her and found her in his arms.

"Natalie, my love." He held her tightly for a moment, then gently released her.

"You didn't kiss me. Don't you want to kiss me, Judah? You've never kissed me on the lips. Mama wouldn't allow that but she isn't here now."

He kissed her as he had often longed to do, full upon the soft, red mouth that clung to his in unabashed eagerness.

"Kiss me again, Judah."

"No, darling."

"Why do you suppose I locked her out there?" She pressed her body against his and the warmth of her was dizzying and wonderful. "Judah, I love you. I want you to love me."

"Natalie, if I loved you less—"

She moved away and he did not follow. The cannon boomed and it seemed to him that even in this room he could smell the burning of the tar and feel the heavy, choking vapors roll over him.

"Judah, come here."

"No, darling."

"We are going to be married. Do you think we would be the first to lie together before the wedding?"

"There is a plague upon the city, Natalie. I could be dead to-night. What becomes of you if I—" He paused. This was an argument for a woman's ears. Natalie was only a capricious child, inquisitive and unthinking. She could not know the seriousness of what she proposed. "Come here and let us talk sense. Sweet one, it would be wicked of us."

"Judah, don't you want me?"

"I have wanted you since I first saw you."

"Come kiss me, Judah."

He could no longer resist the tones of her voice. Perhaps he could kiss her once more without losing all sense. Kiss her again he must.

"Not like that, Judah. Lie down and you can hold me in your arms. Have you never wondered how it would be to—"

"No, I have never wondered. I have always known it would be heaven."

"I have wondered about you. I have stayed awake nights wondering. What kind of a lover are you, Judah? I cannot tell from a kiss."

The cerise sash fell away at the touch of his fingers. The soft gown vanished as though it had been only mist. She was a fragrant freshness and with her he knew an exultation that was different from any experience of the past. Nothing remained that a man could still desire—except within the cool recesses of his mind. There he found a question that clamored to be answered.

It was impossible to sleep. He kept remembering Natalie's face when they had returned to her mother. The girlish innocence of her replies concerning the house, the sweet grave look in her eyes when she said that they had sat in the parlor testing it for comfort and livability. She was a liar of rare talent, with a flair for invention of detail. Granted one did not expect her to reveal what had occurred that afternoon, but it was frightening to observe the ease with which she lied, the enjoyment she took in creating the fabric of falsehood.

"There is a dear little ornament on the shelf in the parlor. I examined it closely and found it to be without a speck of dust upon it. I trust I shall be as watchful a housekeeper. But that isn't what I started to tell you. While I was examining it, it slipped out of my hand. It actually bounced—didn't it, Judah?— as it fell upon the carpet. My heart was in my throat, but the ornament didn't break, thank heaven."

He believed her himself. For a moment he was astounded that he could not recall the incident at all.

He had not stayed long after dinner. Natalie had chattered on about the house and he had been silent, only answering Madame's questions, agreeing that the house was charming.

Very well, she is a liar. You will learn to recognize when she is lying. It will take close study but you will learn. And now, Benjamin, avoid no longer the real issue that confronts you. What of this future bride of yours? Had you ever thought of taking a wife to whom, in a darkened room, you could teach nothing? And are there any questions worth asking when one considers how much you love her?

He sat looking out at the lurid glare cast by the bright torches upon the smoke-filled sky and he told himself that a man who thinks too highly of virginity is a man who thinks too highly of sex. What did it matter that he was not the first man to possess her? What did it matter—unless to him Natalie was only a body?

And, before God, I am not thinking of her as a beautiful adornment for my bed. I love her. I love her dearly.

She was still little more than a child. It was very easy to see that she had been the victim of some scoundrel with whom she had become infatuated. He had deceived her, had taken advantage of her innocence.

Stop telling yourself stories, Benjamin. The girl who lay in your arms today was born without innocence. If you are not a coward you will not fool yourself. If you have any courage at all you will admit the probability that she went as hungrily to the first available lover as she went to you today. And if the thought does not please you at least take comfort in the knowledge that you have faced the truth with yourself.

He suddenly realized that someone was knocking upon his door. How many times had the knock been repeated? He did not know.

"Yes?"

"Mr. Benjamin." It was the landlady, and he opened the door for her. "Mr. St. Martin is in the downstairs hall. He asks if he may see you."

"Mr. St. Martin? Ask him please to come up."

Natalie's father. And at this hour. Well, certainly Natalie had not told her parents what had occurred that day in the dimness of a curtained bedroom. The black woman had tattled. Now St. Martin would charge him with dishonorable designs upon a virgin daughter and for such a crime any Orleanian would approve murder.

But Auguste St. Martin was smiling as he closed the door behind him.

"My dear Judah, I trust you will forgive me for coming so late. You were not in bed, I see. I am so happy I did not awaken you."

Mr. St. Martin seated himself, still smiling. "Such a pleasant place you have, Judah. The landlady so alert and anxious to please. Surely these free women are estimable housekeepers, much superior to the slovenly whites who manage rooming houses." He paused and looked expectantly at Judah. "Have you had a pleasant day, son?"

"Extremely pleasant."

"I am happy to hear it. I returned too late from my brother's to see you and I was disappointed. Now I wish to speak to you of something. True, it could have waited till morning, but the idea suddenly seized upon my wife and me as we chatted this evening. It excited us so we could not sleep till we knew how the idea struck you."

He and his wife had had a talk. What was coming? Judah waited silently.

"This house at which you and Natalie looked today. We have decided that it is not good enough. No, it is a small house, an old house. Inferior. You will live with us when you are married. We will refurnish a bedroom and a sitting room for you. For yourselves you shall have two personal servants, young but well-trained of course." He paused and looked at Judah. "You are favorably impressed?"

Judah said, "You are more than kind, sir." He was watching Mr. St. Martin's hands. They trembled as they drew from his pocket a large folded sheet of paper.

"Look. We are going to build a new house. You did not know that, did you? Yes, a fine house on Bourbon Street. Here is the detail of the ironwork. It will be bows and arrows skillfully wrought. The plan we will have redesigned so that a private apartment for you and Natalie will be incorporated. The house will be beautiful, Judah. An imposing home for a young lawyer, an address to lend prestige."

Judah watched the trembling hands, listened to the words so ingratiating, the voice so pleading. How did Mr. St. Martin know what had taken place? The black woman could not know for sure and Natalie certainly would not admit the truth. Why did a doting father suspect the worst? Would it not be more natural for him to assume that a few stolen kisses would be the sum total of their sin? Why would a man suppose that his daughter's natural impulse was to give herself at the first opportunity? Why indeed?

"Mr. St. Martin, I intend to build my own house at not too

distant a date. It, too, will be imposing and have an address that
will lend prestige."

"Of course, but for now let us all live together. If we are together then Natalie will have her mother with her all day long.
While you are away her mother will be there to watch her, to—
well, a young girl needs her mother."

"Yes, Mr. St. Martin. I see."

"And of course the living in our house will cost nothing and
Natalie's dowry will—"

Judah rose to his feet. "My dear sir, before you continue let me
say that I love Natalie. I do not need any of the blandishments—
material or otherwise—that you have offered. She and I are to be
married as soon as I am admitted to the bar. That was arranged
weeks ago. Nothing has occurred to change the arrangements as
far as I know."

"But certainly not, dear son. I merely wanted to bring an idea
to you which pleased my wife and me. We thought it would give
you a sense of well-being to know that while you were at your
office Natalie's mother would be on hand to—"

"To watch her. You said that before, sir." He knew now why
a doting father would suspect the worst possible behavior of his
daughter. Never for a moment had Auguste St. Martin feared
that Natalie's innocence had that day been taken from her.
Instead, he had been alarmed that Judah's discoveries would lead
to a repudiation of the betrothal.

Mr. St. Martin's eyes, a little hurt and very guileless, met
Judah's. "Yes, it would be a fine thing for you to know that her
mama was with her every moment, would it not? If Natalie
were ill or lonely there would be her mama."

"Yes, sir," Judah said.

And now I am promised a watchdog to protect my interests
while I am at the office. They would promise anything, for it has
not been easy to find her a husband. The gossip has spread all
the way from La Fourche Parish, and the door to a fine marriage
has been closed. There remained only one thing for them to do—
find an outsider reasonably presentable to the girl, an outsider
who knew no Creole gossip, who had no slaves to whisper the
news. They had reconciled themselves to forgiving the outsider
his poverty, his non-Catholicism or any other drawback he might

possess. It was only important to find a husband for Natalie before it was too late.

And he had no regrets that they had found him. He accepted the cold truth that a Natalie without blemish would never have been offered or permitted to a Judah Benjamin. She was his because she would be welcomed into no Creole family. She was his because there was an urgent need to give her in marriage. He was content to take her as she was, knowing well that he could have had her no other way.

This I know, this I admit tonight as I stand here. God help me to remember it if I go forward from this room. God help me to remember always that before I married her I knew the truth and faced it squarely. Let me never expect her to be what she is not. Let me always love her as I love her tonight and give me the strength and decency to never say that I regret the marriage.

In December he was admitted to the bar. In February he married Natalie St. Martin.

The plague had gone and the city had forgotten the horror. The bereaved gathered in the cemeteries, sat upon the iron benches, munched pralines or pain-patate, and took gloomy pride in reciting the last terrible hours of the dear departed. The vendors in *tignons* and fichus circulated among the mourners, selling their wares, and no one would refuse to purchase a plaster image or a papier-mâché cross for the grave. In the cemetery one encountered old friends, displayed one's newest clothes, and heard the latest gossip. New Orleans was herself again. Joy had returned to the city. The sun shone upon Congo Square and upon St. Anthony's Garden, and a newcomer could once again stand on the steps of St. Louis Cathedral and observe the pageantry of the city.

Judah Benjamin was no newcomer so he sat in his office on Canal Street with two letters before him. The first was from his father and he read only a few lines of it.

Dear Son:
    We are in receipt of your news and if I were to tell you that it makes us happy I should be guilty of a great untruth. This Christian whom you have married—

Judah folded the letter and placed it beneath a sheaf of papers in his desk drawer.

The other letter had been delivered by a mulatto boy in fine livery, and it had been written by John Slidell.

My dear Benjamin:
 I am confined to my home with a chest inflammation from which I am all but recovered. My physician however wishes me to remain indoors. It would afford me the greatest pleasure if you would come have a cup of coffee with me. I am certain that you are busy but surely some time this morning you will pause for refreshment and when you do I trust you will note I am only two blocks away.

Your obedient servant,
John Slidell

Judah smiled. Your obedient servant. John Slidell was obedient servant to none. One could only hope that he might prove a benevolent master to Louisiana when he held it all firmly in his hand.

What does he want with me?

Judah thought earnestly but could reach no conclusion. Slidell, the handsome, clever New Yorker of exquisite taste and impeccable manners who was reputed to have on his payroll every thug in New Orleans.

What does he want with me?

Judah looked again at the letter. "I am certain that you are busy."

Well, yes, in a way. Cases were few, but Judah had no penchant for idleness. He was filling in the long, dull days in his office by compiling a work that he found stimulating. He was aware that its title would not catch the eye of the casual reader—*Digest of the Reported Decisions of the Superior Courts in the Territory of Orleans and State of Louisiana.* Each decision was accompanied by an analysis and, in notable cases, by an opinion on what salient point had produced the court ruling. He laughed a little at himself as he wrote. Was this what was needed in Louisiana? Did Louisiana, the great breeding place of legal minds, require a detailed analysis of law by a twenty-one-year-old lawyer? Well, the work would be a useful reference for himself some day. Its present value lay in its creation, in the miraculous way that its preparation shortened the long, unprofitable wait between clients.

In mid-morning he laid down his pen. He would satisfy his curiosity.

The first floor of Slidell's luxurious home bustled with activity. A half-dozen servants were arranging chairs in the parlor, moving furniture to make space for additional sofas which were being brought from other parts of the house.

Slidell, in velvet dressing gown, greeted Judah in the hall. "A small musical evening," he explained. "Just a few friends invited to hear some excellent performances. Come where we can close ourselves away from the confusion."

His upstairs sitting room was bright and spacious. Slidell lounged against silk cushions and clapped his hands for the mulatto boy.

"Coffee."

Judah said, "I regret your indisposition. It has now eased?"

"Oh, yes. It was nothing. However, once before I had such an attack and—"

This was the springboard. From there Slidell's conversation wandered amusingly. He recounted a few anecdotes, some scraps of gossip, a memoir or two from his youth. He preferred French, Judah observed, using it as though his visitor had no knowledge of English. His French was flawless and the conceit forgivable. Judah sipped the coffee, enjoying himself immensely.

Slidell's sedate and perfect behavior in mixed company was compensated apparently by his complete earthiness when talking with another man. His mind rarely strayed far from the subject of women and he remembered and repeated the most amazing details but with wit and a skillful turn of phrase. However, Slidell was a man of sense and good timing. Long before a listener began to tire of his racy monologue, Slidell had tired of it himself.

"And now, Benjamin, what can I do for you?"

Judah raised his eyebrows in honest surprise. "Mr. Slidell, you are very kind but I can think of nothing I would ask of you."

Good God, did the man suppose that no one accepted his invitations unless desiring a favor? Was everyone who stepped into this house a petitioner rather than a guest?

Slidell said, "Let me put it this way then—what can you do for me?"

Judah laughed. "A gracious question, sir."

Slidell frowned thoughtfully. "I asked you here to discover what we can do for each other. Maybe not today or tomorrow but there will come a time. Let us have our sympathy, each for the other, established before that moment comes."

Judah gazed into the searching eyes of Slidell, whose ethics were questionable but whose approach was straightforward. Slidell's father, Judah well knew, had been no higher in the social scale than Philip Benjamin, yet Slidell had learned to fight a duel with all the blaze and dash of a Creole born. Slidell had learned that New Orleans would forgive a man for anything except a lack of fervor.

"Benjamin, the first time I saw you in Stringer's office I felt there was something special about you. Can you believe that?"

"Not very easily."

"Well, then the second time."

"I am still slightly incredulous."

Slidell said, "All right. Last week I saw the reports on your bar examinations. Have a cigar, Benjamin."

"Thank you, no."

Slidell selected a cigar for himself. "How would you like to come into my office? It would pay you, you know. You are a bright boy."

Judah said, "I do not think, Mr. Slidell, that I wish to be a bright boy in an office where there is a bright man."

"I understand. I was the same at your age. However, if you decide to give your time to an office not your own choose mine."

"It would be my happiest hour, sir."

Happiest hour indeed! I do not think, sir, that I would like being seen even on a visit to your office.

Slidell smoked in silence. "You know," he said at last, "you are a fellow much like myself. You are never going to be satisfied with small successes. You will never be content to plod along with modest gains. You will want money. I make a great deal of it. So can you. Where do you live?"

"I live with my wife's parents on Condé Street."

Slidell flicked the ashes from his cigar. "That will not please you for long, my friend. You will want a town house of your own and a huge country place where you can play at being a planter. You will want fine horses and carriages and you will want a quadroon mistress."

"Will I really?"

Slidell chuckled. "I am afraid I shocked you. I keep forgetting how young you are. I am thirty-nine, you know, and perhaps I should not be a corrupting influence upon you but, I can tell you, Benjamin, that—that I understand there is nothing on earth like the attentions of a quadroon mistress."

Judah was silent.

"The thought offends you now because you are newly married but I have heard of these Creole wives. They submit to a man for a time but they are naturally frigid. Within a year they begin to complain that their husbands are lustful beasts and they weep if a man expects more than a dignified good-night kiss."

"How disheartening," Judah said.

"A small inconvenience. A man selects a beautiful quadroon, sets her up in style, and has then someone who will never refuse him. That is, of course, if the man has money enough to pay for such loyalty and compassion. More coffee, Benjamin?"

"Please."

Slidell clapped his hands and the mulatto boy moved silently into the room and refilled the cups.

"Do you think it strange that I am not married, Benjamin?"

"I had not thought of it."

Slidell smiled wryly. "I think of it often. I want a wife but she has to be one of those frigid Creoles I was just talking about. How did you get one, Benjamin?"

"I but asked her father."

Slidell shook his head wonderingly. "There is nothing to compare with the brazenness of youth. To be frank with you, I am now hoping to convince Monsieur Deslonde to give me his daughter Mathilde. Of course she has to mature a little first. She is scarcely through childhood. In another two years perhaps."

Judah stared down into his coffee reflecting on the barbarity of a custom that would hand little Mathilde Deslonde over to John Slidell.

"Of course it will depend on how their finances are. If Deslonde is feeling a little pinched I will put a good thing his way in return for Mathilde. If he is doing well he will bed her down with some Creole boy. I will have to wait and see. God, how I want to sit at the head of a magnificently appointed table and see a Creole wife at the other end of it."

He narrowed his eyes and seemed to be looking into the future, toward the moment when he would entertain on a grand scale, taking pride in his highborn wife. Slidell, the candlemaker's son. Slidell, whose children would be haughty Creoles.

Judah said, "I have a feeling that you will marry Mathilde Deslonde." He stood. "It has been a pleasant visit, sir. I thank you."

"Come again. Any time. Do not forget you and I belong together. Some day we will share the same interests."

Judah smiled. "Sir, you have made me feel rather like the young lady for whom you wait."

Slidell nodded. "It is much the same. I am a very patient man. By the way, how are you and your wife occupying yourselves this evening?" He paused to laugh. "An oafish question—is it not?—considering that you are recently married. I can guess that you will have little interest in attending my small concert."

"I am taking Natalie to the theater," Judah said.

Natalie adored the theater and had seen little of it. He took her frequently, and afterward they would go to a restaurant for late supper. Wherever they went he was aware of the glances that Natalie drew. There was no denying her rare beauty, her style, but there was an indescribable quality that was also hers. No man looked at her with quiet admiration, there was none whose thoughts were a secret from Judah—or from Natalie. The desire that she read in man's eyes produced a storm of emotion within her, and as they were driven home in the carriage she would cling to Judah and they would kiss like lovers who must make the most of every moment. For him there was a strange sense of guilt that heightened the rapture. It seemed evil to want one's own wife as he wanted Natalie.

She would dismiss the servant who awaited her in the dressing room. And now Judah's sense of guilt would fade, for surely this could not be his wife. No man's wife spoke the language of ecstasy so well.

Later she would lie upon his arm and sleep. He would remain awake for a time, wondering if she should be deprived of the theater, the restaurant, and all the excitement that inflamed her frail mind so dangerously. And he would lie there haunted by the realization that it could just as well have been another man in the carriage. Tonight by way of contrast an idea occurred that amused him.

"What is funny?" Natalie asked.

"I have thought of something for which I have a desperate need."

"And what is that?"

"A quadroon mistress."

In the house on Condé Street a remarkable thing was happening. Perhaps not remarkable but unexpected. Though at the time of Penina's birth his mother had been older than Madame, somehow it was strange to see his mother-in-law great with child. She wept no more and laid aside her mourning, fearful, as she said, to place the curse of sorrow upon the unborn.

"New life is always inspiriting," she said. "The house seems to glow with happiness. Since this is so do you and Natalie not wish to entertain, to return the invitations you have accepted?"

Somehow he had not thought of that. She was right. There had been a great many invitations, dinners and parties, a few elaborate masques. Very gratifying, though it was more important that he was bidden to the clubs of the leading legal lights, to their tables at the coffeehouse. The empty, cordial phrases that welcomed one into a man's home were never as sweet as:

"Benjamin, my young friend, would you permit me to borrow the handbook you have assembled on decisions of the territory?"

And the joy of replying, "It would be my pleasure but I have no copy available. Perhaps Mazureau will share with you the one he is reading."

"Judah," his mother-in-law said, "what are you thinking? Would you not like to give a dinner?"

"Indeed, Madame, your suggestion is most admirable but for you to trouble yourself at this time arranging a—"

"I?" She stared at him in amazement. "I am in temporary retirement. Besides it is not my duty to entertain for you. Natalie is your wife. She—"

"But surely Natalie could not—"

"You offend me, son. Do you think she had no training? You will find that your foolish Natalie can plan a dinner and is able to preside as hostess for anyone you will ever know, no matter how far you advance in the world."

"I did not intend to—"

"You will discover you have married a girl who can train a servant, who can judge linens, who can organize a spring cleaning or a levee for a hundred honored guests. You married a Creole!"

"Of that fact I stand convinced, Madame." He had often heard of the rigorous training received by Creole daughters but he had not expected that Natalie—

"The child, for five years, was not allowed a chair that had a back. That gave her the carriage characteristic of our girls. She practiced brewing coffee when she was six and if she spilled any she was punished. Even when she spilled the entire *brûlot* bowl and was scalded I whipped her for her awkwardness. Give her your list of those whom you wish invited. Then rest easy. The problem is in the hands of a Creole wife."

Judah dropped a kiss upon the forehead of his mother-in-law. "Do not be disturbed by my ignorance, Madame. I am only now beginning to understand why a man of my acquaintance will have no bride save a Creole. He is hoping for Mathilde Deslonde."

Madame's eyes glowed with admiration. "Ah, there is a bride for whom any man would hope. A Deslonde daughter is a prize. Even in illness they are not excused from the table. Their mother compels them to appear and to manufacture light and pleasant conversation."

"That is sheer cruelty."

"It creates a hostess of whom a husband can be proud."

Still, it was with some misgivings that he presented to Natalie a list of nineteen names. He would have been not in the least surprised if she had inquired what he expected her to do. Surely her mind was lined with pink velvet and there was no possibility that she would know how to manage all the arrangements a formal dinner entailed. She read the names with care and interest.

When she was finished she asked, "Is there anyone here who feels a slight antipathy toward another?"

"I do not think so."

"It must be considered, you know, for the seating at table. And please indicate for me the most important male guest. He will be at my right. His wife at yours."

Judah nodded wonderingly and placed a mark after the name of Soulé.

"How do we manage the unmarried Slidell, precious?"

She consulted the list. "We extend our invitation not only to Monsieur and Madame Roselius but to Madame's widowed sister, who lives with them. Very simple." She smiled at him, the smile of a wicked child. "You look so stunned, beloved. Did you think I could do no more than a quadroon mistress?"

He turned the list over and stared down at the blank side thoughtfully. "Now as to menu, Natalie, it must be planned—"

"And you could plan it, Judah? Proceed. Permit me to see what you would offer your guests."

"Oh, I should not do too badly. We would have fish and roasts and fowl and *daube glacé* and—"

She laughed. "Of course. Everything is served at every formal dinner. It is only the seasoning and sauces that make one hostess's dinner superior to another. I implore you to leave the matter to me. The St. Martin recipes will grace your table, beloved."

He retreated and no further word was said of the dinner save once, when Natalie reported that no invitation had been declined.

And on the evening named they came, the great legal men of New Orleans.

God knows why they came. I am nobody but they do not seem aware of that.

From his position at the head of the table he admired the fine china. It reminded him of Grandmother Mendes's china that had been sold to keep him at Yale. Forget Yale. It was a heartbreak of childhood. It was long ago. Could he not yet think of it without pain?

Madame had placed all her treasures at Natalie's disposal. The sparkling crystal, the silver with her family crest upon it, the magnificent lace cloth, and the golden epergne. He admired it all but mostly he admired his wife. Natalie, beautiful Natalie, in deep red velvet. With amazement he listened to her sweet, light voice introducing a new topic as another grew threadbare. He heard her remarks, never witty to be sure but always charming. He heard her pretty phrasing as she accepted compliments on the wonderful foods that graced the table. Later in the parlor it was with a high degree of skill that she led one lady to sing for the company and with even more skill that she blocked another's ambition to do the same.

Judah found himself sitting beside Slidell on a settee in the back parlor.

"Excellent dinner, Benjamin. Sort of a surprise party, is it not?"

"I do not understand you."

Slidell's knowing eyes closed wearily. "Yes, you do. We always understand each other. You are absolutely baffled as to what Soulé and the others are doing here. I will tell you." He opened his eyes and turned slightly so that he could look straight into Judah's face. "They want your friendship, the same as I want it. They are wooing you the same as I am in preparation for the day when you can be used."

Something within Judah responded to the cynicism of the man. The defenses that he had built suddenly crumbled and he found himself warming to the honesty of the most dishonest man in New Orleans.

"Benjamin," Slidell continued, "there isn't a son of a bitch here who doesn't know that one day you will be bigger than he is."

"How can they know that? I have had but seven cases."

"Six," Slidell said and smiled at him. "Benjamin, never pretend with me. Every man needs someone to whom he can tell the truth. You've had six cases, but that's unimportant. The big thing is that around you there is that shining something that means success. Everyone sees it. Everyone has read that God-damned book of yours." He paused and sent a winning smile across the room at Mrs. Greenbury Stringer. "Why did you ask the Stringers? They don't belong in this company."

"Mr. Stringer has done a great deal for me, Slidell."

"You have made my point precisely. Has done. He would belong here if there was something he could still do."

Judah said, "Your attitude makes me eager to perform a service for you, friend."

Slidell patted his arm encouragingly. "That's it, Benjamin. Say to me whatever enters your mind." He gazed at the other guests gathered in pleasant conversational groups. "None of them could help you as much as I. Together we could own Louisiana." Suddenly he was on his feet, Mr. John Slidell, the gentleman. Madame Roselius had dropped her handkerchief. With a smile and a bow he restored it, and the lady, entranced by his attention and courtliness, sat gazing at him long after he had returned to his chair. "Sometimes," he said to Judah, "I get so sick of picking up lace handkerchiefs for fat women that I am sorry I was born such a well-mannered Creole."

"It must indeed be a heavy responsibility."

"Did you hear what I was saying about our beautiful Louisiana a moment ago?"

Judah nodded.

"Why don't you come into my office, Benjamin? Together we could do much. I need a quick mind like yours." He cast an eye over the assembled company. "Let us get a breath of air in the courtyard."

"I do not think I will go there with you, Slidell. Once again you have made me feel like a maiden for whom you pant. I do not think I would be safe in the courtyard."

Slidell roared with laughter. "My intentions toward you are clear. I intend nothing but seduction and I have a feeling that once the premise is acceptable you will enjoy every moment of it. Of course if you do not, you can always scream and Mazureau or noble Roselius will come rescue you."

"They are fine men, Slidell. Roselius is the model upon whom I would pattern myself."

"Of course. I was prepared for that. At your age one must have idols. You will recover." His eyes roved the room again. "By the way, Benjamin, do you know how to handle a pistol?"

"No. I am a reasonable man."

"Permit me to teach you. It would give me pleasure to know that you could defend yourself as a gentleman should. If you are going to belong to this city and cherish idols you must be prepared to—"

"Duel? Good God, I? I think of dueling as an exercise of—"

"The half-witted?" Slidell asked smoothly. "So do I, Benjamin, though I am fairly proficient at the game. It is the language of fools but it is the language these God-damned Creoles speak and you had better learn it."

"I do not anger easily, Slidell."

"Confidentially neither do I, but one must have the respect of fools if one lives among them. One must learn to resent, challenge, to shoot, and to act in general like a complete idiot. You will have to learn."

"I will be grateful for your instruction, sir."

"Good. I have fought two duels here and truthfully I liked it not at all. I was not even irked at my opponents but I quivered with rage in the approved manner and issued the challenge. One had accused me of unscrupulous practices."

"Unbelievable," Judah said.

"Unbelievable indeed that a man must shoot another for saying what everyone knew was true. The monstrous thing about it, Benjamin, is that I was somehow cleared of the accusation simply because I shot him in a gentlemanly manner. He was right but because he bled I became a heroic defender of an unstained reputation."

"The other duel?"

"It concerned a woman. I was wrong again but I was the better shot. The fool should have chosen swords. Jesus, I am clumsy with a sword."

Natalie was bending over them, smiling bewitchingly. "Mr. Slidell, I cannot have you monopolized by my husband, who would talk law all evening. Mrs. Grymes wishes to know who the harpist was that evening at your home. Will you not speak to her regarding her chances of engaging him for a musical evening?"

"With pleasure, Madame Benjamin, regretting only that you have not asked of me something more difficult to perform."

He rose and moved to a chair beside Mrs. Grymes. Judah watched him as he conversed with her, the pleasant smiles of the man, the gravity with which he considered her opinions, the artful manner in which he produced in Mrs. Grymes a conviction that all evening long it had been his wish to discuss music with her.

Natalie lingered a moment at her husband's side before moving on to another duty. "Does it go well?" she whispered.

"It goes magnificently."

"Join Madame Mazureau. She is bored with Mr. Stringer."

Natalie moved on across the room. He felt within himself a singing joy and he recognized that here was a memory in the making. For all his life it would return to please or plague him. Their first dinner and Natalie in deep red velvet.

Madame's new child was a boy and he was named Jules. Natalie rocked him in his cradle and sang a Gombo French lullaby, and Judah was deeply touched by her affection for her small brother. He thought the child should be theirs. It seemed a gratuitous insult of Nature that a baby born in this house, at this time, should belong to the St. Martins instead of the Benjamins.

Pov piti Lolotte à mouin
Pov piti Lolotte à mouin
Li gagnin bobo, bobo
Li gagnin doulè, doulè
Li gagnin doulè dans ker a li.

Her lovely face rubbed softly against the baby's cheek, and Judah felt very keenly the injustice of her being childless. But there were reasons why he could reconcile himself to the lack. For instance, the man who bowed to Natalie as they drove down Esplanade one afternoon.

"My instructor at La Fourche Parish."

Judah cast a glance at the tall, broad-shouldered figure.

"He seems to have the qualifications," he remarked.

"He was most admirable but perhaps not as well versed as—"

"There was another?"

"Several, beloved. Then of course from some of the pupils I had instruction, too." She spoke guilelessly, her expression sweetly demure. "I was anxious to learn and you must be happy that I learned so well. Wouldn't you despise a wife who could not spell or knew no mathematics?"

He did not reply. In the beginning it had been impossible to free his mind of his worries concerning her. Now he exercised strict discipline upon himself and no thought of Natalie went to court with him. He was even able, for days on end, to believe that there was no cause for worry.

He looked at her instructor from La Fourche Parish. So he was here in New Orleans? Natalie had wanted him to know. She was having her revenge for the days he had been away fighting a case in Donaldsville. She was telling him not to take her for granted.

They must entertain more, he thought. A very large party perhaps. It would give her something to think about, something to keep her busy. He would be away again in a week's time.

At the theater during the entr'acte he met another member of the La Fourche Parish household. A member with the stamp of the planter's son upon him, the arrogance, the grace.

"My cousin," Natalie murmured, and when her eyes met those of the young man it was there—only for a moment but unmistakable—the look of a man and a woman who have known each other well.

"Cousins, are you?" Judah questioned. "Natalie's father is then your mother's brother?"

The young man smiled. "No, Natalie and I are only distantly related. I am afraid we are but what is known as kissing cousins." His smile widened. "Though within my memory we have never kissed."

Never kissed? Was kissing a formality they had omitted in their haste? He felt a sudden rage descend upon him.

Benjamin, quiet down. Is any of this a surprise to you?

"Am I to be allowed a visit, Natalie?" The question came pleadingly, urgently, and in Judah's ears it sounded as obvious as though the young man had bluntly asked for an assignation.

Judah said, "Come to dinner tomorrow evening. We will be delighted."

"Dinner?" The young man was politely regretful. "I have another engagement." Then with a deep bow to Judah, "Sir, may I claim the privilege of a kinsman and request that I be permitted to call upon Natalie in mid-afternoon?"

"Permission granted," Judah said. "Though it is a disappointment to me that I myself shall be unable to entertain you."

Natalie never appeared at the breakfast table but remained abed until noon. For company Judah frequently had one or the other of her parents. This morning he made certain that it was Madame, for he had a question of importance.

"What are your plans for the day, Madame?"

"Oh, I have a dozen fittings for an entirely new wardrobe. Since the baby came I—"

He raised his eyes from the delicious grillade that had been placed upon his plate.

"I do not think you will keep your appointment. This afternoon there is a cousin from La Fourche Parish visiting. You will, of course, wish to see him. You will want to be here every minute to help Natalie entertain him."

For a long moment Madame was silent and when she spoke she did not look at him. "I will be here, Judah." Wearily she pushed her plate aside. "I will be here this afternoon but it will not always be possible."

Judah said, "I know, Madame. It will not always be possible."

The book, the one so tediously entitled, had gone into its second large printing. No law office in the state could guess how it had functioned without the information to be found in "Benjamin's Digest." The book had helped Judah, of course. It had carried his name to every corner of Louisiana, but the important thing was that New Orleans knew him well. The new man—Benjamin—was the true legal talent of the city. Benjamin, the brain that worked at lightning speed, the voice that spoke in tones of purest gold. Benjamin, the sarcastic, the sympathetic, the savior of the lost case, the winner of the impossible verdict. Benjamin, who won a reversal on the New Orleans Insurance Company case and could now name his own figure for a retainer fee.

He—with Slidell looking over his shoulder—read the pamphlet that was being sold in the hotels and coffeehouses. It was a collection of impressions of New Orleans lawyers. Unsigned, of course, but everyone knew Judge Whitaker to be the author.

> *Benjamin is emphatically the commercial lawyer of our city. He is a man fitted to adorn any circle, however distinguished for elegance or refinement and yet we find him a severe and untiring devotee to his profession. His language is the purest and most appropriate English, his French fluent and perfect. I will dwell long upon this picture as I think it may be studied with advantage by other young practitioners who seek distinction. Benjamin has not been a close student for nothing—*

Slidell greeted this pronouncement with a hoot of laughter. "For nothing! I will agree that it has not been for nothing. What was your fee, Benjamin, on that last harbor case?"

"Satisfactory, my dear Slidell, satisfactory. That is, for now. I am still but a young practitioner. Aren't those the good judge's words?" He gave Slidell a cigar and a smile. "Come on. Let us go to the club and have some coffee. How is Madame Slidell?"

"Benjamin, she is just wonderful. There never was a race of women like these Creoles. God damn it, it's a shame that they will disappear. Their blood will be mixed with Irish and Polish and Swedish and God knows what and—"

"A tragedy, my friend. It should be diluted only by the blood of the sons of candlemakers and fruit sellers. Anything else is an insult to posterity."

"You make me sick, Benjamin. Can't you pretend you're an

aristocrat? Jesus Christ, with the money you're earning you can afford to play the Creole."

"I enjoy watching you play it, my friend. You really play it well —that is, in company."

"Yes, I'm rather successful at it, and isn't Mathilde a dream presiding at my table?"

"A dream indeed, sir."

"God damn it, that girl is out of place anywhere but at a royal banquet. She could entertain an emperor, Benjamin."

"I am certain she could, and if in my travels I find an emperor who needs entertaining—"

"To hell with you. You will not be serious even about important things any more."

They seated themselves at a table in the club. It happened to be Slidell's table but there was also one reserved for Judah. They drew attention, these two. They were greeted, fawned upon, and envied.

Slidell puffed his cigar reflectively. "What are you doing with your money, Benjamin?"

"Spending it. Do you know of a better use for it?"

"I could tell you about an investment that—"

"I have not a spare picayune, thank you just the same. I am buying a plantation in Plaquemines Parish."

"Really?" Slidell was surprised. "Before a town house of your own? I should think you would want one of those Greek monstrosities in the new Garden district."

"I want a plantation house," Judah said.

"In Plaquemines Parish? Truly? It is so remote, so difficult of access. If you do not build a house in town then I think you are foolish not to remain at your father-in-law's. His house is beautiful."

Slidell had spoken the truth. The house on Bourbon Street was indeed beautiful. Mr. St. Martin had spent a large sum on the building and furnishing of it. But a plantation house had become a necessity. To get Natalie away from New Orleans was both his duty and desire.

Frequently she was not at home when he came from the office. She would rush in breathlessly, her eyes alight, her color high.

He never asked where she had been. Suppose she were to tell him?

"I am so sorry I was not here, beloved, to greet you. I was delayed at the milliner's. Such a time I had trying to buy a few simple bonnets. In the end I bought none at all. She had seven bolts of maline in delightful shades and she was taking them from the shelf when at that moment—"

He had not listened closely. He was looking into her sweet, grave face, fascinated by the way she could meet his eyes and prattle on with such seeming guilelessness.

And at that moment the ornament slipped and bounced upon the carpet, did it not, Natalie? Where have I heard a similar story? Oh, my darling, I know all about you. Why can I not tell you that I do? Why is it better that you should think me an easily deceived fool than that you should know me to be a man who loves you despite your weakness? What vulgarian made the rules that a stupid husband is a very acceptable fellow while a knowing husband who forgives because he understands is held in scorn? Why can I only keep your respect and the respect of New Orleans by permitting all to take for granted that knowing the truth I would abandon you instead of giving you an understanding heart to rest upon? You may ask if, in understanding, my pain is less, and I must say in answer, no, it is not less. It is not less.

The plantation in Plaquemines Parish seemed the only solution.

It was called Belle Chasse and was so beautiful that a man could die for love of it. Its white columns gleamed in the moonlight and the river ran silver past the broad galleries. Within, there were twenty high-ceilinged rooms, and he had spent a fortune in carpets and furnishings for Belle Chasse. The chandeliers and medallions, the statuary and paintings were the talk of the river. The library was painted in a shade of blue that reminded him of a house he had known in Charleston. The chamber he shared with Natalie was like nothing he had ever seen before. Even his dreams of the plantation houses owned by his aunts in St. Thomas had provided no visions as lovely as the room that Natalie planned in white and gold.

"Now you have a home worthy of you, my love."

She smiled wryly. "A home in one of the villages that the tribe of Judah inherited along with the cities," she said.

"Inherited? I assure you I did not inherit it. It cost me a year's fees in cash and another year in promises."

She stood upon the gallery and gazed at the wide sugar land and found no magic in the singing of the slaves or in the massive oaks weirdly veiled in Spanish moss.

"It is very sad, Judah."

"Sad?"

"Indeed. Very."

"But I shall be here every week end, my darling, and a dozen guests will arrive with me and there will be great parties and—"

Natalie buried her face in her hands and wept. He drew her to him tenderly. "My love, your parents will be here often and during the week you will be so busy with this great house that the time will fly. On Friday you will have to be ready to entertain God alone knows how many people."

She shook her head. "I want only you and there will be Fridays when you do not arrive at all but will sit in men's clubs and—"

"That is part of my work, Natalie. I did not make the money with which to buy Belle Chasse by ignoring social contacts."

She said, "You have already made enough to keep us forever."

"No, Natalie. No woman lives who loves clothes and luxury more than you do."

She stared at him, her yellow eyes filled with a deep, unspoken sorrow, like the eyes of a small captured monkey he had seen on the docks.

"What shall I do with the clothes you buy for me?" she asked. "Show them to the slaves?"

"I will be here, precious. Every week end and sometimes more often."

"Do you still love me, Judah?"

"I do indeed, Natalie."

"In that case I will try to like Belle Chasse."

When he came down the river on a Friday evening he did not always bring guests. Sometimes he came alone bearing a small gift for Natalie—a lacy shawl or a new perfume from Paris. They would spend the week end as lovers, lost in each other, hopeful that Monday would never come. When the sky was black and the air was filled with the heavy fragrance of the Louisiana night he would lie beside her and wish that he, too, was touched with the flame that never let her rest.

But there were week ends when he did not let himself even think of Belle Chasse. Week ends when he sent a letter to her describing his regret and disappointment.

It was wrong. Somehow it was wrong. Still what did a man do? Toss aside a twenty-thousand-dollar fee for the pleasure of making love to his own wife? One could not outwit Mazureau by lying in a woman's arms. Without effort and application one could not meet the expenses of a house like Belle Chasse.

He was proud of its reputation for hospitality and luxury. The length of the river there was no man's home where servants were more skillfully trained, food more invitingly prepared and served. In every chamber there were flowers in a heavenly blaze of color, and the soft blankets that protected one against the chill and dampness were woven especially for Belle Chasse. A guest found the hours gliding by too swiftly and departure was always the only regrettable moment of a visit to the beautiful home of the Benjamins.

Judah and Natalie breakfasted on the upstairs gallery when he was at Belle Chasse and there was a morning when he became aware of the vile taste of the coffee.

"What is the matter with it?" he demanded.

Natalie looked hurt. "Beloved, it is the same coffee, brewed in the same way as always. Are you sure you do not imagine things?"

By her innocent eyes he knew that she was guilty of something. Of what?

"What is in this cup, Natalie?"

"Coffee, my love."

"With a slight touch of what?"

She turned from him flushing slightly. "Do not drink it, Judah. It is voodoo."

"Voodoo!" He stared at her uncomprehendingly, then broke into sudden laughter as realization came. "An aphrodisiac, I suppose. Well, you are a flattering little minx, aren't you? Personally I had thought myself—"

She said, "Yes, it is an aphrodisiac and no criticism is implied." She sighed and her voice came to him small and sorrowful. "It was only meant to bring you to me more often."

He gazed at the Spanish moss and the river and the slave cabins in the distance. This was what she saw every day. Natalie, the city child, the tormented soul. What should he do about her? What could he do?

"There is a woman," she said, "the mother of the family you bought last month. She works grigri. She told me that it would bring you home to me at least every single week end."

He said, "I am here now, Natalie."

"But you must go. The boatman is waiting."

"Let him wait, my love. I have tremendous respect for voodoo."

As she lay upon his arm she had much to tell him of grigri. With her tousled black hair and her wide, wondering eyes she was half-wanton, half-child as she whispered to him the strange thing that she had heard. He was mildly amused though already his mind had gone to his office. He had missed an appointment with the president of the New Orleans Insurance Company.

"So she gave the grigri to this couple, Judah, and on St. John's Eve they did not sleep at all and he performed a dozen miracles of delight before dawn."

Judah grinned at her. "Any report on how he performed in court next day?"

"Oh, he was not a lawyer. Do you believe the story?" she whispered.

"No, and for the love of God, don't you. You'll only be disappointed." He kissed her mouth and dropped a farewell caress upon her white bosom. "I have to be about the law business, sweetheart."

For six weeks he did not fail in his visits to Belle Chasse. With more than ordinary care he arranged his work so that nothing would interfere. He dreaded the moment in which he must tell Natalie that he would be away for a month.

Slidell had said, "Benjamin, I am going to New York to see Belmont about something I have in mind and I have been thinking that you ought to come along with me. It would be a good thing for you to know August Belmont."

There was no contesting that statement. Belmont, the American representative of the great Rothschild banking house, a power in New York politics, a man whose influence was limitless —and married to Slidell's niece.

"It would not hurt you, Benjamin, to belong to a few good

New York clubs and to know the important people there. We
would stay with the Belmonts of course. Their house is one of
Manhattan's show places, particularly famous for its art gallery."

"Are you planning on taking Madame Slidell?"

"No, oh, no," Slidell had said hurriedly. "We won't have
any time for ladies. This will be all business, Benjamin. All business with August."

Certainly to know Belmont would be worthwhile, to invest time
in such a project would be wise, an insurance for the future. The
man could throw an enormous fee wherever he chose, and Slidell
was tiring of law.

When he told Natalie, she had an idea of her own.

"I do not like Belle Chasse enough to stay alone for weeks
with only cane fields and oak trees for company. I shall live in
New Orleans while you are away."

"Oh, do stay here, darling. Your mother will come and—"

"My mother. For what do I need my mother?"

"Natalie, my sweet, you stay here all safe and snug and when
I return I will bring you a diamond necklace."

Mrs. August Belmont helped him to select it. A score of necklaces on black velvet cushions were brought to him in the marble-
columned ballroom and were judged by gas and candlelight, were
tested against Mrs. Belmont's fair skin, and were tried with every
possible shade of gown.

"Oh, buy that one," Mrs. Belmont advised. "If you do not,
then August must buy it for me."

"Benjamin will buy it for Natalie," Slidell said. "He is the
only man in New Orleans who would buy anything like that for
his own wife. What does that thing cost, Benjamin?"

Judah smiled and slipped the tiny price tag in his pocket. "It
came high, my friend."

High indeed, and in Louisiana there was no one to wear it. He
stopped first at the house on Bourbon Street and Madame ordered
his luggage taken to his apartment.

"Thank you, no," Judah said. "I will but remain tonight and
go to Belle Chasse in the morning."

Madame shook her head. "I think you will want to stay here,
Judah. At least for a while. She is not there. I tried but she would
not listen. She sailed last Thursday for Europe."

There was a paralysis of terror upon him as he opened her

letter. Had he lost her forever? That would depend upon how she had chosen the words she had left for him.

Beloved:

I told you Belle Chasse was sad. You wouldn't want me to be as miserable as I am at this moment. I know how you worry about me in New Orleans with the seasonal fevers and everything so I have saved you the heartache of having me there. Paris seems like a good choice when one considers everything. Judah, my darling, I love you so much that I would never even think of New Orleans or Paris if you could always be beside me. Try to go on loving me as much as I love you.

Your Natalie

He sent for the passenger list of the Thursday sailing. Who beside Natalie was on that ship? Midway down the list his glance came to rest and had need to travel no further. A famous Louisiana name but one known no better in La Fourche Parish, Judah thought, than in the secret chambers of his own mind.

He tossed the list in the wastebasket and walked upstairs. A thousand times he had put Natalie from his mind. Surely he could do it now.

In his room he found a very small boy astride a very large leather valise.

"It is my horse, brother. Do not make me leave him."

Little Jules. It was always a shock to see the child. He never thought of him, hardly remembered his existence. As an infant he had been sweet—well, he was still sweet. Those big black eyes, the brave manner in which he sat the mighty charger of his imagination.

"Come here, little Jules."

He took the child upon his knee. This could be his son. And if he were, would it have made a difference?

"Are you going to tell me a story, brother? I know the one about Bouki and the macaques."

Judah smiled. "So do I, Jules," he said. "So do I."

Every ship that arrived brought a letter from Natalie. He wrote frequently to her. In the care of a captain well known to him he sent the necklace. He sent ten thousand dollars and his love but

she did not return. She wrote as a woman writes when her indulgent husband has permitted her a trip to Europe.

*I am having such a lovely time, Judah. Though I miss you,
Paris is delightful and I am sure you will not mind if I remain
yet a while. You are so busy that you cannot experience any
loneliness. My little house is comfortable and pretty. I have
made many friends and some members of my father's family
live in Paris. With them I am going everywhere and enjoying
the season.*

The house on Bourbon Street at the end of the day was heartache, and Belle Chasse had subtly changed. Its beauty now
seemed that of a well-tended cemetery, its sweetness melancholy,
its peace deathly.

He went about New Orleans with the shadow of Natalie at his
side. He never rode in a carriage that she did not ride with him.
Sometimes he ordered the carriage back to Bourbon Street, and
he himself walked, deliberately choosing streets that he had never
known with her. In that filthy house he had lived his first weeks
in New Orleans. Did the woman with the watery eyes still own
it? He shuddered remembering the mildewed boots of the man
who had died of yellow fever. God, one could imagine the horrors
that house had known in the great plague. The great plague.
The cannon booming in the streets. Natalie walking beside him,
her dark cloak flying wild to show her lovely new dress with the
cerise sash.

Over there was the house of the Free Woman of Color. The
neat little room where he had studied law—where he had studied
law and dreamed of Auguste St. Martin's daughter. Yes, but
before Auguste St. Martin's daughter there had been others.
Could he not think of those others? The milliner's apprentice for
instance. Which had been her house? Had it been on St. Ann or
Dumaine? He could not recall.

"My wife has deserted me," he said to Madame Mazureau and
he smiled as he said it, making certain that she saw the smile.
"She has grown tired of my promises to show her Europe. She
has gone on a trip by herself. A busy man is a boresome husband."

Well-bred people knew how to play the game once the directions had been read and explained to them. They played it
gracefully. No one asked when Natalie would return.

At his club there was always cards and conversation. High stakes and stories of the days when, as the older members said, New Orleans had been New Orleans.

Grymes shuffled the deck, outrageously holding up the game to talk of the past, to laugh at himself for the follies of those other years.

"I received twenty thousand dollars for defending the pirate, Laffite. Forty thousand he paid. Half to me, half to my partner. I resigned a big job—district attorney—to take the case. Would you have done it, Benjamin?"

"I cannot say. It would depend on how much he needed me and how much I believed in him. With me, sir, as of course with you—the fee would be a matter of complete indifference."

Grymes shouted with laughter. "The fee! We were as wild as pirates ourselves in those days. I went to Grand Terre in person to collect, and lived for a week with the Laffites eating and drinking like a Roman emperor. I was paid in golden doubloons and was rowed home with a full escort of buccaneers. It was beautiful, Benjamin, the color, the romance of those days. I stopped at every plantation the length of the river, and there was dancing and gambling and I danced too little and gambled too much. I had not a dollar of my twenty thousand when we reached New Orleans!"

Grymes dealt the cards and no man at the table weighed the values carefully that hand. To consider well seemed suddenly a niggling thing to do.

There was always the club and a card game, friends, theaters, books, work. How could the city be so full and yet so desolate?

He visited with Greenbury Stringer in the small house that remained completely Ohio.

"Glad to see you, Judah. Come in." Mr. Stringer was in shirt sleeves, his feet encased in shabby, restful shoes. It was not only the house that had stonily resisted assimilation into the elegance of Louisiana.

They talked of law, Mr. Stringer asking for explanations of this point or the other. Judah laughed and said to him, "I am getting pretty tired of your questions, boy. Besides they're embarrassing. I don't know the answers to half of them."

Mr. Stringer smiled, remembering. "You've come a long way

from those days, Judah, a long way. Are you tired? It's been a climb."

"I am sharing the load now. I took Bill Micou in, you know."

"A fine man, Bill Micou, and proud as the devil to be with you." Mr. Stringer slapped Judah's knee. "What would you have said if I had told you that you would one day have a staff of trilingual assistants and penmen, an office as spacious as a big home and a man like Micou for a junior partner?"

"I would have said, 'Mr. Stringer, all that will count as nothing unless when that day comes I still have your friendship.' "

Mr. Stringer sniffled and blew his nose. "Judah, you were the nicest boy I ever knew and when all the fancy tailoring and big reputation is forgotten you are still that same boy."

What had he expected to find at Mr. Stringer's house? The peace he had known in those early days? Had he expected to cross the threshold and find himself once again the youth who had needed only Mr. Stringer and a set of law books? What had he sought in wandering about New Orleans? The old familiar smell of the docks, the dampness on his face, the retracing of steps—none of it could bring back the time when he had not known a woman named Natalie.

Six months, and he could endure no more. To go to Paris was irresponsible behavior, he told himself. He was not just anyone who could pack up and go as the mood seized him. He was Benjamin, a leading lawyer of the state. The leading lawyer? Perhaps. He bought a bracelet with yellow diamonds that glittered like Natalie's eyes.

He said to Bill Micou, "I go without a worry. Thanks to you."

The city of Paris, he supposed, was much as he had imagined it. Her charms remained imagined. He did not give Paris a second glance. She was not the woman he had come to see.

His ship, on the return voyage, docked at New York. He stayed a few days with the Belmonts, attended the opera, and spent an hour in the cathedral-like grandeur of a place that was unaccountably his club.

On the way home he made a sentimental tour through South Carolina. Charleston, with the soft light falling upon her candy-colored houses, seemed a village out of toyland. The harbor was no longer of consequence. Charleston was already sleeping, dreaming of the glorious past. He stood on King Street and memories crowded in upon him. Here his father had become an American citizen. Here his mother had flouted Beth Elohim and had opened the store on Saturday. Here he had received word that he was accepted at Yale. That had been a happy day for them all but not happy enough to compensate for—

Benjamin, why do you not grow up? That belongs to another day.

The pretty Seixas sisters, Dr. de la Motta, Mr. Moïse. No doubt they were but a few steps away. It would be pleasant to see them, but in the end he went only to the home of Moses Lopez. The parlor still resembled the reception room of an institution and smelled faintly of yellow soap.

Moses Lopez, aging but still determinedly erect, peered searchingly at him.

"So you fulfilled my predictions. You became a successful man. A great lawyer. I am proud that I played some small part in your career."

"It was no small part, sir."

The old man shook his head wonderingly. "God is good. He let me live to look at you again. Have you seen your parents?"

"I am going from here to Beaufort to visit them."

"You bought them a fine house there I understand. You are a dutiful son."

Judah did not meet the eyes of Moses Lopez. Did the old man not know that his parents might contradict that statement?

"Mr. Lopez, I have hurt them very deeply, I fear."

The huge head of Moses Lopez raised swiftly, ominously, reminding Judah of a charging bull.

"What have you done?"

"I married a Gentile woman, Mr. Lopez."

What business is it of his? Why am I telling him? Do I never outgrow my childishness? In a moment I will tremble as I did beside his coach. I will wonder if I ought to bow.

Moses Lopez said, "A Gentile woman?" His eyes were clouded and thoughtful but he reached out and laid his hand upon Judah's. "Perhaps—I say perhaps—you have done a great harm to your soul. What harm have you done others by your choice?"

The house in Beaufort appeared woefully inadequate. Had he seen it before purchase he would never have agreed to so in-

consequential a gift for his parents. His mother's letter had suggested that he was buying something more suitable than this. Or
did one's standards shift so completely that he no longer knew
what was luxury to those who had lived too long behind a fruit
store?

His sister Rebecca, widowed now, lived in the Beaufort house.
He was pleased to find her a woman of poise, a woman who by
reading had educated herself beyond the circle of her acquaintances. He studied her carefully and came to a decision.

"Sister, would you like to live in a plantation house with
twenty rooms and command a staff of well-trained servants?
Could you learn to do it?"

"I believe so."

Her face was intelligent, her glance direct and pleasant. In
imagination he saw her in expensive clothes and pictured her
hair dressed by a slave who would know what to do with those
flat, dark braids.

"And you, Mama? How would you like to be waited upon by
a black woman whose only purpose in life is pleasing you?"

His mother said, "I could endure it." He thought with wonderment how tall and strong she had seemed to him. She was
only a wisp of a woman with gray hair and tired eyes that responded to nothing that he offered them. Not promises, not
memories, not praise. Her eyes had forgotten how to flash with
anger or glow with love. They were empty, and not even his
visit had brought pleasure. He was a stranger en route to New
Orleans, a stranger from whom it was somehow appropriate to
accept favors.

"Papa?" He turned to Philip. Philip had scarcely spoken to
him. Was this Papa, the gentle little man who had been so
anxious to give his opinions, to share with everyone his hard-
gained learning? Papa, who in his own peculiar way had loved his
children? This was a different man, a sour man who had been
forced to live on an allowance given by the husband of a Gentile
woman. This had been a bitter dose, but it was not all and it was
not the worst. Philip Benjamin was no longer acceptable to his
church. He had been excommunicated for the sin of thinking.
That was the way he put it. The sin of thinking.

"Some day," he had said, "many will think as I do and the

service will be challenged but it will be too late for me. I will be rotting in unconsecrated ground."

"Papa, would you like to live in Louisiana?"

"No. I shall not go there."

The two women showed no surprise. Judah realized they had known this would be his answer.

"Take your mother. She will go. At last she will have a place suited to the elegance of her gold earrings, a place fit for a Mendes."

"You would like Louisiana, Papa."

"I tell you, Judah, I want no part of Louisiana. I want no part of your palace or your fine life. It sticks in me now like a knife that I must ask you to keep this house so that I may live out my days with a roof over my head."

There was no point in argument. What purpose would be served by a family quarrel? Parents were sometimes foolish but never so foolish as the young who made much of nothing.

"It will be my pleasure, Papa, to keep this house as long as you like. A son can ask for no more than to be able to—"

"I know you're able to keep this house. Do not persist in reminding me that I am in your debt."

"I am in yours, Papa."

"Then why did you marry out of your faith? Why did you marry that woman?"

Judah did not reply at once, and in the moment of silence he found the eyes of his mother and sister upon him. Yes, the eyes were asking, why did you? So it was their wish to know, too, was it? Well, then his response would be different. Not just a soothing answer to an angry old man whose unhappiness had half deranged him, but to his female relatives who must understand once and for all.

"Like most of us," he began, "my wife was given a name. It is Natalie. Very simple and very musical, I think. Much more appealing to the ear than 'that woman' for instance. Now as to your question—I married Natalie because I loved her devotedly. Today I love her more than I loved her then. She is a Christian and I am a Jew. These differences never enter any conversation I have with Natalie. Therefore I consider it remarkable that anyone else should find the matter worth mentioning."

"Then," demanded his father, "she is still your wife? I thought you said she lives in Europe. A marriage cannot endure that way. How can you say that she is your wife?"

"I assure you, Papa, she is my wife."

There was a letter in his pocket, a perfumed letter with lines scribbled in her girlish hand. It had been placed aboard the ship with him—though he had not known it—and had been delivered at the Belmonts.

Beloved:

What did you do to me? I weep as I write this, for you are leaving me and I will be unable to get you out of my mind. Was it not wonderful? It all had such a secret air about it that I feel quite like that quadroon mistress you used to have—in your imagination.

I hope I have sent you home happy to that dull Madame Benjamin who, whiningly and complainingly, haunts a dismal place called Belle Chasse. Darling, I beg of you, never make me Belle Chasse's Madame Benjamin again. Do not let us break the spell of what we have had together these last two weeks. When you long for me, slip away to Paris.

You never wanted a married life such as the one I propose but think well before you are sorry for our loss of a mutual hearth. Judah, my love, once the first year was gone did any other man ever have two such weeks with his own wife? Remember there were no worries, no cross words and no ennui.

Again it is not the marriage you would have chosen but are men who return every evening to conventional wives completely happy? No, every man has something that is not as he wishes. You, my husband, have a wife who sits in broad daylight remembering the kisses of a man she married years ago. Come back to me soon, beloved.

Natalie

"I assure you, Papa," he said again, "she is my wife."

They came to Louisiana with him, his mother, his sister Rebecca, and the two youngest, Joseph and Penina. Solomon and his wife moved into the Beaufort house to take care of Papa. The marriage of his parents was ended, and Judah knew there were no regrets on either side.

His mother wept at the beauty of Belle Chasse, walking from room to room, exclaiming on the richness of the furnishings and decorations. This reminded her of something her mother had owned, that recalled a possession of Grandfather Mendes. Judah said nothing, though he well knew that time had indeed put a high value on the household effects of his mother's family.

His sister Rebecca learned to entertain. Belle Chasse was still a desirable place to visit. Her conversation was intelligent rather than delightful. She had wit in place of a talent for silence. She spoke well but lacked the art of leading others to speak well themselves. The atmosphere of Belle Chasse had undergone a change. There was comfort here for the guests as always, despite the fact that the sharp efficiency of Rebecca's efforts was evident. In a Creole household one had the impression that the grace and charm simply happened, that everything glided smoothly into place. In Rebecca's management of Belle Chasse one heard the wheels turn, saw the machinery working. It was no longer a Creole household.

Rebecca followed her brother's career with avid interest, discussed his cases with him, asked questions, praised, commented. Poor sister, doubtless she had heard that he had been unable to come home to Natalie and share with her the burdens of his profession. At first he was amused and touched. Only at first.

If they were to live together, if he were not to dread her company, she must know the truth.

"Rebecca, my dear sister, I have something to say to you. I will say it once then never again, for it is as hard for me to say as for you to hear. It is simply this: I am not a man who likes to talk law with a woman. When at the end of a day I still have a desire to pursue the subject I will go to my club and find Mazureau or Roselius. Do you see, sister?"

"I see."

He turned away so that if it were her wish to cry a little she would think it had gone unnoticed.

"Judah."

"Yes, sister?"

"This is not quite the time to mention it, but I am terribly proud of your handling of the Nassau matter. I read the story of it to Mother and we were both so—"

"What story of it?"

"In the papers that came downriver this morning. It is sort of a personal observation of you written not at all like ordinary articles—you haven't seen it?"

She brought him the paper. He began to read, recognizing at once the style, an imitation of the new form gaining popularity in the New York City journals.

The courtroom is crowded. Today Benjamin himself is to be heard. This is a case of great importance and a king's ransom is at stake. This is the case that has been argued in clubs, coffee-houses, and at dinner tables for two years. Six insurance companies have retained Benjamin to do battle for them. A shipment of slaves loaded in Virginia for transport to Louisiana has been lost. Nineteen of the Negroes mutinied, murdered the captain and forced the crew to change course and make for Nassau. In that port the nineteen guilty of murder were taken into custody. The hundred or more innocent of complicity in either mutiny or murder were permitted to land on the free soil of Britain. Permitted? No, urged, claim the owners of the consignment. Urged by a British officer to fling themselves on the soil of Britain where no man is a slave.

"Is this not foreign intervention?" asks the company that intended to sell the cargo in Louisiana. "Is it not? And are we not insured against foreign intervention? Examine the policy. Of course we are insured against the loss, for it was suffered through the intervention of Britain in the form of one of her officers."

Now listen to Benjamin as he addresses the court. If you would delight your ears, hear his voice. It will give you something of the same pleasure you have experienced at the opera. If you care only to look, then look at the fascinating Benjamin, at the dark face, so cool and calm. You will think him feeling-less till you see the warmth of his eyes. Regard the boyish physique but observe his poise and dignity. Listen to him now. Notice that he never raises his voice but speaks always with restraint, crediting his listeners with an intellect that needs not be harassed by a hysterical advocate.

He speaks:

"No insurance was issued which covers the eventuality here considered. No insurance could be issued to cover it, for this

matter hinges not upon foreign intervention. Is there a policy which insures one against the normal, natural actions of his fellow man? Is there a policy that protects one against a merciful impulse? Foreign intervention? No. A young man gazed upon a shipload of slaves and pointed to Nassau, lying like a land of promise, calling to any anguished soul who could reach its precious soil. Did he act as a British officer? I say that he did not. He acted as a free man who wished his unhappy brothers free. In that moment he was not conscious of queen or country. He did not think of himself as an Englishman or, I submit, was he able to remember those good Virginia businessmen who were counting on a substantial profit. He remembered only that he and the suffering black wretches were one in the eyes of God and he said to them, 'There is Nassau. Hurry!'

"This then is the act against which the plaintiffs claim they were insured. They claim they were insured against the impulse of an individual who values freedom, an individual following a law of Nature, a law older than any agreements made by nations. Is there a policy issued that covers a young man's passion for a free world, a young man's desire to unchain the chained? If so, I withdraw, for in that event perhaps the plaintiffs do actually hold a policy that protects them against loss by an act of human decency."

Benjamin is finished speaking now. He sits. The curtain has descended. The play is over. Oh, the verdict? Benjamin wins. The insurance companies do not have to pay the Virginia businessmen but they pay Benjamin.

In the coffeehouse he is eyed with respect and admiration. Do you realize he has not only saved the insurance companies a great deal of money but has relieved a serious international complication? We could clash with England over a matter like this. Of course, he has presented us with a riddle: When is a British officer not acting in his capacity as a British officer? The answer is—when Judah Benjamin is handling the case.

As he looked up from the paper Rebecca, her eyes aglow, smiled at him.

"I will never talk law to you again, Judah, but is that not a thrilling account?"

"My enjoyment is your pride in me," he said. What would Rebecca think of the conversation he had had with Slidell after the verdict?

"For Christ's sake, Benjamin, I thought you were addressing an abolitionist meeting."

"It would have been a bad case to lose."

"Well, you did not lose it but it took every trick in the book except tears and for a moment I thought—"

"You thought I was going to cry?"

"No. I thought I was. You reminded me a little of myself."

"Come now, Slidell, you never would have thought of endowing a British officer with an impulsive gesture."

"You are touching upon the very thing I mean. The son of a bitch hates us and he did just what he was trying to do—rob slaveholders of their property, and because he was wearing that pretty uniform at the moment, my friend, it was foreign intervention."

"How can that be, sir? The verdict is already in."

"Well, then, what the hell are we standing here for? Let us go open a bottle of wine."

Within a year after bringing her from Beaufort, his mother was dead. She died happily in a bed that had cost him a thousand dollars and had reminded her of "the kind that was in every chamber of my father's house." He was glad he had never shown a sign of disbelief.

It was a bad year. Before his mother's death the headaches had begun. Now they were increasing alarmingly. More often, more painful. A dozen times he was advised by Micou and Rebecca to consult a doctor. He could not do so, he was in the middle of something extremely important. Next week. Next month. Suddenly there was no way of postponing the consultation another moment. There was a day when the office swam crazily before his eyes and he could see nothing but a blur.

Micou drove him to Bourbon Street and leaving him in the care of Madame St. Martin went to fetch a doctor.

"Do not be disturbed, Madame. When the doctor comes I shall be all right."

"Really? Do you think him a witch doctor? Will he work a charm and produce immediate results?"

There were no immediate results. There were a half-dozen visits to the house, a half-dozen more to the office.

"Your eyes must be rested for an indefinite spell, Mr. Benjamin. They are badly overworked. You must not read, you must not—"

"Sir, I am a lawyer."

"Would you care to be a blind one?"

He did not write his news to Natalie. What gain could result from troubling her? The climate of anxiety was not one in which she could be expected to thrive. He told her nothing.

Twice a week Micou or an assistant came downriver to Belle Chasse and acquainted him with the concerns of the office. Slowly and carefully everything was read to him. He concentrated tensely upon the voice, his mind seeing each word black upon a white page. To grasp a situation when it was presented thus was not the same as seeing the vital phrases, the hard core of the matter before one's eyes.

"How are things going, Micou?"

"Splendidly. Your name alone would carry us forever."

"My question does not stem from lack of faith in you. It is only that foolishly people have credited me with an invincibility. I lose but they do not seem to notice. They associate me personally with victory."

"And well they may. Do you not think you could go into court merely to present a case that I had already—"

"No, Micou. I wish I could. I will not argue a case I have not myself studied and prepared. It is too risky."

To Rebecca he was extremely cheerful. "You must read to me every evening, sister. Always have I loved poetry and now I have time."

Now he had time. So much of it that he experienced boredom and moodiness and knew a sickness with life that was new to him. He strolled the sugar lands of Belle Chasse and hated the quiet and the stupid business of producing sugar. To have a plantation house meant that one must plant, though it was shameful that a hundred and fifty people labored from dawn to dark on a project in which their master had no interest.

I do not even know why that man who bends above the shallow wooden box is satisfied with what he sees. What properties in the syrup are pleasing to him? And what is the working name for the shallow wooden box?

For a lawsuit he had always studied the practical and theoretical points involved. He knew the essentials for sailing a ship or building a railway. Yet here on his own land he had not troubled to learn the smallest detail of sugar making.

He sent for the plantation manager.

"What is that shallow box called?"

"A cooler, Mr. Benjamin."

"What is its purpose?"

"Well, the impurities in the sugar settle to the bottom. That's a step in the open kettle process."

"You had better take me around. Show me everything, and in the showing pretend you have been assigned the task of explaining to a blockhead. On second thought there is no need for pretending."

He learned about the making of sugar. He also learned about drainage, fertilization, the selection of seed. Within months he was dictating articles for publication on chemical principles, analysis of cane, and methods of employing vacuum pans. His land became a focal point for the planters of the neighborhood. Belle Chasse won the State Agricultural Society first prize for loaf sugar, but Judah was tired of sugar. It had no continued enchantment, for what one learned was negotiable. One could pass a proven fact to another and that which had worked once would work again. The business was without surprises, without the possibility of finding oneself in sudden, sharp combat with a trained adversary. His manager knew as much as he of the saccharometer, the polarizer, and the other machinery he had installed. Belle Chasse would now produce sugar of absolute chemical purity world without end.

He roved the house, reflecting on the changes, the differences. Sometimes he stood in the doorway of Natalie's dressing room and pictured her as he had seen her so many times. On that brocade chair she had sat while a slave, kneeling at her feet, slipped silk hosiery and little silver pumps in place.

As he walked through the chambers he knew that no servant had arranged those flowers that had blazed so colorfully. No servant had created the serenity and well-ordered routine of the household.

"I am going to Paris again," he told Rebecca and Micou.

They only smiled and wished him a pleasant voyage. Each had wondered how long he could live without Natalie.

• • •

He came back to Louisiana with a new idea. Politics. Something of the flavor of law could be found there. He wanted a very small office. It must not be of statewide importance. Something related only to New Orleans. Board of Alderman? Splendid.

Slidell said, "Are you mad? What do you want that for?"

"It will give me something to do. Besides, since I am not even of your political faith, I do not see that—"

"You cannot be elected."

"Why not?"

"You stated it yourself. You are not of my political faith."

"I am popular in New Orleans and, by God, I think myself capable of holding so unpretentious an office."

Slidell laughed. "You can't hold any office unless you are elected, Benjamin. And you will not be elected."

Slidell was right. Judah was defeated and stunned by the turn of events.

"I will tell you truly, Slidell, I am not a conceited man but I was certain that I could aspire to something so modest."

Slidell put his arm around him and laughed till tears started to his eyes. "My poor Benjamin, it was dreadful what was done to you. A handful—mind you a handful—of unprincipled wretches circulated the rumor that you are anti-Catholic and overnight the whole city had accepted the vicious lie."

"What! I? Slidell, my wife is Catholic, my friends are Catholic. How can people believe such a story?"

"Voters believe anything, Benjamin. Next time you run for office you can hire the same unprincipled wretches to tell this Catholic city that it was all a hideous invention. Politics is rough and tumble."

Benjamin stared at Slidell. "Somehow I am not angry at you. I do not know why I am not. I suppose it is because a man cannot feel anger toward an alligator. But I will permit myself the luxury of saying—Slidell, you're a bastard."

"I? Surely, old friend, you do not think I would circulate so vile a canard against you."

"Old friend, I think you would dig my eye out for a picayune."

"Oh, how are your eyes, by the way?"

The question so solicitously voiced, so out of place in the tenor of the conversation, made Judah smile. "It is no wonder you

. . .

never infuriate me, but I can tell you now, friend alligator, you will not run me out of politics."

Slidell said, "God love you, Benjamin, you are not even in politics. What is the news? Personal news, I mean."

Judah shook his head. "There is none."

None? In his pocket there was a letter.

Beloved:

I am incredulous. After ten years of marriage we are to have a child—

With what joy he would inform Slidell, Micou, Rebecca, and anyone willing to listen, what rejoicing within himself there would be—if the child were born no later, no earlier, than April.

"You did not give me an answer regarding your eyes, Benjamin. Can you use them again? How are the headaches?"

"The headaches have disappeared."

Slidell shrugged. "You don't need to see. I heard you got fifteen thousand dollars one dull afternoon for simply listening to two possible presentations of a case and naming the one you thought more effective."

Judah said, "But dull afternoons come infrequently, Slidell."

"What the hell do you do with your money? You ought to have a room at Belle Chasse stacked with it by now."

"Oh, I have. One can scarcely open the door to my library."

It occurred to him as he spoke that something must be laid aside for the child. It was not too early to begin building an inheritance. He must examine his expenditures. Money was slipping through his fingers. There must be more reasonably priced tailors in town than his. There must be a way to run Belle Chasse more economically.

The problem of Belle Chasse disappeared that spring. The rains came and the river rose. Though the Benjamin levees held, neighboring ones did not, and the result was ruin for all. Water seeped into the sugar land destroying the growing crop and even the seed cane. Flood rushed across the parish, and wild deer, frightened and hungry, huddled at the very door of Belle Chasse, asking to be saved from starvation. Judah, sitting in his library, knew that never again would he come down a placid river on a Friday afternoon to beautiful Belle Chasse. Never again.

"It will cost a fortune to repair and replace everything," Rebecca said.

"Yes, sister. A fortune."

In his hand he held the full knowledge that someone else would restore Belle Chasse, if restored it was to be. In his hand he held a notice that the respected gentleman for whom he had endorsed a sixty-thousand-dollar loan had disappeared, and that he, Judah, was obligated to redeem the defection.

Belle Chasse was gone by the end of April. All of it. The proud house, the ravaged sugar land, the furniture and paintings. He saw his slaves gathered together in wagonloads, looking heartbreakingly like the puzzled deer who had turned to him for help.

But even their faces and the loss of Belle Chasse were driven from his mind, for to his office came the letter he had awaited.

Beloved:

A girl was born April 15th. She is beautiful. Hurry to me so that together we may count her little pink toes. She is so little —so lovable—

The child was named Anna Julie Marie Natalie and was brought to him on a satin pillow. Yards of fine lace adorned the impressive garment in which her nurse had dressed her. He gazed down at the small face and saw at once that the baby lacked only a pair of bright gold earrings to be a tiny Rebecca Mendes Benjamin.

Natalie, slim in yellow organdy, looking as though her body had never known the miracle of producing life, reached for his hand. "I call her Ninette. It sounds warm and soft. Am I foolish, beloved, or is she not much prettier than other babies?"

"You are not foolish. She is the most beautiful child in the world." In a moment Ninette would be whisked away from him. He could not allow that. He plucked her from the satin pillow and Natalie smilingly dismissed the nurse.

"I was not sure, beloved, that you would care to hold her. Most fathers only look and adore and save their fine broadcloth."

"I am different," he said. "I want to hold her."

It was probable that never again would he have thought of entering politics had it not been for Slidell. Slidell owned New

Orleans, did he? And politics was rough and tumble? Well, other people could learn a few grappling holds.

He would run for the legislature, another insignificant office. It would take work, a little scheming, a few speeches. How he would laugh at Slidell if he managed to defeat him.

A hired cabman who drove him to his office one morning provided the key that could open the door.

"Mr. Benjamin, I would vote for you but I do not have a vote. I own no property and therefore—"

"No property? Do you own this cab?"

"Of course, but it is not a piece of land."

"We will see."

That fight in itself was as good as any Election Day scuffle. Certainly cabs were property. If a man owned a cab, he owned property, did he not? All that could properly be demanded at the polls was a license showing cab ownership. With vigor and enthusiasm Judah fought for the unenfranchised cabmen, whose property often represented a value greater than that of a weed-covered lot. He won his point. Cabmen were property owners. They could vote upon presentation of a license.

Election Day came, and Judah, in the newspaper office, awaited the returns with eagerness. The fun of beating Slidell, the joy of crowing over him if victory should come!

It came. It came with a cry of fraud. This was only natural. Louisiana expected fraud in her elections. Always there were repeat votes, trickery, bloodshed, and often murder. Automatically she cried fraud. It was expected and justified and her cries were part of the background sounds like the "Ramoné la chiminée!" of the chimney sweeper or the call of the strawberry man. But Judah was sickened at having his name linked with such shabby practice.

Slidell was thunderstruck. "You licked me! You, the clear-eyed boy who said that politics did not have to be dirty."

"I assure you I am still a clear-eyed boy. I thought only of the legitimate ownership of cabs. I had no part in or knowledge of the fraud."

"Sh, you fool. Stop calling it a fraud. You won. Louisiana loves a winner. Tomorrow she will have forgotten any irregularity."

"Irregularity! A delightful euphemism. There were counterfeit licenses presented. I am not going to serve, Slidell. I am going to denounce the man responsible and I am going to—"

Slidell said, "You cannot do that, Benjamin."

"Why not?"

Slidell, with the edge of his spoon, drew designs on the table-cloth. A small box with a neat X inside. "Benjamin, you went into this race for fun. The men who managed you were playing the game seriously—"

"But I did not know that they would—"

"You knew it was a game never played by strict rules of sportsmanship. Nevertheless you joined because it amused you. If you get drugged and robbed in a Swamptown whore house you do not have a right to protest. You know Swamptown's reputation and you have no business going there."

Judah said, "I do not go to Swamptown, and I find it depressing that, for the purpose of allegory, our politics can be compared only to a whore house."

"You find it depressing, Benjamin, that everyone is not pure and clean. Well, some are. Let us talk of those for a moment. If you announce that you, too, suspect treachery in this election you are not simply exposing a few bottom-drawer rascals. You are putting into the minds of the voters the thought that your entire party is corrupt. You are smearing men like Henry Clay and Daniel Webster."

"Oh, I do not think that is necessarily true. Moreover, why are you so concerned about the good name of my party?"

"I am not even slightly concerned about it, but I cannot sit here and be still while you contemplate making a God-damned fool of yourself. Jesus, Benjamin, every man elected to anything has made a compromise with his conscience. Even the shiniest, loftiest knight in armor has to be elected before he can give whatever it is he has to give. And yet, Benjamin, there is this: Once he is in office there is nothing to prevent him from serving with the greatest honesty of which he is capable. Never forget that, my friend."

Judah smiled. "You are very persuasive, Slidell."

"I am trying to be. You were made for politics. If you were in my camp for a few years I would secure for you any office you desired—barring the presidency. That, too, I will deliver one day, but to a good Protestant."

"And when he is in office will he be allowed to serve with the greatest honesty of which he is capable?"

Slidell thoughtfully sugared his third cup of coffee. "Benjamin," he said, "I will never bring any pressure to bear upon him. I will only hope he remembers who his friends were."

"Oh, he will remember, Slidell. Who are you backing at the convention?"

"Polk. He is not my ideal but Belmont likes him and can get New York for him. I will get the South."

"Then he is our next president."

"I am sure of it. But to hell with politics, Benjamin. What do you hear of Natalie and the baby?"

"They are in splendid health."

"And Rebecca?"

"I bought her a house on Naiades Avenue and she is contented. It is too far for me to visit often but she made many friends in the Belle Chasse days and during holiday time the children come to her."

Slidell was drawing again with the edge of his spoon. "A house in New Orleans for Rebecca." A small square. "A house in Beaufort for your father." A slightly larger square. "A house in Paris for Natalie and the baby." An enormous square. "Also a sister, a brother, and innumerable nephews and nieces in schools and colleges all over the South. My poor Benjamin, I trust the St. Martins permit you to live with them free of charge."

"As a matter of fact they do."

"I am so relieved." Slidell sat back in his chair and looked at Judah earnestly. "Go serve your little term, Benjamin, then if you have had enough go home quietly but, for Christ's sake, don't make any enemies, old friend."

Judah said, "At some point in your lecture you made sense, Slidell. I do not remember just when or where but I am convinced. I promise you that never again will I go to a Swamptown whore house unless—"

"Unless what?"

"Unless I discover that the effects of my last visit were, after all, not disastrous."

Polk was nominated, and though it was a foregone conclusion that he would carry Louisiana, Judah fought ardently for Henry

Clay. Louisiana really had no choice. The state was without a registration law and the successful candidate was the man who won the greatest number of parishes. It was a mathematical certainty that Polk must be victorious in Louisiana. Slidell's election army was limited only by the amount of ground it could cover, and enough steamboats had been chartered to guarantee a Polk decision in many an uncertain parish. Clay, the selfless, inspired statesman, was as anachronistic as a gladiator, and no vote was cast for him with hope but only as a mark of esteem.

Polk became president and Slidell was appointed minister to Mexico.

"A small reward for your efforts," Judah said.

"It is what I wanted. War with Mexico is a distinct possibility. The man who can avert it will be highly regarded."

"The man who can avert it is highly regarded now, Slidell. He is known as God."

With a flourish, a wagon of baggage, and the memory of a huge testimonial dinner, Slidell departed for Mexico. Judah's business led north that autumn. New York, Washington. He had been admitted to practice before the United States Supreme Court, and New Orleans was seeing less of him now. There was a new partner in the firm. Bill Micou was frequently ill and another pair of strong shoulders had been desperately needed.

"You know Bradford, do you not?" Judah asked August Belmont.

"By reputation I know him. He will be very good for you I think."

"How is Slidell doing?"

"He is sitting on his handsome posterior in Texas, I understand. The Mexicans decline the honor we have conferred upon them. They do not want Uncle John."

"What a rage he must be in."

Belmont laughed. "John doesn't really know what a rage is. He is utterly cold-blooded. His emotional temperature is a result of outside climate which he simply reflects. Within him there is no mechanism that makes for heat."

"Are we going to have that war with Mexico?"

"Yes, we are. I hope no one shoots John."

Slidell came home, and there was indeed war with Mexico. It was strictly a military man's war and lacked the spark to fire an average American's imagination. It had nothing in common with the glorious goal of the Revolution or the honest flame of resentment that 1812 had ignited. The army was at war with Mexico. The people, though they felt themselves uninvolved, wished the army well. It was, they admitted, their army even if it had marched away on some bloody errand not very clearly understood. When it was over the Rio Grande was the new border and a great many Spanish-speaking people were Americans. Very odd. Still if the results pleased the army one must be content, and changes were to be expected with the years.

The years. Judah was only aware of their passing when something startling occurred such as that Washington's Birthday afternoon when he made an address and became conscious of a very enthusiastic supporter in the first row. A slim, black-eyed boy who applauded vigorously at each pause. A nice little fellow, delicate looking, aristocratic, perhaps fourteen or so. My God, it was Jules. Of course. Somehow he remained a baby in one's imagination.

I scarcely ever see him. He is asleep when I come home and with his tutor when I breakfast. Besides which, I guess I look without really seeing him.

When Judah stepped down from the dais he made a point of greeting the slim child who was his brother-in-law. He saw the flush of pleasure in the pale cheeks, the pride that relationship had been acknowledged so publicly.

"Brother, may I walk home with you?"

Judah had not intended to go to the house on Bourbon Street but he realized an explanation, no matter how gentle, how logical, would come as a dash of cold water.

"Are you going home at once, Jules? How delightful. I thought I would have no companion on the way."

He felt the slim, young arm slip through his.

"Brother, I am perplexed."

"Perplexed, Jules? Why?"

"You are said to be so brilliant a speaker and to have a mind unequaled by any other and yet—brother, I understood everything you said. How can that be?"

The years. Polk gone before one had grown accustomed to him, before one had admitted aloud that he had been a good president.

Polk's last dinner at the White House was given in honor of the incoming Taylor. The guests, therefore, were of two camps. Judah felt a deep weariness as he looked at Taylor. Taylor had been his man. He had worked hard for him and now he felt only a sad conviction that all was sound and fury. Only after a man had been president did one know whether or not he was worthy of the expended energy and eloquence.

Slidell, at the punch bowl, handed Judah a drink. "You are going to be invited into Zack's cabinet."

"God forbid. I cannot afford to accept and he will be insulted if I refuse."

"Moreover, you will be happier as a state senator."

"Am I to be a state senator?"

Slidell put down his cut-glass cup and said, "I hear they are going to try with you. How do you feel about it?"

Judah grinned sheepishly. "I believe I am beginning to like Swampton, Slidell. It is not bad once people have learned that you intend keeping the place clean and tidy."

"If you become state senator you'll have to live in Baton Rouge. They're making that the capital, you know."

"I guess I can stand Baton Rouge."

"You haven't seen it, friend. That reminds me—how are your eyes?"

"I had a talk with them and told them about my expenses. They have promised to serve me. I am going to California on a land grant case."

"California! For Christ's sake, I believe you would go to the moon. That trip will eat up months in travel and trial. How much can you get that will cover the—"

"It is an opportunity to exercise my polished Spanish, Slidell."

"To hell with your polished Spanish. You work too hard. You will be dead at forty if you do not slacken your pace. But drink up, do not let me worry you."

Judah was not invited into Zachary Taylor's cabinet. In a yellow journal that was left upon his desk he read a small, sly item neatly marked for his attention.

A prominent lawyer was considered for a high appointment then forgotten when someone whispered in the right ear a story concerning the lawyer's much-discussed wife. The right

*ear belonged to a certain Brave Soldier who is something of
a prude at heart. He paled and trembled at the realization of
how close he had come to introducing into his official family
a lady whose beauty is exceeded only by her fascinating
reputation.*

New York, commercial interests, the annual trip to Paris. The
courts of New Orleans scarcely saw him. His work for the firm
was mostly in Washington now. Bill Micou was dead. The firm
was Benjamin, Bradford and Finney. Railroads occupied his
mind. Dreams of connecting Jackson, Mississippi, and New
Orleans. A small dream. The big dream was the Tehuantepec
Railroad crossing Mexico, shortening the journey to California
and opening commercial possibilities that would revolutionize
the entire transportation system. So bright a dream and not beyond the reach of those who would work for it.

Ninette was no longer an infant. On his last visit he had
established a camaraderie with her that he hoped would last forever. She had remembered him this time, had run to meet him,
an enchanting cloud of ribbons and lace and irresistible smiles.
A small Parisian angel who knew no word of English.

"Natalie, in the interests of her education she must—"

Natalie grinned impishly at him. "No, indeed, Mr. Benjamin.
I know about these young men who give English lessons."

In Louisiana he had been safely elected to the state senate. On
his first night back from Paris, Auguste St. Martin had brought
him the latest copy of the *Delta* and lit the gas above the chair
where Judah sat.

"Read the editorial, son."

Judah said, "Now? I would prefer to talk with you." It was
a sweltering evening, the air thick and humid. The elaborate
glass globe shielding the flame seemed to have instantly heated.
"I will read it later." He reached to extinguish the gas but, becoming aware of his father-in-law's disappointment, he picked
up the paper and read.

*Benjamin is sagacious, possesses great tact, and would make a
very brilliant senator. His appearance among the gray heads
would startle Washington. His boyish figure, his gentle, innocent expression and manner would render him a most un-
senatorial figure. But when he should rise and in the most*

graceful manner proceed to pour forth the most subtle and ingenious arguments then would the old senators say, "That's a devilish smart fellow." Then would the ladies declare, "What a love of a man!" So beautiful yet so wise, so gentle yet so terrible in sarcasm.

But Mr. Benjamin will hardly be elected to the senate because he is the acknowledged leader of several great enterprises in which our city and state have a greater interest than in being ably represented in the United States Senate.

"What is this, sir? What do they mean about Washington and the United States Senate? I am going to Baton Rouge and the Louisiana State Senate. I do not understand."

He walked around the corner to the house of Ed Bradford. "What is this, Ed? Just talk or—"

"Talk? My God, Judah, it is only a matter of saying you want it."

"But there are men like Kenner and Hunt and Downs."

Bradford said, "Planters remember you as a planter. Americans know you are an American. The Creoles think you belong to them. And everybody all over Louisiana is delirious at the thought of a railroad from Jackson and one across Mexico. You are the railroads as far as they're concerned. Judah, your election would be a great thing for us."

He left Bradford and went to Royal Street. Slidell, a picture of domestic tranquillity, was reading *Jeanne d'Arc* aloud to his two little daughters. They curtsied prettily and departed. Baby Mathilde and Rosina, the golden-haired joys of Slidell's middle age.

Christ, isn't it hot, Benjamin? What do you want to drink? How was Paris and the family? What about the Senate proposition? Do you like it? What can I do to help you? Name it and you have it."

Judah said, "Have I really, Slidell? It is not an easy thing to request."

"What is the difference? Hard or easy, it is yours."

"Very well, friend, I will be frank. I want to be senator from Louisiana and this is the favor I ask: Do not help me. Do not say a good word for me. Please, for the love of God, Slidell, do not endorse me."

Slidell threw his head back and roared. "Oh, what a crime that I cannot repeat this to anyone." He flung his arms around Judah and rested weakly against him. "Long ago I told you that you could say anything to me and I guess you believed it. Don't you think I have any feelings that may be injured?"

"I do not know, Slidell. I only know that today no man believes I was anti-Catholic and no man believes I engineered the cab vote fraud. I exonerated myself without explanation, without denial, simply by conducting myself so that no thinking man could believe the charges against me. But, by God, Slidell, I would have to sprout wings to overcome the effects of having your support."

"How could I support you? I have my own party, my own man to work for."

"You have torpedoed your own candidates before when it seemed expedient to do so. Do not do it this time, I beg of you."

"I will fight you tooth and nail."

"Thank you, old friend."

They shook hands warmly.

One hundred covers were laid at the St. Charles Hotel for the friends who came to pay honor to the new senator from Louisiana. Tomorrow he would depart for Washington. The speeches were numerous. The wishes warm and trite. Here were gathered the most articulate, the most eloquent men of New Orleans and it seemed remarkable that none could raise a champagne glass without employing the phrases: "a man who—", "honor and devotion" or "in all the years I have known him."

Judah's eyes wandered about the room searching for Mazureau or Roselius, for the others who had been at a dinner party long ago. Natalie in deep red velvet—

"Gentlemen, I give you the new senator from Louisiana!" It was Slidell. The champagne glasses were raised again.

Natalie, the gracious, charming Natalie. The house on Condé Street. All in the past now. My God, where did the years go?

"It is my proud boast that Judah Benjamin is my friend. Always we have held conflicting opinions, always we have argued but, gentlemen, the respect we have felt for each other—"

Respect? Slidell, I have never respected you. I have never even trusted you. And yet there has been something solid and real between us. What have I felt for you? What is its name? And why do I feel it? Is it because you were kind enough to introduce me to August Belmont and New York? Is it because you talked me out of behaving childishly in the matter of the cab votes? Is it because you offered to lend me a hundred thousand dollars the day I knew Belle Chasse was lost? No, it is none of these things, for I was drawn to you when first we met and I can no longer avoid the truth, the obvious. There are qualities within you, Slidell, that I understand far better than an honest man should understand them. You are my friend because I recognize in you the ambitions, the desires that are also mine. And in me, what did you find, Slidell? What did you find that, after our first conversation, made you willing to discard your beautiful French vocabulary and speak to me in pure Manhattan? Somehow, somewhere in our development something happened that made us different but not so different that I do not understand and like you better than any man on earth.

"Benjamin, as you all know, is not of my party but I would be a strange Louisianian if I did not love him for his fighting spirit and his purity of purpose. I am an old man now. The road ahead leads only into the sunset but as long as I live I will be proud that I could call Judah Benjamin my friend."

Afterward he walked Slidell to his carriage.

"I will not see you in the morning, Benjamin, but I will be in Washington before the year is out."

"Really? I thought the road ahead led only into the sunset."

"You bastard! Good-by. Good luck."

They shook hands and parted. Judah walked up Gravier Street. New Orleans. Is it all over between us, little city? Walking in the darkness, feeling the damp touch of the night upon him, smelling the indescribable odors that belonged to New Orleans, he experienced the sadness of a last adieu. Why was it so? He would be back. Of course he would be back, but the thin, sharp pain of parting persisted. He walked past a score of walled-in gardens and felt a kinship with the houses, dark now behind their lovely ironwork balconies. Congo Square where the slaves had danced on Sundays before the city fathers had judged their conduct lewd. With a little imagination it was possible to hear them now.

Danse Calinda, bou-djoumb! Bou-djoumb!
Danse Calinda, bou-djoumb!

The river. Exchange Alley. St. Anthony's Garden. He lingered a moment outside the door of Greenbury Stringer's office, then walked on. The old house on Condé Street. The little house that had belonged to a lady who had rushed off to St. Bernard Parish the year of the terrible plague. He walked by the courts and the coffeehouses and over to the market.

And at last he stood upon the steps of St. Louis Cathedral. It was over. The adventure that had begun here had drawn to a close.

Good-by, New Orleans. May all go well with you, little city. God knows you owe me nothing.

Five

WASHINGTON

Charles Dickens had superciliously looked at America's capital and had called it the city of magnificent intentions. No one was certain of his meaning. Did he refer to the aims of government? Or was he laughing at a nation that would erect temples of classic design in a sea of mud? Surely he must have been amused at the pretentiousness of buildings that reared their spires and domes and cupolas above streets where pigs wandered unconcernedly. In dry weather one contended with Washington's choking dust; on wet days carriages were mired hub-deep on the principle avenues. Malaria, mosquitoes, and prostitution flourished unchecked, but there were few who admitted to the presence of such unwelcome visitors.

Theaters, hotels, and restaurants blazed with light and gaiety. One heard accents of all America, of all the world in the markets where ladies shopped in person for the delicacies to serve at their highly competitive dinner parties. If one were not fortunate enough to be in Washington society one could still catch a glimpse of the Baroness de Bodisco of the Russian Embassy—she who had been Harriet Williams of Georgetown. Any day one could see the dashing Mrs. Clement Clay of Alabama and her faithful mulatto girl, Emily, or perhaps even Countess de Sartiges, wife of the French ambassador. Every afternoon Pennsylvania Avenue had a sparkling equestrian parade to offer, the gentlemen of Washington society in whipcord and top boots, the ladies devastating in velvet habits and plumed tricorns.

There were no homes in Washington. Only hovels, mansions, and well-kept private houses where ladies of good breeding and bad investments rented rooms to congressmen and their wives. An establishment of one's own in Washington was an expensive undertaking, and many a lady preferred to entertain for her husband at Gautier's elegant restaurant and live modestly in two nicely furnished rooms. Congenial housemates were easily come by, for landladies were beginning to let it be known where Northerners would find a welcome and in which houses Southerners would hear no nasty words such as "abolition." Of course those who came from their states with money to burn selected at once a stately residence and either staffed it from the large Negro population of Washington or brought their own servants.

Judah settled himself in a quiet hotel and took up his duties as the junior senator from Louisiana.

Both Pierre Soulé and himself, he discovered, were regarded as temporary members. Soulé was to be sent as ambassador to Spain and President Pierce had publicly expressed the wish that Judah might accept a Supreme Court appointment.

"My God," Judah said to August Belmont, "it is an honor that would ruin me. I cannot work at law for the salary a Supreme Court justice receives."

Belmont laughed. "Tell Pierce. I am sure you will find him very sympathetic to the complaint that you cannot live on less than fifty thousand a year. How much do you think he earns?"

"I know what he earns. It is what he spends that makes his income more comfortable than mine."

"Is your Senate seat now secure, Judah?"

"Of course. That was only a straw-clutching performance by the Soulé faction of your Democratic party, my dear August. I have never thought of myself as a native of the Island of St. Thomas. I scarcely knew of what they spoke when the issue was raised."

Belmont said, "They could never make the charge stick if it came to a real fight. You were a minor when your father was naturalized, weren't you?"

"Of course. The whole thing is quiet and done with now. No thanks to Soulé. I can tell you I boiled with fury."

"Did you really?" Belmont asked earnestly. "No one remarked that you were angry. You are just the reverse of Uncle John, who pretends anger when he feels none. With you no one knows when you are steaming mad."

"I would not say that no one knows, my friend. There are moments. Soulé, thank God, will soon be off to try his hand at talking Spain out of Cuba."

Belmont shook his head. "I suppose that means another war? I still recall that we were going to talk Mexico out of California."

"That war I am still fighting. The career of the Tehuantepec Railroad is seriously in doubt owing to a few lingering memories cherished by our Mexican neighbors. One president agrees to the project. We sell stock and use the money to purchase equipment, to hire surveyors and five hundred laborers, then that president is out of office and the new one abrogates all commitments of his predecessor."

"That must be exasperating."

"Yes, August, you can take my word that it is. Twice I have been to Mexico trying to settle the matter. The new president is weighing in his mind the charming possibility that none but Mexican nationals may be permitted to build or share in the profits of—"

"That makes it simple. You need only become a Mexican national."

"Be quiet. You will have my senate seat in jeopardy once more."

Within three months Soulé was on his way to Spain, and the governor of Louisiana surprised no one with his choice of a successor.

Slidell, Mathilde, the two young daughters, and fifteen servants arrived to create a week's wonderment in Washington. Slidell took over the largest, most luxurious house available, and Mathilde took over the position of leading Senate hostess.

"What is the news of Louisiana?" Judah asked.

"Political or social?"

"Both."

"Well, politically I could not find anyone I liked better for this job than myself. I tried but I finally had to admit there was no one around to handle it better than I."

"What a coincidence that the governor agreed!"

"Yes. Well, he is an agreeable fellow. Socially the big news this season was a wedding in our family. Mathilde's sister married Captain Beauregard. Do you know him?"

"Of course. A splendid chap."

"I think him rather stuffy, a typical military man. He is a widower, you know. Rather good Creole family."

"Rather good indeed, Slidell. Beauregard would be so pleased that you approve."

"Do not tell him that I do. It will only increase his conceit. What about you coming here to live with us, Benjamin? I think we could find a cot and a cubbyhole somewhere."

Judah said, "Madame Slidell showed me the cot and the cubbyhole you had in mind. I would save it if I were you. In the event that the British Embassy burns down it will be suitable quarters for Crampton and all his attachés."

"I would rather have you, Benjamin. Do come."

"Thank you, old friend, and please do not think me ungrateful, but I have another plan in mind."

The plan had been with him for weeks. Rarely had he been able to banish it for more than an hour of any working day. At first it had sidled shyly into his thoughts and had raised no objection to being considered impractical. Now it clamored loudly and had become a demanding voice, talking him down, silencing his most sound and sensible arguments.

Slidell and his family had done nothing to further the cause of clear thinking—the sight of Mathilde making a home in this ugly city of gambling houses and saloons, Slidell's daughters greeting him at the end of a day.

He wrote to Natalie and received an answer by the first possible ship.

Beloved:

I have read your letter over many times and I do not see how I can refuse what you have asked of me—not that you really asked. You are a proud man, my darling, and your letter is written so carefully that you do not risk refusal—you only invite debate. Well, I will not debate with you. I see clearly the possibility that you may not get to Paris every year in the future. There is one solution. Only one. I must come to Washington.

Long ago, after your first visit to me here, I begged you never to break the spell of what we have. It is a curious marriage, I grant you, and yet it is one from which the magic has never faded. I will come to you in Washington for such is your wish, beloved, and let us try to keep the spell unbroken, the magic bright.

I love you, Judah. I love you so much as I sit here writing to you my heart pounds with the excitement that you never fail to create within me—

On the one fashionable street where no window looked upon an open sewer or a rubbish heap, Judah rented a house. The spiral staircase and bronze chandeliers appealed to him. The paneled library and great double parlors had architectural purity unsurpassed by any house in Washington.

It would be three months before Natalie arrived, and Judah furnished the house from the shops of New York, selecting with care everything from carpets to crystal, from bedsteads to tapestries and paintings. In Philadelphia he purchased the carriage Natalie would use—lined in peach-colored satin, her initials in tiny gold letters upon the door. From Virginia he sent the horses, matched grays. His office in New Orleans bought and shipped the perfectly trained servants Natalie would need.

All was in readiness two weeks before she sailed from France. He was pleased with his work. Again and again he went over the house assuring himself that he had forgotten nothing. He was especially charmed with Ninette's apartment in pink and ivory and with Natalie's dressing room and its wall of mirrors. He was anxious for Mathilde's opinion, so the Slidells crossed the street to examine and suggest.

Mathilde said, "You have left nothing undone, Mr. Benjamin. The house is delightful. Far nicer than ours."

"Madame, you are very kind but I cannot forget the exquisite appointments you and John have lavished upon your home."

Mathilde pursed her pretty mouth. "We have the mirrors and brocades where the guests may enjoy them," she said. "My boudoir is rather like a nun's cell."

Slidell laughed. "We have to save somewhere, my love. Only Benjamin can afford to live like this."

"And how Benjamin wishes he could afford it," Judah said. "Next year I am really going to start saving a few miserable dollars. Madame, is there nothing you see that could be improved upon? Is there anything Natalie will want that is not here?"

Mathilde shook her head and gave Judah a long look. "Mr. Benjamin," she said, "if Natalie wants anything that is not here, she is a woman who will not be happy in heaven."

Until he saw Natalie in company with them he had not realized how differently American women wore their clothes. Why, they had no style, no style at all. They were countrified, their formal gowns worn self-consciously, the flowers in their hair quite ridiculous. There were no flowers in Natalie's hair. The sleek smoothness of it was sufficiently ornamental and the sophisticated satins that clung to her figure in classic simplicity made comedy relief of the laces and ruffles and flounces and flowered materials that Washington ladies adored. She was more than thirty-five now, but no young girl welcomed a comparison between herself and Mrs. Judah Benjamin, for youth that dared stand at Natalie's side appeared not fresh but raw, not sweet but flavorless.

Sitting quietly with Supreme Court Justice Campbell and Mrs. Campbell, Judah watched Natalie across the ballroom floor as she danced and he thought how the years had never dimmed her radiance, how his yearning for her had never lessened, how—

A voice whispered softly in his ear. "Yes, Senator, she is the loveliest thing alive."

He turned to the dark, friendly girl beside him, a rather large girl with an intelligent face and the easy grace common to expert horsewomen—Mrs. Jefferson Davis, wife of the Secretary of War.

"I am alarmed that my mind is so easily read," he said.

"Oh, I did not read your mind. I simply guessed. Who would not think her beautiful? I never see her that I do not feel like an awkward, outsized daisy blooming beside a gardenia."

Judah laughed. "Madame, when I see you with my wife I think only that beauty comes in many designs. Is Mr. Davis with us tonight?"

Varina Davis sighed. "Yes and no. He came to the ball but he is closeted with some gentlemen in another part of the house." She lowered her voice. "It is just as well really. There are so many Northerners here. I grow quite nervous at times, for Mr.

Davis is very quick-tempered and Northerners never try to be polite."

"Dear me, after that remark, Mrs. Davis, I think we should have a cooling drink to your grandfather who, I believe, was governor of New Jersey."

"Eight times." She grinned. "I cannot help it, Mr. Benjamin, I am completely Mississippi. I hope my poor Granddaddy would forgive me. Northerners really do not care what they say to us. Last night at dinner the gentleman—gentleman?—to my left asked me if I owned slaves. I said to him, 'No, sir, I do not. They own me.'"

"A lovely retort," Judah said.

A lovely retort which I am getting damn sick of hearing, Madame. I like you. You are a nice girl, but that answer truly has the edge worn off it. And what are you going to say when someone is not flattened by this reply and says to you, "Then, Mrs. Davis, are you not terribly afraid of being sold away from Jeff one day?"

"I think I would like that cooling drink, Mr. Benjamin, but please do not fetch it. I am tired of sitting here. Let us move about."

He offered his arm and they skirted the dance floor, Mrs. Davis making *sotto voce* remarks about the guests as they walked. Sam Houston, wearing conventional attire save for a scarlet necktie, brought forth a brief, disdainful "Texans!" from Mrs. Davis.

"Texans are not Northerners, dear lady."

"I know, but isn't it a pity? Don't tell my husband that I made nasty comments about this brilliant company."

"Wild horses will not drag the information from me."

Besides which, Madame, both you and I know that if you could not speak freely with strangers you would expire. Surely you are never at ease with Jefferson Davis, hero of the heroic Mexican War!

At the table where the punch bowls stood in pleasant, icy invitation Judah and Mrs. Davis encountered Natalie and her recent dancing partner.

"I want to go home," Natalie whispered. "As soon as is convenient and polite for you."

"In about ten minutes," he responded.

She smiled sweetly at him. "That will do well, beloved."

In the carriage she leaned back wearily. "I am fond of dancing," she said, "but, Judah, they do not dance. Who was that awful man, my last partner, the one at the punch bowl?"

"That was Mason of Virginia."

"He is no credit to his state. The repulsive lout chews tobacco."

"In a ballroom?"

"Perhaps not exclusively, but I assure you a ballroom is one place where he does chew it."

So many strangers, so many rustics sent to Washington by adoring constituents. She had been extremely patient and amiable, making a dogged effort to like the people who populated his world. Well, the effort was not all one-sided. The ladies of Washington had been urged by their husbands to accept Mrs. Benjamin just as Mrs. Benjamin had been urged to accept them. Did Natalie know this? Did she know that gossip had swept north from Louisiana and west from France? Did she know that Varina Davis and Virginia Clay and others felt themselves extremely self-sacrificing because they did not snub Natalie Benjamin? The idea would amuse Natalie. She would laugh at the notion of being judged by people who came from places like Natchez, Mississippi, and Huntsville, Alabama.

"Is that Mason a Virginia gentleman, Judah?"

"My dear, he is a genuine Virginia gentleman. In colonial days his grandfather bore the same distinction."

Natalie said, "How impressive. I suppose that means his table manners were as good as any Indian's. Do people actually take pride in springing from such stock?"

"They do, Natalie."

"How is it that I have not been unfortunate enough to have this person as a guest? His name has appeared on none of my invitation lists."

"He is probably on your very next one."

"I do not think so. My next dinner includes no Americans. The guests will be from the French and German embassies."

"Yes, I remember now."

She had arrived in Washington with a sheaf of introductions and at least half her dinners had excluded Americans. Odd how she never seemed to realize that she was an American herself and that her husband was a small part of the United States government.

"Do you not think, Natalie, that we could mix a few Americans with your European friends? I do not mean Mason or any of the Texans but perhaps—"

"We have had the Slidells with the French. Is that not enough? With others there is always a language barrier."

"Mr. and Mrs. Jefferson Davis speak French."

Natalie laughed. "Really, Judah, you cannot have listened very closely. She is not completely impossible but he pronounces all French words as though they were English. He thinks it perfectly absurd that the French will not accept good, solid Anglo-Saxon pronunciations and he is not the one to give in to their ridiculous whims."

"All right, darling, not Mr. and Mrs. Jefferson Davis."

Not the Clays either or the Chesnuts or the Cobbs. Not any Americans when it could be avoided. What did it matter after all? Surely she was entitled to give dinners for the French and Germans if she chose and if she invited no senate or cabinet members —well, it was her home. And when she did entertain government circles she was a tireless and charming hostess.

"With the exception of Louisianians I never saw an American who knew the difference between food and excellent food," she had said while planning a Washington menu. "They have no standards. There is no satisfaction in having appealed to the appetite of an American."

"I am insulted. I am not a Louisianian."

"Beloved, you are a Louisianian. You could be nothing else. Americans—even Carolinians—are easily pleased, thoroughly unselective. They are satisfied with anything. Why offer them that which they cannot possibly appreciate?"

So the best wines, the most elaborate dishes were withheld from Americans. Natalie had no belief in their ability to distinguish between an ordinary delight and a superb experience.

Now turning to her in the carriage he said, "I believe you would find Mary Chesnut lively company if you knew her better."

"I know her well enough, beloved. She is brilliant, witty, and indulges in the use of opium. That might account for her liveliness."

"I believe she suffers an affliction of the nerves, Natalie."

"No doubt. Any woman would who believes as she does. She says that gentlemen in possession of plantations have all sold their own children along with the black mothers at one time or another."

"An evil allegation. Did you reply?"

"I did indeed. I said, 'Speak for Senator Chesnut, Madame. I will speak for Senator Benjamin.'"

They climbed the stairs together, tiptoeing softly in the upstairs corridor. At Ninette's door he paused and looked questioningly, pleadingly at Natalie.

"Why not?" she whispered. "She is our child."

Like conspirators they entered the room for a good-night glimpse. Ninette, sleeping sweetly, never stirred, but there was a reassurring motion from the other room. The nurse was alert to every sound, to any danger. Fondly, foolishly they blew kisses at the slumbering child and withdrew to their own chamber.

Madame St. Martin was ill and felt unequal to joining her husband and Jules on their visit to Washington. There was talk that perhaps Natalie would return with them to New Orleans, but actually she had no desire to test the discomfort of railroad travel. Ninette would make the journey instead.

"She will stay the winter in New Orleans," Natalie planned. "Then Jules will bring her back to us."

"Jules!" Judah said. "Surely that boy could not be expected to—"

"That boy! Jules is almost twenty years old, beloved."

Almost twenty? Jules? Of course. But where did the time go? Judah saw the eyes of very young Washington ladies upon his brother-in-law and knew that the boy had the equipment for wholesale heartbreaking.

"You danced with that girl from the Italian Embassy all evening, Jules. I felt desperately sorry for your castoff love of only yesterday."

"Oh, I explained to her that never before had I seen an Italian with golden hair and that it startled me so I was not myself all evening."

"The explanation satisfied her?"

"Of course. Did you ever notice, brother, that ladies accept any explanation, no matter how ridiculous, if only you remember to look deeply, pleadingly into their eyes as you speak?"

"No," Judah said drily. "My experiences have been different."

"There was another girl," Jules said.

"Another?"

"Yes, this is interesting, brother. She paid no attention to the music or the dance. She wanted to talk. She asked me if I owned slaves."

"Yes, Jules. And you said that indeed you did not, that they owned you."

"I said no such thing. What an idea! I said, 'Yes, Mademoiselle. We own slaves. What about it?' I thought this, brother: I thought that perhaps it is unpopular to own slaves, but since we do own them, why quibble about it? Why do we not give up pretending that we do the slave a great favor by owning him? Let us be honest and face up to whatever follows."

Judah put his arm about the boy. "God bless you for bringing a fresh viewpoint to town."

"My fresh viewpoint endeared me not at all to the young lady. She left me alone to finish the dance by myself."

Judah sighed. Even among the young it was happening. The bitterness was penetrating, spreading evilly. It was only a matter of time. A matter of time.

The visit of the St. Martins passed all too quickly. It seemed that on one day they had arrived and on the next were ready to depart taking Ninette with them. Judah felt a deep sadness when she raised her little face for his kiss. Why was it so? He had said good-by to her so many times. The melancholy of parting was lightened none by Jules, who sheepishly displayed a book he had taken without asking.

"I was going to steal it but I have no criminal instincts. I must confess. I wanted a little something that was yours, brother, and so I took this from the table beside your favorite chair. Do you actually read Horace in the original for a frivolous half-hour's relaxation?"

Judah said, "Though you are welcome to the book, Jules, I wonder that you need a memento. You will return to us shortly with Ninette."

"Of course, but I just had the impulse. I do not know why."

For the rest of the day it was impossible to shake off the feeling that a warning bell had sounded. He told himself that nothing but loneliness for Ninette was responsible for the heaviness of his heart.

"I miss her terribly already," he said to Natalie.

She smiled. "The time will fly, beloved, and she will be back. Actually, you are too busy to miss anyone very much."

Before the Supreme Court he had the case of the steamer *Gipsey* to fight for Benjamin, Bradford and Finney; in the Senate the constant sour interchanges of sectional grievances. Seward of New York, hating the South and its institutions with a fervor that flared at white heat, fought anything that might prove compatible with southern existence. Too, there were the great land grant entanglements, which, as chairman of the committee, Judah must examine with special care; and always there were the railroads—the Jackson-New Orleans and the Tehuantepec.

Natalie bringing a bottle of wine to his desk one midnight touched him softly upon the cheek. "Beloved, what are you doing so late?"

He turned to smile at her. "Would you really like to know?"

"I would."

"I am workng upon an address entitled 'The Roman Lawyer in the Age of Cicero.' "

She said, "I am interested in a New Orleans lawyer in the age of Franklin Pierce."

"I know, my darling, and I am terribly flattered and grateful but I will have to make this address in Virginia and—"

"You are going away?"

"Only to Virginia. That is not going away."

She said, "Slidell's house I can see from my window but you were there till four o'clock this morning."

"I know. There is so much heavy talk these days, Natalie. I was amazed when I realized the time last night." He put down his pen. "Come sit on my knee and I will try to be a more companionable fellow. I think Cicero's lawyer was very dull and pompous and somehow—"

She said. "Do not blame it all on Cicero's Roman lawyer."

She poured the wine and he pushed aside the address upon which he had been working. Tomorrow he must find a chance to finish it.

"You did not sit on my knee as I asked you to do."

She smiled coolly. "Beloved, do me no favors."

"Favors?"

"I know you want nothing in the world at this moment so much as to turn a subtle phrase for your Roman lawyer."

"Come kiss me and see how much I care for a subtle phrase."

She walked toward him, the wine gleaming crimson in the glass she offered him. "If we kiss," she said, "there will be flame. It has always been so with us. But I am one who likes to walk into a room where the fire is already burning invitingly. To build one somehow robs the occasion of its welcome."

He took the glass from her and set it down and when the wine spilled across the pages of "The Roman Lawyer in the Age of Cicero" he did not even notice.

Sumner, the gentleman from Massachusetts, was on his feet. The Senate gallery snickered at the unavoidable comparison of his enormous height and weight to that of the slim, slight gentleman from Louisiana.

"I wish to ask the Senator from Louisiana if in South Carolina or in Louisiana itself a colored citizen of Massachusetts can, without any crime, be seized and thrown into prison and then, on failure to pay certain alleged jail fees, be sold absolutely into slavery."

"Sir, you suggest that South Carolina and Louisiana are capable of acting in a manner outrageously opposed to constitutional rights."

"I am pleased that the Senator from Louisiana has signified his awareness of the Constitution."

"Oh, I am aware of it, sir. I was about to ask if you were familiar with it. If so, then you are acquainted with the provision that requires full faith be given in each state to the public acts, records, and judicial proceedings of sister states. Do you acknowledge the obligation imposed by the Constitution for the return of fugitive slaves from free states to those by whom they are owned?"

"And before I answer that question," Sumner said, "I will ask the Senator if he is ready to introduce an act of Congress that secures colored citizens of the North their rights in South Carolina and Louisiana?"

"I have heard of the Yankee method of evading a question by asking one. I put my question with a sincere and earnest desire to ascertain whether the gentleman really recognizes any constitutional obligation to provide for the return of fugitive slaves."

"Before answering the question of the Senator—"

Sumner was interrupted by laughter from the gallery but there was not much humor to the debate. There was only bitterness. Judah was glad to be free of Sumner and the Senate, to go home to the quiet of day's end.

Natalie was on the chaise longue in the sitting room of their suite. Behind her the draperies were open and the winter sunset, pale and silvery, furnished a striking background. She wore a deep purple robe and in her hand was a bouquet of hothouse violets that matched dramatically. This, he knew, had been the day for calling upon the wives of cabinet members. Evidently she had made no calls.

"You are not ill, sweetheart?"

"No, today I simply could not face the ladies and their conversation."

He came to the chaise and sat down beside her, smiling encouragingly. "I know. Prattle."

"Prattle? I could tolerate pleasant prattle. I am no intellectual giant, beloved, but the things of which they speak! You would not believe it. No one should mention the matters which they discuss so glibly."

He stared at her incredulously. Mrs. Davis? Mrs. Orr? Mrs. Crittenden? This was not possible.

Natalie threw herself back upon the cushions and laughed. "From your expression I see I have misled you. You think they speak of love-making. That is truly funny. These creatures do not make love. They mate! The body is no shrine of delight to Americans, I can tell you. Would you like to know anything about Mr. Clay's bilious attacks?"

"People are sometimes obsessed with such matters, dearest. For myself, since coming to Washington I have heard enough of bunions, earaches, and rheumatism to do me for a while."

"Truly, Judah, it is beyond belief. Babies regurgitate. Wives suffer monthly discomforts. Husbands develop boils. They speak of birth—in detail of course—of upset stomachs, of sore toes and abscessed teeth. My God, beloved, for twenty years we have been married and I know more of Mr. Davis's digestive tract than of yours."

He smiled. "Surely they have other topics."

"Oh, yes, but not less dreary ones." She breathed deeply of

the violets. "No one has read a book she wishes to discuss. No mention of poetry or music. No one has a delightful experience to relate. These subjects are reserved for mixed company. When there are no gentlemen present there is no conversation. There are only revolting disclosures such as one might expect from peasant women."

He said, "Mrs. Davis is an exceptionally well-educated girl."

"Really? Do you mean that I may expect one day to hear in Greek or Latin the dismal details of Mr. Davis's headaches, which are sometimes accompanied by nausea? I am not well educated. I was taught nothing except what is coyly known as 'charming deportment.' I trust you are not disappointed in my inability to join in a fine, straightforward American conference on what is to be done for night sweats or nosebleeds."

The last silver brightness was fading from the winter sky. Shadows were crowding thickly into the room. Natalie, with the violets in her hand, was a charming silhouette against the dying light of day. The fire crackled and its orange deepened as the night moved in upon them. Did Natalie know that her displeasure with the Washington ladies was only a symptom of the dark restlessness that afflicted her?

"So you see," she said, "I did not go cabinet calling today. Instead I stayed at home and the milliner came with some plumes and veiling. After that a bootmaker arrived and the woman with the new gloves from Paris and I grew very tired of them all and left word that I was not to be disturbed again and at that moment—"

He tried not to listen to the sweet voice that sang so false a song. Did she have to manufacture these foolish stories? Was there a strange, unexplainable thrill in compounding her guilt, in adding an outrageous lie?

The only question was who. A man had curiosity as well as susceptibility to pain. Rather like having an itch upon one's ankle as one is being hanged. But the itch was real, the curiosity persistent. The young nobleman who assisted Count de Sartiges, the one with the surprising streak of white in his dark hair? No, that was a poor guess. Sumner of Massachusetts must really have exhausted him. It had been obvious at a glance, of course. The hothouse at the German Embassy was growing violets. He could place him now. Lohengrin in the handsome uniform of King

Frederich Wilhelm's guard. A blond captain with eyes of blue ice that doubtless melted irresistibly at the right moment.

Natalie raised her arms in a graceful, indolent stretch, a yellow-eyed kitten in the warmth of a cozy room. "We must think of dressing for dinner, beloved."

"Yes, Natalie. Are we going out this evening?"

"Oh, indeed. Did you forget?"

"I forgot." He rose from the chaise and lighted the gas. The flame shimmered upon the satin draperies and the luster of the deep carpet.

"Draw the curtains," she said. "There is a cold wind rising."

He walked to the window and looked out upon the city of Washington, bleak and depressing in the rawness of winter.

"Indeed, my love," he said, "the cold wind has already risen."

Mathilde Slidell cast a critical eye over the breakfast table, signified her satisfaction, and withdrew, leaving her husband and Judah alone. It was seven o'clock on a Sunday morning, the only hour of mutual convenience they had been able to find.

"You have discoursed with a certain degree of engaging logic, Benjamin. Are you ready yet to relieve my suspense? Are you going to introduce the land bill?"

"Yes, I am going to introduce it. I believe it is time those vague eighteenth-century titles were settled once and for all. Doubtless you will get a clear claim to the twenty thousand acres of the Houmas tract. That is all you are interested in, is it not? I cannot believe you care that people in Alabama, Missouri, Florida, and other places will also profit if their claims are as good as yours."

"You think then that my claim is valid?"

"You know well that if I did not I would have it removed from the bill's consideration. However, I cannot find any evidence that you did not buy in good faith."

Slidell thoughtfully buttered his toast. "I must warn you that you will be accused of getting a slice of the Houmas tract in return for introducing the bill."

"No, thank you," Judah said.

They smiled across the table at each other. An offer had been made and refused. They understood each other well.

"I am very grateful to you, Benjamin."

"Do not be. This bill is not being introduced for your benefit. It is to clear up the confusion about Indian sales, haphazard surveying methods, and obscure titles. And, my friend, do not yet begin counting your profit. I am putting into the measure a stipulation that withholds absolute title for two years, giving that time for the institution of suits by people who think they can produce better titles."

"Very fair of you, I will admit. Distressingly fair. Two years is a long time for an old man."

"I know, my poor decrepit Slidell, for you the road ahead leads only into the sunset."

Slidell grinned, reached for the pepper and then did not use it. He sat motionless with the silver shaker in his hand and Judah knew that he was deliberating whether or not to voice a thought that had come to him.

At last he decided. "Benjamin, I think the sunset's going to be a blaze of glory. Do you remember that I once told you I would some day deliver the presidency to someone?"

"I remember."

"Well, before the sunset closes in I am going to do it. I have my man now."

"Congratulations. Who is the poor devil?"

"Jim Buchanan."

"Buchanan? Would he make a good president?"

Slidell said, "Who knows? He'll make one hell of a good candidate."

"That's enough, is it?"

"Oh, for Christ's sake, Benjamin. Nominating a man for the presidency is like getting engaged to a respectable girl. You can only pick out something that looks pretty exciting. There's no way of getting an advance sample."

"Buchanan looks pretty exciting to you, Slidell?"

"Well, he was our ambassador to England. It has a nice sound. Don't you like him?"

"Does it matter? My faith in you is such that I am at this moment convinced he will succeed Pierce."

"And I will tell you something, Benjamin, you will work for Buchanan. You will campaign for him. You will be a Democrat."

"Why do you think I will leave my party?"

"You will not leave it. It will leave you. It will become impossible for you to subscribe to its policies. It is dying and sometimes the dying make horrible sounds."

Judah drank his coffee in silence. He knew that what Slidell said was likely to prove true. Surely he could not remain within a party whose precepts were beginning to attract abolitionists and bigots. Any party had a fanatic fringe of adherents but if the fringe should suddenly become the main body—

"Of course," Slidell said, "I won't get to work on this thing anyhow till after you are back from South America."

Judah, stunned, set his cup down and stared at Slidell. "Where did you hear that I was going to South America?"

"I hear so much, Benjamin, that I do not remember all my sources. Ecuador, I believe. Your firm was chosen above all others because of your brilliant Spanish and your unsurpassed knowledge of Roman law."

Judah said, "I cannot discuss the matter now."

"Why not? Your mission is not to assassinate someone, is it?"

"I am quite certain, Slidell, that you know the purpose of my mission to Ecuador as well as I, including details which have not as yet been disclosed to me."

Perhaps Mathilde, too, would know all that Slidell knew. He could no longer delay the time when he must tell Natalie. The voyage was at least a month in the future, still, Natalie must not be kept in ignorance of matters known to others.

He took her driving that afternoon behind the matched grays. All Washington drove on Sunday. The length of Pennsylvania Avenue to Georgetown was the fashionable route. It was a pleasant day, spring in the offing but the air still holding the crisp sparkle of winter. Natalie, in ermine-trimmed black velvet, bowing to acquaintances along the way. They played a game. A chilly bow to those from northern states. A smile for southerners.

"Quick, Judah, here comes a border state. What is the proper procedure?"

"Bow formally and smile slightly. That will meet the emergency, I believe."

"Oh, dear, I became confused. I smiled formally and bowed slightly."

He regretted the end of the drive. They had laughed a great deal together today. Now he must explain about Ecuador. Was there any point in mentioning prestige or fee? None whatsoever, he decided. It was not as though she had ever urged him to increase his legal stature or to earn more money. Achievement to her was a matter of complete indifference.

Her maid took her wraps and brought coffee to the upstairs sitting room.

Natalie said, "I always want coffee. Despite my years in Paris I remain a Louisianian."

"It is a claim none would care to relinquish," he said. "By the way, dear, I think you should visit your mother. What would you think of going to New Orleans for a few months?"

"Could you go with me?"

"No, I could not. That is just the point. I find I will have to go to Ecuador shortly—"

"Ecuador! My God, that's at the end of the world."

"Not quite. The Galapagos Islands are slightly more remote and I shall have to go there as well."

"Can you not take me with you?"

"No, darling, I cannot. The journey and the living conditions will be far too unpleasant. But I am loath to leave you alone in Washington."

Loath? God Almighty, I cannot do it, Natalie.

"I think Washington will be lonely for you, dearest. Tell me you will stay in New Orleans during my absence."

She looked down into her coffee and smiled. He understood the smile. She was thinking that once he had asked her not to go to New Orleans. New Orleans then had been his city. He had inherited another now.

"When are you going to Ecuador?"

"At the close of the present Senate session. In perhaps three weeks."

"Then we have time to discuss the matter further. It need not be now, beloved. Today I have something else to mention. I am going to New York for a few days."

"New York?"

"Yes. I want to see about some clothes. I hear New York has some truly marvelous dressmakers."

Clothes, was it? Why, she would not be found dead wearing the work of an American dressmaker.

"Do you wish to stay with the Belmonts?" he asked.

"No. I have an invitation from the Baroness something-or-other at the German Consulate. I don't remember her name. Her brother is in the embassy here."

Be careful, Natalie. You are getting very close to honesty. He has asked you if sometime it would not be possible to hide away with him for a few days. You have said that it would not be but now it is different. I am going to Ecuador and you must have your revenge for being abandoned.

Strange how her mind worked. Though, as far as she knew, the rendezvous was unguessed by her husband, still within her there would be the sense of having repaid him for choosing Ecuador. Very curious that she thought of it as revenge, for, by God, it was. As a reward for his cleverness, for his brilliant ability to read her correctly, he had the joy of picturing her lying with the blond captain. He watched her thoughtfully as she refilled the coffee cups. Of course it was not actually revenge she sought but justification.

"Ecuador," she said suddenly, sharply. "I never heard of a man having to go to Ecuador." Her eyes were sullen and hurt. "And I was so happy all day."

"And are you not happy now? The thought of New York should delight you."

"I would rather be with you," she said.

"Then why go to New York?"

"Why go to Ecuador?"

"There are things I must do, Natalie."

She smiled sardonically. "Because you are Judah Benjamin. Permit me to say, beloved, there are things I must also do because I am Natalie Benjamin."

A week before his departure Natalie left. He had not offered to accompany her to the station. He could not be positive that New Orleans was her immediate destination though it seemed that he had won his point. She clung to him when they said good-by.

"You know I love you, Judah."

She was so appealing with her small Parisian hat perched upon the black curls, a bewitching veil shading her yellow eyes.

"I would not have cared how bad the living conditions were in Ecuador."

"You would have cared, Natalie."

"But not to have been asked." She looked at him sadly. "I am a woman who lives for love and not to have been asked—" She turned from him. "Good-by, beloved."

He caught her before she crossed the threshold and kissed her once more. "Natalie, sweet one, remember that I love you."

She laughed shakily. "I remember," she said, and he knew well when she would remember. It would be when she was taking her revenge for Ecuador.

"Do not wait till you reach New Orleans to write," he said.

"I won't," she answered and was gone.

She kept her word. She wrote from New York.

Beloved:

When you get this my ship will be at sea. Perhaps you have already guessed that I am not on my way to New Orleans. I am going back to Paris and never again will I return to America. The spell was broken, the magic tarnished there in Washington. I regret that you did not take a quadroon mistress instead of a career. I could have made a quadroon mistress weep with loneliness for you but I have no weapons with which to fight law. For a woman who has only love to offer it is a depressing thing to have her love welcomed only in moments when John Slidell, the firm of Benjamin, Bradford and Finney, two railroads, and the United States Senate are not holding her husband's attention. This happened before, of course. It happened at Belle Chasse when you had to go north to meet August Belmont and you had no need for me, no wish to take me with you. But that is in the past now. So is my residence in Washington. I hope, beloved, that you will come to Paris when you can, for there I am happy in the knowledge that you made the voyage to see me, to hold me in your arms. Nothing in Paris claims your time except me. No one in Paris is important to you except me. I will be waiting there with all my love.

Your Natalie

P.S. You will be wondering about Ninette of course. A sea voyage has been prescribed for my mother so that all the St. Martins will come to Europe in June bringing Ninette along. If on your way to Ecuador you have time you may like to stop at New Orleans and visit her.

He folded the letter and put it away. On the day that Ninette had left something within him had known that never again would they all live together in this house. It was finished forever, the dream in which they had been a family as other families, living under a common roof. He took the letter from his pocket and read it again with a towering rage rising as he read. God damn it, what did she think life should be? A never-ending love affair? Did she think a man could live without any desire save that which could be satisfied in bed? She had given herself none the worst of the argument in her letter. She had not considered that he had been generous beyond belief, long-suffering to the point of idiocy. She simply left him when displeased as though it were perfectly within her right to leave.

He paced the floor fuming, his mind composing the letter he would write to her. It was time surely that she knew a wife had duties and responsibilities. Millions of women, the world over, had true grievances against their husbands but they did not quit a home as though it were a hotel room for which there was no further need. When he wrote he would tell her—

Oh, good God, what is the use of this performance? Quiet down, Benjamin. You will tell her nothing except that you love her.

He dropped into a chair and his anger vanished as he remembered that she was not a woman like other women and could not be judged so. His rage had flared in stupid disregard of the evidence presented. He had reacted as a man suddenly shattered by totally unexpected news. There could be no shock or surprise where Natalie was concerned. She was the way she was, and his was an immature mind indeed if it could not remain cool and logical in its evaluation of her behavior. Yes, she thought life should be a never-ending love affair. That was the way Nature had constructed her. What was the matter with him that after all these years he had permitted himself to shake with fury?

What would have happened if he had been able to speak to her when his anger had first risen? Would he have told her that things had to be different in the future? If so then indeed things would have been different. Would he have been fool enough to give an order that she could not obey? Would he have forgotten that a man who makes rules makes his own noose? What can one do about a broken rule? One can only be very strong or very weak and either way there is no victory.

He rose from the chair and walked through the house as years ago he had walked through Belle Chasse, feeling the presence of Natalie beside him as he walked. Her dressing room, again as at Belle Chasse, heartbreaking with the ghost of her perfume. The empty wardrobe, the mirrored wall that reflected only a lonely man. And the thought came to him that he would wander so if Natalie had died and been carried from this house in a white casket.

If it were so, if she were dead, I would be thinking now how wonderful life had been when she lived. I would be thinking that if I could see her breathe again I would not ask for a greater joy. So, Benjamin, she was not carried from this house in a white casket. She lives and you will see her again, will hear that sweet whisper in your ear, will look upon that lovely face and she will smile at you. So be glad you have her still. Write and say that in July you will come to Paris.

There were things to be done. He had been through this before in New Orleans. First, people must be taught how to act. They must not wonder if it was poor form to mention Natalie's name. They must not be uncomfortable with him, perplexed as to whether or not they must shape their conversation to the needs of a grieving man.

He dispatched a note to Virginia Clay.

Dear Lady:
    Short notice, I realize, but could you and Clement possibly come for dinner? Very quiet, very intimate. Natalie's ship has sailed and I find myself rather at loose ends without her here to tell me what to do next. Do come this evening if you can.

                                              J. B.

He sent similar notes to the Cobbs and to the Bayards. He did not write to the Slidells. Instead he walked across the street and visited with them.

"I had a letter from Natalie. I wanted to report to you that she is on her way."

Mathilde said, "Her mother will be pleased to see her."

Judah managed to show surprise. "Did I not mention that

her plans were changed? She is not on her way to New Orleans. She is returning to Paris."

"To stay?" Mathilde asked.

"Yes. She was not very pleased with Washington."

Mathilde said, "I do not see how a lady knows one city from another. One's home, one's family, and one's friends are all a lady needs. The city certainly goes unnoticed, does it not?"

Slidell scowled at her as she sat fanning herself with a look of great calm and innocence upon her face. "Natalie was born homesick for Paris," he said. "If you were a proper Creole that would be your feeling, too."

Mathilde's lips thinned. "My home is where you are."

"Very touching," Slidell said. "Remind me to be touched for two new gowns and a few bonnets. Go get us a drink, little wife, and—er—send it in."

Mathilde disappeared and Slidell turned to Judah. "What can I do for you?"

Judah smiled at Slidell. "I wonder how many times you have asked me that question. I wonder how many times I have been glad to know that you would ask it."

"Well, what can I do for you?"

"Come to dinner at my house tonight."

"With pleasure. We were supposed to go to the Davises and you know how glad I will be to get out of that."

"You cannot get out of that, friend. Varina is a nice girl. You must not do that to her. Besides I have a much larger request to make of you. I am going to put my furnishings up for sale. I wonder if you will take charge and—"

"Certainly. Do not give it another thought. The house will be empty when you return from South America. Anything else I can do?"

"You might tell the Davises that Natalie has sailed. Doubtless they, too, are under the impression that she was bound for New Orleans."

"Doubtless," Slidell said. "I shall correct the impression. The second Jeff brings up the victory at Buena Vista and how he charged magnificently, flinging himself at the enemy with no thought of personal danger, I shall say, 'By the way, talking of Buena Vista, Natalie Benjamin has gone to Paris,' " Slidell poured the drinks then leaned comfortably back in his chair. "Benjamin," he said, "I love that girl—Mathilde."

"Of course you do. Why would you not?"

"Because she is a little sharp-tongued, a little waspish at times, but I'll tell you something. You can depend upon her not to use a dinner table as a forum for gossip or irresponsible guesses concerning other people's problems."

Judah studied the frosted side of his glass. "A splendid virtue," he remarked.

"Yes, well, it has no part in this conversation but I like people to think highly of Mathilde, so I just mention that she is naturally closemouthed and trustworthy in company."

"That is the result of her good breeding."

"Indeed. Besides which the first time her good breeding fails I shall beat the hell out of her."

Judah smiled. "I do not think you will beat Madame Slidell, my friend, but I understand the point you are trying to make."

And so the annual voyages to Paris were begun again. He had no home. He needed none. A suite in a hotel, an office, these were enough for him.

Slidell said, "At the risk of being tedious I must ask you again —what is the matter with my house?"

"I work too hard to live among my friends, Slidell."

"You work too hard for anything. Christ, Benjamin, nobody else holds a Senate seat, a full-time working partnership in a law firm, a—"

Judah laughed. "I have been told before that I am spreading myself rather thin. It sounds familiar."

"You will kill yourself."

That was the year Judah made the decision to become a Democrat. He had no regrets, no doubts, for his old party had shamelessly merged with those whose declared aims were repulsive to him. At their convention in Philadelphia the entire Louisiana delegation had been expelled for no other reason than its adherence to the Roman Catholic church. Immediately upon receiving this information he announced that he was now a Democrat.

Slidell said, "You will come to the convention in Cincinnati, won't you? I have a hell of a fight on my hands. Pierce's friends still have a lot of life left in them."

"I have not said I like Jim Buchanan."

"Do you like Pierce?"

"No."

"Then come on, let us get the nomination for Buchanan."

They went to Cincinnati and they got the nomination for Buchanan. Slidell seemed to have almost singlehandedly defeated the forces of Franklin Pierce. His tactics and strategy were magnificent to watch, his leadership perfect and unfaltering. He knew the favorite whisky, the favorite cigars of every delegation, the weakness and strength of every wheelhorse. The failings of Buchanan became virtues when explained by John Slidell, and with some rare sensitivity he knew the moment to shift emphasis or relinquish a claim in entirety. He knew how to take a man into his confidence and yet tell him nothing. He knew the value of a good laugh, a suppressed sigh, or a great exaggeration. He knew when he was not liked, when it was time to disappear and leave Judah to carry on the conversation. And in the end he knew how to gain control of the visitors' tickets and pack the galleries with howling Buchanan supporters.

Buchanan and Breckenridge! We want Buchanan and Breckenridge!

Dan Sickles, a broad-shouldered, young New Yorker who had been on Buchanan's staff at the Court of St. James's was beside himself with delight. He had assisted in the battle and his enthusiasm for Buchanan, though childish, was genuine and, to Judah, rather touching.

On the train returning east Judah commented to Slidell on Sickles's exuberance. "He is a devout worshiper, isn't he? It is good to see someone whose admiration for a nominee is without cynicism."

Slidell leaning back against the red plush seat stared up at the swinging lamps in the car ceiling. "Well, yes," he said slowly, "but let us not talk too much about Sickles's admiration for our worthy candidate. One of these days we may have to claim that Sickles always hated Jim and that he is making up lies to defeat him."

"I am unable to follow you."

Slidell turned his attention from the swinging lamps to the

long ash on his cigar. "I have information," he said, "that
Buchanan has been sleeping with Sickles's wife."

"What? My God, what would a woman want with Buchanan?
He is sixty-five."

"Hell, Benjamin, I am sixty-two."

"Very interesting. Is that intended as a testimonial to our
candidate's irresistible appeal? I doubt the story, Slidell."

"I hope voters do. If Sickles ever hears the talk he will ruin
us. Voters are awfully God-damned fussy about the sanctity of
the home, and make no mistake, that young behemoth would let
everybody know."

Judah studied the scenery. Very dull. Cows feeding docilely,
little houses, green fields. Would Sickles really let everybody
know? Did any man of education and worldly experience ever
disclose for public viewing the torments with which he lived?
Of course not. It was unthinkable.

He said, "Slidell, I have a feeling that Mrs. Sickles is not
sleeping with Buchanan. I think the whole thing is just talk.
Moreover, even if true, her husband would certainly not advertise
the matter. At the next stop we must get some coffee. You look
thoroughly done in. I thought you would be in a mood for rejoicing."

"I feel let down, Benjamin. It is all over now."

"Really? I thought we still had to elect our man."

Slidell said, "You know Buchanan will be a shoo-in. Why do
you always talk as though you didn't know where presidents or
babies come from?"

"It worked with the Mississippi delegation, Slidell."

"But you're talking to me now."

"True, friend, but we still have to elect our man."

"Barring scandal that will be too easy to be fun. Your old
guard picking out Millard Fillmore helped us tremendously. Who
the hell is going to vote for Fillmore? Finishing out poor Zack's
term is all the White House Fillmore's ever going to see."

"You have forgotten the new party and its noble Frémont."

"No, I have not. I am remembering them both. They must have
a plank in their platform which pledges them to an early death.
Sort of a political suicide pact. John Charles Frémont and the
Republican party. Jim is a sure winner."

Nevertheless, the campaign was energetic. Judah went on tour to speak for Buchanan. It was the first time he had seen Maine, New Hampshire, and Vermont. He looked at the people, mostly abolitionists, mostly suspicious of the South and its ways. It was a curious thing, what misunderstandings existed between the two sections of the country. Yet when they met together, a Louisianian staying at the home of a man in Maine, there was mutual respect, an exchange of opinions.

"I do not see it your way, Mr. Benjamin. There are things about your state that I can't go along with."

"Granted. That is why you do not have those things in Maine, sir. Louisiana never asked Maine to accept customs that are pleasing to Louisiana."

Judah looked across the table at his host, a decent man with intelligent eyes and a firm mouth. Here was a man who liked business and profit no less, no more than a man from the South. Why did the South believe that these Northerners cared more for money than they themselves? Here was a man who could be stubborn when he believed himself right. So stubborn that he would starve before surrendering a point. He would not sacrifice principle any quicker than a man from Alabama or the Carolinas. Yet the legend persisted that Yankees would sell anything for a profit.

I am not in love with New Englanders but they must not be underrated. They can fight and they will fight without asking what percentage is guaranteed on the investment.

Some of these ideas he took back to Washington with him and offered to Slidell.

"Benjamin," Slidell asked gently, "are you trying to tell me what Northerners are like? Long ago in another incarnation I was a New Yorker and I can tell you that if anybody ever blows the whistle those sons of bitches will fight. But I have something more pleasant to talk over with you. How would you like to live in Spain, my friend?"

"Spain? I never really thought about it. Why should I now?"

"Well, Jim—if elected—wants to repay us a little for our efforts. He thought of giving me the ministry to France and you the Spanish ministry."

"Actually, Slidell, I had figured on receiving a silver cigar box— suitably engraved of course. Or perhaps a nice cravat pin."

Slidell said, "Come on, tell me. What is your reaction to the plan?"

"Really, Slidell, it is ridiculous. If Buchanan is elected I want only an occasional invitation to eat that excellent White House food. Are you going to France?"

"Of course not. That would be a dull job. I just thought perhaps you would like Spain. Perhaps Natalie would like Spain." Slidell paused. "I'll tell you what, Benjamin. I'll get the French post for you. How would you like that?"

The French post. A house in Paris and trying it all over again. Natalie and Ninette. To have them with him once more—

But why would it work in Paris? Consider the reasons for failure, Benjamin. What would be different? How does living with Natalie in Paris improve the chances of happiness together? Once and for all, Benjamin, give up.

"You are very kind, Slidell, but I think I will stay in America."

"I, too. I will tell Jim he has a couple of staunch Louisianians to deal with. Let him buy us each a small, sentimental token such as a few blocks of real estate in the heart of Washington."

Judah had not listened. Sitting there in the morning room of Slidell's house with the sunlight streaming through the gauze curtains, he was looking into a world gone suddenly gray. Without warning, without the opportunity to brace himself against it, the thought had come to him that it was all over, that never again was he to have a home with Natalie.

But that could not be so, for if it were then all roads lead to nothing, all effort to despair. He got to his feet.

"I must go, Slidell."

He could remain there no longer contemplating the bleakness of a world devoid of the hope that sometime, somehow—

"You are sure you do not want me to work on Paris for you, Benjamin?"

"I am sure, friend. As a matter of fact I am positive."

The celebrities of Europe seemed to be channeled into America through August Belmont's ballroom as their less distinguished countrymen entered through Castle Garden. At the Belmonts' affairs it was a poor evening if there was not an Italian nobleman, an English poet, a French artist, or a German composer.

Judah looked with interest upon his dinner partner, the

great Rachel, the muse of tragedy herself. She was an exquisite thing gowned in floating black chiffon, her hair brushed to a glistening sheen and permitted to hang loosely as though in wild and natural state. She wore one huge diamond on a delicate chain about her throat, and the diamond was no brighter than the long, slanting eyes that were reputed to have driven men to suicide.

"Are you going to attend my American debut?" she asked.

"I am afraid that joy is to be denied me, Madame."

She fixed him with a freezing glance. "At great cost I have been brought here. My salary is tremendous and you do not feel any compulsion to see me perform?"

"Compulsion I do feel but time I have not. I am contrite. Can you forgive me?"

The black eyes softened. "Rachel always forgives. That is why she is a great artist. Within her there is understanding and sympathy."

"How comforting! How kind!"

How affected! Her French was interesting. It was extremely artificial, as befitted France's greatest tragedienne. Who would respect an actress who did not speak in accents more elegant than those used by ordinary people? Still, beneath the polish there lurked the unmistakable tones of another Paris, the Paris of slums and hunger.

"You are Parisian, Madame?"

"But of course Rachel is Parisian. In France there is only Paris as in your country there is only New York."

"I cannot agree. In France there are many lovely cities. In this country there—"

"In all the world there is only Paris and New York. Rachel plays for percentage as well as salary and small cities are useless places."

"You are a true artist, Madame."

She smiled graciously. "What is your business, sir?"

"I am a lawyer."

"Very dull, is it not? Still there must be satisfaction in saving some poor wretch from the guillotine or from long years in prison."

"Oh, I suppose so, but poor wretches are such bores I never bother to save them." How natural it was for an actress to think only of criminal law, to be unaware of the less dramatic branches.

Belmont, at whose right Rachel sat, suddenly turned to her. "Is Benjamin talking railroads?" he asked.

"Railroads?" The black eyes flashed with new interest. "He has not mentioned railroads. You have railroads, Mr. Benjamin?"

"Not with me, Madame. I regret."

"Do tell me. I adore railroads."

He strolled with her in the conservatory after dinner. She moved as a light breeze, her beautiful hands as expressive as her voice. The tender, tropical plants were her brothers, their troubles her heartbreak.

"Poor desolate things, not understood, not tenderly loved."

Judah said, "I have an idea Belmont's gardener understands them and if Belmont doesn't love them he is wasting a lot of money."

She frowned and he realized he had furnished the wrong cue. Her next speech was now without the proper lead-in but she continued as planned.

"They are so like me. Misunderstood, forced into a climate they abhor, forever exiled from their spiritual home." She turned to Judah, her eyes wet with tears, her small hands clasped in an attitude of prayer. "Try to understand them. Try to understand me."

"Oh, Madame, I assure you that I do."

"No, no. You see only Rachel, the greatest actress alive. Do you see the true Rachel, the woman? Do you know I never wanted the theater? It is make-believe. It is unreal. I wanted the reality of life. A home, a husband, children." The tears ran prettily from her eyes, not reddening her nose or distorting her face in the slightest. "The real Rachel, the real woman is a creature of simple tastes. I wanted only to cook and to bear children for a man who loved me well. No wonder I play tragedy so magnificently. My life is tragic."

"Yes, Madame. That is evident."

There was probably a good whist game in progress in the card room. Still, there was no denying that entertainment was being offered here in the conservatory—indeed a private performance by Europe's immortal Rachel. How old was she? Surely not more than thirty.

"Mr. Benjamin, would you think me mad if I said that we

have met too late? If I said that we had been meant for each other and that our destinies have somehow gone awry?" Elaborately she placed herself against a latticed wall, her arms high above her head, her pointed breasts accentuated by her pose. She looked at him with stricken eyes. "The moment I met you I knew. I felt it in my heart. Mr. Benjamin, it is no accident that we were born to the same faith. Did you know that I am a Jewess?"

"Your fame, Madame, is very great. It could not have escaped me that you are known in some quarters as the Jewish Sorceress."

"You see? Fate made us right for each other but we did not meet until tonight and now it is too late. Sorrowfully, heartbreakingly we must part. Happiness is over for us before it has begun." Her eyes closed, the unbelievably long lashes glittered with tear drops. "Kiss me good-by. At least we may have our sad farewell."

A man who travels without his wife grows accustomed to all methods of approach. This, however, was quite new, and of course never before had the huntress been so dazzling. She moved away from the lattice and came toward him, her full, red lips raised to his.

"We will say good-by," she breathed and kissed him.

It was a kiss to be expected from Rachel, the Jewish Sorceress. Warm and clinging. Was there any reason why he should not have a mistress? By what rules of justice was he bound to austere behavior? Was there any logical reason why he should not return her kiss, why he should not open his arms to her and draw her closer? Yes, there was a reason and it had nothing to do with logic or justice. It was only that her kiss stirred him so mildly that he was able to pretend a complete indifference. She stepped away from him and regarded him hostilely, her eyes narrow and chill.

"Are you numb?" she asked.

"Numb, Madame? Not at all. But am I supposed to burn for a lady who has just said good-by to me?"

He caught the small hand that flew for his face and held it tightly. Had she only intended to slap him or would she have used those long, shining nails?

"Rachel kissed you, you fool. A man exhibits emotion when Rachel kisses him. What is the matter with you?"

"Something very serious, I am afraid. I am in love with another woman."

"Who mentioned love? Love is for quiet. For excitement love is not needed. Sometimes the greatest delight is found with one who is almost a stranger."

"I fear I am far too conventional."

"You are far too civilized. It was no part of Nature's plan that male and female must love each other. Nature intended only that they must meet and experience an irresistible urge."

"As you say I am too civilized."

"Are you in love with Mrs. Belmont?"

"Good heavens, no. I am not even that interesting. This is going to shock you. I am in love with my wife."

"A wife is only a convenience, never an expert in the art of rare excitement. A woman who has lived, who has known true desire—Mr. Benjamin, take me, for instance—"

"My dear, I do not think I will."

He sighed and released the small, beautiful hand. It was a pity in a way. She would be a spectacular mistress. Very expensive of course, but he could not save a dollar with or without a mistress.

"Shall we go to the ballroom?" he asked. "Shall we join the others?"

Rachel smiled a slow, bitter smile at him. "You have left me in no mood for gaiety. I fear now for my American debut. Is it possible that I will not appeal to Americans?"

"You will appeal to Americans, Madame."

"But to be less desirable than a man's wife. I can scarcely credit it."

"Well—" He shrugged. "It is only fair to tell you that I am a man who likes buxom women of the strictly domestic type. My wife is a great cook and though she is plain she is good-tempered and bears a child regularly every year. You know, she is the woman you wish you were, the woman you dreamed of being before the theater ruined your life."

That time he had to be very quick to catch the little hand and he was startled by the stream of gutter words that flowed from France's great tragedienne. Some of them, he thought, might just possibly be new even to Slidell.

"Calm yourself, Madame. Quiet down."

"Quiet down? You are an impossible man. I have been insulted. I have been—"

"No, no, Madame. If you could but believe it you have been
deeply, passionately admired. You are beautiful beyond dreams,
Rachel. You are a poet's lyric in the flesh. You are music for the
eye and you are every man's youthful dream of love. Does that
make you feel better? If it does not, I have something more to
add."

"You may add it, sir," she whispered meltingly.

"Very well. It is this: Neither one of those railroads is ever
going to make me a God-damned penny."

Buchanan was elected. Miss Harriet Lane, niece of the bachelor
president, was installed at the White House as hostess, and Washington had a brilliant social season. Entertainment was plentiful
and lavish. Judah, at his desk, found himself laying aside for future consideration the envelopes that obviously contained invitations. Here was a letter from Paris. Not, regrettably, in
Natalie's hand. Jules. Since the St. Martins had settled in France
they wrote more frequently than they had ever written from
New Orleans. This was a rather excitable explanation as to why
Jules did not want his Louisiana property sold.

> *It is mine with full deed to it granted on my twenty-first birth-
> day and I think, dear brother, that my father was not correct
> in telling your New Orleans office to sell my property as well
> as his. Your Mr. Finney did manage beautiful prices for all
> Papa's holdings but Papa is old and was a Frenchman to begin
> with. I am an American and want to live there again one day
> so, dear brother, will you see that I keep my lovely little piece
> of Louisiana?*

There were nine pages of elegant handwriting expressing the
same thought in many ways. Judah smiled. Jules had no need
to worry. Finney had already questioned Auguste St. Martin's
right to lump all the properties together without any authoriza-
tion from Jules.

Judah suddenly became aware that someone was standing at
his desk. He looked up from the letter. A big fellow with a
pleasant smile. Very familiar looking. Who was he? Judah
searched his mind as he accepted the extended hand, hoping that

his visitor would not guess how false the "delighted to see you" truly was.

"Mr. Benjamin, I tried to catch a word with you the other evening at the White House but there was such a crowd there."

"Indeed."

"Teresa has missed you at her at-homes."

Teresa?

"We certainly thought you would drop by—if not to see us at least to see what we've done with the house."

Oh, of course. Dan Sickles. He had been elected to Congress from New York's Third District. Judah remembered hearing that Sickles now occupied the home that had been furnished for Natalie. No, he had no wish to see it.

"You are very kind, Mr. Sickles."

"I want you to know Teresa. I am very proud of her. She has developed into a magnificent hostess."

Judah was puzzled. Developed? From what? Was it odd that Mrs. Sickles should be a competent hostess?

"I am certain she manages that lovely home with great capability, Mr. Sickles."

Sickles laughed heartily. "Well, I wasn't so certain she would. This sort of thing is new to Teresa. After all she's only twenty-one years old and—"

"Twenty-one? Really? Twenty-one?"

Oh, Slidell was insane. How could it be possible that Jim Buchanan and a girl of that age—?

"Of course at the embassy in London she entertained but no one dared criticize there or they would be criticizing Mr. Buchanan and the whole American representation. Here it is different. This city is filled with cats but Teresa gives them nothing to meow about. Do come see us, Mr. Benjamin."

"I will indeed. Thank you again."

Dan Sickles, his wife, and the invitation went completely out of Judah's mind till the night of Senator Gwin's fancy dress ball. It was a spectacular affair with every member of Washington society present. Vice-President Breckenridge costumed as a viking chief brought Mrs. Representative Pendleton to Judah.

"Will you guard this lovely lady while I fetch a tankard of mead?"

Mrs. Pendleton in red, white, and blue satin with thirteen glit-

tering stars in her hair was slightly apologetic for her magnifi-
cence. "It seemed like a good idea when I thought of it. After all,
my father did write 'The Star-Spangled Banner,' but now I feel
I have overdone things a little."

"Not one whit, Madame. Your costume is the envy of all ladies
present, I feel sure." His eyes wandered to the dancers. "I have
heard that the stars in our flag are, in some quarters, thought of
as spurs. Does that explain your brother's costume?"

She smiled fondly out at her brother, Barton Key, United States
attorney, handsomest man in Washington. Tonight he was wearing white satin breeches and a cherry velvet jacket.

"He is, of course, a huntsman of some sort," Mrs. Pendleton
said. "I can't think why he chose that costume."

I can, Madame. Look at his partner. Obviously she wished to
wear a cherry-colored habit and prevailed upon him to appear
conspicuously as her possession. Though perhaps it is the other
way around.

"Who is the young lady with the enormous black eyes?"

"Where?" Mrs. Pendleton asked innocently.

"In Barton's arms. His partner. Do you know who she is?"

"Oh, yes. She is Mrs. Dan Sickles. Dan could not be here. He
asked Barton to escort her."

"She is quite a beauty, isn't she?"

"I suppose she is, now that I look at her. I hope no one mis-
understands the poor little thing. She holds onto Barton as
though she were drowning. It's because she feels so insecure in
society, you know."

"Naturally. Of course."

And is there a chaise longue in the same place where we had
one? Does Dan Sickles come home and find her sitting there
musing upon the revolting conversation of Washington ladies?
Does Dan Sickles live with jealousy or has he learned to put it
from him?

"If I present you to Mrs. Sickles, Senator, will you ask her to
dance? Just in a sentimental mood I would like to take a turn
with my brother."

You would like to take a turn with your brother and warn him
that he is fooling no one, would you not, Madame? You would
like to say that none can mistake the looks that pass between him
and Mrs. Sickles. I cannot oblige. Perhaps you are one who does

not know it but I have lived in the house in which Dan Sickles lives. I know every corner of it and I do not even wish to visit there.

"My regrets, Madame, but I have asked Mrs. Slidell, and since here is our good Breckenridge I think I will now leave you."

He found Mathilde, a bored harem girl, appropriately sitting at the side of her lord and master. Seward of New York was violating etiquette by talking politics.

"Dance with me," Judah whispered to Mathilde. "For heaven's sake, Madame, dance with me."

Slidell's sharp ears missed nothing. "What is your trouble, Benjamin? What has happened that you need my wife for protection? Go dance with the gentleman, Mathilde. You will never have a more anguished proposition offered you."

Seward smiled. "Pray do dance with the gentleman, Madame Slidell. I have my hands full with one Louisiana senator. Two would be more than I could bear."

Slidell said, "Well, I'll tell you, Seward, one New York senator is often too much for me."

"Why, Senator Slidell, you underestimate yourself."

"Why, Senator Seward, you missed my point. Say, Benjamin." Slidell turned completely away from Seward and lowered his voice. "Did you see Barton Key dancing with—"

"I think I noticed them in passing."

"They wore the wrong costumes. Night clothes would have saved them a hell of a lot of time when the ball is over."

"John!" Mathilde gasped.

"Pardon me, darling. I am just a horrid old man."

Judah danced with Mathilde, observing that Barton Key now had his sister, Mrs. Pendleton, for a partner. Evidently she had simply comandeered him, leaving Teresa Sickles to search for other company. A glance revealed to whom Teresa had turned in her loneliness. It also proved that President Buchanan's long suit was not discretion. He stood with his back turned toward Teresa, a man obviously suffering from an attack of injured feelings.

Mathilde, it was plain, understood the situation but she looked away from Buchanan and made no comment. Instead she said, "Mr. Benjamin, I want to say you are a very distinguished something-or-other in that costume. What is it?"

Judah laughed. "It began as an early Spanish explorer then turned slightly bridle path as the explorer's boots showed signs of pinching. My goodness, regard Mrs. Davis. Who is she tonight?"

"Madame de Staël. Let us not go near the Davises. In keeping with their costumes they are speaking what they think is French. We won't be able to understand a word they say."

"He seems not to be enjoying himself."

"His neuralgia is bothering him. My horrid old man says it is not his neuralgia at all but only his distaste for being a mere senator from Mississippi after having been the glorious Secretary of War under Pierce. Mr. Benjamin, can't you do something with John to make him more charitable in his opinions of people?"

Judah said, "Could we bear it if he changed, Madame? Aren't we terribly pleased with him just the way he is?"

She smiled. "Yes, I think you are right, but Mr. Davis *is* suffering with neuralgia and not mere distaste for his lastest position."

It was difficult to decide who had judged Davis's malady fairly—Slidell or Mathilde. Judah wondered a few days later at a Senate session whether Slidell had not diagnosed correctly. Surely Davis was as touchy and petulant as it was possible for a grown man to be, as full of quibble and bad temper as a prima donna. One could scarcely address him without receiving an almost insultingly short reply. Was this neuralgia or the irritation of a man who functions in a position he considers beneath himself?

The Army Appropriations Bill was under discussion and it was clear that Jefferson Davis did not think any but himself qualified to speak on the issue. When Judah asked him a question the answer came short and sarcastic.

"The Senator from Mississippi," Judah said, "has given a sneering reply to what was certainly a very respectful inquiry."

Davis looked at him chillingly. "You, sir, attempted to misrepresent a very plain remark."

"The Senator from Mississippi is mistaken and his manner is not agreeable at all."

"If the Senator from Louisiana happens to find it disagreeable I hope he will keep it to himself."

"When directed to me I will not keep it to myself. I will repel it instanter."

Davis's lips twisted in a sour grimace. "The trouble," he said, "is that I had no idea I was to be met with the arguments of a paid attorney in the Senate chamber."

"Did I rightly hear the words 'paid attorney,' sir?"

"Yes, those were the very words."

Judah said, "I have marked them well. May we continue with the discussion?"

They continued with the discussion and when it was over Judah wrote a note to Jefferson Davis, a note in which he asked satisfaction for the insult.

Slidell said, "You are out of your mind, Benjamin. The son of a bitch will kill you. He's a crack shot."

Judah sighed. "What could I do, Slidell? Could I take his arrogance and say thank you? Could I live in the same world with a man like that once he found he could direct his contempt against me and not be challenged?"

Slidell jumped to his feet and paced the room nervously. "My God, couldn't you have laughed a little, pretended that you were amused? I am not sure you even remember which end of a gun shoots."

"It'll come to me," Judah said.

"This is the stupidest thing you ever did. I can't tell you not to do it again because you won't get another chance. Christ Almighty, Benjamin, think of something. There must be a way out. You have simply asked to be murdered."

Judah said, "Sit down, Slidell. Please rest yourself. Years ago you told me there was a language of fools. Well, Jefferson Davis speaks it. To live in his world I must speak it, too. If I get killed, that is a pity but I could not have lived with him and accepted insult calmly. You see that, don't you, Slidell? Besides he is not a maniac. He will not shoot to kill."

Slidell ran his hands through his coarse white hair. "I could beat your head in for getting yourself into this. At least look frightened, Benjamin."

"I am so frightened I could be sick."

And in that moment he remembered the dining room in the widow's house in New Haven and the buck-toothed boy who had threatened to strap him. The blurred room as he had risen from the table to meet his tormentor, the same sickness now, the same cold terror.

Slidell came to him and flung his arm about his shoulders.

"Benjamin, you have a great brain. It is a crime to let Davis blow it to pieces. Back down, for Christ's sake, Benjamin. Back down."

Judah smiled at Slidell. "You know I cannot do that. Listen to me now, we must be sensible. If the worst should happen—will you personally go to Paris on the first boat available and tell Natalie?"

"I will, Benjamin. I promise."

God Almighty, were those tears in Slidell's eyes? Slidell could weep? Then anything at all could happen, anything was possible.

"Come on, Slidell, I am not dead yet. Pull yourself together. Let us have a drink."

Slidell blew his nose and opened a bottle of whisky. They drank together, then sat quietly with no further words between them. The day darkened and Judah thought he must tell Slidell to go home. Mathilde would be wondering and waiting. He could not go with him. He must stay and write to Natalie. He must write the letter that Slidell would deliver if Davis aimed to kill. Natalie, my darling—

In the gathering shadows there was a figure in the doorway. Bayard of Delaware.

"Senator Benjamin, I have been requested by Davis of Mississippi to carry a message to you."

"I will accept it," Judah held out his hand.

"There is no note. He wished me to say that he tore yours up upon receipt and that there will be no duel. He offers you full satisfaction in the form of a public apology upon the floor of the Senate tomorrow morning. He said to tell you that he was wholly wrong and will so declare himself in session."

Slidell jumped from his chair. "Davis!" he cried: "Davis will apologize?"

Bayard, conscious of his solemn duty, did not respond to Slidell's joyous excitement. "I have repeated the words, sir, which Senator Davis requested me to deliver." He turned and left the office.

Slidell leaped to Judah's side. "Did you hear? What do you make of it? He backed down. Davis backed down."

Judah said, "That's not the way to put it, friend. Let us not suppose Davis is afraid of me. He knew he was in the wrong and he is willing to make amends. Let us drink to Davis. He has acted like a man."

"Go ahead, Benjamin. You drink to him. I will just drink."

"You are not giving him his due. It takes a brave man to apologize."

Slidell grinned. "What kind of a man does it take to challenge Davis to a duel?"

When word came to Judah that his father was dead he felt no more than a slight and passing grief. This old man, Philip Benjamin, of whose passing he now heard, was a stranger, an aged and unhappy man to whom life had long been a burden. He hoped only that his father had not known that death was near, had not realized how soon he was to be laid away in unconsecrated ground, without prayers, without notice of the Sephardim.

Will I mind when my time comes?

Curious to sit in a smartly furnished office with a corps of assistants answering one's mail, to look out upon the buildings of Washington, D.C., and to be thinking that one would lie in one's grave alone and outcast. Long ago he had made his decision but he had been so young then. Death had seemed so far away. How would he decide today? In a choice between his marriage to Natalie and a grave within the walls of Beth-Hiam how would he decide? The answer was simple. The unmarked grave, the unholy earth. For him there had been no other way. And yet there was a strange, primitive terror in knowing that one must go into the uncharted hereafter with no voice to speak a prayer for one.

And sitting there at his desk he prayed silently for Papa, hoping that he might be heard, hoping that Papa's soul might rest in the unconsecrated ground where he, too, must lie one day.

"Senator Benjamin, you have not forgotten your luncheon appointment?"

His mind was on many things as he walked toward his club: the case that would shortly be pleaded before the Supreme Court, the obnoxious—though reasonably witty—remark of Wade of Ohio that Judah Benjamin was an Israelite with Egyptian principles. Slavery. God, it was in everyone's thoughts. No action, no word today could be divorced from the flaming issue. One was for or one was against and one must stand somewhere. Even

a man who could not see slavery as a sound economical investment was forced to champion it because there was no camp for
moderates. To say slavery was not a hundred per cent right was
to say all Southerners were Simon Legrees. To say slavery was
not a hundred per cent wrong was to say all Northerners were
fanatical abolitionists. There was no room for a coolly stated
opinion, no room for reason.

As he approached the club he observed that a crowd was
gathered in the doorway. The entrance was blocked by a neck-
stretching mass of people talking excitedly. He knew none of
them but as he drew near he caught snatches of conversation.

"Never had a chance, poor devil. I seen it happen. I tell you
he never had a chance."

"I seen it, too. There he was just walking along the street and
the next minute there he is full of bullets, dying on the sidewalk."

There were no attendants at the door. Judah pushed his way
through the crowd. Inside, in the main foyer, there was no need
to ask questions of club members who stood pale and shaken.

"We carried him inside," someone said. "He was shot right
out there in front of your old house."

"Is he dead?" Judah breathed.

"Yes, he didn't live a minute. Doctor May happened to be here
but he could do nothing. He has gone for the coroner."

Barton Key, the handsomest man in Washington, lying bloody
and torn on the floor, his head resting on a hastily rolled throw
rug. Key, who had been so brave and gay in his cherry velvet
jacket. No shot had touched his face and it was strangely calm and
tranquil.

Slidell detached himself from the knot of men bending over
Key. He came to Judah's side.

"I have to have a drink," he said. His forehead dripped with
perspiration, his lips were white.

"Who did it, Slidell?"

Slidell stared in amazement. "Who did it? Dan Sickles did it.
In full view of passers-by he murdered Barton Key. Right out
there." Slidell waved his hand weakly. "He was like a crazy man."

"Where is Sickles now?"

"He's over in your house. I mean *his* house of course. He didn't
try to escape. Get me a drink, will you?"

There was no barman at work. Judah poured a dozen drinks, set them upon a tray and carried them to the foyer. He brought one to Slidell, leaving the others for those who needed them.

"Sit down, Slidell."

So far he had not fitted the pieces together. Contact with murder was certainly a nerve-racking experience, but Slidell was more unstrung than members who had been intimate friends of Key. He drank his whisky at a gulp and mopped his wet forehead.

"God Almighty," he moaned.

"Are you all right, Slidell? Do you want to go home?"

"Yes. Let us go."

It was only a step away. Mathilde had gone to her room half fainting. She had heard the shots and a servant had brought her the news.

"My God," Slidell said. "Key murdered by Dan Sickles! Murdered, Benjamin, in cold blood!"

"I know, Slidell. Try to stop thinking about it."

"I can't." Slidell pressed his hands to his forehead. "Sickles must have been crazy."

Judah nodded. Poor Sickles had not learned how to live with jealousy. He had not learned to close his eyes and to take her as she was. He had expected too much of her, too much of Key. Sickles had not known how to grasp whatever happiness there was or how to bear the anguish a man assumed at the altar with a woman like Teresa. God, what he must be suffering now, poor miserable Sickles. For him there was no going back. Never again could he hold Teresa in his arms. No matter what happened now Key would always stand between them. Sickles stupidly, blindly had made certain that Teresa would never forget Barton Key. And Judah found himself picturing the inside of that house where he had lived with Natalie, where Sickles had lived with Teresa. He could see the room in which Sickles must have kept his guns. He could see him taking the revolver, placing it in his pocket, walking down the spiral staircase toward the door. Sickles, who had not learned to live with jealousy.

Slidell said, "Jesus, Benjamin, I'm really shaken."

But he wasn't. Not now. The color had returned to his face. He had ceased mopping his forehead. "It was a close one, Benjamin. We are out of that lucky."

"We? What do you mean, Slidell?"

"It could have been Jim! God Almighty, that man who just got murdered could have been the President of the United States. But for the grace of God it could have been James Buchanan!"

Judah smiled faintly. But for the grace of God, the man with blood on his hands, the man who had walked down the spiral staircase with the revolver in his pocket could have been Judah Benjamin.

The years. Where did they go? They were so full of travel, of work, of money earned and spent before one had a chance to count it. The Jackson–New Orleans Railroad was at last a noisy, smoking reality, and Juarez of Mexico was looking with favor upon the Tehuantepec project. In the darkness and turbulence of the times Judah was re-elected to the Senate, and three days later John Brown was hanged in Virginia for his raid on Harpers Ferry. He died bravely, being conscious that his actions would be remembered as long as there was an America. He knew himself to be a symbol, and there is no courage like that of a man who goes through the motions of dying, knowing full well that he will live forever.

"We are entering upon dangerous times," Slidell said.

"You have not overstated the case, my friend."

The Democratic convention was held in Charleston, and the secession of the Southern delegates was recognized by many as a foreshadowing of a more formidable secession. Judah went with the Louisiana delegation into the dim half-world of uncertainty. He could not support Stephen Douglas.

"I want to know," he declared publicly, "the principles of the party for which I act. I want to find them written in letters of light so that no man dare misconstrue them. Can we go before the people and ask their votes with the avowed purpose of presenting opposite sets of principles in the two sections of the country? I will support any available man who can honestly stand on a platform satisfactory to the people. That far I will go, though I have no stomach for a fight in which I have my choice between the man who denies me all my rights openly and fairly and a man who admits my rights but intends to filch them."

At their convention the Republicans nominated Abraham

Lincoln, and Slidell was of the opinion that Lincoln could be elected if the Democrats did not unite.

"That observation is not as shrewd as some you have made, old friend. Of course Lincoln will be elected if we split ourselves into two factions. What can we do? Can you support Douglas?"

"No, of course I cannot. He is a traitor to the party."

"Then you will have to choose Breckenridge and Northern Democrats will not have him. I wish I could be here to see the thing through."

"I envy you for getting out of this mess, Benjamin."

"I will not get out of it. I expect to find California seething with doubts and questions."

He was right. California had taken very seriously its political responsibilities. It was often difficult to convince those he met that the purpose of his trip was, as it had been a decade earlier, a land-grant matter bearing no relation to the unrest of the day.

Election Day came while Judah was in San Francisco. He was instantly sought for comment and opinion. Was it true that there would be secession of the Southern states now that Lincoln had been elected? Actually, he had not the slightest idea. He had been out of touch for three months with the climate of Washington. Still, since he had never been one to argue that Lincoln's election must force secession, he saw no reason for raising fear. He made a brief and empty address to San Franciscans, assuring them that "a better understanding and appreciation of the Constitution would hush forever the discordant din which now stuns our ears."

What would Louisiana do? What would Louisiana ask him to do? Bound for Panama and home he paced the deck of the ship guessing what the future held. Abraham Lincoln. He remembered what Slidell had said of the Republican party—pledged to an early death. In the darkness and puzzlement of the moment Judah could only wonder to whose early death the party was pledged.

In Washington he heard the news immediately. South Carolina had seceded from the Union. Slidell had, of course, saved the Louisiana papers for Judah. He read that he opposed secession. He read that he thought secession necessary. A minister of New Orleans had used the pulpit to advocate the repudiation of the compact with the Federal Government. Angry letters from citizens screamed that continuation within the Union was impossible. The superintendent of the Louisiana State Military Academy, a man named William Tecumseh Sherman, had said that all the congresses on earth could not make the Negro anything else than what he was, that he must be subject to the white man.

"What does Buchanan say?" Judah asked.

"What can the poor bastard say, Benjamin? He's out of office soon. No one cares what he says."

"I care. He must say something."

"Well, he feels they had no right to secede but that the government has no right to whip them back into line."

"That's a fine, strong stand he has taken. We can be very proud."

"Don't be hard on him, Benjamin. He is trying to please everyone."

"But he pleases no one, Slidell. At least a man who takes a positive stand has some admirers. This way Buchanan brands himself a weak-spined—"

"Forget it. It doesn't matter now. Whatever Buchanan says will be drowned out in the roar of voices that fill the country." He gestured toward the pile of Louisiana newspapers. "Our state feels this thing pretty strongly."

"So strongly that I should say we have a mandate, Senator Slidell."

Slidell raised his feet and rested them upon his desk where he could make a comfortable study of his boot tips. "Not quite yet. There is going to be complete Southern secession but it has not so far happened. And when it does, Benjamin, remember that we, to, have a right to reach personal conclusions. Do not become emotional. Think carefully."

"What does it matter what we think? If Louisiana—"

"Wait a minute. You are still an innocent, clear-eyed boy, aren't you? Listen to me. Shortly, very shortly, there is coming to the men of this country an opportunity that rarely comes. A man can be a hero no matter what he does. Stick with the Federal Government and, by Jesus, that is patriotic. Go with your state and, by Jesus, that's patriotic, too. Are you following me?"

"At your heels, friend."

"Benjamin, do you know you are the greatest legal mind alive?

You can be chief justice one day if you like. Already in the past you could have had a cabinet job, a Supreme Court appointment, or the ministry to Spain. You are not just a Louisiana senator. You are a man of national fame and importance in legal and political circles. Lincoln would welcome you with open arms."

"Somehow the proposition finds me lacking in enthusiasm, Slidell."

"All right then, forget government. Just take a little sign that says 'J. Benjamin, Attorney' up to New York City and ask August Belmont where to hang it. You'd run all those Northern boys right back to law school."

"Slidell, for God's sake—"

"Now hear me out, Benjamin. I am only presenting a side you may not have considered. You have to think well before you make a choice."

Judah walked over to the desk and leaned close to Slidell. "Listen, I have no choice. No choice at all. Do you understand that? If my mother was being lashed by our next-door neighbor would I have a choice? Could I stand by and debate the advantages and disadvantages of embroiling myself?"

"Don't get sentimental. Be realistic, for Christ's sake. Benjamin, this is going to be a war and you have a hell of a lot to lose."

"Everyone has."

Slidell smiled. "But I don't like everyone, Benjamin. I like you. Think about it for a while. Think about war, *this* war that's coming."

And Judah knew that Slidell had seen what he had seen. The Federal Government under Lincoln, the Republican, would never let the South go in peace. The North would fight for union, the South for its life. If the North lost, the Union was disbanded, but if the South lost, it lost its life. The hazards were not the same. The North was a man wagering half his fortune. The South would be gambling all, including survival itself.

"Benjamin, you run the chance of throwing away the biggest legal career in the country. You aren't rich enough to act noble on impulse. You never saved a cent. You can't just jump into this without thinking it over."

Judah said, "Are you thinking it over, Slidell? Where do you stand on this matter? Now tell me, what are you going to do?"

Slidell took his feet off the desk and looked at Judah in astonishment. "What am I going to do? Don't be ridiculous. You know what I'm going to do. I'm a Creole."

The galleries were crowded with Southern sympathizers. Today Senator Slidell would announce his state's secession from the Union. Then Benjamin would speak. The information was that both carried pistols. God alone knew what might occur. Was it safe to attend the session? Certainly, it was safe. Besides, how many more such dramas could one expect to see? Mississippi, Florida, Alabama, and Georgia had already followed South Carolina.

Slidell, very erect, his white hair crowning the straight six feet of still powerful physique, took the floor. His announcement was as advertised. Louisiana was no longer a part of the Union. Briefly Slidell stated the case as Louisiana saw it. His declaration was unembellished, lean and functional. The crowd was silent, breathless, waiting for Benjamin, the dark man in the well-tailored clothes, who would not raise his voice but who would lull the senses and fill the mind with food for thought.

He rose and spoke for the last time to the Senate of the United States.

"And now we part to meet as senators in one common council chamber of the nation no more forever. We desire, we beseech you to let this parting be in peace. I conjure you to indulge in no vain delusions that duty or conscience, interest or honor, imposes upon you the necessity of invading our states or shedding the blood of our people. You have no possible justification for it. However, if you are resolved to pervert the government framed for the protection of our rights into an instrument for subjugating us then we must meet the issue that you force upon us as best becomes free men.

"What may be the fate of this horrible contest no man can tell, but this much I will say: The fortunes of war may be adverse to our arms, you may carry desolation into our peaceful land and with torch and fire you may set our cities in flame but you will never subjugate us.

"You are told that the South is in rebellion without cause and that her citizens are traitors. Rebellion! The very word is a confession: an avowal of tyranny, outrage, and oppression. When, sirs, did millions of people rise in organized, deliberate rebellion

against justice, truth, and honor? Men do not war against bene-
factors. No people ever rose or ever will rise against rational and
benevolent authority.

"Traitors! Treason! Ay, the people of the South imitate and
glory in just such treason as leaped in living flame from the lips
of Patrick Henry, just such treason as encircles with a sacred halo
the undying name of Washington."

It was the last time he would ever speak here on the Senate
floor. It was over. Never again would he see this city. He had
asked a question when he had come as junior senator. What will
happen here? What would happen indeed? War would happen.
It had to happen.

And so he belonged in this place no more, and with applause
and shouts from the galleries ringing in his ears Judah Benjamin
walked out of the Senate chamber and out of the United States
of America.

Six

MONTGOMERY

It had been a pretty little city, sleeping peacefully among the
wistaria vines and dogwood. It had taken a certain amount of
pride in being Alabama's capital, but a quiet sort of pride, not
vulgar enough to draw attention, not active enough to disturb
a deep, sweet slumber. The city had built two hotels and a
lovely little capitol on a green hill in acknowledgment of the
honor that Alabama had bestowed upon her, then had gone back
to drowse among the flowers. It was nice to be the capital, but the
main business of any small city was to be clean and flower-filled
and to get plenty of rest. Alabama understood about such things,
and for the fifteen years that Montgomery had been the capital
her legislature had gone about its work gently, yawning a little
in the lazy, fragrant atmosphere, rather anxious to go back to
sleep itself. There was not a man or for that matter not a child
in all of Montgomery who did not know that a raised voice or
a quick movement was both unnecessary and rude. No swift
pursuit of anything on God's earth could ever bring more pleasure than lying still and peaceful in the shade of a good, full tree.

And it was to Montgomery they came, the men who would form
a new nation, the men who wished to give and the men who
wished to receive. They came by the score and then by the
hundred, the statesmen, the politicians, the office seekers, the speculators and contractors. They poured into Montgomery and
screamed with dismay to find it unprepared for this distinguished
onslaught. Why couldn't a little city have thirty hotels and at

least twenty restaurants? It was outrageous. Montgomery opened its eyes, stretched, made a gesture or two of hospitality, then seeing how futile the effort was went back to sleep. Only now the sleep was feverish and troubled. In dreams Montgomery knew that the two neat little hotels were overcrowded and dirty, the flowers trampled, and the lovely little capitol filled with men who had no love for Alabama but only need of her.

The people looked at the new flag that flew above them. They thought it was a very pretty flag. Everything was sure to be all right when one considered the way President Davis sat a horse and how there wasn't a little boy anywhere in the South who didn't know all there was to know about shooting a gun.

In the front bedroom of Mrs. Cleveland's house, Judah Benjamin looked out the window at Montgomery, Alabama. He had tried the Exchange Hotel and the Montgomery Hotel and he had chosen Mrs. Cleveland's. God knew it was not much but it was cleaner than the hotels and there was more hope of having the bed linen changed.

Across the street there were small houses set in well-kept gardens. A woman cutting flowers caught his attention. It did not matter very much to her about the new flag, indeed at the moment she and the flowers were equally unconcerned that they lived now on Confederate soil.

If she continues not to care, not to notice the difference, then all will be well with us. It is only when she begins to notice—what will happen here, I wonder. What will happen here?

He turned from the window determinedly, admitting to himself that he had gone there only to delay thinking, only to put from his mind the things that troubled him. Where else could he go but to the window of his room? To kill time in town was a boresome business. Every adventurer accosted one on the streets or in the hotels, wanting influence brought to bear in his behalf for a position, a commission, or a special privilege. Judah sat down and found that he had chosen a rocking chair. He rocked back and forth experimentally and suddenly laughed. God, if Slidell could see him! Benjamin with nothing to do. Benjamin sitting like an old woman in a rocking chair. Benjamin wondering how to consume two hours!

He left the chair, turning to look at it well so that it would not trap him again. A rocking chair. Was it to sit in a rocking chair that he had followed his state? Was it to live in a shabby rooming house? Or was it to have his hard-earned reputation for honesty and integrity wiped out?

All right. You have said it now, Benjamin. Go read the papers. Everyone else has read them. See what they say.

He walked to the chest of drawers. There were papers waiting for him. Northern papers that had picked up and reprinted an item from the New York *Independent*. By next week everyone, both North and South would have read it.

THE EARLY HISTORY OF A TRAITOR
by
Francis Bacon

Judah, in the little room in Montgomery, Alabama, stood remembering. Francis Bacon, the boy with the friendly smile. Bacon, who had been his star of hope in those dreadful early days at Yale. Bacon, who had been so kind.

The class of 1829 at Yale College was the finest body of young men that I ever saw. There was one of the class whose name cannot be found on the list of graduates, or in any annual catalogue after 1827. He was and still is a handsome fellow. He haled from a great state of "the chivalrous sunny South," bright-eyed, dark-complexioned, and ardent as a Southern sun could make him. Soon there was a mysterious trouble in that class. Watches, penknives, and sums of money disappeared unaccountably. The losers constituted themselves a volunteer "detective force," set their trap baited with thirty-five dollars and soon caught the thief. He confessed. On opening his trunk in his presence they found the missing valuables. He begged pitifully not to be exposed, and they agreed not to inform the city magistrates or the faculty of the university but ordered him to clear out at once and forever.

That little thief in later years became a senator of an important Southern state—not the one from which he originally haled. Today he is advocating and justifying the theft of the Federal Government's property. Time has not made and can never make any change in the rascal. Had these early filchings been a mere boyish escapade, a momentary yielding to temp-

tation, they would not deserve mention now, but they were systematized theft. Had the fellow not at length reproduced his private morality in public life, I would have allowed the secret of those early crimes to remain in the hearts of the few men who then knew and now remember it.

Ah, Bacon, they told you I confessed and you believed them. They told you I begged not to be exposed and you believed that, too. And now you have hated me all these years because you championed me and were made to feel a fool for having done so. How bitterly you hated yourself for having befriended me. The bitterness shows, Bacon, that after all this time you could give the press such an article. You feel free now of the shame of having been taken in. How ironic it is, poor Bacon, that in the end your desire for justice serves only the bigoted and the merciless.

He read the article again. No one could miss who was here described, and for the benefit of those who might not guess his identity immediately one newspaper had obligingly supplied a few additional clues.

He thought of Ninette as he stood there. Would the canard appear in Paris journals? Would she read it? What would she think? How would Natalie explain it to her? It would come as news to Natalie herself, and it was perhaps the saddest thing about their marriage that after twenty-eight years he could not tell how good a case she would make for him to the girl who was their daughter.

Suddenly, unbidden, a memory came to him. Natalie in deep red velvet, Natalie moving gracefully among her guests. The parlors in the old house on Condé Street. The first dinner. Why did that memory always return? Had there been something significant, something pivotal that he had missed? Did the memory come as a sad ghost chiding him gently for not having recognized that the evening had offered more than the opportunity to entertain Soulé and Roselius? Was there something that should have been different? And if it had been would he now know what Natalie was really like, how much, how little he could depend upon her? Where was the connection between that night and the words she would muster in his defense?

What could have been different? Natalie was always Natalie

and I was always I. And regrets are for those who have nothing
new to disturb them.

There was no shortage of present heartaches concerning Natalie. When would he see her again? How should he answer her
letter which had been forwarded from New Orleans? And could
she live comfortably on ten thousand a year? She would have
her annual twenty-five thousand no more. Early in January he
had raised a hundred thousand dollars and had sent it to England
to be paid in yearly installments to her. Ten years was all he had
been able to provide for. Only God could tell what those years
would bring, but one hundred thousand dollars had been all he
could manage. As it was, he had had to sell everything he owned
including stock in the Jackson–New Orleans Railroad and a
piece of land in Texas which he had taken once as a fee. He had
called in all outstanding debts and in the end had had five
thousand dollars to send to his sister, Rebecca, and fourteen
hundred dollars for his own use. Rebecca could live for some
time on five thousand dollars. After that he would do what he
could.

He had tried to explain to Natalie the reasons, the essential
meaning of their new and reduced circumstances. He might have
saved the ink. Finance was not a matter Natalie could be expected
to discuss.

Beloved:

*Oh, talk not to me of economy! It is so fatiguing. Money is a
fit subject for a woman only if she is a harlot or a shopkeeper.
Otherwise it is quite unsuitable. If you have money, do send
me some. If you have not then of course you cannot send it.
Only let us not, after all these years, begin talking like coarse
wretches dividing up a handful of coppers.*

*Now as to this magnificent new country—the Confederacy?
—Beloved, I am ill thinking about it. A gentleman who is a
lawyer here has handed down an opinion which turns my
blood to ice water. I am sure he knows nothing you do not
know, but in your enthusiasm you may not have thought as
objectively as he. This gentleman tells me that, no matter how
lofty your purpose and ideals, you are guilty of treason and that
should the Federal Government apprehend you, you may easily
be hanged. Is this the truth, Judah? I pray it is not. Do you*

*know how much I love you? Have you thought well about this
dangerous thing you have done? I could not live with the
thought that horrible people had dared to lay rough hands
upon you, to hurt you, to kill you. Oh, beloved, if this lawyer
has spoken truly, I beg of you, before it is too late, go to
President Lincoln and tell him that you have been wrong and
that you are sorry. Perhaps you are laughing at me. Do not
laugh, for my heart is breaking. Judah, my husband, if you
have willingly walked into treason, I plead with you, for the
love of God, retrace your steps. Ask yourself very honestly:
What am I doing here?*

It was a pity that someone had thought it necessary to alarm
her. Still, it was inevitable that she should hear or read the
dangers inherent in rebellion.

What am I doing here?

He gazed around the room. It was years since he had lived in a
room so lacking in comfort and luxury. He considered the rocking
chair that had trapped him and the stack of newspapers that
damned him as a thief.

What am I doing here?

He thought of his position in the Confederacy. Attorney general of a country that had only district courts. A member of Jefferson Davis's cabinet. Almost thirty years of struggle and drive
to reach the top. Almost thirty years and the ultimate is reached
—attorney general in Jefferson Davis's cabinet at a salary of six
thousand dollars a year!

What am I doing here?

It was not an easy question to answer. On a platform addressing
a multitude of Southerners it would be easy. There he would
speak of this sweet land and her principles and virtues and he
would speak of the bravery and selflessness of her sons. People
would applaud, even cheer, and they would say that the question
had been answered clearly and fully. But here in this little room
he wished to tell himself the pure truth, and the pure truth was
not found so simply. He could not lay it out for inspection as
though it were a bolt of cloth.

Do I believe in the Confederacy? I said that I did and the
price of saying it was very high, but I do not believe in the Confederacy as Jefferson Davis believes. I do not think Mississippians

are finer and braver than New Yorkers. I do not think Georgia
more honest than Maine. I do not think South Carolina more
noble than New Jersey. And, by God, I do not think the person
of Jefferson Davis any more sacred than that of Abraham Lincoln.

What am I doing here? Natalie, I will tell you.

I am here because the brain has grave limitations. A man can
think clearly only up to a point. He can think coldly, objectively,
but mostly for others. Never completely for himself. I do not
admire or even like Jefferson Davis. I do not think slavery is essential to our well-being. I doubt the Confederacy can win a war.
You see, I can regard the whole matter unemotionally, unsenti-
mentally. What am I doing here? I will tell you, my darling. I am
a Southerner.

The President and his wife lived in a modest, clapboard house
set in a small garden. The house stood on a corner and had been
given a new coat of paint in recognition of the honor that had
come to it. White paint of course. A president must have a white
house.

Judah wondered if informality was to be the keynote of the
new administration's social policy. The Negro who opened the
door smiled broadly and admitted him without question. In the
background the three Davis children romped and squealed, and
the general atmosphere was that of any Sunday afternoon in the
home of any prosperous American business man.

"This way, sir, Mr. Davis is expecting you."

He followed the butler across the hall. From the top of the
stairs Varina waved to him and called a cheery, "I will see you
at dinner." If he had felt himself in the home of an average
American it was because he had been meant to feel that way.
The Confederacy had broken with the cold formality of the
North. This was Southern charm unleashed at last.

Jefferson Davis was at his desk in a bright little room. He wore
a rustic-type suit of some slate-colored material and around his
neck there was a black silk handkerchief. Judah instantly received the message which Davis' attire was at such pains to deliver. You see, your President is a simple Mississippian, too hard
at work to give fancy clothes a second thought.

"Good afternoon, Mr. President."

"Ah, Mr. Benjamin. So nice of you to come early. I hope my

note was no inconvenience to you. I thought we could have a good talk before the others arrive. Do sit down."

Judah seated himself. It was not his prerogative to make conversation. That was up to the President, and the President seemed unable or unwilling to begin. So it was the matter at Yale he wished to discuss, was it? Judah waited, looking expectantly into the chill, fine-featured face.

I could help you, sir, but I will not. Find your own way to New Haven and I will meet you there.

Davis moved a mountain of documents from one end of his desk to the other. "We have not really had a personal talk, Mr. Benjamin," he said. "Actually we do not know each other well and I feel that a greater intimacy would be both a pleasure for me and a service to the Confederacy. When I am asked questions concerning you I find myself somewhat at a loss to reply."

When you are asked questions concerning me? Come, sir, you can do better than that. Who would ask questions concerning so obscure an office as that of the attorney general?

"Mr. Benjamin, it is a sad fact that in all the years preceding our withdrawal from the Union a large portion of our Southern people did not seek to acquaint themselves with events and personalities upon the Washington scene. Today they clamor to know everything about the men at the head of their government and I must be ready with the answers."

Judah nodded. "You must be ready to defend your choices against all opposition."

Davis said, "There is no opposition. I would not tolerate opposition, for if my decisions are not trusted I am of no value to my country. Still, people have a right to know. I truly believe, Mr. Benjamin, there are citizens here in the South who knew nothing of me at the time this government was formed."

"Well, Mr. President, that prepares me to accept with humility the public's ignorance of my own insignificant accomplishments."

Davis smiled briefly. "I have, of course, made it a point to inform everyone that you were nominated for the United States Supreme Court and that Buchanan offered you the ministry to Spain. Naturally I do not possess the facts with which to explain why you chose to refuse these appointments." Davis paused and looked encouragingly at Judah.

Judah looked back at him pleasantly but in silence and the

pause grew long and uncomfortable until at length Davis spoke again. "Your legal career has, of course, been creditable and it is on that basis you were appointed attorney general. I am willing to accept the verdict of those who say that you are the country's greatest legal mind. Your political career is, regrettably, a matter that comes under question."

"Sir?" Judah asked sharply.

Davis smiled a quick little smile. "I do not mean that *I* question it, Mr. Benjamin. I am speaking of the people. *They* want to know. You see—between the two of us—Louisiana's reputation has long been an ill one. I think you will admit this freely yourself. It certainly predates your entrance into politics by many a year, but the fact that Louisiana's elections have often been a stench on the air leads people to inquire— Sir, this is painful and revolting to me but I must hear from you an explanation of the cab votes, of the introduction of the land-grant bill that gave John Slidell twenty thousand acres of the Houmas tract, and of the railroads you were so active in promoting."

It was incredible that a buck-toothed boy known so long ago, so briefly, was responsible for this degrading inquisition. A buck-toothed boy and Francis Bacon—Bacon, who had never intended harm to the innocent. But today Jefferson Davis had read the newspapers, had been disturbed by what he read, had begun to wonder about matters that he had hitherto been willing to dismiss. And a buck-toothed boy had brought him, Judah Benjamin, into the Confederacy under a cloud.

Judah rose to his feet. "Mr. President," he said, "the cab votes, the Houmas tract matter, and my railroad activities have long been known to you. I was invited to be attorney general while you were in possession of this knowledge. What has occurred that makes an explanation necessary now?"

Davis experimented with the inkwell. Would it be better two inches forward on the desk? No, no. Back where it had been was the proper location for it. "I am examining these matters, Mr. Benjamin, only so that I may be on firm ground when I am challenged concerning the integrity of a cabinet member."

"I see. For a moment I thought you had read the papers that came to town this morning, the papers that speak of an outrageous episode at Yale."

Davis smiled, not briefly now but warmly. The smile that made people forget that they had thought him a cold man. He said, "I will be very frank with you. I did read the article concerning Yale. I did not want to embarrass you by remarking upon it, but I am happy and relieved that you have mentioned it. The article will cause comment. We must be ready to refute it."

"Mr. President, how does one refute such a thing?"

"Why, by proving that it could not have happened, by giving reasons why one has been unjustly accused."

"I see. It hadn't ocurred to me that it would be so easy. As a matter of fact, I had thought it would be a rather difficult undertaking to dispute the word of Francis Bacon, who is an eminent physician, a world-famous religious leader, and a very great gentleman."

Jefferson Davis stared at him, his light eyes filled with something that was almost horror.

"You will not explain, Mr. Benjamin?"

"To whom will I explain, sir? Men who do not know me will believe Francis Bacon. Why should they not? And am I to insult those who already trust me by assuring them that I am not a thief?"

"Why does Francis Bacon accuse you?"

Judah came close to the desk and met the eyes of Davis. "I will tell you why Francis Bacon accuses me, Mr. President. Francis Bacon accuses me because he believes me guilty."

Davis lowered his eyes and sat very still.

I owe him more. He is the President and he is entitled to know the truth. What can I say? Can I say that I was a Jew where Jews were not wanted? No, for I can accept his sympathy, no more easily than I was able to accept his sneers, and when it comes to it, there is little difference.

"Mr. President, I am from a state whose civic honor you challenge. I am accused of introducing a bill for the profit of my fellow senator. I was elected to a minor office with the help of counterfeit cab licenses, and certainly I am responsible for the sale of stock in a Mexican railroad which to this day does not exist. Sir, I am a lawyer. I have infinite respect for testimony, and yet I ask you to take my word against all evidence that has been presented. I assure you that I am not a thief and that you may, in defending me, feel yourself on firm ground."

"You give me that assurance, sir?"

"In the name of all that I hold sacred, Mr. President, I give it."

Within the small, bright room there was a moment of still-ness. Jefferson Davis gazed coolly, speculatively upon the face of his attorney general. At length he spoke. "Mr. Benjamin," he said, "between us the matter is closed."

The first cabinet meeting took place in a room at the Exchange Hotel. The members sat around a table and talked about the future of their country—the Confederate States of America. "If there is a war—" There seemed no other way to begin a sentence.

President Davis, sitting tall and proud at the head of the table, listened as each man spoke. A facial nerve twitched as he listened, and one of his eyes—some said it was sightless—was filmed and seemed inflamed.

Mallory of the Navy Department said, "I propose that we take it for granted there will be war. If there is not, all the better. Still, I think we should be ready for it."

Walker of the War Department looked down his nose at Mallory. His disdainful expression as he surveyed the Florida ex-senator suggested that he was thinking not of Mallory's words but of Mallory's mother, who had been a washerwoman.

"Anyone agree with me?" Mallory asked.

Walker said, "My dear fellow, why should there be war? We do not intend to make war and the Yankees are not interested in anything except money. I am willing to wager that all the blood spilled in this controversy I will be able to mop up with my pocket handkerchief."

Davis scowled. "Mr. Walker, I am sorry you are so willing to gamble on peace. It would give me a feeling of greater security to know that you are thoroughly aware that there are no cer-tainties."

Walker looked hurt. "Mr. President, I have proceeded on the theory that we are in an extremely dangerous situation."

"Well, now, which is it, Mr. Walker? I cannot reconcile your talk of Northern unwillingness to fight with our 'extremely dan-gerous situation.' Do make the effort to clarify your thoughts, sir."

"I think I can do so. I do not believe the Yankees will have any taste for meeting us in mortal combat but if they do, my department will be ready." Walker's glance rounded the table looking for support and approval.

"Very well. Now if we are agreed, gentlemen, that war is a lively possibility, what must be our first important step? Give your opinions please."

Walker and Mallory spoke together.

"A strong army."

"Plenty of ships."

Everyone laughed. Davis smiled slightly. "Mr. Reagan, do you believe our first need is an adequate supply of stamps for the post office?"

Toombs, Secretary of State, brilliant, mercurial Toombs, whose shirt was slightly soiled, held a surprising silence.

Memminger, the German-born South Carolinian, leaned across the table toward Davis. "Sir," he said, "I do not wish to put upon my office an unmerited emphasis, but how does a nation function unless the Treasury Department is immediately—"

"We digress," Davis said. "I asked opinions on the matter of our first step. Our very first step, remember. Now, gentlemen, what shall it be?"

Judah said, "Cotton."

Davis nodded. "That is correct. Cotton." And Judah felt like a precocious child whose reply has pleased but rather astonished his teacher. "Cotton, gentlemen, is the muscles and sinews of the Confederacy. Mr. Benjamin has gone directly to the only first step possible. We must immediately cease shipping cotton to Europe."

Judah said, "Mr. President, that is not what I had in mind. My idea was quite the reverse."

"The reverse? You mean to continue shipping?"

" 'Continue shipping' does not accurately describe the course I would suggest, sir. I believe that we should gather every bale of cotton in the Confederacy as quickly as possible and transport it all to England and France. We will sell it there and with the money buy arms."

Davis said, "It would be a great mistake to put England in so comfortable a position. Her economy rests heavily on her mills and she needs our cotton desperately. In fact she cannot do without it. If we withhold our cotton England *must come get it.* Now, suppose we go to war, suppose we are blockaded, suppose we need assistance. England has to have cotton, doesn't she? She would even have to break a blockade to get it. Do you see that, sir?"

Judah did not reply. Around him others nodded and murmured approval of the President's cotton policy, but he said nothing and Davis spoke again.

"Do you see that, sir?"

Judah said, "I do not see England coming to get our cotton, sir."

"But she will have to. She will have no choice."

"She will have a choice, sir. She will have a choice between closing her mills and supporting slavery—and the English have no stomach for slavery."

And suddenly the warm, rich taste of peaches was in Judah's mouth and he was a child in the fruit store on King Street. Rebecca, his mother, was there, and her gold earrings flashed in the sunlight. She gave him a beautiful, silky-skinned peach and she told him a simple truth and he was telling it now to the fathers of the Confederacy: The English have no stomach for slavery!

Toombs said, "They may have no stomach for slavery, Benjamin, but England's too smart to cut her own throat. Business is business, you know."

"No, I do not know," Judah said. "And I would ask the Secretary of State to explain his meaning. I would like to know if he believes that the Confederacy values the almighty dollar above high principles, if he believes that to grow fatter and richer the Confederacy would support a system despicable to its way of thinking."

"Of course I do not believe the Confederacy would—"

"Then why, in the name of God, are you so swift to think that other countries are without conscience or ideals? Here in Montgomery, Alabama, Mr. Secretary, we did not invent integrity and honor. I am a little tired of hearing that other countries will sell anything if only the price is right."

"Well, their history shows that—"

"And we are in the enviable position of having no history as yet. When we acquire some it may make us more tolerant."

Toombs made no answer and Judah suddenly became aware of the silence in the room. He had forgotten this was a cabinet meeting. He had behaved as though on the floor of the Senate chamber. He turned to Davis.

"Mr. President, I am sincerely apologetic. If you will pardon me I will then ask the same consideration of the Secretary of State."

Davis said, "Mr. Toombs has no apology due him. You spoke your mind in defense of a country you obviously admire. Let us say Mr. Toombs insulted a friend of yours and has been rebuked. As for myself, sir, I do not know for what offense you ask pardon. I was extremely interested in your remarks."

"Thank you, sir. However—" Judah smiled across the table at Toombs— "I am sorry for engaging in an irrelevant argument with you."

Toombs said, "Forget it. I am always saying the wrong thing."

A heartening admission from the Secretary of State!

"Now then," said President Davis, "the first step, of course, concerns cotton. We will ship not another bale of it and await the outcome of that strategy. Now as to the next step—"

After the meeting Judah went to the bar with Walker for a glass of sherry. As he stood beside the tall, bony man Judah could not help but remember what Mrs. Chesnut had said of him on Sunday at the Davis house.

"Some ladies are praying for a Napoleon of the South," she had whispered when the Secretary of War had entered the room. "It wouldn't do a bit of good. If Napoleon himself came back to earth Walker wouldn't give him a commission."

She was probably right. Not Napoleon, but it was a certainty that no well-spoken Alabama boy would have a bit of trouble.

"I hope you don't mind if I ask you a few questions, Mr. Benjamin. You do agree, don't you, that we should all know each other's thoughts?"

"Up to a point, sir."

"Well, if I ask you something you do not choose to answer, you just say right out that—"

"Have no fear, Mr. Walker."

"And do feel free to ask my advice and opinions."

"Oh, I will, sir, whenever I have the need of them."

Walker took a sip of his sherry and said, "Just now at the meeting, sir, when you mentioned England's distaste for slavery, I got the feeling that you didn't care very much for the institution yourself. Sir, would you like to state how you feel personally on the subject?"

Judah considered the matter. Should he say that he had written *Uncle Tom's Cabin* and had permitted Mrs. Stowe to sign her name to it? He looked long and hard into Walker's thin, pointed face and felt an aversion for the man.

And yet if I do not try to be one with him and Toombs and Davis, what am I doing here?

"Mr. Walker, I have owned slaves. As a matter of fact I still own a few house servants. It is the custom in our part of the country and has been convenient for many of us. If the South had said, 'Let us free them all,' I would have replied, 'Splendid. Let us do it.' But when the North assumes it is her right to take them from us then I am in rebellion. I would have responded similarly to any arrogant gesture from the North."

Walker said, "You do not believe slavery is a blessing for the Negro?"

"Oh, Mr. Walker, who believes that?"

"I do, sir."

"Really? How extraordinary."

"I do not see why it is extraordinary. Without us they wouldn't be Christians, sir. They would not have their health carefully guarded. They would have no advantages."

It was an inferior sherry but Judah sipped it thoughtfully, slowly. "Mr. Walker," he said, "you are in a position to answer a question that has always troubled me. Why is it, if slavery is such a blessing, that a slave who performs a noble deed is freed by his master? A slave—we will say—has saved your child from drowning or from the bite of a poisonous snake. With tears of gratitude in your eyes you instantly cut off that good black lad from all his blessings. No more contacts with Christianity for him, no more careful guarding of his health, no more advantages for this fine boy. I am perplexed, Mr. Walker."

Walker said, "Well, now, Mr. Benjamin, they're an ignorant people. We all know that. They cannot always see how lucky they are to be slaves. Consequently in rewarding them we give them the thing they think desirable. It is like giving a child a shiny, useless toy."

"Sir, freedom is a shiny, useless toy? You cannot mean it."

"Not to us it isn't, Mr. Benjamin, but to a lesser people—"

Walker paused and peered sharply at Judah. "You do believe they're a lesser people, don't you?"

"I have no proof that they are. I know they are uneducated but we are responsible for that. I think it unfair to withhold learning from them and then judge them as lesser people because they have no learning."

"But learning is withheld from them for a purpose. They were born to labor so there would be no point—indeed it would be cruel—to give them a taste for a culture they can never possess."

"How can you be so sure they were born to labor?"

"They were created the white man's inferior, Mr. Benjamin. It is very apparent. Why else did God make them a different color?"

"I will admit to being not fully informed as to God's plan, Mr. Walker. However, if He made the Negro black in order to mark him as a slave, He was, I think, rather subtle. He could have conveyed His intentions to us more clearly by supplying the Negro with two pairs of hands or perhaps with the strength of a large horse."

Walker shook his head. "Your ideas are very confusing to me. Are they generally understood by others? For instance, Mr. Benjamin, did President Davis understand your views on slavery?"

"President Davis has not heard my views on slavery, sir."

"Well, I think he should, don't you?"

"Oh, he'll hear, Mr. Walker. I feel very sure he'll hear."

The warm spring night closed in on Montgomery, and Judah lay on a lumpy mattress and could not sleep. It was early April and the heat was already intense, but was Louisiana cooler? Surely he was accustomed to warm weather. But in Louisiana he had had a good mattress to lie upon. Always? Well, no, but he had been very young in the days when New Orleans had offered him a bed as uncomfortable as the one he now lay upon.

Would the North obligingly evacuate Fort Sumter? Not likely but there were those who still believed that it was possible. Toombs had sent a commission to Washington to inquire into the matter. To naïvely ask, in fact, if the North wouldn't please take its horrid soldiers out of the fort and leave it for Southerners to occupy. Judah tried to picture Seward as Secretary of State. Obviously it had been easy for Abraham Lincoln to see the man in so exalted a position. For Judah it was impossible. Seward had not received the Confederate commissioners. Instead he had asked Judge John Campbell of the Supreme Court to meet and treat with them. The commission was satisfied with the message that Campbell brought. Sumter would not be reprovisioned. It would be evacuated. Judge Campbell's word was good. No one could doubt Judge Campbell, and yet the pledge had not been his. He had merely delivered Seward's assurance, and Judah knew Seward.

Perhaps if the pillow were turned over it would present a smoother side. If he could only get to sleep. If he could forget thinking about—

Would Virginia secede? If it came to a fight—and of course it would come to that—they were going to need Virginia.

A slight breeze stirred and he was grateful. At the window one could make the most of it and perhaps the bed would seem more comfortable if he sat for a while in that abominable rocking chair. He went to the window and looked out into the blackness, feeling the soft, warm breeze upon his face, thinking suddenly about the cabinet. Toombs, who hated his job, Walker, who was incompetent. Memminger, who had been esteemed till he had presented his tax plan. Now people were remembering that he had been raised in an orphanage. Mallory, Reagan, Benjamin— Davis's cabinet. Why did it exist? Did Davis ever listen to a word spoken by any one of them?

He thought of Varina, the sweet, serious-minded Varina, who loved Davis so deeply that her eyes softened when she spoke his name. "He is not well, you know." She said it often, so often that one could not miss her meaning. "Be tolerant of my dearest," she was saying.

"He has had a great deal of grief," she had said to Judah. "His health has always been imperfect and of course he suffered so when his first wife died."

"Yes, it must have been a blow to him."

The daughter of Zachary Taylor, Davis's bride for only a season and then laid in her grave. Varina had been a small child when this sorrow had struck, yet she spoke as though she had lived through it with Davis.

"It was awful for him, Mr. Benjamin. He is so sensitive."

Sensitive? Oh, indeed, but unaware that others were also capable of anguish.

What shall I do if he ever speaks to me with the contempt he so freely offers Walker? I will not take it from him. And yet— did I accept his invitation into the cabinet without knowing him to be a captious man? Is serving the Confederacy less important than my precious honor?

Slidell had written from New Orleans and in the letter had remarked, "I expected you here by now. Somehow I do not see you and our revered President standing each other very long."

Why not, Slidell? I came to serve the Confederacy. I will forgive anything but an insult and perhaps that, too, in the end. I do not know. I must wait and see.

The breeze was gone. The air was heavy and hot. He felt no nearer to sleep. A footstep sounded in the night. The young man who lived in the house across the street returning from drill. Everywhere all over the South, the salesmen, the farmers, the clerks, the factory hands were drilling. In the North they were saying it was a rebellion of aristocrats and slaveowners. He smiled to himself. How convenient that would be for generations yet unborn. Everyone in the future could think—or say—that of course his forebears must have been aristocrats and slaveowners. Hadn't they been in the Southern army? He wondered if anyone would ever say, "Naturally my family fought against freeing slaves. The didn't want no free niggers taking their jobs in the sawmills."

He thought of Beauregard at Charleston glowering out at Fort Sumter. Slidell's brother-in-law, the elegant Creole, who was a general now. In the tradition of West Point he was a soldier. What would he think of an army that only yesterday had been selling shoes or peddling vegetables or adding a column of figures? And what, when it came to that, would an army of boys from Alabama and Mississippi think of Beauregard?

Could I sleep? No, I am not sleepy and there is no point in getting into that dreadful bed and lying there in misery.

He dressed and walked over to the Exchange Hotel. Mallory was at the bar. He had not really known Mallory in Washington. Their circles had been wide apart. Judah had heard a lady remark that Mallory was so notoriously dissolute that a woman was compromised by being seen with him. He had thought the lady full of hope rather than truth, for the Florida senator had seemed a safe though dull man. But tonight he had been drinking. His color was high and the Irish blue eyes were not as mild as Judah remembered them.

"I have been meaning to have a word with you, Mr. Attorney General. The time never seemed right but I'm a little drunk, I think, and that's a good time for a word or two."

Good God, does *he* want to know where I stand on slavery?

"I read the thing about you in the paper. It was you although the New England coward didn't have the daring to say so."

Judah stiffened. "You *are* a little drunk, sir."

"I'm not so drunk that I can't tell you what I think. I understand things lots of people don't understand. I'm a Roman Catholic and don't think I haven't had to fight more than once just because I wasn't a Baptist or a Methodist. Right now I am the only member of the cabinet who didn't meet with immediate approval. I'm a Roman Catholic and I can imagine, sir, what it must be like in certain quarters to be a Jew."

Judah said, "In certain quarters it is a fine thing, sir."

"But not at Yale and don't tell me it was. You're talking to a man who has an imagination."

Judah stared down at the bar. It needed mopping. A fastidious man could not long endure the bar of the Exchange Hotel.

"Come on, Mallory. I'll walk home with you."

"Oh, that'll be fine. I was dreading the walk alone."

"Where do you live?"

Mallory grinned. "Upstairs. Where do you live?"

"At Mrs. Cleveland's."

"Fine. I'll walk home with you, but not just yet. First we'll have a drink to the Navy."

Judah said, "Indeed. To the Navy."

Mallory nodded solemnly. "And what a fine day it will be when we get one," he said. "I guess after the Navy we'll have to drink to the War Department. Damned if I will. To hell with Walker and the War Department. We'll drink next to the office of the Attorney General."

"No, nothing can follow the Navy. That's the ultimate."

"Right you are." Mallory stared at the whisky bottle thoughtfully then pushed it away. "I don't often drink. Really I don't. Tomorrow I'll be a sober man. You'll never recognize me as the fellow you were with tonight."

Judah said, "That, Mr. Secretary, will be a very great pity."

The door of Judah's office flew open and a young boy, excited and breathless, bounded into the room.

"Mr. Attorney General, sir, I have been requested to tell—I have been told to request—I have been asked for your presence—President Davis wants to see you."

The boy was not more than sixteen and he was carrying a message from the President. What a wonderful moment it was for him. No one should laugh or even smile or use the moment to deliver a crushing lecture on the correct approach to a closed door.

"Thank you," Judah said gravely. "Please say that I will join the President shortly."

"Yes, Mr. Attorney General, sir. Thank you." The boy hurried away, his mission triumphantly accomplished.

Judah read a few of the letters upon his desk, answered one with a brief line or two, and considered the Montgomery morning from his window. Then he walked down the hall to Davis's office.

"Good morning, Mr. Benjamin. Are you well this fine morning?"

"Yes, thank you. And your health, sir?"

"It is perhaps improving but I have no time for that. Sit down, if you please. I have news of the most serious nature. A federal fleet is on its way to reprovision Fort Sumter. The United States Government has broken its word."

"Or at least Seward has, sir."

"Seward represented the United States Government so they must answer for the consequences. Now, here is the question: What steps shall we take?"

Judah said, "Have we assurance that reprovisioning is their intention?"

"They are sending food and soldiers to Sumter, sir. The crooked paths of diplomacy can scarcely furnish an example so wanting in courtesy, in candor and directness as was the course of the United States Government toward our commissioners in Washington. Judge Campbell is outraged at having been an unwitting tool of their perfidy. He has resigned and is joining us."

Judah's eyes wandered from Davis's stern face to the whitewashed walls of the office. Down in the street someone was whistling the tune that had taken Montgomery by storm. There were words that went with the tune, something about taking a stand.

"What does Mr. Walker think?" Judah asked.

"I have not told Mr. Walker."

Mr. Walker was the Secretary of War but he had not yet told Mr. Walker. This was only Davis's business and he would discuss it with whom he chose and none other.

"What is your opinion, Mr. Benjamin?"

"I believe, Mr. President, that the United States Government must be informed that Fort Sumter cannot be peaceably reprovisioned."

Davis closed his eyes and massaged his eyelids vigorously as though to exorcise a torment that lay behind them. "Is that your best opinion, sir?"

"I have no other. Fort Sumter has become a symbol. For the United States to lower its flag there is to recognize the Confederacy. For us to permit its continuation is to advertise our inability to function as a nation."

"Then to put it bluntly—you say fight."

"No, Mr. President, you misunderstood me. I am no hothead. No one has ever heard me say that war is glorious or desirable. However, since we have declared ourselves a nation we must behave as one. We must not grumble threateningly and make empty gestures in the manner of an unorganized mob. We must clearly and coolly state a policy and then adhere to it."

"Quite correct, Mr. Benjamin."

"We must say that Fort Sumter cannot be peacably reprovisioned. Then let the decision be theirs. All this, of course, is my opinion, Mr. President, the opinion you requested. I trust you will not consider that I am urging or entreating you to act upon my advice."

"Naturally. Naturally. Your opinion is what I desire. That is what a cabinet is for—to give opinions." Davis reached into his desk drawer and took out an apothecary's box. From it he selected a large, white pill and swallowed it with a noisy gulp. "Dyspepsia," he explained.

Judah nodded. Dyspepsia and a large, white pill. A remarkable man, Jefferson Davis. Perhaps none other lived who could maintain a dignity as severe as his, a manner as haughty while gulping down a large, white pill.

"When I was Secretary of War to President Pierce in the old government," Davis said, "I gave of myself unstintingly as you no doubt know. I hoped I was effectively taking from the shoulders of my president some of his cares and doubts, but never till I, too, headed a government did I know the value of a cabinet. I did not know what it meant to have loyal, thoughtful men surrounding me, to be able to share with them the problems of state."

"We trust we are a comfort," Judah said.

"You have helped me immeasurably to formulate a plan which I think is the one we must act upon. If you have work of your own, sir, please feel free to retire."

"Thank you, Mr. President." Judah rose and went back to his own office.

What would I do if I were Secretary of War and failed to receive the war news upon its arrival? And what shall I do when he confers with Walker on matters that concern my department? Will he let Congress know the dangers we face today? Or will Congress read in the newspapers that we are at war? Suppose he tells the United States Government that he will not permit Sumter to be reprovisioned in peace, what will Lincoln do? Certainly he is too smart to attack us. That will lose him the border states and he must know it.

There was a cabinet meeting called a few hours later. Davis had evidently informed his advisers of the crisis upon which they were to advise him. Now he had additional news for them. In his hand he held a telegram.

"As you know, gentlemen, through the proper channels we warned the United States Government that Fort Sumter could not be peaceably reprovisioned. Now I have this telegram from General Beauregard which reads as follows: 'An authorized messenger from President Lincoln just informed me that provisions

will be sent to Fort Sumter peaceably or otherwise by force.'
Now, gentlemen, please speak your minds."

Toombs of Georgia needed no second invitation. "Mr. President, we walk into a trap if we interfere with the relief fleet. It is what Lincoln wants. The North is apathetic. Most Northerners are in favor of us going our way in peace, but once we wound or kill a Northern soldier or sailor we have not a friend in the North, perhaps not in the world."

Davis waited impatiently for Toombs to finish, shifting his position, biting nervously at his lip.

"Mr. President, we are mistaken if we judge Lincoln to be no more than a stick-whittling rustic. He is diabolically clever, his countrified manner is a pose and he fooled many a man with it. There is nothing candid, nothing simple about Lincoln. He is the devil in homespun, Machiavelli with an Illinois accent."

Toombs looked to dwarfish Vice-President Stephens for support. His fellow Georgian was not even aware of the imploring glance.

"Mr. Toombs," Davis said, "what would you have us do?"

"I would have us govern our territory in peace and let others make the mistakes."

"But Fort Sumter is within our territory."

"Mr. President, it is South Carolina's contention that Fort Sumter is within her territory. When she seceded that was her cry. I see no reason for the Confederacy accepting wholeheartedly her every quarrel and claim. Let the Yankees have Fort Sumter. Let South Carolina scream. Mr. President, I submit that we cannot exist by inheriting or honoring every delusion enjoyed by residents of the separate states."

Walker said, "Mr. Toombs, South Carolina has every right to expect us to protect the fort. That fort is part of South Carolina."

Toombs fought alone. His argument was not without validity. Still it carried within itself its own rebuttal. If Lincoln was truly a brilliant *provocateur* intent on drawing the South into error, then it might as well be today as tomorrow. If Toomb's view of him was justified, he would never let the South live in peace.

With passion Toombs fought on, surrendering at last in a rage, silenced but unconvinced.

Davis dictated the telegram to which Walker signed his name.

If you have no doubt of the authorized character of the agent who communicated to you the intention of the Washington government to supply Fort Sumter by force, you will at once demand its evacuation, and if this is refused, proceed in such a manner as you may determine to reduce it. Answer.

No man left the State Building till he had seen Beauregard's reply.

The demand will be made tomorrow at twelve o'clock.

So it was war, and war meant many things. Men, guns, munitions. It meant ships and factories and tools and railroads. Taxes and government bonds. Uniforms, food, and horses. It meant medicine and chemicals and fuel. It meant small things, too, such as making an impression upon an Englishman whose opinion of the Confederacy would be printed in a London newspaper.

Davis said, "I wanted to have a few words with you, Mr. Benjamin, before Russell arrives. I consider his visit very important."

It was possible to overrate its importance, but Judah said nothing.

"The London *Times* can help us a great deal in winning the sympathy and support of the British people, therefore Russell's view of us can be of monumental worth."

Russell's view of us? It cannot help. Let us not waste our time, sir. Let us instead consider Congress's insane rejection of Memminger's sound tax plan. Do they think wars are won with fists and oratory?

Judah held his silence.

Davis sat massaging his temples. "I have a terrible headache," he said.

"I am very sorry, Mr. President."

"Well, no matter. I am growing accustomed to living with pain." He winced as though one of the pains to which he had not yet grown accustomed had seized him. "First of all, Mr.

Benjamin, I trust you will invite Mr. Russell to dine with you this evening."

"Sir, I have no home here. I can only invite him to the hotel and that is execrable fare to offer a man whose good opinion we seek."

"Well, that cannot be helped. Personally I cannot entertain him and—" Davis lowered his voice— "to be honest I am not as concerned with the food as with the company. I do not wish him marooned for the evening with anyone who, in the London newspapers, can be made to appear ridiculous if Russell is in the mood for lampooning."

Judah said, "May I remind you, sir, that no one is safe if Mr. Russell is in the mood for lampooning?"

"True, true, but there are people in Montgomery who may not be properly understood by an Englishman and thus become easy targets for scorn. Mr. Benjamin, before anyone else has the opportunity to extend a dinner invitation to Russell I hope you will do so."

"I will make the effort to be first, sir."

"Thank you." Davis's eyes went to the immense mass of letters upon his desk.

Judah knew the interview was not ended. He had begun to understand Davis well. The gaze leaving his face and going to the mail did not mean "I am busy and I am finished with you." It meant "I have something else to say and I am uncomfortable about saying it." Judah searched his mind. There must be a way of helping this harassed man who had a headache.

"Is there anything especial to which you would like me to draw Mr. Russell's attention?"

He saw that he had helped. Davis seemed to relax slightly. "Well, not exactly, Mr. Benjamin, but—" the thin little smile— "the question of slavery is bound to arise and I would appreciate your not drawing Mr. Russell's attention to any unorthodox convictions you may entertain."

So Walker had carried the news to Davis. It was to be expected.

"Mr. President, in speaking to the press I will always reflect the Confederacy's convictions."

"Of course, I knew that."

"I would also like to say that never—but never—will there

come a moment when any general, any newspaperman, or anyone else of consequence will hear from me any word inimical to the interests of this nation."

Davis raised his eyes to Judah's face. "Sir, you are the first man who has offered me such vigorous and unequivocal support. I want you to know that I am deeply moved." He rose from his chair behind the desk with his hand extended to Judah.

Judah took the thin, strong hand in his. "Sir, I fear I am being credited with a more all-embracing pledge than the one I actually made."

Yes, Mr. Davis, you are placing a curious interpretation upon my words. I have not sworn to dedicate myself to you and your interests. You are not the nation, sir. Davis and the Confederacy are not interchangeable. Do not look at me with such touching gratitude, sir. I have not given you anything. It is only the Confederacy to which I am willing to give.

It was late May now. Both North and South watched with breath held tensely. Armies gathered and no one believed that it was only to eye each other with haughty gaze. Any day, any hour there would be news.

In Montgomery, Judah sat at his desk and considered the matters Davis had marked for his attention. Methodically he checked through the assortment of memorandums. Not one item could be properly designated as the business of the attorney general. Davis simply ignored the departments to which, in all good faith, these advices and problems should have been forwarded. It was with amusement that Judah observed the absence of communications rightly belonging to Mallory or Reagan. Davis permitted them to manage their departments without interference. Davis had no interest in either ships or postage stamps.

A thin, middle-aged man wearing a clerk's alpaca coat walked into Judah's office and placed on the desk a note bearing the War Department's imprint. Judah experienced a sudden, instinctive feeling that this was no ordinary clerk. Something—a bustling self-importance perhaps—radiated in waves from the rather nondescript person of the man.

"Good morning," Judah said. "I don't believe I know your name."

"It is Jones, Mr. Attorney General. J. B. Jones. I just arrived a few days ago but you are going to see a lot of me. I am head clerk of the War Department."

"Splendid. Are you enjoying your work?"

Jones smiled a self-conscious, puckered little smile. "It is very new to me. I am not really a clerk by vocation. Before the war began I was a newspaper editor and writer."

"A writer? J. B. Jones. Of course. Quite recently I read something of yours. It was called 'The Story of Disunion.' "

Jones colored with pleasure. "Imagine your having read that. I am pleased."

"What are you doing here, Mr. Jones? I mean in a clerkship. Surely they could have found something more suited to your ability."

"Well, sir, you see I plan to keep a diary to be published at some later date—a diary of personalities and events associated with the early days of our nation. I was presented to the President and when I explained my intention to him he was most enthusiastic about the idea. Together we decided that clerking in the War Department would afford me the finest vantage point."

"Indeed." Judah slid open a drawer and brushed a few letters into it then closed the drawer carefully. "It sounds like a fascinating project—the diary. Good luck with it, Mr. Jones."

"Thank you, sir," Jones said and departed.

So the new nation had a biographer. J. B. Jones. Had Davis noticed those sharp eyes? Or had he been misled by the fussy, schoolteacherish manner of the man?

And what was the note from Walker? He opened it and read. Walker could fill three pages with nothing. Here he discoursed on a machine that would produce percussion caps and desired an opinion concerning patent rights. Amazing how he could write so many words without giving a scrap of information that would be useful in answering his questions. The man had been a successful Alabama lawyer. How could he write so ramblingly? And didn't he know anything about patent rights?

Maybe he does and is simply being courteous, making the effort to render unto my department the things that are my department's.

There was a knock at the door. The page had been taught

by someone—could it be Jones?—that one did not burst into a cabinet member's office.

"Mr. Attorney General, there is a gentleman here to see you."

"Did he state his business? What is his name? Has he an appointment? You remember, don't you, that you are supposed to—"

"I know, but this gentleman is special."

"Son, never interrupt me."

"Your pardon, sir. He got me upset. He's a foreigner. His name is St. Martin."

"What! Why didn't you say so? Send him in. Never mind!"

Judah rushed out of the office. His father-in-law? Jules? God in heaven, what was either doing here? Had something happened to Natalie? Or Ninette?

It was Jules in the outside office. Jules rushing to him with outflung arms.

"Brother, I am so glad to see you. Are you busy? Can we talk? I have so many troubles. You must help me."

Judah hurried him into the privacy of the office.

"Tell me, Jules, what has happened?"

"What has happened! Beauregard has fired on Sumter! There is a war and so—"

Judah nodded. "We will talk of the war, dear Jules. First let us exchange some personal conversation. How is Natalie?"

"She is very well."

"And Ninette?"

"In excellent health."

"Your parents, Jules?"

"They are reasonably well."

"Fine. And you, my dear, young brother-in-law?"

Jules's face fell. "Me. I am very sick," he said.

"What is the matter with you, Jules?"

"Oh, I will tell you, Brother. Do not fear. At once when the noble Beauregard fires upon Sumter I sail for my home, Louisiana. I will be a soldier for New Orleans. My mother cries, my father cries, several young ladies do me the honor of crying also —but I sail. In New Orleans I tell everyone I have come to be a soldier. And what happens?"

"I do not know, Jules. What happens?"

"I go to be an officer. I am a Creole. I am educated, I have qualities of leadership, and I detest sleeping on the ground so I wish to be an officer. Whom do I meet in the office where I go to be an officer? I meet our family doctor. He looks at me in surprise and we converse. Shall I tell you our conversation, Brother?"

"As it pertains to the main point."

"Oh, only as it pertains to the main point. In that case I can save much time. He tells me that I cannot go to war. That my heart is so bad I would not live a week. This he says he has known always. Did you know it, Brother?"

Judah felt his own heart flutter. "No, I did not know."

"He said my father knew it but my mother did not. Brother, why did my father not tell me in Paris?"

"He could not, Jules." No, how could Auguste St. Martin tell his boy, who loved Louisiana, that he could not fight for her?

"Very well, I can understand. To proceed: I leave the place where they give commissions. I do not have to be an officer. I will be just a small soldier. But I cannot be a small soldier, Brother. The doctors everywhere, even strange doctors, put their ears against a man's chest and listen. Very rude of them."

Judah said, "Jules, my boy, has it occurred to you that every man cannot be a soldier? There are other ways of serving one's country."

"Not for me, Brother. I must fight. I have come to ask you to use your influence. Surely you, in your high position, can impose your wishes upon little medical men. You must tell them to accept me. Actually, what does it matter if a simple soldier dies of a weak heart?"

Judah sighed. Jules had brought to the Confederacy the one thing of which it had no shortage—sentiment. If one could only annihilate the enemy with brave words, if one could but bombard him with the gallant speeches of young men who thought they wanted to die on the field of glory. One grew a little tired, even a little impatient.

"We will speak of all this again, Jules. For now let me attend to a few matters here. Then we will see about making you comfortable in Montgomery."

There were no rooms available in the entire city. Mrs. Cleveland had not even a vacant bed. She did, however, find a mattress which was placed on the floor in Judah's room.

"I have made myself a great nuisance to you, Brother. I am sorry."

"Nonsense. I am glad to have company." Judah gazed at the small room with Jules's belongings now added to his own. "We will manage."

"But so badly. You must get me in the army. You cannot live in so crowded a room."

"I will learn how, Jules. Now shall we freshen ourselves and go see what the Exchange Hotel has for dinner this evening?"

"Indeed, Brother. I am very hungry. Is their food good?"

"It is horrible, Jules. I do not believe you have ever in your life been subjected to such dreadful service or eaten such a dinner as will be your fate tonight."

"You excite my curiosity if not my appetite."

The dinner was as Judah had feared, but Jules ate without comment or criticism. Judah was disappointed. A complaint would have been a helpful beginning for a campaign which, if successful, would see Jules on his way back to Paris.

At bedtime Jules was talkative enough. He lay upon the mattress resplendent in a nightshirt of china silk upon which his initials had been embroidered.

"I see Madame, your mother, is still busy with her embroidery."

"How can you see that from Montgomery, Alabama?"

"The initials upon your ravishing nightwear, my boy."

Jules raised himself on an elbow and stared at Judah. "Brother, you cannot believe that only my mother embroiders."

"Oh, pardon me, Jules."

Pardon me indeed. What is there about you that makes me think of you as a child? God knows you are not. You are twenty-six years old. You are a man. And I am willing to wager that—weak heart or no—the young ladies of your acquaintance are well aware of the fact.

Jules said, "What do you plan to do about me, Brother?"

"I plan to turn off the gas and make you go to sleep."

"You are tired?"

"Yes, Jules."

"Surely you can say in a few words if you will help me enter the army."

"Tomorrow, Jules, we will talk." Judah extinguished the light and lay down on the hot, lumpy bed. "Good night, boy."

There was a moment's silence. Then: "Brother."

Judah laughed. "A moment ago I scolded myself for thinking of you as a child, Jules. Now I do not know. Would you like a bedtime story?"

"A very small one. I would like to know if you do not think Natalie should have come with me. Is her place not here?"

"I think it is not."

"She is a Southerner."

"You are smarter than that, Jules. She feels no kinship with the states whether they are United or Confederate. She is a French woman. An accident of birth does not guarantee loyalty or even liking for a geographical location."

"You reason everything coldly, Brother. It is your lawyer's mind, I suppose."

"My lawyer's mind is now reasoning that the hour grows late."

"Still, I think she should be with you in your hour of trial. If you were angry with each other I could understand, but as it is I am bewildered."

The young voice coming out of the darkness puzzled, pleading, gave rise to a sudden fear Judah had never known before.

"Is Ninette bewildered?" he asked.

"Oh, no. Ninette is never bewildered. She is like you."

"Has she ever spoken as you have just spoken, Jules? Does she wonder why she and her mother live in Paris?"

"I do not think so, but *I* wonder, Brother. I think it is because my sister is selfish."

"No, Jules. Never think badly of Natalie. In all the world no one knows her as well as I. You have my word for it—we understand each other. Our way of living is ours and need suit no other person."

Gossips have been very gentle of your feelings, Jules. Strange that you have never been faced with the truth about your sister. And if you were, you would not be less bewildered. Suppose I told you that no one man has ever been enough for Natalie, that I know and accept the knowledge with the same bitter resignation that I would accord to a doctor's verdict that she was incurably ill. Suppose I told you how her mind works. You would not understand a woman who pretends to herself that she has been neglected and takes lovers only to repay her husband for his cruel indifference. Oh, would you understand that? Then try this, Jules. Even as she tells herself that she would never yield to temptation if she were sufficiently desired by that husband, she places an ocean between herself and him. Why? Because in her heart she knows the truth: one man is not enough. And, Jules, if you take from this that she can be dismissed as an unfaithful wife, you are a fool. To call her unfaithful is to call a magpie mercenary. They both yield to compulsions, uncomprehended and unnamed. What does any of it matter? I love her dearly. And when shall I see her again?

"Brother, I guess I have talked enough. I will say good night. I will let you sleep."

"Oh, very kind of you, Jules."

Sleep? Now?

It was decided. The capital of the Confederacy would be moved to Richmond. Word came that the city had gone mad with delight at the news. The citizens could scarcely wait to receive President and Mrs. Davis. It gave Virginians something exciting to think about, gave them the chance to forget that forty of their western counties were in revolt, that the Old Dominion was shrinking. Forty counties had refused to secede from the Union. Confederates who thought seriously of the matter were outraged. Would the United States recognize this parcel of illegitimate counties and pay it the honor of accepting it as a state in its own right?

Davis said, "It is typical Yankee logic. The Yankees say we have no right to secede but they look with approval upon these counties that are in secession from Virginia."

Judah said, "But the counties are not in secession, sir. Virginia seceded and they have declined to accompany her. They are remaining with the parent body. You cannot remain and be in secession."

Davis blinked his eyes thoughtfully. "I do not see that. Virginia is the parent body for those counties, not the Federal Government."

"Ah, there is the entire question, sir. State or nation? The question will be argued as long as any American, north or south, still survives."

"Particularly if the American is a lawyer," Davis said. "I wish, Mr. Benjamin, that our case against the Federal Government could be tried in a courtroom. I would rest easy if you were representing us."

"Thank you, sir. Personally I would not rest until I knew who had been hired for the defense."

Davis smiled. "A modest man, our attorney general. Mrs. Davis remarked only last night upon that characteristic of yours, sir. She finds it most surprising and admirable in one who has known such singular success. By the way, she is expecting you to accompany us to Richmond."

"Very kind of her, but are we not all moving east together?"

Davis hesitated. "No, not exactly together. I do not think it advisable for the government to descend upon the city in one grand mass like an invading army."

"I shall be honored to go with you and Mrs. Davis, sir."

What a favorite I will be with the Secretary of State and Walker of the War Department. What is he trying to do? Kill them with insult? And am I the instrument chosen to do them in? I do not like the feeling of being an instrument. It is very new to me and very unpleasant.

"On second thought, sir—I may be forced to forego the honor. I have my wife's brother with me. He is not in the best of health and I am reluctant to have him travel alone. Perhaps Mr. Toombs or Mr. Walker—"

"I have not invited Mr. Toombs or Mr. Walker, sir," Davis said. "I have invited you and I do not see that your wife's brother creates any problem. Can he not ride with us?"

"It would be a tremendous privilege for him to do so, Mr. President, but I must tell you that he is working as a war clerk. As Jules St. Martin he is a suitable companion for any gentleman who lives but, as a war clerk, in the private car of the President—"

"Mr. Benjamin, this is the Confederacy. We have left stupid, stiff-necked customs behind us. Mr. St. Martin will be my guest and no one, I assure you, will think it odd or inappropriate."

Well, no one will say so at any rate. You have defeated me. I can offer no further objections without being childish or rude. I am in for it, sir. I am now open to the enmity of all the cabinet, all their friends, supporters, and well-wishers, to say nothing of those who have only an honest affection for protocol. You are a dangerous man to know, sir. Your favor can do more harm than your disdain.

"You are very kind, Mr. President."

"Then make your plans. We will go to Richmond together. I pray God that success awaits us there." Davis closed his eyes and Judah saw that he was indeed praying.

Well, prayer was certainly among the things for which the Confederacy had desperate need.

Confederacy had [...]

Seven

RICHMOND

As seen from one of its seven hills Richmond was beautiful. Its
broad streets, its noble trees, and the shimmer of the gently flow-
ing James made Southerners proud that Richmond was a Southern city. One knew she was a Southern city because she flew the
Confederate flag. Certainly it was not the face of Richmond that
made her recognizable as a sister of Charleston, New Orleans, or
Montgomery. There was no family resemblance at all. Richmond
had a primness, a stiffness more reminiscent of her enemies than
of her friends.

The South was supposed to be langorous and dreamy. Where
were the palmettos, the violently colored flowers, the sensuous
breeze that carried strange, heady fragrances? Richmond had
nothing like that to offer. She was plain and sensible and had no
patience with any living thing that behaved in a theatrical manner. Plants in Richmond were respectably shaped and colored,
with no foolishness about them.

The men of the Confederacy were glad to see Richmond. Decent food, clean dishes, and tablecloths. Plenty of space—at
least when compared to Montgomery. Everyone had a room and
a good bed. It had been a wise move. Richmond was the proper
capital of the Confederacy. It was not Washington, of course.
Nothing here could boast the elegance of Washington's best, but
for men who had known that best, Montgomery had been a
sobering note, had taught them to appreciate Richmond.

The city, of course, was not herself at the moment. Her people were living under the influence of continual excitement. Every day brought its thrills and wild demonstrations. They had cheered their president and Beauregard, the hero of Fort Sumter. They had seen their own Joseph Johnston, who must certainly be the greatest general alive, since he had been entrusted with command of the mighty Army of Virginia. They had listened to flaming words from a score of orators and had listened to the band play "Dixie." They had heard a thousand rumors and a thousand promises.

Into Richmond had poured the heroes of the nation, the men of the South carrying their flags, the Lone Star of Texas, the magnolia of Mississippi. The gentlemen, the roughs, and the farm boys. The soldiers of Louisiana—the white-gloved Washington Artillery, every man an aristocrat whose uniform had been made by his own personal tailor and, for contrast, the New Orleans Tigers, murderous, gutter-bred scum more dangerous than the enemy. The pretty girls cheered everyone. The war was new. Every man was an adored hero. Richmond was insanely in love with the Confederate Army, and if the brilliantly colored uniforms, the flashing banners and the glitter of bayonets were not sufficient, God had hung a comet in the sky.

Courage was high. Every man and woman felt the exultation of the times, the delirious joy of being alive during these fateful, glorious weeks. To live in Richmond now, to hear the first heartbeats of a new nation, surely it was an experience the world must envy. The people had heard Yancey of Alabama say of President Davis, "The man and the hour have met." And they had been there at the hour and had looked upon the face of the man.

And what a man he was, their president. Intelligence, compassion, and valor were there for everyone to read upon his handsome face. His love and trust of them, his fellow citizens, were implicit in the way he roved the city without fear of incident, an adored neighbor. Seated upon his horse he was a soldierly figure, a living legend, on foot he was an inspiration to all.

The home he would have among them was not yet ready. It was being redecorated and there were a few repairs to be made. It would be comfortable and dignified but not so overpowering that it would be a building rather than a home. The people had had enough of presidents who lived in palace-like residence and made themselves both incomprehensible and inaccessible. The

Confederate White House would be a charming home sheltering a man and his family. Richmond smiled delightedly at the thought of his family. The adorable children and the wonderful, wonderful First Lady. Why, she was so much like other, less distinguished women that she was actually pregnant again.

The social season came early that year. No one left Richmond for the summer. Leave Richmond! Hospitality was the order of the day. Nearly all the ducks on Chesapeake Bay fell victims to unprecedented demand. Oysters and terrapin graced every table. The government circles included many a hostess who had not forgotten to take her menus and recipes when she left Washington.

Judah rented a furnished house that was only a short walk from his office and once again he had a home. It was not the home he would have asked a gentle Fate to grant him but if it lacked the ingredients from which happiness is made, it lacked also those which produce heartbreak. Jules would make an excellent and entertaining guest and the house servants he had been boarding on a farm in North Carolina had now been summoned. The furnishings of his house were not dismal or tasteless either. That was a stroke of luck. Judah, sitting in the presidential suite at the Spottswood Hotel, was grateful that his landlady had spared him the little gilt chairs, the potted palms, and the poisonous shades of green that one found in the carpet and sofas of the Davis parlor.

Davis, lying on the greenest, most ornate of the sofas, stirred restlessly. A discussion of the gathering of federal forces at Manassas had been under way and every fiber of Davis's being seemed to rebel at lying beneath a woolen throw while armies gathered within a hundred miles.

Judah said, "Sir, Mrs. Davis asked you to lie quietly."

"She sets everyone to watching me as though I were a child— though I will admit to feeling rather weak today. Tomorrow I shall be better."

"Of course."

"Can you believe I am actually chilly?"

"When one is ill the heat of summer often fails to warm the bones."

"Have you ever been ill, Mr. Benjamin?"

"I once knew a year of blinding headaches."

"Really?" Davis looked at him with a new interest. "Where did they strike? Across the eyes? Or back in here? I get them across one eyebrow and sometimes with a terrible distortion of vision and an inclination to nausea. How did yours behave?"

"Abominably, sir. They drove me into politics."

"Are you completely cured of them?"

"Of the headaches? I believe so."

"You are very fortunate. The doctors do not expect me to be cured. They hope only to give me some relief. I have complications, of course, with neuralgia and dyspepsia." He pulled the throw closer to his throat. "No one really knows how sick I am at times."

"I think Mrs. Davis knows."

"No. No. I tell her white lies to keep her mind at ease." He sighed. "We are wasting time by discussing personal matters. We must even forget for the moment the activities around Manassas, for that can only be speculation. The things that I called you for are the things we must concentrate upon. First, of course, Toombs. I am sure he is quite right in resigning. His heart is with the army. He will make a first-class general. What do you think of Hunter as a successor to him? Virginia is not represented in the cabinet and I believe that she should be. What are your thoughts on Hunter, sir?"

"He is certainly a Virginian, Mr. President. His other qualifications have for the moment escaped me."

Davis closed his eyes and lay still. "Hunter," he said at length, "is a man of integrity and he is extraordinarily articulate."

I have no one to suggest and he has. So why cavil? Moreover, he does not want a suggestion. He needs only someone to listen. I wonder why Varina will not do for these moments in which he tests his ideas by speaking them aloud?

"Do consider Hunter, Mr. Benjamin. If you find yourself objecting to him on any solid grounds I wish you would inform me." Davis opened his eyes and regarded Judah thoughtfully. "We have other matters to consider as well. The desire for recognition by more established nations fills my mind. I believe we should have proper representation in England and France."

"Indeed, Mr. President."

"When our first battle is fought and won we should send men

of consequence to insure that recognition. To England I think of sending Mason of Virginia."

Mason of Virginia. Judah thought of Natalie dancing with Mason, damning him for a revolting lout who chewed tobacco. Would England be more favorably impressed than Natalie?

"He is a gentleman," Davis said. "A conservative man, a true representative of his homeland. I do not think we could do better than Mason. It is France that has me puzzled, Mr. Benjamin."

"Why France, sir?"

"For France we need a man who speaks the Emperor's language with a grace and fluency that will not shame us. It would also be helpful if with equal facility he spoke the language of the Empress—providing, of course, he is fortunate enough to be granted an audience with the royal couple. It goes without saying that our man's manners must be polished, his standards of excellence extremely high, and his mind keen as any which he will encounter."

Judah smiled. "May I inquire, Mr. President, if you have knowingly described John Slidell?"

"What!" Davis was startled. "Mr. Benjamin, I have described you, but regrettably I cannot spare you for even so important a mission. I need you here. Can you suggest a man with talents comparable to yours?"

Judah said, "I can, sir. John Slidell."

"Mr. Benjamin, John Slidell is a rogue!"

I should be angered, I suppose. John Slidell is my friend but of course he is a rogue. It would be ridiculous to contend that he is not.

"Mr. President, no American's French or Spanish is superior to Slidell's. His mind is sharp. His taste and tact are exquisite. Moreover, as you know, his wife is a highborn lady whose linguistic abilities are equal to his. If, as you say, we are fortunate enough to have the royal couple receive our envoy, Madame Slidell's elegance would be very creditable to the Confederacy."

"But John Slidell's past would not bear scrutiny."

"I assure you, Mr. President, the Emperor is in no position to question any man's past."

"I have always disliked the devious ways of John Slidell."

"The Emperor and his advisers would make short work of any man who understood only candor."

"I am sorry. I cannot see that Slidell's usefulness to us would be great enough to outweigh his unsavory record."

"No matter, sir. I am not sure that Slidell would be interested in—"

Davis sat up abruptly. *"Slidell* not interested! Why, Benjamin Franklin did not consider a similar mission beneath him."

"You are right. But then Slidell is not Franklin and so many other things are not the same. Do lie down, Mr. President. Mrs. Davis will be very cross."

"Not with you, Mr. Benjamin. I am sure you have done your best."

Judah rose to his feet at the sound of Varina's voice. She was standing in the doorway, a medicine bottle and a spoon in her hand. It was absurd and old fashioned, of course, but he still preferred the custom of Louisiana ladies who withdrew from the gaze of all but the immediate family once their pregnancies became apparent. Varina's way had good sense on its side, but grace and beauty could in time disappear completely if good sense were too highly esteemed.

Varina advanced into the room and to her husband's side. "It's time for your medicine, dearest."

Davis made a sour face and nodded. Varina poured a spoonful of dark red syrup and Davis opened his mouth and swallowed.

"And now it's time for your nap. You promised that you would—"

"I know, I know. But there are things Mr. Benjamin and I must discuss."

Varina shook her head. "Not now," she said firmly. "An hour's rest is what the doctor said and—would you like a cup of tea first? The waiters have just brought—"

"No." Davis glanced from his wife to Judah and back again. "Suppose I omit the nap and retire early this—"

"That will not be satisfactory at all," Varina said. She was smiling but the dark eyes were determined. "I have, however, a suggestion that might be helpful if Mr. Benjamin agrees. You rest for an hour. Meanwhile Mr. Benjamin and I will have tea, then he can rejoin you."

Judah said, "The suggestion pleases me enormously."

Varina drew the draperies, darkening the room. She brought Davis another pillow, kissed him lightly, and led the way to her own sitting room.

It was far nicer than the parlor. The hotel had used a simpler motif in the furnishings and the room had a winsome appeal. The waiters were arranging trays of pastry and thin sandwiches upon a drop-leaf table. Varina dismissed them, taking an evident pleasure in making her own arrangements.

Judah watched her large, brown hands as they moved among the tea things. They were fine hands, graceful and capable, and it seemed completely right that they should be sunburned. Never since he had known her had her face and hands lacked the bronze tint that she had brought from the plantation lands of Mississippi. It was plain to see that never had she ridden veiled and gloved. What long odds one could have had on the likelihood of Jefferson Davis, the proud and cold-eyed widower, falling in love with a tomboy.

She passed him his tea and said, "Sir, I am afraid you have let yourself in for something when you consented to enter my sitting room. I did not tell you till I had you safely trapped that the children are expecting to join us."

"That will be delightful," he said.

"How kind you are. I know children are not soothing companions but I assure you they will simply clutch at a few goodies and then depart." She left him for a moment to return with the three little Davises.

"Mr. Benjamin, may I present Margaret to you? She is six years old and she is a very nice girl. Jefferson Junior is four and he is trying very hard to be as fine a man as Jefferson Senior. And this is Joe. He is two and Margaret and Jeff Junior are raising him for me."

Gravely the children came to Judah's side. The little girl curtsied. The boys bowed with baby awkwardness, almost unbalancing themselves in the effort.

Judah smiled at them all but his attention was caught by Joe, a cherubic little thing with the warm, dark eyes of his mother.

"Now," Varina said, "Mr. Benjamin will excuse you while you make your selections."

Instantly they turned to the pastries and sandwiches, Margaret cautioning her brothers not to touch. Judah watching them wondered if Davis knew how blessed he was. Fifty-three years old and the possessor of a young and lovely family. Varina was filling a plate for the children to take to Catherine, their Irish nursemaid. He studied her with a wondering interest. What had drawn her to that humorless, dyspeptic man? It was difficult to guess.

The children said their good-bys politely and were gone..

"They are darlings," Judah said.

"How is your Ninette, Mr. Benjamin? I remember her as an enchanting child in Washington."

"Washington. 'The eternal landscape of the past.' "

"I recognize that as a Tennyson quotation but I protest the idea of Washington warranting enough importance to be our eternal landscape. I am glad to be away from it. And you have not told me about Ninette."

"A very tall young lady, Madame, according to the latest advices from Natalie."

Varina had no choice now. "And how is Natalie?"

"Very well. Thank you for inquiring, Madame."

The dark lashes fell concealing the look in Varina's eyes. She passed a silver tray of small, jewel-like pastries to him. "I wish they would get our house finished," she said. "I detest hotels." She paused and looked slightly embarrassed. "Of course I didn't actually mean *our* house. I know it isn't ours and I fully realize that when the permanent government is installed Mr. Davis may not be president."

Judah said, "Madame, Mr. Davis's election is as certain as anything in the world has ever been."

"I think your optimism is colored by your admiration for the President, sir."

"Oh, I do not truly think so."

She looked at him with warmth and friendliness. "Mr. Benjamin, I want to tell you that nothing in this entire new world of ours has given me more pleasure than the relationship between yourself and the President. To me it is truly wonderful."

"Madame, I have appreciated—"

"You cannot guess how much he admires you. It is not, I

would have you know, the ordinary admiration for a large legal reputation. It is the man, Judah Benjamin, he respects—and to see you so considerate and sympathetic to him. Sir, I wish to say that a great load is taken from my mind by the fact that there is one man in the cabinet whose affection for my husband is deep and true."

It was all very well for philosophers and men of God to expound the theory that dishonesty must be avoided. But how was this done? In a case like this for instance? Would it be noble to tell Varina that she was mistaken? That actually no affection existed? Did one brutally strike out at a sweet and innocent woman and thus uphold the banners of honesty? Could one be proud of such a glorious triumph? What an insufferable prig a man would be who said to her, "Restrain yourself, my dear lady. I do not care for your husband but he is the President." Damn Mrs. Davis for translating loyalty to the Confederacy into loyalty to Davis, for accepting courtesies as evidence of sentimental attachment. Damn her for not being cynical and suspicious. Why was it that one was caught in a web of dishonesty only when one talked to the honest?

Varina took a fruit tart from the silver tray and looked at Judah pensively. "You know that dreadful incident out of the past was really a splendid thing, though I did not realize it at the time."

"Dreadful incident, Madame?"

"Yes, my husband yielding to ill temper and his subsequent apology to you on the floor of the Senate."

"I beg of you, Mrs. Davis, put the memory from your mind."

"I treasure the memory, Mr. Benjamin. Your courage in challenging my husband makes me proud to know you."

Judah laughed. "Madame, you have placed me in a difficult position. I must either wholeheartedly agree that I am not less brave than a lion or else belittle your husband's marksmanship."

She did not laugh with him. She turned her face away and said, "Sir, there is much you and I could discuss that would not fall into the category of idle chatter. There is a ground upon which we could meet that might prove as valuable a piece of ground as any the Confederacy possesses. And yet though your kindness and courtesy are unflagging you choose to speak play-fully to me. Why is that, sir?"

He sipped his tea and thought of his sister Rebecca. He thought of the day years ago at Belle Chasse when he had told her that he disliked speaking of law to a woman. But that woman had been his sister and it had been within his right to discipline her. This woman was Varina Davis, wife of the President of the Confederate States of America. What should he say to this woman?

She was waiting for his answer. Quietly she waited, her gaze direct and unwavering. There was certainly the opportunity here for an evasive reply but the answer must be worthy of a woman who would ask the question.

"The companionship of ladies has always been a delight to me. With a lady I will talk by the hour of flowers, children, even clothes, Madame, but I have no taste for a conversation that involves politics, law, or national problems."

Varina said, "Apparently you have never known a lady who could discuss these subjects intelligently."

"It has always seemed to me, Madame, that a lady who had a grasp upon politics and kindred subjects would serve only to ruin a gentleman's evening. I am a man who loves poetry and books and music. Men speak of them too rarely. If ladies begin to talk of politics the country has lost its last bulwark of culture and a sort of barbarism will overtake us."

Varina smiled. "Mr. Benjamin," she said, "you are rather wonderful. I had expected you to humor me. I had expected you to deny that your conversational approach has been insulting to what I regard as my excellent education."

"I am sure your education is excellent, Madame. We will talk of poetry and plays, of music and of those delightful children."

She said, "I beg of you, Mr. Benjamin, do not dismiss me with so much finality that you will find it impossible to contact me on a stormy day."

He said, "Madame, if you hear that I am searching for you you will know that it is to offer my protection. It will never be that I am expecting you to walk with me through the storm."

"I have never known a man like you before. To my kinsmen, my husband, and to all men I have ever met I have seemed a woman of strength and dependability. In fact—" She paused and her eyes became thoughtful and slightly troubled.

"Madame, I offer you something far more valuable than anything you have requested. I offer you this—the promise that to me you will never seem strong and dependable."

He saw the sudden rush of pink that had risen beneath the tanned skin, the hint of lightning in the dark eyes.

"Mr. Benjamin, I am not sure I like this promise of yours."

He said, "I think in time you will come to regard it highly."

The offices of the War Department were crowded to the doors. As each successive dispatch was received excitement increased. The entire cabinet was present, waiting, hanging on the words that came from Manassas. A great battle was in progress. Secretary Walker strode to and fro cursing because he was not at the side of President Davis, helping him in his hour of glory and peril.

"Is the President actually directing the battle?" someone asked.

Walker said, "Of course. That is why he went to Manassas. It will be a great triumph for him and our government, gentlemen."

The offices grew more crowded, the dispatches came more thickly. Nothing decisive. Conflict under the hot Virginia sun on a July afternoon. Terrible slaughter. Dreadful suffering. We know war is like that. Do not waste words with such foolish remarks. Tell us who is winning. The telegraph clicked on inanely, giving the frantic listeners little more information than that it was very unpleasant to be a soldier today at Manassas.

The afternoon waned and there was still no word that told the final outcome. Some thought the telegrapher unwilling to send dreary news. Others thought perhaps a drawn battle had resulted. There were those who would have settled happily for a drawn battle.

No one was willing to leave the offices. Few had eaten. Tempers were short. Dusk settled over the city without the answer that all awaited.

Howell Cobb said, "This is incredible that we sit here not knowing. Why doesn't Davis send us word?"

Secretary of State Hunter gave him a thoroughly disgusted

glance. "Do you think he has nothing else to do but send telegrams?"

Judah grew thoughtful. Davis might have something to do other than send telegrams but there was one he would surely send.

If I am not mistaken about him there is one telegram he has not neglected.

Quietly Judah left the office and walked to the Spottswood Hotel. Varina, surrounded by ladies, received him in the poisonous green parlor. The ladies all talked at once, their excitement a shining thread that snapped suddenly at the realization that it was Mrs. Davis's prerogative to announce the contents of the telegram she held in her hand.

"A tremendous battle has been fought, Mr. Benjamin, and we have had a great victory. The Yankees are in shameful retreat."

Her cheeks were feverishly red, her eyes bright with exultation. "But Colonel Bartow has been killed. I must tell Mrs. Bartow."

"May I suggest, Mrs. Davis, that some other lady be assigned to handle that sad business for you?"

"No. No, sir, it is my duty."

He returned to the War Department and gave the news. There were cheers and lusty slaps on the back for everyone, smiles and tears of joy.

It was not till later that resentment boiled in the hearts of the men who had waited so eagerly in the War Department offices. Davis had notified only his wife! Who had ever heard of so cutting an insult to cabinet and congress? And he had not directed the battle at all. The enemy had been driven from the field before his arrival. No one demanded that the President take part in battle but hadn't he led the public to think it was his intention? Even now was he not by implication suggesting that he had been the force behind the victory? It had been Beauregard's victory. General Beauregard, the hero of Fort Sumter, the adored little Louisianian with the sad, soft eyes.

The President, on his return from Manassas, answered the call of the cheering mob and spoke to them from the balcony of his hotel. Inside, there was a brilliant party in honor of the victory. But there were questions. If the Yankees were in shameful retreat, why were they not pursued all the way to Washington?

"Why weren't they, Mr. Benjamin?"

Mrs. Chesnut, that rather frightening woman, was at his elbow.

"I was not at Manassas, Madame. You must take your questions to Mr. Davis."

"Do you think I will hesitate. This victory could be our ruin, you know. It could lull us into a fool's paradise of conceit at our superior valor."

"Your husband, Madame, is aide to the President and a general besides. He will be a far greater fount of information than I."

Mrs. Chesnut said, "Very well. I respect your reluctance to discuss the matter, but you know as well as I that the disgraceful behavior of the Yankees will now awaken every bit of manhood that lies within them. It was the very fillip they needed. We must strike again before they reorganize."

Judah grinned. "Do you hear voices, Madame? Jeanne d'Arc did."

"I hear no voices but that doesn't stop me from knowing that this battle is not going to win the war."

"Then you belong to the pessimistic school of thought. There are two, you know."

"I know. The demented school thinks the war is over. Does the President belong to that school? Is that why he did not order immediate and swift pursuit?"

"Madame, when you have reconsidered your words you will regret them, I feel sure. Would you like to dance?"

Perhaps the enemy could have been ignominiously driven right into the streets of Washington. He did not know. He was not a military man. Perhaps Davis and Beauregard and Johnston had been too pleased at the triumph, too ready to accept what they had, a little fearful of pressing their luck. No one knew. No one would ever know what might have happened. He was certain of only one thing. He was certain that the failure to pursue would be argued for many a year to come.

Beloved:

Ninette and I are well. I will say that at once because it is the thing you wish most to hear. It is autumn in Paris, the leaves fall and it is a sad time for a woman in love with a man who lives in Richmond, Virginia, C.S.A.

Judah paused in his reading. Any time was a sad time for a man in love with a woman who lived in Paris. And it was autumn here, too. In fact it was the day after the election and the end of the provisional government. Mr. Davis—with no one contesting his election—had become the first duly elected president of the Confederate States of America.

Speaking of those very important letters—C.S.A.—Judah, I suppose congratulations are in order. To be Secretary of War sounds very wonderful. I remember when I was in Washington your President Davis held that post to Franklin Pierce. Everyone honored him for his high place, therefore I know you have come up in the world of the Confederacy. So congratulations, beloved, but forgive me, I am only a woman. I think in terms that will probably amuse you. I think only that your new office sounds more treasonable than the old and I wake up asking myself what will happen to you if Mr. Lincoln is more fortunate—or more capable—than Mr. Davis.

Judah looked up from the letter. There were four more pages. He always read the beginning at once to assure himself that all was well with her. Later at home he read the entire letter slowly, savoring each word, feeling her close to him.

Now there were less pleasant matters to face. Commissary General Northrup's proposal that a whisky ration be issued to the troops. Had the Commissary General ever looked at the troops? Some of them were practically children who had never before been away from home. Northrup, Davis's classmate and friend at West Point, had no acquaintance with a fighting army that numbered among its heroes wide-eyed, innocent farm boys.

It wasn't enough that there was an alarming amount of sickness. Thousands in camp where suffering with mumps, whooping cough, and measles. Fifteen thousand soldiers in the hospital. Was Northrup insane, allowing his mind to dwell on whisky when so much else was needed? The first duty was to organize measures for aiding the sick and to devise means of keeping the healthy out of hospitals. A whisky ration!

Would the North obligingly hold off its next offensive till the sick were well again? And, if there were enough troops, would the Confederacy be able to arm them? Captain Huse, the chief

purchasing agent abroad, had been requested to speed his ship-
ments. It was a large ocean and no one seemed to appreciate the
need for haste.

The small skirmish with the State of Georgia was a matter for
concern. Arms which the state had purchased and received,
Georgians were unwilling to sell to the Confederacy. They were
Georgia's possessions, intended for the protection of Georgia. Let
the Confederacy get her own. This was the attitude of North
Carolina as well. It was only natural. The new nation had been
fabricated completely out of the material of distaste for a central
government. It was the love of a man for his state that had created
the nation, and when one said that, one had described and
doomed the baby that had been born of this passionate romance.
How could a nation be sustained by men who cared only for the
segment of it which was personally known and loved?

He thought of Walker and wondered how Walker had always
had so much time to complain about his miserable desk job. Like
Toombs, Walker was a general now. No doubt he was happier
than he had ever been at this desk, but surely no man could
honestly say that the position of Secretary of War left one with
nothing to do. Or was it possible that Walker had not visited
army posts and hospitals, had not examined the complaints of
generals and governors, had not worked on a system of leaves
and bonuses to stimulate re-enlistments, or had not concerned
himself very much with the problem of arming the Confederate forces?

Hunter had said, "Confidentially I shall feel more willing to
plunge into the work of the State Department when Election Day
has come and gone. If Mr. Davis is not elected, certainly I will
not be in the new cabinet and I am loath to institute policies that
may not please my successor."

Of course Hunter had meant that he did not intend to work
himself to death until he was sure of his job. Why hadn't he been
able to see that no one would run against Davis? Beauregard, the
only man with even a remote chance of defeating him, had not
wanted the presidency. Beauregard was a Creole. What had the
presidency to offer that could compare with the drama and glory
of the battlefield?

If Davis had only believed that Beauregard was no political

rival. Beauregard was a fine general, a successful general, but the people's adoration of him had not increased his popularity with President Davis. Now that Davis was secure in his office there was hope that he would forgive Beauregard for having earned the praise of Confederate citizens.

Perhaps Davis would even be more tolerant of General Johnston. Johnston was certainly a man with a chip on his shoulder, a man who lived expecting insult and slight, but he was an able leader, a general of extraordinary ability. An effort should be made to keep him well-fed on a rich diet of respectful words and special treatment. Too bad Davis antagonized him at every meeting instead of seeking a way to placate him.

"I simply cannot understand him," Davis had said sadly. "One must agree with him or invite sarcasm. He is touchy and irritable and resentful of the slightest criticism. Constantly he is watching for his authority to be challenged and in advance of the challenge he is already in an ill-humor. How can you be so cordial to him, Mr. Benjamin?"

"It is relatively simple for me. I do not find him unique."

The newsboys shrieked on every corner from Maine to Florida.

MASON AND SLIDELL REMOVED FROM BRITISH SHIP

The Yankees had dared to halt the *Trent,* a British vessel that had sailed from Cuba carrying the Confederate envoys to Europe. The captain of the U.S.S. *San Jacinto* had actually fired two shots across the *Trent's* bow. It was sensational and unbelievable. Had the United States gone mad? Did they not know that the British lion was not a docile house cat? England would not accept this violation of her neutrality. She would declare war.

The Yankees had actually boarded the *Trent* and had taken by force passengers sailing under the protection of the English flag. Slidell and Mason were in a Northern prison while the American captain responsible for the act was being hailed as a hero. Oh, England would never swallow such insolence without a fight.

Judah read the accounts carefully. Slidell had taken the incident with the debonair grace one would expect of him. He had

said to Mathilde, "I will see you in Paris, darling," and had left
the ship, a Yankee prisoner.

Davis said, "England will have to declare war on the United
States."

"I do not believe Seward will be found lacking in explanations, sir."

"It is an unexpected piece of luck for us. If Seward should offer
no acceptable explanation, then England must fight." Davis
smiled almost boyishly. "I do trust Mr. Seward is without the
proper words for the occasion. I hope he becomes most stubborn
and refuses to give up the prisoners."

Judah looked away from Davis finding it impossible to return
the smile. Slidell was well past sixty-five and he was in a Yankee
prison. Smile with Davis over that? Hope that Slidell would be
indefinitely detained while Mathilde lost her mind with worry?

Davis said, "What is your guess, Mr. Benjamin? What will
England do?"

"England will demand the immediate release of Mason and
Slidell. She will quite rightly demand apologies."

"Do you think she will accept apologies?" Davis asked with a
sharp note of disappointment in his voice.

"I do not know, Mr. President."

Succeeding editions of the newspapers brought further word.
Mason and Slidell were imprisoned at Fort Warren in Boston
Harbor. Slidell's daughters aboard the *Trent* had clung desperately to their father. Mathilde had been pale but had made no
demonstration. These were the things that Judah noticed in
the accounts.

I should rejoice that England is furious. I should be praying for
Seward to grow obstinate, but I can think only of Mathilde, pale
and troubled, Slidell in prison, Slidell who perhaps cannot adapt
himself to discomfort.

"The indications are that the United States has made so great
a hero of the Yankee captain that they cannot now repudiate his
act," Davis said. "England, I understand, is sending troops to
Canada in the event that the prisoners are not released. We might
have a miracle worked in our behalf, Mr. Benjamin."

"Sir, I trust that Mason and Slidell have been well treated.
Have you had any word on that subject?"

Davis shook his head and looked quizzically at Judah. "You are worried about Slidell, are you not? I am sorry to have given you no inkling that I, too, am concerned for him and Mason. You must remember that Slidell and I have known each other for a very long time. I would be inhuman if I did not regret what has happened to him."

Judah nodded.

"But, Mr. Benjamin, I implore you to remember that this is war. Slidell's experience is unpleasant, of course, but if his incarceration should be of great assistance to us Slidell would be the first to rejoice. If it meant his death he would welcome it gladly."

Haven't you the wrong man in mind? Aren't you confusing him with Nathan Hale? I can tell you that Slidell is turning the air blue and what he is saying is impartially directed toward the United States and the Confederacy.

"The doubtful expression you wear, Mr. Benjamin, suggests that you are underrating your friend Slidell. He is as selfless as any of us. The Confederacy has made us all one. The Slidell to whom I spoke about representing us in France is not the Slidell of the past. He is a new man under a new flag, an eager patriot."

Judah's eyes wandered away from Davis's face. Curious the naïveté that the man possessed. Slidell had sold himself to Davis as he had sold Buchanan to the Democratic convention in '56.

Slidell, at Judah's house after the interview, had said, "Benjamin, I don't know what you've gotten me into. This will be an interesting job but he seems to think God and right have some connection with winning recognition. You know, Benjamin, at heart he's still a starry-eyed West Point cadet."

"You just get us French recognition, my friend."

"By any means whatsoever?"

"Now wait a minute. We just want to be recognized, not pointed at."

"Benjamin, you bastard, you don't trust me. You've known me thirty years and you still don't trust me. Why not?"

"As you say, I've known you thirty years."

Slidell had laughed. God, how Slidell could laugh when something struck him funny. Poor old boy locked up in Fort Warren.

"Mr. President," Judah said, "I would consider myself underhanded if, unknown to you, I engaged in communication with someone in the North. However, I am very anxious to insure Slidell's comfort and good health. Would you frown upon my contacting August Belmont and making certain that he is doing whatever can be done for Slidell?"

Davis stared. "Why, Mr. Benjamin, what would Belmont do for Slidell? Belmont is an enemy of Slidell today."

"His wife is Slidell's niece, sir. He—"

"Mr. Benjamin, brother fought brother at Manassas. All over our two countries families are divided in their loyalties. It is sad but true."

Sad indeed but not true with people like Slidell and Belmont. If they met right now, sir, they would embrace and exchange a few stories. Belmont would bring a case of brandy and a packing box of delicacies to Fort Warren. Belmont would call you a dirty name and Slidell would say the same of Lincoln and they would laugh together. You would be shocked, sir, revolted, for they are men you do not understand. They are men who see no virtue in brother fighting brother. In fact the idea would repel them. They were not raised on the proper legends.

"Since you have asked, Mr. Benjamin, I will say that I do not think it appropriate for you to communicate with August Belmont."

"Very well, Mr. President."

And after two months Seward apologized, explained, and released Mason and Slidell. The Confederacy mourned that such an excellent opportunity had been lost. England at war with the United States would have assured a Confederate victory. The Southern newspapers satisfied themselves with acid comments on the Yankees' cowardice and willingness to knuckle down at the roar of the British lion.

It was announced that Mason and Slidell were about to sail again, and at Judah's request Davis sent a message through the British legation to Slidell. The message simply stated that if for any reason he wished to retire from the mission his decision would be respected and understood.

Davis was deeply touched by the reply. Wordlessly he handed it to Judah to read.

I must make the most of every hour. For me the road ahead leads only into the sunset.

· · ·

Already it was January. Judah sitting before the flames of his library fire found it difficult to account for the months since Louisiana had withdrawn from the union. January, 1862. Where had the time gone? And what had been accomplished? He raised his eyes from the fire. Above the mantel was a portrait of Natalie that had been painted in Washington. Natalie, lovely and proud, in soft coral satin, her yellow eyes bright with secret amusement.

He became aware that Jules was moving chairs out of the way, carrying a small table closer to the fire.

"You are dissatisfied with the arrangements of our library, Jules?"

"Brother, we are going to play cards and I prefer to play where I will not freeze."

"We are going to play cards? I did not know."

Jules said, "When you announced that you would remain at home this evening I decided to give you the advantage of my company—despite a very attractive possibility."

Judah laughed. "Your company will be very welcome but please overlook no attractive possibilities for my sake."

Jules drew his eyebrows together thoughtfully and studied the design on the back of a playing card. "Ever since I arrived in Montgomery last spring I have been wishing to say a similar thing to you, Brother."

Judah said, "I am afraid I do not understand you, Jules."

"I think you are afraid you do. I mean it the way it sounded." He glanced at Natalie's portrait. "Since I am her brother it occurs to me that I have perhaps limited your—er—social life by living with you."

"I have no—er—social life, my sophisticated young relative, and no wish for any."

"This is impossible. You are not so old."

"Oh, I do thank you."

"And despite the fact that you have gained a little weight recently you are still the fascinating Benjamin. There are many ladies who would be charmed by your attentions."

"Why, Jules, you are an evil influence. You will have me looking at the ladies wondering which of them would fall into my arms if I but speak the word."

Jules said, "I advise you not to speak it unless you are ready. The best drawing rooms are full of eager females, Brother."

"I give you my word, Jules, I do not care."

"Remarkable." Jules's eyes were filled with the wonderment he felt. "When I do not care it will be because I am dead. But of course, Brother, your mind operates on a higher plane than mine. That no doubt is the explanation. I just thought that I would assure you of my complete reliability in the matter of secrecy in case you—"

"I do not, Jules."

"Very well, Brother. You do not."

No, I do not. Instead I go to Worsham's gambling house and watch the wheel spin. For the risking of a few dollars Worsham offers a pleasant fever of excitement that cannot end in regret or self-disgust.

"Shall we play cards, Brother?"

"If you are determined to entertain me, Jules, I guess I had better be entertained. Yes, let us play cards. What will it be? Cribbage?"

Jules did not reply. The butler had appeared in the doorway. "What is it?"

"Mr. and Mrs. President, sir."

"Who? You are mistaken. Brother, would it be—"

"Oh, yes, indeed. Listen." The voice of Davis, the muffled light laughter of Varina. "Go greet them, Jules, and bring them in please."

"Of course if your house is to be an annex to your office—" Jules shook his head and went about his errand.

Good God, the informality of the Confederacy had finally reached its zenith. This was the end of privacy, the Davises dropping in on the Secretary of War like any Mississippi couple calling on a neighbor.

Jules ushered them into the room. Varina, pink-nosed from the cold, Davis, as always, the patrician face on a golden coin.

"Mr. Benjamin, I trust you will forgive us for arriving unexpectedly," Davis said.

"My only regret is that I must receive you here. Alas, there is no fire in the parlor."

Varina said, "This room is lovely and it is so warm." She seated herself close to the fire and looked approvingly at Jules, who brought her a glass of port.

"It is indeed charming," Davis said. "I like its intimacy. It lends itself to thoughtful conversation." He, too, accepted the port from Jules with pleasure. "We will try to make our visit brief. There is, however, a matter or two which I did not feel could wait till morning."

"I am at your service, Mr. President."

"My thanks, sir." Davis considered the contents of his glass. "The subjects I would submit for discussion are of a highly confidential nature." His eyes wandered to Jules, who was encouraging the fire with an additional log.

Judah felt a sudden wave of resentment. If Varina was no risk to the security of the South then, by God, Jules must have the same trust accorded him in his own home. This was one place where Davis would not command. Who had asked him here? If he was seeking complete privacy let him use an office, not a man's residence.

Judah said, "I am so sorry we must confer alone, sir. I wanted to hear from Mrs. Davis all the pleasant facts about the new baby. Most of all I wished to enjoy the decorative touch she brings to our somber quarters. However—" He shrugged. "Jules, have a fire built in the morning room. When it is burning brightly you can invite Mrs. Davis to play chess with you in there." From a shelf he took a chessboard and the box of ivory pieces and laid them upon the table.

Varina looked up at him and smiled. She had not missed the point.

"You will play, Madame?" Jules asked her.

"With pleasure, Mr. St. Martin."

"Very well. The fire will be ready in a brief moment." He started from the room.

Davis sighed almost imperceptibly. "Mr. St. Martin," he said, "do not trouble yourself. Please be seated. After all, as a war clerk there is little you do not learn of your nation's problems. And Mrs. Davis, I fear, reads in my face the daily report of all that occurs."

Varina moved to a chair at the card table. Jules seated himself and set the chessmen upon the board. In silence Davis watched the game begin. There was a faraway, absent-minded look in his eyes. It was only with the first pawn moved by Varina that he seemed to come back to the library and the matters at hand.

He said, "A thought came to me this evening, Mr. Benjamin, and I naturally desired to discuss it with you. Why should we not transfer General Beauregard to the Mississippi Valley?"

"What are the reasons for such a transfer, sir?"

"Well, Joe Johnston does not need him."

"Indeed? I cannot conceive of anyone declaring himself not in need of Beauregard. Did Johnston say that—"

"Oh, no. You know Johnston. He will shriek to high heaven at having Beauregard removed. He enjoys testing his bitter tongue. Beauregard, too, has strained badly against authority. He has a peculiar Latin temperament, theatrical, oversensitive. His ambition will destroy him if not checked."

"I do not think ambition will destroy Beauregard, sir. He desires only to serve the Confederacy well. When there was talk that he could be president he never in any way fed the flames of his supporters' enthusiasm."

Davis said, "If his supporters knew him as I do he would be no hero to them. He is an insufferable egotist."

"Really? I confess to never having seen that side of the man. I knew him for many years in Louisiana and—"

"And he was well-liked there?"

"Yes, he was."

"I find that incredible. However, he is a Creole and I suppose appeals to the artificial, dramatic atmosphere of the Creole—"

Varina said, "Darling, for heaven's sake!"

Davis stared at her blankly for a moment before realizing why he had been reprimanded. Then suddenly, there it was, the Davis smile that came so rarely, so irresistibly.

"Mr. St. Martin," he said, "my sincere apologies. I had forgotten that you and General Beauregard share a common heritage. Anything I may have said that was uncomplimentary to Creoles or Creole characteristics I deeply regret."

Jules grinned. "I took no offense. We Creoles have our faults— even General Beauregard and myself."

Judah turned away. Jules had taken the magnificent apology as though every day in the year a clerk received apologies from the

President. This interchange, Judah thought, had not improved the position of Creoles any in the President's estimation.

"As to Beauregard, Mr. Benjamin, write to him tomorrow, if you please, informing him of his new assignment. The order, of course, must properly issue from your office."

Now wait. Is this the moment? Shall I say to him that I will not bury Beauregard in a western command? Shall I fight for Beauregard? Shall I say the order will never be issued with my name on it? Shall I? What would be my reasons for so doing? And are any of them good reasons? Well, the Confederacy needs Beauregard in an active command. Yes, but if Davis's mind is made up nothing can save Beauregard. I can resign and the Confederacy will still lose General Beauregard's contribution to the winning of the war. Now as to the man Beauregard—what about the unfairness of his treatment? What about it? Did I give up my legal career to fight for Beauregard? Certainly not. The man Beauregard must fight for himself. And as for my name upon the order which transfers him west—well, Benjamin, what serves the Confederacy better? That Beauregard hates you or that he hates Davis? Grow up, Benjamin, let a general hate you, let a general damn you from here to the Mississippi Valley. What does it matter? You came here to serve the Confederacy. If you are not ready to serve in every way, even in small, nasty ways then you should be sitting now in that delightful New York club of yours having a drink with August Belmont.

"I will send him his orders in the morning, Mr. President."

"Good. Good. Now about Roanoke Island. I wanted to speak of that, too. I have definitely concluded that the Federals will not attack it. General Huger agrees with me."

Varina turned from the chessboard. "Dear, *please* pronounce his name correctly. It is pronounced U-zhee. Remember?"

"I don't see why," Davis said. "However, I will try to remember." He turned back to Judah. "I know that General Wise believes that the Federals will take the island, but Wise is simply a political general. They are always hysterical. Huger is a West Point man so we're bound to accept Huger's opinion over Wise's."

"Are the Federals bound to accept Huger's opinion?" Judah asked.

Davis acknowledged the question with a brief smile. "Mr.

Benjamin," he said, "we are in a little trouble on this Roanoke Island matter. Wise, being Huger's subordinate, of course can do nothing, but as a former governor of Virginia he carries a great deal of influence. He is protesting loudly the administration's refusal to reinforce Roanoke Island."

Judah nodded. Wise was protesting loudly indeed. And people were beginning to listen.

"Mr. President, do you think we might talk very quietly to Wise and tell him quite honestly that we have not the means to arm additional men for the island's defense?"

"No, no. He would blurt it out to the world. Such information could never be trusted to a non-West Point general. From the housetops he would shout our poverty of arms."

"But he is shouting now."

"That's because he dislikes me personally. I do not know why."

"If the island is attacked—"

"It will not be attacked."

"But, Mr. President, *if it is,* the administration will be soundly blamed. Since we cannot strengthen the island, why do we not withdraw the men?"

"Because it would be a grievous sign of weakness."

Judah said, "To my non-West Point mind the most grievous sign of weakness would be to get thoroughly whipped."

"We will not be thoroughly whipped even if attacked. Our little force will protect the island with great determination."

"And I, Mr. President, consider it immoral to place so much reliance upon the naked valor of men."

"That is because you have never been a soldier. A soldier glories in the battle, Mr. Benjamin."

"You must know, sir. You have fought and I have not, but it is difficult for me to accept that a man who yesterday planted a rose bush in his own garden today wants nothing but the pleasure of dying on a bleak little island that even history will neglect to mention."

Davis's cold face was impassive. "As you say, you have never engaged in battle. You cannot know the exultation that grips a man as he faces the enemy."

"I can only guess, Mr. President. I can only guess."

"Mr. Benjamin, I have often noticed that civilians do not understand the soldier's philosophy. Civilians pity soldiers. Nothing could be more absurd. A soldier does not feel imposed upon. He feels inspired. He feels himself more favored than other men."

Judah's eyes went to the chessboard. He kept them there, watching the long fingers of Varina as they hovered above a bishop, hesitant, fearful.

"Mr. President, I am sure your great courage is responsible for the emotions you experienced in battle. I humbly submit that all men are not grateful for the opportunity we are giving them to die so thrillingly. Lesser men prefer a chance at survival. I have a very long list of desertions that suggest that this might be the case."

Davis frowned. "There is always the 'summer soldier,' the 'sunshine patriot.' "

"And there is always the man who is no coward but will fight more readily for a government that has indicated its wish to save him. Mr. President, can we not withdraw the troops from Roanoke Island?"

"No, it would advertise a sorry weakness."

"Sir, the troops stationed on that island deserve a chance—"

"They will not be attacked. Have you a suggestion for restraining Wise's inflammatory denunciations of our policy?"

"It is unthinkable that we tell Wise of our inability to arm additional men?"

"Such a confession to Wise would be mad, sir. He would consider it his duty to inform the world that we cannot protect Roanoke Island."

"And you will not consider withdrawing the troops that are stationed there?"

Davis shook his head. "The idea is unsound."

Judah said, "You then find me barren of suggestions."

"Not so." Davis leaned forward and slapped Judah encouragingly upon the knee. "I believe I have stimulated your thinking. In the night a plan will come to you as a result of our talk." He turned to Varina. "Are you ready to go, dear?"

She smiled and nodded. "I am sorry, Mr. St. Martin, we cannot finish our game."

"Oh, I think we can, Madame." Jules moved his queen. "Checkmate," he said.

Varina studied the board. "How did you do that? I am suddenly helpless. Come, husband, help me. Can I get out of this?"

Davis walked over and glanced at the problem. "No, you are defeated. Surrender, my dear."

Varina scowled in mock rage at Jules. "You are an evil wretch, Mr. St. Martin. You could have done that at any time. You simply spun the game out to the length of the gentlemen's conversation, did you not?"

Jules smiled beguilingly. "Oh, Madame," he said. "We Creoles!"

Lacking the elegance and international flavor of Washington, Confederate government circles very wisely pretended that what they had always desired was plain and simple regionalism. It became smart to scoff at other days and other dinners, to remark contemptuously upon the golden spoons at the federal White House. It was even patriotic to regard as odious Washington's support of world-famous singers and actors. Somehow the appreciation of fine music and the wish to hear Shakespeare read by great professionals proved Washington's shallow character. It was stylish to believe that Northerners had no imagination, no resources with which to entertain themselves.

Virginia Clay, sitting next to Judah at one of Mallory's dinners said, "I have just been thinking, Mr. Benjamin, how much we missed in the past by depending on mere display for our pleasure. The to-do there was over getting tickets to hear Adelina Patti sing, the mad rush to New York to witness the performance of Rachel."

Rachel. Virginia Clay pronounced the name as Mr. Davis would. Did she know no better or was this more regionalism? Perhaps there was a growing belief that any pronunciation good enough for Alabama was good enough for France. He sighed, remembering Rachel. She was dead now, the Jewish Sorceress with the beautiful hands, the eyes that could weep on signal, the voice of an angel. It was a thousand years since he had stood in August Belmont's conservatory with her—no, it was only seven years and yet—

"And what applause and acclaim we lavished on those people."

"Were we mistaken?" Judah asked.

Mrs. Clay pouted girlishly. "Oh, it was splendid of course. I do not wish to detract from foreign celebrities, but I am of the opinion that today we are happier. Here we are united in interest and in heart, all one people with a mutual love and understanding and a wholesome enthusiasm for our own talents."

He looked into her shining eyes. She was still walking on clouds as a result of having appeared in an amateur production of Sheridan's "The Rivals." All the ladies who had had roles in the play were extremely pleased with themselves. Why, there hadn't been a seat vacant in Mrs. Cora Ives's double parlors!

"Truly, Mr. Benjamin, at the risk of seeming conceited I must say that our talents appeared very acceptable to me. We rehearsed untiringly and everyone enjoyed it. Secretary Mallory, who had seen the play in New York and in Washington, declared no other cast was so brilliant and so able."

"You were charming, Mrs. Clay. Utterly charming."

"Wasn't Connie Cary beautiful?"

"Beautiful indeed."

"Wasn't Miss Herndon bewitching?"

"Bewitching, Mrs. Clay."

"Of course in my role—"

"You were enchanting. Your performance gave the utmost delight to the President, to the cabinet, and all of us fortunate enough to witness it."

"I was not looking for a personal compliment, sir. I only intended to make the point that we can create our own entertainment."

Our own machine tools as well, our own matches and lead pencils and brooms and cutlery and streetcars. Every day someone tells me that what we are producing is superior to the Yankee product. So far I have not seen the evidence that we can forego forever the product of the low-minded, conniving, shopkeeping Yankee or any proof that we have a substitute for the voice of Adelina Patti or the art of Rachel.

After dinner there was dancing in the parlor. Judah watched it for a while then wandered into the library where Mallory was displaying to his guests a model of a new invention.

"A man named Leavitt designed it. He said it will work. I do not know but I will try it out."

"What is it?" someone asked.

"An underwater craft. I am rather taken with the idea of a ship that will submerge, leap to the surface, fire a shell, and then submerge again. If successful it could work havoc."

"Incredible!"

The assembled company stared at the odd little contrivance and shook their heads.

Jules whispered to Judah. "Will it work, that thing?"

"I haven't the slightest notion. There seems to be no reason why it should."

A gray-haired lady, a relative of the British consul in Richmond, moved closer to them, obviously eager for conversation. For a moment Leavitt's invention was the wondering subject of her remarks.

Then: "Mr. Benjamin, I have the extreme pleasure of knowing your wife."

"Really? You met her in Paris?"

"No. Not in Paris. It was in the south of France—oh, about a year ago. An exquisite creature—Mrs. Benjamin—as delightful to know as to see."

Judah murmured a gracious word.

The beaming, gray-haired lady turned to Jules. "She was accompanied by your older brother. Not so handsome as you, perhaps, but still very handsome. My family and I were terribly taken with him."

The rhythm of the conversation lost not a single beat. Jules smiled, bowed, and said, "I am so happy you liked him. He is my favorite brother."

"That wouldn't surprise me," the lady said. "He is a splendid chap." She smiled at Judah and Jules and moved away.

Jules said, "No ship can operate under water and I do not really care. This party is a stupid bore. Do you think we can leave?"

"Of course we can."

So you are taking me home, Jules? You are taking me where I can repair my shattered nerves in privacy. But it was you who received the shock. Not I. A dozen times I have heard of this older brother of yours. I would say that I know him well except that his appearance keeps changing.

When they reached home Jules retired at once. Judah did not detain him though he wished desperately for the proper, comforting word to offer. Were there any words?

If I tell him I have long ceased to sorrow, if I say that it is an old story with us, if I extend to him the philosophical props appropriate to a moment of disillusionment? No. He must rationalize it for himself.

Judah poured a glass of port and sat down beside the fire. In a moment he would get a book and read till sleep overcame him. He raised his eyes to Natalie's portrait. The south of France, my dear? Who was he? The lawyer who told you I would be hanged for treason? I will give you a message for him. Tell him they will never hang Benjamin. Tell him that when you have forgotten the south of France, Benjamin will be alive and will be holding you close and listening to sweet whispers in his ear.

He rose from his chair. There was a book that had been sent him from Louisiana, a French law book that he had been intending to—

Was that the bell? At midnight? Whoever it was could stand in the cold. The servants were asleep and he did not propose to— there it was again. Who on God's earth dared to ring his bell at this hour? Doubtless it would be rung once more and then there would be silence. Three times was usually enough to convince anyone that a door would not be opened.

To his surprise he heard the footsteps of his butler in the hall and a moment later—"I will see if the Secretary is at home, sir."

"He is at home and I intend to speak to him."

The voice. Whose is it?

"General Wise, sir," the butler said.

The announcement was unnecessary. General Wise was in the room, a slight figure in Confederate gray.

Judah said, "Good evening, Governor Wise." Would the man take his cue from that greeting?

"I wish I were governor again," Wise said.

Judah sighed. The interview could have been relatively easy. The man had chosen to make it difficult.

"Let us pretend that you are, sir. Governor Wise calling without appointment upon Judah Benjamin is a flattering surprise. When we identify ourselves as General Wise and Secretary of

War the encounter loses its pleasant flavor. General Huger is your superior and you are here without his permission."

"I suppose by army regulations I could be shot for this."

"I will make inquiries, sir."

"Your suave sarcasm that I've heard a lot about is not going to scare me, Mr. Secretary. I'm here to tell you that Huger is a fool!"

"Governor Wise—"

"Call me general, if you please. I am willing to accept the consequences of my rash act."

"Very well, General."

And I am willing to accept your rudeness only because I know the burden of your complaint, sir, and I know you to be right. Roanoke Island. God help us all, for Huger is, as you say, a fool and the President will not withdraw the troops.

"Mr. Secretary, Roanoke Island will be attacked by the Feds."

"Kindly concede that this is by no means undeniable."

Concede it yourself, Benjamin. Of course the island will be attacked.

"Mr. Secretary, the Feds can't be blind to the advantage of occupying it. Huger commands the whole North Carolina district and has all the men. I have only that little island to defend, but that is where the action will take place. You must make him send me reinforcements."

Judah looked into the haggard face of General Wise. Here was sincerity in the form of an unpopular political general.

"Sit down, General, please. Since you are here we will discuss the matter."

"What is there to discuss? The island will be attacked. Everybody knows it except those God-damned West Pointers. I want to avert disaster. To hell with retreating in good order or fighting these fine rear-guard actions."

"I entreat you, sir, to be calm."

"Calm? I've come to you because I'm desperate. I talk sense and no one listens. For the love of God, Mr. Secretary, do something. Reinforce us or take us off that island."

You ask from me what I asked from Davis and you cannot win with me, General, because I could not win with Davis.

"General Wise, have you considered—"

"I have considered nothing except the dangerous position of my men, who look to me for leadership. They are boys, Mr. Benjamin, plain boys who want to return one day to the farm or the river. What do you people think they are? Do you think they're a contingent of handsome, gallant West Pointers, all riding coal-black horses and dreaming of glory?"

"I think I know the Confederate soldier, sir."

"You don't know him as I do. My sons are Confederate soldiers. One of them is with me on Roanoke Island."

Was there a door open somewhere? Surely a draft had caused that sudden chill. Wise's son on Roanoke Island? Good God, Davis, did you know that? His son, do you understand? Would you be so obstinate if it were your son? Yes, I think you would be. I will acknowledge, Mr. President, that I believe you would face that which you demand of others.

"Mr. Secretary, I see you lost in thought. May I ask if you are considering the reinforcement of the island?"

"At the moment I am considering another matter. For your information, sir, I am and always have been strongly opposed to the practice of an officer having his own son in his command. Do you agree that it puts an added strain upon the officer?"

"I do not."

"Would you accept without argument an order removing your son from Roanoke Island?"

Wise's face flushed with sudden, violent rage. "Is that a casual or a deliberate insult? Do you imply that were my son safe I would have no further interest in the island?"

"You are overwrought, sir."

"I value the life of every soldier in my command as highly as the life of my son. I did not come to ask favors for myself or for him. Will you reinforce Roanoke Island?"

Judah said, "I do not believe reinforcement is indicated by any logical thinking."

"Will you withdraw the troops?"

"Not on the strength of any evidence so far presented to me."

"Then my handful of men remain to be maimed and murdered. They suffer and die by reason of the brilliant opinion handed down by a God-damned New Orleans lawyer."

Judah said, "You have made further discussion impossible. I bid you good night, sir."

Beloved:

We are well, Ninette and I. With interest I follow the news of the Confederacy. Much space is taken in our papers with the progress of your government. I do not understand all the things I read about recognition and not recognition but I do understand that Slidell's coming here has to do with the matter. Of course you know more than I do about Slidell's mission, but the small things that would not be communicated in dispatches may be of some amusement to you. I will relate the things I have heard from friends at court, dressmakers, milliners, etc., etc. Nothing is first hand, for the Slidells have not called on me and I did not expect them to do so. Mathilde dislikes me as you no doubt have always known. Parenthetically, beloved, I do not mind your being fond of Mathilde. No wife could be jealous of her. It would be the same as suffering jealousy over a marble statue.

To return to where I began: The Slidells have taken the court by storm. The Emperor always has time for Slidell. They drink and laugh together and behave as though their lives had been incomplete till now. Eugénie and Mathilde—well, from the moment Mathilde was presented they have been as two school chums reunited after years of separation. They speak Spanish together most of the time, Mathilde worships in the private chapel, and they confer on dress materials and coiffures. It is a great friendship. As for the girls! Here the gossip really gets exciting. These two golden virgins have the court gentlemen in a continuous fever. The Emperor's bastard half-brother, who as you must know is a powerful force with the Emperor, wants Rosina so badly that it is said he would urge recognition of the Confederacy for one small frolic with her. They say he trembles when she enters a room. I can tell you—on authority from a very fine dressmaking establishment—that he would not be disappointed if he was able to realize his dream. Those virgin Slidell bosoms need no padding. The girls, however, are in no danger of being seduced, and there are many reasons why De Morny and the other gentlemen can stop trembling. Eugénie is very pious and she regards the Slidell girls as pious women everywhere regard virgins. She would ruin the future of any man who even kissed one of them. Also, Madame Slidell rides on the stag and boar hunts with the girls, accompanies them everywhere, and watches them with anxious eyes. And thirdly, Slidell never found a man in America he thought was good enough to marry either of his girls. Therefore he certainly didn't bring them here to have them bedded down for a brief season with some reprobate of Louis Napoleon's court. Of course it is a great help to a beautiful virgin to have a father like Slidell. Not having been eligible for sainthood any time in his life he knows every trick in the seducer's repertoire. Nobody can fool him. At the court balls—where I am told some curious incidents occur in the darkened recesses and corridors— Slidell sits proudly with a tempting daughter on either side of him, his arms through theirs, guarding them relentlessly. They dance with no one, and Eugénie approves. Dancing, she believes, is sensuous and not at all correct for the young and innocent. Eugénie's endorsement of Slidell's policy will certainly keep the Emperor from requesting a waltz. What would Slidell do otherwise? He could not refuse the Emperor. Of course he could say, "It is an honor for my daughter, your Majesty. May I ask you to wait till she slips into a chastity belt?"

I don't suppose any of this has a single thing to do with the Confederacy, but still in my foolish, impractical way I think it has.

Beloved, when will you be free to visit Paris? Why, instead of Slidell, did you not come? I want you so, Judah. I want you so. Do you ever want me as much as I want you? Do you ever lie awake nights thinking of me?

When the letter was completely read he could not help but shudder at the thought that it might have fallen into enemy hands. Several mailbags traveling from Europe to the Confederacy had been unexplainably lost. Letters had turned up in the Northern press that had been extremely embarrassing to the parties concerned. But nothing so succulent as this. This! My God, it was almost unbearable to speculate on the sensation it would have caused. He must warn Natalie. She must not speak of the

Slidells, the Emperor and his court so freely. And she must never
—till she was in his arms again—speak of love or longing.

The Slidells. It was a fine thing that the royal couple had accepted them so enthusiastically. It could prove very helpful. It
could also mean nothing at all. Certainly anybody on earth
would enjoy having the Slidells for companions. It was a long
way from being favorites at court to having one's nation recognized and accepted by the government of Louis Napoleon. The
charm of the Slidell family would not necessarily make the Confederacy more attractive than the solid, established firm of
Abraham Lincoln and Company. Still, it was a start and a good
one when one considered how Mason was faring in England.

Judah took from his desk Mason's most recent letter. It had
been sent to Secretary of State Hunter, given to the President for
consideration, then handed on to Judah. Mason had as yet arrived exactly nowhere. His expectancy of an interview with Lord
Palmerston, the Prime Minister, had already dwindled and he
spoke hopefully of a meeting with the Foreign Secretary. An
audience with Queen Victoria was not even dreamed of by
Mason. It was not mentioned and certainly such a glittering
possibility had never entered Mason's mind. Judah smiled, knowing full well that it would have been Slidell's first thought.

It amused him to speculate on how Slidell would have resisted
any efforts to pass him over to a mere Foreign Secretary. And what
a different man Slidell would have been in the London post—a
model of serious deportment, his rectitude most appealing to Victoria and Albert, his Christian ideals inspiring to one and all.
Mathilde would crochet lace instead of hunting the stag and boar.
The golden virgins would modestly conceal their bosoms and it
would be Victoria's court instead of Louis Napoleon's, but the
Slidells would still—in a quiet English way—take it by storm.

Judah sighed. There was only one Slidell family. They couldn't
be in France and England, too.

Natalie's letter and the few minutes spent in amused con-
templation of the Slidells were the lighter side of the day. From
here in it must be strictly business. Unpleasant business, too,
from the look of it. Here was another of those telegrams report-
ing constant drunkenness in an officer. The man must go. A good
officer but unreliable. Why did so many of them drink them-

selves into insensibility? How could they do it when the lives
of their men depended upon clear, sober thinking? From local
governments every week there came the warnings and frightened
cries. "Our army was routed in panic, their leader intoxicated."
That was today's message. They were all similar. "Send us a new
leader. We beg of you let him be sober."

He will be sober when he leaves Richmond but I cannot guarantee his condition by the time he reaches you. I wish I could.
The truth is, little town, that all Southern officers are gentlemen
and all gentlemen carry liquor well and somewhere in that statement is a fallacy I am not prepared to challenge.

Here was another message, as serious in its way as the problem
of drunkenness. It concerned that curious eccentric, General
T. J. Jackson, the mathematics professor from the Virginia Military Institute. At Manassas he had been dubbed "Stonewall."
How the people loved to fasten a formidable nickname upon a
man. It seemed to give them a sense of invincibility, a pathetic,
childlike belief that no man could fail when he carried a name
calculated to chill the enemy.

The document that now confronted Judah was one upon
which immediate action must be taken. Eleven officers, with the
approval of their commander, General Loring, had signed what
amounted to a complaint against Jackson. Despite terrible suffering to the men, Jackson had marched them across the bleak winter mountains to the exposed and cheerless village of Romney.
The men were now sleeping in snowbanks and muttering loudly
and threateningly about their almost unendurable privations.
The officers admitted that Jackson himself slept in the snow, but
this fact did little to mitigate the suffering of boys within whom
no flame of fanaticism leaped high and warm. Only picked men
could stick it out with Jackson, and continued hardship
would cause mass desertions and certainly destroy all hope of
re-enlistments.

Judah studied the letter. The suffering of troops always moved
him to deep pity. Many of these soldiers were so young, so unprepared for the rigors of war. West Point officers did not understand
that a citizen army was an army of citizens who fought like de-
mons because the thing they desired most in life was to get out of
the army. These citizens had enlisted to fight and fight they

would. But freeze for a purpose they could not understand? Never. And certainly that iron-faced general who sucked a lemon with as much pleasure as a normal man consumed a sweetmeat would never communicate his purpose to the troops. Desertions were sure to follow. The Southern army had already evidenced in its first winter of the war that it saw no dishonor in desertion. It was simply an independent man's right to leave when he chose.

Judah thought the matter over well, then telegraphed Jackson to order General Loring's command out of the village of Romney.

God knows I have no idea what Jackson wants with Romney. He has confided in no one. He never does. He may have plans of great importance, but lacking information I can only proceed in one way. Jackson is not concerned with desertions as I am. He has not even thought of re-enlistments and what we are to do if the boys do not sign up again. This, God help me, is my problem. I must handle it in the way that seems least dangerous to me.

From the streets sounded the terrible melancholy of death. Was it possible that the sobs of the people who lined the sidewalk could be heard above the sad strains of the "Funeral March"? Or was that imagination? Judah sat at his desk and stared unseeingly at the work before him. How could a man work when a boy had died without reason and was now being borne to his grave? He had not been mistaken. Their sobs, the moans of the heartbroken Richmonders were rising to this office above the muffled drumbeat, above the slow hoofbeats and the tread of sorrowing men.

He gave up his miserable attempt to apply himself to the business before him. He leaned back in his chair and for a moment regarded the flag of the Confederacy that hung upon the wall. Then he closed his eyes and surrendered to the dreadful sorrow of the music that filled his office.

Jones, the Confederacy's biographer, stood at the window watching the procession. A good view could be had from this window and Jones had respectfully requested permission to borrow it so that his diary could record the funeral with accuracy. He had not, however, been given permission to chatter. Judah looked at him narrowly. The man's easy flow of talk bordered on disrespect. This was the office of the Secretary of War. What had made Jones so at home in it?

"A tragic loss. Simply tragic. I must say, though, that it is a beautiful funeral. A fitting tribute to one who was Virginia's most promising young man."

Judah did not open his eyes. He did not want to look at Jones. Jones, who so obviously enjoyed a beautiful funeral.

"So young to die, poor boy. Ah, well, General Wise will have to take comfort from the knowledge that all Richmond weeps with him for the loss of his son."

You do not weep, Jones. You are excited and pleased. You are at this moment framing the phrases that will go into your diary. And I do not weep. Do you know why I do not weep, Jones? This would be an interesting entry, too. I do not weep because no tears are left. I spent them all when the island fell.

"The people loved Wise so much when he was governor they have practically all turned out to honor his poor son. This is really the first big war funeral Richmond has had, too. But I suppose before this horrible business is over there will be many more."

He could not have licked his lips. That must be an illusion. "Well, I guess that is about the end." Jones turned almost cheerfully from the window. "I'll get back to my work. Terrible this had to happen right after the fall of Fort Henry. I guess we're in for disasters now. I do thank you, Mr. Secretary, for allowing me to use your window."

When he was gone Judah walked to the window himself. The streets were quiet now. The casket had been taken into St. James Church. What would the papers say tonight? Coming fresh from the graveside the reporters would be in no mood to minimize the tragedy of Roanoke Island.

He was displeased with the weakness that caused him to wince at the thought of the newspapers. Dear God, after all these years was he to begin worrying over newspapers? Did it really matter what they said of a man? Already they had accused him of willfully, cold-bloodedly murdering General Wise's son. What more could they say?

There was a knock upon the office door and at his word Jules walked in. Jules looking subdued and white-faced.

"Jules, you watched the procession and it depressed you."

"Brother, I do not want to talk about the procession. It was barbaric, an emotional orgy, a—"

"No, no. It was a military funeral. My friend Jones assures me there will be many more."

"Your friend Jones!" Jules twisted his lips in contempt. "Do you know what he is telling the clerks? He is saying that you will be flung from your high office, that the President must ask for your resignation. He is also saying that you deserve public condemnation."

"Tell him not to fear. I will receive it in full measure."

"Brother, it is being said—"

"Jules, dear Jules, I know what is being said and I know what is being thought but I make it a rule never to be disturbed till I know what is being done."

"But you should have that Jones expelled from the War Department, from the Confederacy in fact. He lacks respect for you."

Judah smiled. "Do you think I could win this treasure from Jones by having him expelled?"

"No, but—"

"Of course assuming that I retain my position long enough to issue the order."

"Brother, I came to say that Jones should be discharged." He sighed. "I see you will not listen so I will go back to work."

"I think you should, Jules. And do not be rude to Jones. He will tear you apart in his diary."

"I do not care."

"But he will tear me apart, too."

Jules smiled wanly. "You are already doomed," he said and opened the door. On the threshold just raising his hand to knock was another clerk. Jules admitted him and departed. Judah looked with curiosity upon the young man. What was he doing here? A young, untrained boy who did not know a clerk in shirt sleeves did not enter the office of the Secretary of War.

"There are several letters ready for you to sign, sir."

"Why didn't Jones bring them to me?"

The boy reddened. "I have brought them, sir."

"Are you now Chief War Clerk?"

"No, sir."

"Where is your coat?"

"Outside."

Judah looked sharply at the boy and was satisfied that no impudence was intended. Here was innocence and inexperience. Jones's insolence was very apparent. He had sent the lowliest of the clerks to the office of the discredited Secretary of War.

"Did Mr. Jones not tell you to put on your coat?"

"No, sir. Nobody did. Shall I get it?"

"No. Give me the letters."

The boy awkwardly laid them on the desk, and it was at that moment that there was a tap upon the door.

"In response to that sort of sound, son, you go to the door, open it, and inquire as to the business of the person who has knocked."

"Yes, sir."

Judah continued to sign the letters, aware of the considerable whispering on the threshold. At length the young clerk returned to the desk.

"Sir, I am informed that General Wise is outside requesting to see you."

General Wise. God, why had he thought it necessary to come? What could be gained? What could they say to each other that would not live forever as a gnawing, never-forgotten bitterness?

"Tell General Wise I will see him at once."

"Yes, sir."

The boy departed and Judah got to his feet. This would be an ordeal. Wise would be in a mood for murder. And who could blame him? He walked to the window again. His back was turned when he heard the footstep behind him that he knew to be that of General Wise. Turning he faced the General and was startled by the awful pallor of the man's face, the glint of madness in the eyes that stared into his. It would be unthinkable, ridiculous to greet him in any fashion ever devised. Judah kept his silence till Wise spoke. When he did his voice was low and savage, his lips trembling with his passion and hatred.

"I have come from the church where I have gazed upon the dead face of my son. The people who were his friends are filing past his casket, looking upon him for the last time. Soon we will bury him. In the interval, Mr. Secretary, I thought I would like to talk to you."

"If such is your wish, sir, I am at your service."

"I know that in cases such as this it is frequent for a grieving father to be softened by his tears. In one's sorrow one feels very close to God and it is supposed that this experience gives mortals the Godlike wish to forgive those who have sinned against them. I have come to tell you that no such emotion has been mine. God has given me no flaming desire to forgive my enemy or to pray for the murderer of my son."

If Ninette were dead and I believed myself facing the one responsible I would not be different from this man. He must speak or die himself.

"I want you to know—I feel you should know—I feel you should never forget that you personally killed my boy. War is one thing. I could accept his loss if it had been useful to his country. This was not war. This was murder. He died unnecessarily, meaninglessly. He died because you would not listen."

The quiet coldness of Wise's tone was deserting him now. His voice was rising out of control, hysterical.

"God knows what pleasure it gave you to belittle my advice, to ignore my pleas, but today my son is dead because you reveled in the feeling of power it gave you to say, 'To hell with General Wise. To hell with Roanoke Island.' "

"I assure you that such was never my attitude."

"It was your attitude. You proved it by ignoring our needs. You could have saved the island. You could have saved my son. But he lies dead now. Murdered. Murdered by a God-damned Jew."

Why did I not guess it would come to that? Inevitable, was it not? And yet I never grow accustomed to the shock of it.

"I deeply regret the death of your son, sir."

"As your illustrious predecessors regretted the death of Jesus Christ? You do not change, do you? Through the centuries you remain the same. Lying, stealing, murdering. You are a race without honor, without conscience, without pity."

The sick feeling of outrage is passing, sir. I can endure quite a lot of this but how much more is there that I must endure? Are you satisfied yet? Consoled? Avenged?

"Now I go to bury my boy. He will not rest while a Jew controls the policies of the land he died to save, but I will pray for him and I will pray that Jefferson Davis clears you evil, stinking Jews out of our country. I have another prayer, too. Listen well to this one. I pray that some day I may see the murderer of my son mourning for his flesh and blood as today I mourn for mine. That is what I wanted to tell you, sir. That is what I had to tell you."

Wise walked to the door, flung it wide, and sobbing noisily rushed away. Judah closed his office door quietly.

Let no one bother me. Let me pace the floor in peace. Let me remember that he is a man maddened by his grief. Yet how is it that his grief was not too maddening for him to remember that he was speaking to a Jew? Benjamin, be charitable. Wise is a man whose sorrow has shattered him. He does not remember that you offered to take his boy from Roanoke. He does not know you would have taken them all had the choice been yours. He knows nothing but his sorrow and he strikes blindly, hoping to hurt, and in the hurting ease his own pain.

So the age-old insults could be forgotten but Roanoke Island, no. It would never be forgotten. To pace the floor, to wring one's hands, to feel a sickness in the soul would do nothing for men who had perished on a lonely little island. There was nothing that could be done for them. They were gone. They were as much in the past as though their graves had been dug a century before. But the island could not be forgotten.

Pacing, turning, passing the door, he saw it open slightly. The young war clerk was back again.

"Don't you knock on doors, boy?"

"Sir, I'm sorry but—"

"Go away. I have not finished signing the letters. I'll ring when I—"

"But it's the President, sir. He sent to inquire if you are in your office. He is on his way to you. I thought you should know."

So Davis had not gone to the funeral of Wise's son. Did he expect the carnage to be so great that it would be folly to establish a precedent? And he was coming here instead of sending for his Secretary of War. How sensitive of him to feel that a man whose resignation was to be requested should receive the blow in the privacy of his own office.

The door popped open again. "He's here, sir."

"He?" Judah asked chillingly.

"The President, sir."

"Then say 'the President,' damn it. And stand up straight when you say it."

God Almighty, it was for this nation that men gave their lives, their careers, everything they had to give, and sloppy little simpletons dare to—Benjamin, you're making a case for yourself. The truth is that you want to shout at someone and that boy is available and vulnerable.

The boy was standing very straight now, the door had been thrown wide and Davis walked into the office.

"Good morning, Mr. Benjamin."

"Good morning, Mr. President."

The door was closed. They were alone. Each man looked for a moment into the face of the other and then away. Roanoke Island, the violent accusations of the newspapers, the funeral of young Wise. I must have your resignation, Mr. Benjamin. All this would come but not yet. Judah saw that there was something else that must first be met.

There were deep lines on Davis's face. He frowned and they grew deeper. His neuralgia was troubling him today.

"Please seat yourself, Mr. Benjamin."

"Thank you, sir. Will it disturb you if I stand?"

"Not at all." Davis looked down at some papers he held in his hand. Letters. What was the point of exploring any lesser matters when Roanoke Island loomed so large?

"Mr. Benjamin, I am in possession of several communications concerning General T. J. Jackson. Distressingly enough he requests permission to resign from the army."

"Because I ordered him to withdraw Loring's command from Romney."

Davis consulted one of the letters in his hand. "He says that with such interference he cannot expect to be of much service in the field. Letters have all but flooded my office. The Reverend McFarland for instance—" Davis thumbed swiftly through the pages he held. "Oh, yes. Here. He says in part: 'If a God-fearing man like Jackson feels it necessary to resign I will regard his action as evidence of the Lord's disapproval of the Southern cause.' "

Davis looked at Judah questioningly. The look said, "What do you say to that, Mr. Benjamin?"

Mr. Benjamin said, "Of course you will not accept Jackson's resignation."

"If he should persist in requesting it—" Davis left the sentence unfinished.

Judah walked to his desk to do nothing but rearrange the pile of unsigned letters. Why was it necessary to discuss Jackson and his resignation? Davis had come here on the matter of another resignation but he was apparently in no haste to reach the point.

"Mr. President, Jackson will not persist. Though perhaps he is the most God-fearing man in our armies, he is also the most ambitious."

Davis was taken aback. "That is not my understanding, sir. I have heard he is a most modest and humble man."

"So have I but I have found it impossible to accept him on his own evaluation. His modesty and humbleness I have not seen proved. His dusty uniforms, his battered hat are no less affectation than Jeb Stuart's gaudy plume and flaring gauntlets. General Stuart is also a God-fearing man, an excellent soldier, and, I understand, a fine Christian."

Davis nodded. "I am sure he is all of that."

"Well, sir, does it not strike you as odd that no one ever finds Stuart on his knees deep in prayer? Somehow no journalist, no congressman ever enters Stuart's tent and finds him communing with his God. In Jackson's case it is entirely different. One never hears of him but what he is either praying, patting a child's head, or finding a lost cow for an old woman. I would that Jackson saved a little of his great heart for the unfortunate men he commands."

Davis stood idly rearranging the letters in his hand. "You do not regard General Jackson very highly, sir."

"He may be a first-rate general. I am not yet certain. Jackson, the man, I do not admire and this latest piece of pettiness I despise."

"Pettiness? You call it pettiness?"

"I do indeed. No man loves the warrior's laurels more than

Jackson. He will not leave the army. He could not be driven from it."

Davis shook his head. "I disagree. The man is sincere. He wishes to resign."

"In that case, sir—if he is truly in earnest—General Jackson's character becomes even less admirable in my eyes. I have no liking for a man who, in wartime, having a contribution to make, will withhold it because his nice little honor has been roughly handled by the government."

Davis seated himself and looked at Judah thoughtfully. "I am afraid you are too severe in your judgment of Jackson. He fancies himself unappreciated."

"And so he reacts like an opera tenor who believes that the management is not sufficiently aware of his talents. I do not expect soldiers to behave like tenors, sir."

Davis smiled thinly. "Regrettably they sometimes do, Mr. Benjamin."

"Beauregard does not. Johnston does not. Both of them have great cause for considering themselves unappreciated. Neither has offered his resignation."

"Beauregard and Johnston are full generals. They could not resign without infinite discredit to themselves. Jackson's case is different. Moreover, in having taught mathematics for some time at V.M.I. he has absorbed something of a civilian viewpoint. He has ceased to think as a West Point man should. He has become more the professor, more the scholar, and I understand him well."

Judah nodded. "Perhaps you do, sir."

"Well, if I did not understand men then I certainly would not belong in the position the nation has assigned to me." He paused. "Mr. Benjamin, while on the subject of the nation—" He paused again and made a rustling noise with the letters.

"Yes, Mr. President, while on the subject of the nation and those who do not belong in positions assigned to them. Let us get to that, sir. I have read the newspapers, so do not hesitate in fear of wounding me."

Davis scowled. "The newspapers. I have so deeply deplored their intemperate attacks upon you that I have considered suppressing them."

"Mr. President, I beg of you never to consider such a move. The liberty of the press is sacred."

Davis sighed heavily. "I commend the tolerance with which you can view the newspapers." He rose and walked to the window. "Mr. Benjamin, I heard this afternoon there is to be a congressional investigation into the fall of Roanoke Island." Davis stared down into the street. "Sir, I cannot retain you as Secretary of War."

Judah said, "I should have guessed that on the evening you called upon me and your wife played chess with Jules St. Martin. Who replaces me here?"

"I am thinking of Randolph."

"A good choice. A Virginian. I have observed that Virginians are partial to them."

Davis wheeled suddenly from the window. "Virginians are not dictating to me. No one dictates to me. My decision to replace you as Secretary of War is for your sake. I will not have you further condemned in the event that there are more reverses for our armies to meet."

"You are very kind, sir."

Davis said, "My plan is to remove you completely from a post so much discussed and so little understood by the people. With your permission, sir, I will give you a new office. Would you consider becoming Secretary of State?"

Judah stared in frank and utter amazement at Davis. "Has Hunter resigned?"

"He will. He is very unhappy, you know."

Hunter was indeed unhappy. In the presence of the entire cabinet Davis had replied to a Hunter comment with, "When I want your opinion, Mr. Hunter, I will ask for it." Davis was right. Hunter was unhappy.

Davis left the window and walked to the center of the office. "Mr. Benjamin," he said, "I would not consider myself worthy of the presidency if I permitted a group of vindictive scribblers to erase you from my cabinet. I am a man of staunch loyalties. You will always find me fighting at your side, defending you, giving the lie to those who would defame you. If you have made a grave error—well, your assignment has been difficult."

"If I have made a grave error?" Judah felt a cold, quiet rage rise within him as he spoke. "Do you by any chance mean Roanoke Island, sir?"

"Roanoke Island is in the past. Discussion of it is as useless as it is painful."

"Mr. President, you and I are engaged in a vast and perilous experiment. Someday our names will be in history books. Patriots or traitors we will be called depending on the matter of success or failure. There will be a mistiness about us, the impenetrable haze that enfolds all historical figures. Nobody will quite understand us. Today while we live, sir, let us understand each other. Let no mistiness exist between you and me. In the matter of Roanoke Island I have submitted to unmerited censure. I am reconciled to the fact that for all the years to come people will believe me responsible for its fall. Sir, I am not reconciled to your believing me responsible for it now."

Davis said, "Mr. Benjamin, no one man is ever responsible for a military disaster."

"The congressional investigation may reveal a different opinion but I will not worry that question now. It is, however, my purpose to learn one thing from you—I feel compelled to ask if you believe you are outwitting Congress and the people by changing my status in the cabinet?"

"I do not seek to outwit them. I have no desire but to serve my country well, but I will do it in my way, letting no one frighten me into any course I do not wish to pursue. I ask only for the help of God and the great Confederate Army."

"Yes. Well, I do not presume to identify God but I feel myself on firmer ground where the great Confederate Army is concerned. It is composed of people. I should like to see your popularity unimpaired with them."

Davis said, "My popularity does not concern me. Do you accept the new position?"

"If you need me, I will serve."

"I need you, sir. For the time being the matter of your elevation will rest silently between us. It will probably be a month before you assume your new duties. Now I will leave you." He walked to the door and opened it wide. "It's been a good talk, sir." He turned suddenly, unexpectedly then to Judah, his face alight with the celebrated smile that had melted hearts the length and breadth of the Confederacy. In full view of the clerks in the outer office his hand reached for Judah's and clasped it warmly. Then he was gone, disappearing with his soldierly stride behind the filing cabinets and high desks of the outer office.

Judah stood looking after the tall, retreating figure. Did he think that they would give him peace now? He had satisfied the letter, not the spirit of the law as spoken by those who wanted Benjamin removed. True, Benjamin would be Secretary of War no more. He would simply rise to the most important of cabinet positions. They would not be satisfied. They would not be silenced. Here in Virginia, Wise would guarantee that they were not satisfied or silenced.

He became aware of someone standing quietly beside him. It was Jones, Chief War Clerk Jones, the Confederacy's biographer.

"I see you have returned," Judah said.

Jones inclined his head politely. "Sir, I apologize for the ineptness of the lad who served you while I was otherwise occupied. Mr. Secretary, sir, could you possibly find time to finish signing those letters now?"

Judah looked long and hard at the little man, the deferential clerk with his spiteful eyes carefully veiled. Judah laughed.

"Not quite so humble, Jones," he said. "We are all entitled to one bad guess a day."

Judah, making every effort to concentrate upon his reading, could not help but hear the rattle of newspapers, the constant sighs of Jules.

"Jules, for heaven's sake, stop torturing yourself. Throw those newspapers out."

Jules's eyes came slowly, sadly away from the front page of the Richmond *Examiner.*

"Brother, they must not do this. They must be made to desist from blaming you for the fall of Roanoke Island, for the loss of Forts Henry and Donelson." Jules pointed dramatically to a headline. "Here, for instance, you are actually accused of—"

"Do not tell me. Let me guess."

"Very well, Brother. I will not tell you. I will let you guess. It begins with a T."

"I suppose it is not trustworthiness."

"No. It is treason, Brother. I am appalled that President Davis permits you to be so badly abused by the press. It is not enough that he smiles at you and offers you a pleasant handshake. He must *do* something."

Judah made no reply.

"But the President does nothing so I, Jules St. Martin, have decided to fight a slight skirmish for you, Brother."

"What?" Judah put his book down and leaned forward in his chair. "What do you intend to do?"

"I intend to administer an antidote for all this poison. I am in a position to do so for I have met a journalist who admires you."

Judah laughed. "The man must be mad. Where has he been? Can't he read? Can't he hear?"

Jules walked to the writing desk, flipped open the inkwell, picked up a pen, and assumed a position of eager amanuensis. "Now that you know my plan we can work on it together. He wants a story about you. It will show the public Judah Benjamin as he really is, for I myself am to furnish the details."

"Who is this journalist, Jules?"

"I met him at the Spottswood Hotel last night. We had a drink together. I am to meet him there again tonight. I intend to tell him of your great legal achievements and how you were a pioneer in revolutionizing the Louisiana sugar industry. But let us begin at the beginning. When were you born? I always forget."

"I was born," Judah said, "on the sixteenth of Ab in the year five thousand five hundred and seventy-one."

Jules had begun to write. Now he glanced up in surprise. "I thought you were born in August, Brother. But wait. What is it you have said? It sounded like—"

"That is the way my birth was entered in the archives and I will be surprised indeed if history does not record the fall of Roanoke Island also by the Hebrew calendar."

"I know what you mean. There are a great many ugly references to be sure. To counteract some of these I intend to tell how you are a member of New York's most aristocratic club."

"Oh, do not miss doing so. It will enshrine me in the hearts of the people of Arkansas and Tennessee."

Jules looked at him for a long moment, then laid down his pen. "I am being a fool, Brother?"

"No, Jules, not a fool but take my word—there are two things in life more dangerous than all others combined. One is New Orleans in fever season. The other is a journalist who promises to print a story just as it is given to him by a member of the family."

"I wanted so much to help you."

"You have already done so. To have your loyalty means much to me. Now do throw those newspapers away and we will have a glass of sherry together."

"It appeals to me as a fair bargain," Jules said. "Are you at home for dinner this evening, Brother?"

"No, I am invited for an informal repast at the Presidential Mansion. Are you at home?"

Jules busied himself with the decanter. "No, I, too, have been invited to a very small, exclusive gathering," he said.

"Have a good time, Jules."

"You, too, Brother, though I cannot imagine it at the Presidential Mansion."

Sundays there were not as dreary as Jules supposed. The children were permitted a half-hour or so with the guests, and Judah enjoyed the children. Little Joe with the wonderful dark eyes, and the new baby, William Howell, who was always exhibited for a brief moment. The guests were even interesting at times.

The mansion itself was a pleasant place. Varina had succeeded in removing the stiff, history-conscious appearance it had first worn. She had remarked that some of her own belongings must be installed before the atmosphere would please her. They were installed now—her own belongings. Judah recognized a few of them. A pair of porcelain flare vases and a mahogany writing desk outlined in brass. So Varina had attended the auction in Washington. The auction at which all the furnishings he had bought for that ill-fated venture in domestic bliss had gone to the highest bidders. Well, that, too, was in the past. This was now, and the flare vases and the mahogany writing desk belonged to Jefferson and Varina Davis.

Mrs. Chesnut, of course, was speaking. The woman was rarely

still. "She rebuked me. I do not say that I did not deserve it but it was a positive rebuke just the same."

"Who rebuked you, Mary?" Varina asked.

"Sally Tomkins. You know, the woman who opened that hospital at Third and Main. I went to Pizzini's and bought loads of delicious confections for the wounded. She received me nicely when she saw all I had brought but then—"

"What then?"

"Well, nothing really. I merely said to her, 'Are there any Carolinians here?' She turned white with fury. Her uniform was no whiter. She said, 'Madame, I never ask where the wounded come from.' Now, wasn't that a rebuke?"

Connie Cary grinned. "A mild one," she said. "Considering."

"Incidentally I was fortunate not to have arrived at Pizzini's earlier. Directly outside the window on the sidewalk, within full view of the ladies eating their ice cream, one of those New Orleans Tigers engaged in a fight with another New Orleans Tiger and decapitated him."

"That isn't all the Tigers have done on the sidewalk within full view of the ladies," Judge Trescott whispered to Judah.

"I know. Those of us who love Louisiana wish we could claim only the Washington Artillery as our own."

Davis caught Judah's eye and rose from his chair. Judah followed him into the room that was used as an office. It was a pleasant room with a desk, a couch, a few chairs. Nothing unnecessary except a sheaf of winter leaves and a crayon drawing of Franklin Pierce.

"Do sit down, Mr. Benjamin. I can stand just so much Sunday chatter then my head begins to ache. Is it not peaceful in here?"

"Very, sir."

Davis was silent, obviously enjoying the quiet of his office. He closed his eyes and rested his head against the small cushion that was affixed to the chair back. Judah began to wonder if he had been intended to follow Davis here.

"Mr. Benjamin." Eyes still closed.

"Yes, Mr. President."

"On Friday you mentioned that when I had time there was a matter—"

"Oh, it can wait. It is not important and I am reluctant to bring Monday's business to you on Sunday, sir."

Davis said, "Proceed freely. It is more restful here than in the drawing room no matter what we discuss."

"It is this then, Mr. President. Before I leave the office of the War Department to my successor I would like to see harmony established between that office and General Joseph Johnston."

Davis opened his eyes. "We cannot hope for harmony with Johnston. He delights in argument."

"And I wish to see General Beauregard restored to a command commensurate with his rank and ability."

Davis sighed and looked regretfully at Judah. "Believe me, sir, you are inclined to overestimate Beauregard."

"Then may I repeat, sir, that the War Department must make every effort to reach a congenial understanding with General Johnston? He is, after all, the leader of Virginia's armies."

"And in strictest confidence I say to you that I wish he were not. I would be content if General Lee had his command. Lee is an amiable man, never childish or contentious. He does not argue."

Judah thought of Lee, the courtly desk general. No, he did not argue. When crossed he kept his grand and godlike silence. Not so Joe Johnston, whose sarcasm was pure poison, whose doubts of Davis's military genius were painfully evident. Curious the things the people never knew. Could they sleep nights if it were known to them that a president sometimes dislikes a general so intensely that he prays for him to make errors and denies the support necessary to success? Could they face a terrible war if they dreamed that a general, such as Beauregard, could be dropped into an obscure command for the sin of being popular?

There was a soft tap upon the door. "Dinner is served, Mr. President."

Davis stood. "I guess we shall have to face their fire, Mr. Benjamin."

Judah had Connie Cary beside him at the table. She said, "Do I have a smudge on my nose?"

"Of course not. Why do you ask?"

"The President's secretary—Mr. Harrison—keeps looking and looking at me."

"Does he have a smudge on his nose?"

"No, of course not. Why—" She turned a pretty pink. "Oh, I do not. Do I? Do I keep looking and looking at him?"

Judah laughed and turned from her to conceal the sigh that followed. He had thought of Ninette. How sweet it would be to have her near him now. To watch the bright unfolding of her first romance. What a joy if this were Ninette sitting beside him, happily, nervously in love with Burton Harrison.

But no man could have all things. Was he not to be Secretary of State with a salary of nine thousand dollars a year? And had he not willingly chosen everything that he now possessed?

Mallory, red-faced and riding the high road of excitement, said the fall of Nashville, Tennessee, meant nothing at all.

"Won't you take a loss like that in exchange for a victory like the one we had?" he demanded. "If we can give a miserable little city such as Nashville and in return get a victory like sinking two warships and crippling another I say it is damn good."

Memminger of the Treasury looked unhappy. He was tired of hearing about Mallory's great naval victory. The Treasury Department had had no victories at all.

Reagan said, "You did a good job, Mr. Mallory, the *Merrimac* is—"

"God damn it, her name is the *Virginia,* not the *Merrimac.* That was her Yankee name before I dug her up and made an ironclad out of her. The *Virginia,* Reagan, not the *Merrimac.*"

Watts, the Attorney General, chewed thoughtfully upon his tobacco, then closing one eye aimed expertly for the cuspidor. "*Merrimac* or *Virginia*—we still lost Nashville," he said.

"Well, the *Virginia* will even the score tomorrow. How many Yankee warships will you take as a fair trade for Nashville?"

Judah sat with Mallory the next evening and did what he could for him—he let him weep.

"Benjamin, it's a God-damned shame. We worked so hard. We tried so hard."

"I know, Mallory."

"She was such a brave little devil, that *Virginia.*"

Somehow that was the saddest thing of all. Mallory mourning the ironclad, not for the loss of its deadly usefulness, but as though the *Virginia* had been a living, noble creature. Judah looked into the stricken eyes of the Secretary of the Navy. Headlines, neither North nor South, ever shrieked of the heartaches of men who sat at desks and wept when the battle was over.

"She was the most gallant little thing I ever saw."

Perhaps in Washington Gideon Welles was saying that tonight of the *Monitor*. Another Secretary of Navy. Another ironclad. Another story.

"Your glass is empty, Benjamin."

"I think I'll keep it that way. Thank you."

"Mind if I fill mine?"

"I think it's coming to you."

Later he put Mallory to bed and went home. Walking slowly through the night he was chilled by the late winter winds and the realization that the year so far had brought nothing but defeats and discouragement. Mill Springs in January and the death of General Zollicoffer. Roanoke Island. Forts Henry and Donelson. Nashville. The fatal injuries to the *Virginia*. Somewhere in between, like small significant punctuation marks, there had been the bloody skirmishes, the dead and dying in mountain passes and by the sides of cold and lonely rivers. Were there to be no victories? Was it possible that the tide would never turn? Could it be that the Confederacy was unable to furnish a contest, that there would be nothing more than a steady, downhill road to surrender? He thought of Manassas from which the Yankees had run like frightened children. Well, they were men now.

In mid-March Judah was officially appointed Secretary of State. The newspapers screamed their anger. The congressional investigation into the affair at Roanoke Island had not yet been concluded and the Richmond *Examiner* bluntly charged the President with complete indifference to Congress.

We have martial law. For Secretary of State we have a man whose motives are definitely suspect. Our president is no president but a dictator who acts as he chooses without regard for Congress or the rights of citizens. Is this the dream for which we formed a new nation, the Utopia for which we fight?

Davis read the editorials and smiled coldly. "These article writers will die one day of the poison they ferment within themselves," he said. "They seem to me like mad men striking their heads against a wall, knowing nothing else to do in their frustration. 'Replace Benjamin,' they shouted. Well, I have done so. I have given them Randolph in the War Department but at the same time I have shown my contempt for their opinions by elevating the man they sought to destroy."

Judah said, "May I hope that my elevation was also directed somewhat by your belief that I would ably discharge the office of Secretary of State? At the moment it seems I am nothing so much as a rather large portion of vengeance heaped upon the press and the public."

"You will be a magnificent Secretary of State, sir."

The findings of the congressional investigation were revealed at last and came as a surprise to no one.

Blame and responsibility attributable for the defeat of our troops at Roanoke Island is attached to General Huger and the former Secretary of War Benjamin.

The papers paid little attention to General Huger.

New Orleans fell to the Federals that April. New Orleans. It was impossible to picture it in the hands of a conquering army. New Orleans with her gentle laughter and her happy heart. And General Butler of Massachusetts, striding beneath the iron balconies, searching the sun-drenched courtyards for dangerous characters, marching his men on Royal Street. Butler had wanted to hang the commissioners who had gone to Washington requesting the evacuation of Sumter. Butler had presented a hero's sword to the blundering captain who had removed Mason and Slidell from the *Trent*. He was the commanding general of the New Orleans occupation.

Judah thought of his sister, Rebecca, and of the young nieces who were with her in the house on Naiades Avenue. One could only pray. One could only be grateful that Natalie, Ninette, and the St. Martins were in Paris.

Constance Cary, who identified every friend with the corner of the Confederacy from whence he had come, did not forget that New Orleans was Jules's homeland.

"Has this hit you very hard, Mr. St. Martin?" she asked.

"No, no. I am ruined, that is all," Jules replied.

Ruined indeed. Judah remembered the letter Jules had written years before when St. Martin property was being sold. "Will you please see that I keep my lovely little piece of Louisiana?" Well, he had not been able to oblige Jules. Butler had it now. And Jules had nothing in the world but his job as war clerk and his salary of fifteen hundred dollars a year.

"But it is a fortune, fifteen hundred dollars," Jules said. "An income to be respected when one considers that with it I manage to live in a luxurious home where there are two servants, the best of food, the finest sherry. I cannot complain. Let the small-salaried man worry."

The small-salaried man was indeed worrying. Prices were spiraling. But was it he—the man with the family to support—who walked abroad in the dark hours and scribbled upon the streets and buildings? Every morning there was a new message to read. "Rally around the Old Flag" or "God Bless the Stars and Stripes." Who was responsible? Many were arrested, many more suspected, but there was always another inscription at the street corner. "Will the Old Army Never Come to Save Us?"

And the old army was coming. It was virtually in the suburbs of Richmond, and Johnston, the hope of the people, the head of the army, lay wounded at Seven Pines. Who will replace him? Who can command our army? Well, there is Lee, the desk general. The President favors Lee. Doubtless it will be Lee in Johnston's command. And Johnston, from his bed of pain, said, "It is a good choice, a great thing for the Confederacy. Lee will have the support and confidence that was withheld from me. He will never be given responsibility without authority. He will not be expected to fight both the Federals and the administration." And Lee fought the Federals. Within a few weeks they were twenty miles from Richmond and General McClellan was doubtless trying to explain to Lincoln how it had happened that suddenly he and his army were back at the base from which they had begun their offensive.

Judah did not hear from Rebecca for some time and when her letter came it was postmarked La Grange, Géorgia.

My dear brother:

We are finally here safe and sound in La Grange. Our lives have not been at all difficult considering everything. For a while we were permitted to stay in our house without any trouble, then one night it happened. A federal lieutenant came to the door and told us that the military authorities wanted the house at once. We must be gone by morning! Even though the order was harsh I will say that the man himself was gentlemanly and kind enough. I had a few bottles of bourbon and cognac from Belle Chasse(!) and after I offered him a drink and he had sent for a few of his friends to join him he told me I could keep all my furniture and belongings if I knew somewhere to move them. Well, that was more than I had expected. A lady with whom I had become friendly owned an empty house directly across the way and I was in possession of the key. So I felt very relieved about the whole thing.

All night long we gathered our belongings together. The lieutenant had said that he would send men in the morning to move the furniture. When morning came it was a different story however. With the first crack of dawn a strange and very insolent young fellow arrived in command of a squad of soldiers.

"Madame," he asked, "are you the sister of the arch rebel, Benjamin?"

I said I was the sister of the Secretary of State.

He said, "In that case you can remove nothing from this house except yourself and the other relatives of the arch rebel. This is a military order. Leave the property at once."

Friends took us in and we were not hurt in any way save for material losses. When we could no longer impose upon our friends we rented rooms for a while on Iberville and finally left to make our way into Confederate territory. I hear there is now a reign of terror in New Orleans. Everything is going satisfactorily with us, dear brother. I hope the same for you and I pray that your wife and daughter are well. I know you must be terribly busy but do write to me if you find time. We are all very proud of you and send our love.

Rebecca

Down on the street there were shouts and roars of laughter. He walked to the window. Hood's men. The Texans. He might have known. Only the Texans still frolicked like lighthearted schoolboys. It was a paradox of war that, once the high excitement had faded, only a man could laugh like a boy. He watched them at their horseplay. Rough, young giants who brawled and yelled and expressed in loud voices their admiration for the pretty girls who passed. No one resented them, no one in Richmond feared them. They were full of hell and fight and sentiment. They wanted to be liked and they wanted to be noticed. Lee had noticed them. He and the lemon-sucking mathematician had used them in every desperate encounter. The Texans had been prominent in the victories that had saved Richmond. Judah at the window stared down at the tall, broad-shouldered men of Hood's division. They were not afraid to fight. They were not afraid to die. They saw war in terms as simple as their own courage and honesty of purpose. What would they make of the documents that lay upon his desk, the documents that he had read and reread and studied till dawn?

His secretary entered the office and dropped a stack of newspapers upon the table. "These are from New York, sir," he said.

"Thank you."

Judah glanced at the clock. There was a moment or two before he was expected in Davis's office. What was going on in New York? Well, the hospital fund had been enriched by nineteen hundred and twenty dollars and eighteen cents. This had come from Mr. and Mrs. August Belmont, who had permitted a group of volunteer fund raisers to charge admission to the Belmont art gallery. August, Judah remembered, had also donated two thousand dollars the previous month to a similar fund but that did not make this particular newspaper treat him more kindly. August was an antiadministration man.

The money collected at the Belmont art gallery had been used in a very practical manner, Judah observed. With it the lady volunteers had bought and sent to a base hospital "a cargo of ice, potatoes, onions, cabbages, lemons, anti-scorbutics, and tonics. Also beef stock, crackers, and farinaceous food."

He thought of Mrs. Chesnut and her lovely purchases at Pizzini's Confectionery Establishment. She would scorn the idea of bringing onions and cabbages to the wounded. The poor boys should have only strawberry ice and mauve-colored bonbons. Potatoes and lemons for the brave lads? Never. How horrid after they had fought so hard. Dear Connie Cary. Would she carry beef stock to a homesick amputee? Certainly not. He must have a layer cake. Only a coarse Northern woman would allow a word like "scurvy" to enter her mind.

Judah glanced again at the clock, picked up the documents that lay upon his desk, and walked across the hall to Davis's office.

"Go right in, sir. The President expects you."

They were waiting for him. Davis, Memminger, and the man who had crossed the ocean for this meeting. Judah had not bargained on finding him here as the discussion opened.

Davis was in fine spirits this morning. No sign of headache or dyspepsia. "Do sit down, Mr. Benjamin, and we will proceed. You have, of course, read the contract, weighed the merits of the transaction, and are ready to give your opinion."

"I am ready," Judah said, "to give my opinion to you and Mr. Memminger."

The stranger, a round little man with a skin that seemed to have been polished, smiled slowly. "Mr. President, perhaps I should withdraw."

Davis looked at Judah thoughtfully, blinking his eyes slowly as he considered the matter. "I am not at all certain that privacy is needed. If there are objections I see no reason why they should not be made known to Erlanger and Company."

Judah said, "My objections will certainly be made known to Erlanger and Company, Mr. President. I thought it a courtesy, however, to let you know them first."

"We will not stand on ceremony, sir," Davis said. "If you think we are being offered a bad bargain I believe you should say so plainly."

The Frenchman leaned across the table. "Mr. Benjamin," he said, "there are three things which I would have you know so that you may be comfortable in unburdening your mind. One, I am thoroughly acquainted with the emptiness of Mr. Memminger's treasury. Two, I have given several months to the study of what Baron Erlanger's banking house can offer to lend you, and, three, Mr. Slidell thoroughly approves the transaction as outlined in the papers before you."

Judah swallowed the wrath that rose to choke him. He said, "The emptiness of Mr. Memminger's treasury, sir, is for Mr. Memminger to mention if he chooses. It is not and never will be a proper subject for your notice."

The man from Erlanger's spread his hands and shrugged. "All Europe speaks of how unfortunate it was that your government did not ship every bale of cotton in the Confederacy abroad before the blockade began. It was a great mistake not to have done so. How is it that you never thought of it?"

"That, too, should not trouble you, sir."

"The governments of Europe are aware that you are in financial trouble. That brings me back to the second observation with which I attempted to put you at your ease."

"Very kind of you," Judah said. "Your second observation concerning Baron Erlanger's banking house and what he can offer us—my dear sir, Baron Erlanger's offer strikes me as being but one point away from unabashed robbery. It violates all the proprieties of international finance."

Both Davis and Memminger were shocked and dismayed, but the representative of Baron Erlanger was an old hand at the banking business. He smiled and regarded Judah with pitying eyes. "Mr. Benjamin, you will get no offer as good as ours anywhere and in your heart you know it. Mr. Slidell approves a hundred per cent."

"Who the hell is Mr. Slidell?—Pardon me, Mr. President— Really, my dear sir, may I remind you that Mr. Slidell is a man appointed by this department, a man who can be recalled by this department? Do not give me Slidell as an authority on business or as a North Star toward which this government must gravitate. I say your offer is ridiculous."

"In what way, Mr. Benjamin?" Davis asked quietly.

Judah spread the papers out before him on the table. "Mr. President, they offer to underwrite an issue of twenty-five million dollars in Confederate bonds. This is very generous of them. They ask nothing in return but all profits in excess of seventy per cent of the sale price, plus a five per cent commission for disposing of them, plus an eight per cent discount for anticipating any and all of the installments, plus a one per cent commission for handling the sinking fund and interest!"

Davis stared at the papers, squinting his eyes at the spidery handwriting, at the prettily formed numbers and zeroes. "I confess that the point you make, Mr. Benjamin, escapes me."

"The point is that of the twenty-five million dollars involved, the Confederacy receives little more than fifteen million and even this amount will be reduced under the redemption and commission provision. Baron Erlanger will make an enormous profit, for it is my guess the bonds will sell well in France and at a good price, too."

Davis turned to Memminger. "Do you understand, sir?"

"Yes, Mr. President."

"Is Mr. Benjamin overzealous in our behalf, do you think?"

Memminger shook his head. "Mr. Benjamin is quite correct. Baron Erlanger is driving a very hard bargain but—" Memminger fell silent.

"But what, Mr. Memminger?" Davis prodded.

"But the treasury is greatly in need of funds." Memminger sighed and turned away. "I do not know what else to say."

Davis's eyes went sadly to the Erlanger papers there on the table. "The transaction could bring us an unlooked-for blessing," he said. "If a great many Frenchmen owned Confederate bonds it would create a nationwide interest in us. It might lead to the French recognizing us."

"Sir," Judah said bitterly, "the French have already recognized us. They have recognized us as pigeons!" He pushed his chair back from the table. "My advice is to decline the contract."

Memminger gasped. Davis stirred uneasily and said, "Let us not be too hasty, Mr. Benjamin."

"Sir, it is in my power only to give advice. It is not possible for me to reject the proposition. My advice I have given. The rejection—if such eventuates—is up to you."

Davis nodded. He turned to the Frenchman. "Does the Emperor look with favor upon the selling of Confederate bonds in France?"

"Indeed, sir. He and Mr. Slidell have talked to Baron Erlanger regarding the issue and the Emperor is most enthusiastic. I believe he would resent a rejection of the—"

Judah jumped to his feet. "President Davis has confessed his innocence of business and business methods, sir. I take it as cheap and underhanded of you to exploit with lies and misrepresentations the possible outcome of our failure to transact this—"

The Frenchman said, "Do you think you can float the loan in England?"

"No. Nor in Russia or Spain but—"

Davis said, "Gentlemen, I care little for the turn this conversation has taken. Let us talk business coolly. Personally, I will be candid. I understand only that the treasury is very lean and that no one but Baron Erlanger is willing to extend a helping hand."

Judah said, "A helping hand, sir? You are mistaken unless the hand of a pickpocket is in that category."

Davis did not reply. Deep concern lined his face. It was obvious that he feared the Frenchman would depart hurt and humiliated. Judah sighed. Bargaining with the man from Erlanger's was going to be difficult with Davis refereeing the contest.

"Now if Erlanger would take profits only above eighty instead of seventy," Judah murmured.

"Eighty!" screamed the Frenchman. "We are not in business to give charity, sir. Perhaps we could talk about seventy-two."

"I will not talk about seventy-two and I will not talk about eight per cent interest."

For an hour they argued, then adjourned for lunch. In the afternoon the bargaining began again with Davis and Memminger as nervous spectators.

It was four o'clock when the Frenchman said he would agree to profits above seventy-seven per cent and a seven per cent interest.

He is beginning to make sense at last. He will settle for something that is not utterly shameful, something that has some aspects of a bona fide loan.

"Fair enough," Davis said suddenly. "I like that. Gentlemen, you have finally arrived at something equitable to all parties. I salute you both." He clapped Judah on the back. "A splendid fight for the Confederacy, Mr. Benjamin." He turned smiling to Memminger. "You are again in business, sir."

Judah closed his eyes and sat rigidly at the table. Another hour and he would have had a deal that was not a complete rout for the Confederate government. When he opened his eyes the Frenchman was grinning at him, trying hard not to burst into loud, derisive laughter.

Davis was speaking of Slidell now, how so much of the credit was due him for having begun the negotiations, how he personally would write and commend him on his interest in matters that did not really fall within his province.

The man from Erlanger's nodded and glanced sidewise at Judah. "I shall report everything to Mr. Slidell." He reached across the table and patted Judah's shoulder. "He will appreciate the details," he said, and now roared with laughter.

The first letter that Judah received from Slidell that concerned the Erlanger loan made no actual mention of the loan at all. The letter dealt with many things that were of interest to the State Department, then:

> *Old friend, I must use this paragraph for personal news. I have lived long enough to realize every father's dream. I have seen my elder daughter married to a fine man. On Wednesday last my darling daughter Mathilde walked down the aisle and took for her husband the oldest son of Baron Erlanger. It is a wonderful family, as rich in virtue as in worldly possessions, and of course one day she will be the Baroness Erlanger which, I may add, means nothing to her as it was a true love match.*

Judah replied immediately. He wrote:

> *Slidell, you old bastard, years and years ago I told you that you made me feel like a maiden whom you were pursuing. I will tell you now in language more genteel than you will understand that I still feel like that maiden—after she has been caught.*

It looked very peculiar in code.

> *Beloved:*
>
> *We are well but our lives are not exciting so there is really little to say of them. Ink would only be wasted on my small day-to-day adventures with friends and tradespeople. I realize that of course Ninette's activities should fill a letter. I wish I could cover pages with charming stories of her beaux and her popularity but both are nonexistent. Alas, there is not a suitor in sight. And still it must be said that she is not an unattractive girl. No beauty perhaps but still well-featured. Her skin is lovely and her eyes are just like yours. She is serious-minded to a fault, which is probably the real difficulty. She reads continually but it is never a love story. As a matter of fact love seems revolting to her, if you can believe it. I would think I*

had raised a candidate for the nunnery but her approach to religion is intellectual rather than emotional.

The wedding of young Mathilde was not reported in your newspapers so I will tell you that it was—according to our papers—breath-taking. A fortune was spent on it and Slidell is getting ready to toss another fortune to the florists, the dressmakers, the wine merchants, the jewelers, etc., because Rosina is marrying the Comte de Saint-Romain next month. As I told you once, Slidell never found any Americans he thought worthy of his golden virgins. He did better over here. He and Mathilde Sr. are truly having a time rushing between Paris, St. Cloud, Vichy, and Biarritz keeping Eugénie and Louis Napoleon amused. I wonder if Slidell really came to serve the Confederacy.

I did not write even a word of condolence to Mathilde when I learned that her sister Caroline had died. It would have looked as though I were trying to re-establish an acquaintance with her. God knows I want no such thing. I am sorry for General Beauregard. If you see him present my sympathies. His heart must be broken, for, from all I have heard, I do think he loved Caroline. And to think of New Orleans being in Yankee hands and him unable to enter there to be at her side when death came—it is tragic. Poor General. Poor Caroline. If you were not near me as I lay dying, Judah, I would not be able to face death with resignation. I would cry out and fight against it.

It was a dreadful, depressing thought. The time since he had seen Natalie could be reckoned now in years. He had been in Paris the summer of 1860. Now it was spring of '63. He thought of the song the soldiers sang so mournfully and ceaselessly. The popular song of the day that was responsible for more than half the desertions.

> The years creep slowly by, Lorena
> The snow is on the grass again
> The sun's low down the sky, Lorena
> The frost gleams where the flowers have been
> But the heart throbs on as warmly now
> As when the summer days were nigh. . . .

He looked at the portrait of Natalie and knew how the soldiers felt when they sang "Lorena." No wonder they deserted. "If you were not near me as I lay dying—" Who could guess when the war might end? Perhaps never again was he to see Natalie, never again to hold her closely to his heart. Beauregard had not known when he left Caroline that she would die alone.

Sitting there in the library before the portrait of Natalie he knew an overwhelming misery. Without help he could not face the lonely, frightening future. Beauregard had not known—

And after a time Judah went out of his house and walked the few squares to Beth Ahabah and stood in the dimness of the synagogue. His eyes sought the east wall where traditionally, re-assuringly the Ark, containing the precious scrolls, would rest. It was there, the Ark, a promise and a deliverance. And in the quiet he spoke to his God.

I have not rejected Natalie. I will never reject her, for I love her more than I love my soul. And perhaps if I have not come to apologize for loving her I have no business here at all, but I have come. I have come because my heart is heavy and I am a man who has never made a confidant of any and it is to You that I must speak. I ask You to consider my sins. If they have been very great, forget me, forget my prayers. But if I have been deserving of one blessing, let it be that I shall again feel Natalie's hand in mine and see her smile.

He became conscious that he was not alone, that a man had materialized in the dimness and was standing only an arm's length away. He faced him and saw that it was Beth Ahabah's rabbi. A man with a stern face and a touch of irony in his cultivated voice.

"It is, I believe, our Secretary of State."

"It is, sir."

"I have prayed for you."

"I have come."

"You are in need of guidance and strength?"

"Is not every man?"

The rabbi said, "These are grave times for the Confederacy."

"I did not come here to plead a case for the Confederacy. In God's house I ask for no victories on the battlefield. Both armies march certain that God marches with them and only time will show who was right."

The rabbi sighed. "We should be proud of you, Mr. Secretary, but you have not let us be proud. You have not joined us and yet in a way you are ours." The rabbi had clear gray eyes. They went to the Ark and he said, "All who worship here must fight for you, sir, against the dreadful attacks that are made upon you. Yet we are denied the pride of claiming you belong to Beth Ahabah."

Judah said, "I can never be recognized as a member of any congregation. When I die there cannot even be an *escaba* made for me."

The rabbi smiled faintly. *"Escaba?* The Ashkanazim prayer for the dead is simply called *yizkor.* We can only hope it does as well as the *Ladino escaba."*

"It was not my intention to impress upon you that I was instructed at Charleston's Beth Elohim. Here within the walls of God's house I but reverted to words known and used as a child."

"A pity a man does not always think of his religion as he did in childhood."

"I have never ceased to think of mine with love and reverence, but I would not change any act of the past."

"Not any act?"

"Not any," Judah said.

"How long has your marriage endured, Mr. Secretary?" And the question was asked as though all along they had been speaking of Natalie.

"Thirty years."

The rabbi looked directly into Judah's eyes. "Have you been happy?"

"Can any man claim that his thirty years of marriage have produced only undiluted bliss?"

"Have you always loved the woman you took as wife?"

"I have always loved her."

"Have you been faithful to her?"

"I have always been faithful."

The rabbi's dark, stern face softened. He said, "It is only the ancients who could weep for you, sir. A modern clergyman finds wonderment and encouragement at meeting a man who, within this sacred house, can say that he has been faithful for thirty years."

"It was not difficult. I told you that I love her."

"A pity that she is not of our faith. I will pray for you, sir. I will pray that when death comes you will know neither fear nor sorrow but will be reconciled to lying excommunicant from —from—you will pardon me, I trust, for not knowing the Sephardic word for consecrated soil."

Judah said, "I came here to pray that when the war ends I may find my wife safe and well."

"I will pray for that, too, Mr. Secretary. My prayers are that every man engaged in this fierce struggle will be reunited with his loved ones. But I interrupted your meditations. I will leave you to yourself."

Silently he moved away and Judah stood alone once more in Beth Ahabah thinking that it had been a mistake to come. A synagogue was not an office which one visited for an interview with God. God had no office. If He wished to listen to one's prayers He would listen as well in a library. And the rabbi had at first thought he had come to be restored to good standing, to atone for his marriage, to do penance for it.

No, I should not have come.

And yet when he left the synagogue and walked slowly home, down the tree-lined streets, he found that his heart was no longer heavy, his thoughts suddenly free of fear and foreboding.

It occurred to Judah that women were frightfully maligned. Suppose when gathered together they did chatter like monkeys. Were men different? Here was the cabinet of the Confederate States of America seated around this table. Did they sit in solemn, thoughtful silence awaiting the President? They did not. Judah had brought a sheaf of notes gathered at his conference with Mercier, the French Ambassador to the United States. Mercier had been permitted to pass through the lines for a brief meeting, and his remarks and comments Judah thought worthy of study. But the running conversation here at the table made it almost impossible to recall or associate the atmosphere of the meeting with the notes before him.

Memminger and Mallory were having one of their arguments. Mallory, having discovered long ago that Memminger could be tormented into a fury, delighted in baiting him.

"Well, I wouldn't have mentioned it, Mr. Memminger, had it not been for the bread riot," Mallory was saying.

"Bread riot!" Mallory had as usual found a sore point and Memminger was obligingly responding to the goad. "You don't mean bread riot. You mean Yankee-inspired demonstration. Those were not decent Richmond housewives. They were vicious women in the pay of the enemy."

"Oh, I don't think so," Mallory said. "With bread at a dollar and a half a loaf I don't see the necessity for the enemy paying them to riot."

"You don't? Then tell me this: if they were decent, law-abiding women who were suffering hunger why did they march down Cary Street breaking the shop windows of merchants who sell no foodstuffs?"

"They wanted to call your attention to their plight. It's a hardship, you know, to have Confederate dollars rated at thirty to one."

Reagan said, "Mallory, for God's sake, don't tell Memminger that."

"Why? Doesn't he know it?" Mallory asked innocently.

Memminger said, "Of course I know it. In time the depreciation of the Confederate dollar will be arrested. I am doing everything."

"You're doing too much. That damn practice of controlling prices is starving us to death. The farmers are selling more produce to the speculators than they are to the legitimate markets."

Memminger spat contemptuously in the general direction of the cuspidor. "Mr. Mallory, would you appreciate my ideas on how to run the navy?"

"Hell, yes. Have you got any real good ones?"

"I have. Look to your own speculators. What are your blockade runners but speculators? Do they bring in anything that can be sold for sane prices or anything that will help win the war? No, they carry Paris bonnets and jeweled slippers and fine wines and—"

Mallory said, "Sure, there are cases of that, but usually the blockade runners bring—"

Reagan said, "They bring satin and perfume and kid gloves. We all know that, Mallory. Every speculator's daughter and

wife, every whore, every newly rich hag has Paris clothes while
the boys in the hospitals need medicine that nobody brings in.
You get no five hundred per cent profit on medicine." He turned
to Seddon, the mild little aristocrat who rarely said a word. "Remember when I told you—" He paused and looked suddenly perplexed, staring at Seddon as though he had never seen him before. "No, it wasn't you I told. It was Randolph when he had
your department."

There was a brief silence at the table during which everybody
looked at Seddon, remembering that he was the fourth secretary
of war. Seddon, conscious of the eyes upon him, felt that it must
be his turn to say something. He said, "I feel very optimistic
about our economy. I know that prices can be regulated and
finances restored to normal. However—" he sighed—"the tragic
blow we have suffered that can never be repaired is what weighs
so heavily upon me now."

"Yes, yes, indeed," Memminger said.

Watts shook his head. " 'In the midst of life we are in death.'
Just a week ago today we all believed him on the way to sure
recovery." He chewed reflectively. "I never witnessed such a
funeral. It was magnificent."

Reagan wrinkled his nose. "It was too magnificent," he said.
"Too many black plumes for so humble a man as Jackson. He
wouldn't have wanted all that show. You know how modest he
was."

Seddon's eyes brimmed with tears. "A simple prayer would
have been all he would have wanted. I often think that—"

Mallory said, "Jackson isn't the only general we lost this
month! What about Earl Van Dorn, Seddon?"

"Horrible," Seddon said. "Horrible."

"Oh, I don't know." Watts shifted his quid. "He got what
was to be expected."

"You are a cool one, Watts," Mallory remarked. "Do you mean
a man must expect to be murdered whenever he goes to bed
with somebody else's wife? God help the Confederacy if—"

Reagan said, "I believe Van Dorn was guilty of the affair and
that the husband had every right to murder him, but I feel sorry
for Van Dorn just the same."

Memminger was shocked. "How can you be sorry for him? Aren't you sorry for the poor husband driven mad by—"

Mallory said, "Remember when Dan Sickles murdered Barton Key? That was really a scandal."

"What happend to Sickles?" Reagan asked.

"He was acquitted. He's a brigadier general in the Union army right now. Forgave his wife, took her back—"

Memminger gasped. "And they are happy together?"

"Not very. Teresa Sickles is quite insane, I hear, and lives almost completely on morphine."

Memminger seemed satisfied.

"Personally," Mallory said, "I think if there's any shooting to be done, the wives ought to get it instead of the lovers. I don't think Barton Key raped Teresa and I don't think Van Dorn—"

Seddon said, "Mr. Mallory, really! This conversation has become—"

He broke off, rising to his feet with the others as the door to the cabinet room opened and Davis came in. Judah noticed at once that Davis was in a testy mood. The twitching facial muscle, the pallor that advertised one of Davis's smashing headaches. He greeted no one but launched immediately into the business of the day.

"If there is anything you had planned to present at this meeting forget about it. I have called you here for a particular and very important reason and I will be deeply annoyed at the introduction of any extraneous considerations."

Everyone was quiet. Judah looking around the table saw a flicker of amusement in Mallory's eyes. He knew the reason for that. Mallory had said that Davis often reminded him of a cranky schoolteacher he had known at Key West. "So help me God, Benjamin, I won't be surprised if some day Davis takes to whacking us with a ruler."

"As you undoubtedly know, General Lee is in Richmond," Davis continued. "He spent the entire morning with me and we discussed matters of great moment. I have prevailed upon him to remain and present these matters to you. He plans to march his army into enemy territory. Briefly, that is the issue. Naturally you may ask questions of General Lee. Before he joins us are there any quick questions that come to your mind that you would like to ask of me?"

Judah stared down at the pages of the Mercier interview. He had asked his questions of Davis two hours earlier and the answers had raised only dissatisfaction within him. Mercier, the French Ambassador, had made it plain that he would be deeply impressed by the Confederacy's ability to hold her own territory. That, after all, was the proper function of a nation.

Reagan said, "Mr. President, I have a question."

Davis smiled icily. "Yes, Mr. Postmaster General?" And the use of Reagan's official title indicated that he thought it rather preposterous of Reagan to have a question.

"Why is General Lee planning to invade the North?"

"That is not a quick question, sir."

"But," Reagan persisted, "when General Johnston had Lee's command he never—"

Davis's face twitched in sudden spasm. "May I point out to you that General Johnston is now operating in the west? We are only concerned at this time with the counsel of General Lee. Are there any more questions?" Nobody said a word and Davis hit sharply upon the small bell on the table before him. Immediately Jules, looking ridiculously fashionable in his clerk's alpaca coat, popped into the room.

Judah smiled to himself. He never grew accustomed to watching Jules play his role of war clerk. Frequently he overplayed. Judah often thought he aped too completely the innocence and awe of the wide-eyed boys who, at their first glimpse of the President, sometimes trembled in nervous excitement.

"Ask General Lee to have the kindness to step into this room, Mr. St. Martin."

Every eye was now fastened on the door through which Lee would enter. Curious the effect he had upon men. Lee, the Virginian's Virginian. Judah glanced down at the map Davis had spread out on the table but his eyes soon returned to the door.

I do not believe in magic or invincibility. I do not even believe very much in Virginians and I know Robert E. Lee reasonably well by now, but I will be watching when he steps into this room.

The general moved with a silent, masculine grace that was the natural product of his ancestry and training, his physique and self-discipline. He wore full-dress uniform today with sword and yellow sash. To look upon him was to see physical perfection, and no one lived who would at any time be uncertain as to whether or not he had ever met Robert E. Lee.

The general greeted the President and the others and took the chair that had been provided for him at the table.

Davis said, "I see no reason for wasting your valuable time, General. I have already informed the cabinet of the basic issue. Let us proceed."

"Very well, Mr. President. I would like to begin by saying that it has long been my belief that the best defense for Richmond is to keep the enemy concerned as to the safety of his own country. To give battle in Virginia certainly puts a burden upon our people and—"

Lee paused and frowned as the office, the street, and seemingly the city suddenly were filled with a fearful clanging of every massive church bell in Richmond. Davis leaped to his feet and threw open the door.

"What is that infernal din?" he shouted.

Jules shouted back at him. "We are sending word to discontinue it."

The voice of the great bell closest to the building faded first and as the ringing at more distant points showed signs of dying Seddon beckoned to Jules.

"Tell them to be quiet till the cabinet meeting adjourns."

Davis came back to the table.

"What was that racket about?" he demanded.

Seddon looked uncomfortable. "We are testing the bells for volume and to acquaint the war clerks with the sound of them. They are to assemble for the defense of the city in case they are ever needed. The bells are to be the signal."

Lee smiled. "I trust nothing personal was intended. It will be a sorry day when I am dependent upon war clerks to hold Richmond. How many of them are there?"

"More than a hundred in my department," Seddon said. "The entire clerks' battalion would number around seven hundred, I imagine. Of course in case of—"

Davis said, "General Lee, before the clanging began you were speaking of something very important."

"Yes. Well, my goal, as you know, Mr. President, is Pennsylvania. I would cross the Potomac and move at once into—"

Reagan said, "General Lee, I—"

Davis raised his hand to silence him.

Lee graciously waited, indicating that he would accept a question or comment from Reagan, but Reagan was for the moment crushed. Lee continued, "The enemy would thus be drawn from Virginia and I could feed my men upon Pennsylvania provisions. Need I mention that my men are hungry?"

Watts shook his head. "It is a shock to hear it from you and to know that it is true."

Lee's mouth tightened and his eyes burned resentfully. "It is true. They are also badly clothed and many are without shoes. I rely on Pennsylvania to reclothe my men, to put shoes upon their feet and flesh upon their bones. I would also like to recruit some sleek Pennsylvania mounts for the cavalry."

Davis nodded and turned to Judah. "Are you disturbed by anything General Lee has mentioned?"

"I am disturbed by what General Lee has not mentioned. I am thinking of Vicksburg."

You know I am disturbed. I told you so this morning. Do you not know me well even yet? Did you think I would forget Vicksburg because the general wears a yellow sash? Did you think I would be convinced because I hear the proposition from the lips of the Virginian's Virginian?

Lee said, "Mr. Secretary, I am thinking of Vicksburg, too. I am thinking that our advance into the North might alarm the Federals sufficiently to withdraw from Vicksburg and in that way raise the siege."

"You see, General," Davis said, "Mr. Benjamin and I have discussed sending troops to Vicksburg."

Seddon looked surprised and Judah saw the expression in Lee's eyes as they rested wonderingly upon a secretary of war who was obviously excluded from discussions of troop movements.

Davis said, "General Lee, Mr. Benjamin thinks the Army of Northern Virginia could save Vicksburg for us."

Lee nodded. "It is a possibility, but who guards Virginia meanwhile? In a choice between saving Vicksburg and saving Richmond surely—"

Reagan could no longer hold his silence. "My feelings then⊤ if you don't want to save Vicksburg—"

Davis scowled. "Reword your thought, Mr. Postmaster General. Certainly we *want* to save Vicksburg."

Reagan sighed elaborately. "Well, if you can't see your way clear to saving Vicksburg let General Lee stay here and guard Virginia. Why should we invade the North? I thought we just wanted to establish a nation down here and be let alone."

Lee stared sadly at Reagan. "The truth is I have no choice, sir. I must have provisions."

Reagan set his jaw stubbornly. "We have plenty of food in the Confederacy. It is only a matter of distributing it properly." He tossed a small, defiant glance at Davis, aware that he was criticizing Commissary General Northrup, the President's West Point classmate and friend. "I think the army ought to be used to keep the Yankees out—not to go around acting like Yankee brutes themselves."

Lee's voice was freezingly polite. "I trust, sir, the behavior of my army on enemy soil will erase such a picture from your mind."

"Well, you're going up there to take their food, their horses— that is if they will let you. General Lee, you're going to have a fight on your hands."

Lee did not laugh with the others. He said, "It is a very likely possibility."

Davis's mind came back to the room. It was apparent that it had been in Pennsylvania. "Our vast army on Northern ground," he said, "would certainly be a powerful argument for our independence."

Lee studied the flag on the wall behind Davis. "I am relying on the quality of our army, not its vastness. There are never enough men, and conscription has not solved the problem."

Seddon said, "How can it? The states will not co-operate. Each governor satisfies himself as to how many men he will furnish."

Lee said, "Yes, that is why General Beauregard's idea appealed to me. If you remember, Mr. President, it was his thought to avoid national conscription entirely and to permit each state to handle the matter for itself." Lee looked directly at Davis as he spoke. "State pride would have been stimulated and we would have benefited from the natural healthy competition that would have flourished."

Seddon's dull eyes lighted briefly. "Why, that's a brilliant idea," he said.

Davis glared at him. "Mr. Seddon," he said, "prior to the Confederate Congressional Act of April, 1862, no American had ever been forced into the army, and nobody's 'brilliant' idea would render conscription one whit less repugnant to our people."

Lee gave his attention to his gloves, painstakingly laying one very smoothly and evenly upon the other. "While on the subject of General Beauregard," he said, "since he is now in South Carolina—"

"Since we were once more obliged to relieve him of a command," Davis said as though furnishing Lee with the proper words.

Lee was willing to compromise. "Since General Beauregard has recovered from his illness," he began again.

Davis threw himself impatiently to a new position in his chair. "I will let that pass, General, though it is obvious that Beauregard feigned illness. It was a theatrical trick aimed at causing the administration to seem heartless in ordering his removal."

Lee was silent for a moment. When he spoke he said, "If Beauregard can be spared from the defense of Charleston—"

"He can be spared, sir."

"I would—in opening the Pennsylvania campaign—be greatly assisted if Beauregard furnished a diversion southwest of Washington. He is deeply respected by the Federals. His mere presence would give magnitude even to a small demonstration."

"You will have your demonstration, General," Davis promised. "It will be Beauregard or someone else but you will have it." He glanced around the table giving each man one of his quick, cool smiles. "I guess that is all we can discuss now. I would appreciate it if each of you will immediately write me a note setting forth your thoughts on this matter. Now you are free to depart, gentlemen. Thank you. Mr. Secretary of State, please remain."

The others got to their feet. They filed past General Lee offering handclasps and earnest wishes. Their notes to Davis were still unwritten, their advice in almost every case still unheard, yet all wished Lee a great victory and a safe return. There was not one of them who did not know that the decision was made and that advice from the cabinet was valued at the same level as a word of counsel from Davis's houseboy.

When they were gone Davis turned to Lee. "I asked Mr. Benjamin to remain so that he might acquaint you with our progress in securing recognition from England to France."

Lee turned his attention to Judah. "Have you made progress, sir?"

Judah said, "By special arangement with the Federal Government, Mercier, the French Ambassador, visited me yesterday. You have had a string of dazzling triumphs, sir. I find foreign nations extremely cordial at the moment. Following defeats they have been rather less so."

Lee's handsome head rose proudly. "If there had remained any way in which I could be made to feel my responsibilities more deeply your words would have filled the need."

Judah fingered the pages of the Mercier memorandum. "We must prove we are a nation, General Lee. We must prove it with victories and with our ability to defend ourselves. I never fool myself regarding that which I can achieve for the Confederacy. My contribution can only be small. Our chance of success rides with you."

"I do not underestimate the power of diplomacy, Mr. Secretary."

"General Lee, the power of diplomacy works its most potent magic when supported by strength of arms. Diplomats are at their best when they are backed up by a formidable army. Yours is swiftly earning such a reputation and I believe that reputation would be clinched if you electrified the world by raising the siege of Vicksburg."

Lee turned to Davis. "Is it Vicksburg you value above Richmond, Mr. President?"

"If we lose Vicksburg we have completely halved the Confederacy," Davis said. "The Mississippi River is lost to us—and yet if we lose Richmond we have lost a precious symbol. It will sound a dreary note in the homes of the people and in the councils of foreign nations."

Judah looked from one to the other. These were military men, trained to judge coolly, to see clearly. But so was Huger and he had advised Davis poorly on the matter of Roanoke Island. Still, there was something almost absurd in the idea of a lawyer pressing his own civilian notions against the judgment of professional soldiers.

"Let me not color your thoughts, I beg of you," he said. "I think too much in terms of what affects the State Department. You have delayed your departure, General, to hear news of progress in statecraft. There is little progress beyond Mercier's visit and the fact that I am now tempting his emperor with one hundred thousand bales of cotton."

Lee shook his head. "I had hoped that rulers of great nations were immune to temptation. Will he not feel his integrity insulted? Isn't there a risk involved in seeking to deal with him in that manner?"

"Risk indeed with Louis Napoleon, General. There is a risk he will take our cotton and pretend he never saw us before. In the matter of England now—"

"England! Surely you do not dare offer England a purely materialistic—"

"Oh, no. England is very virtuous. She promises nothing and lives up to her word. Her honesty of purpose delights you, I see, General. Ah, well, you may rest assured she is incorruptible. She is even extremely rude to our envoy, I may add."

Lee said, "I pray God our armies will win for the Confederacy everything her people need to be free and at peace. As for diplomacy, I know nothing of its devious ways. Mr. President, you have further need of me?"

"I can think of no unselfish reason for detaining you. Will you walk as far as my office with me, General? Good night, Mr. Benjamin."

"Good night, Mr. President. Good night, General."

"Good night, Mr. Secretary."

Judah stared out at the spring dusk that was closing in on Richmond. Out there beyond the spires and hills lay the battlefields from which Lee had come triumphant and proud. The

Virginia battlefields on which Southern men had died. The
Texans, the Georgians, the Carolinians. Boys who had asked
no questions, for they had had none to ask. They believed it
was all as simple as they saw it and there was nothing to question,
nothing to doubt, nothing to distrust.

He looked about the room. The cabinet room. Here it was
decided, the fate of those boys. Suppose one of them had listened.
Suppose at random a big Texan or a white-gloved Louisianian
or one of those mean-faced little gutter rats of the Tigers had
been chosen for a place at the table. And, by God, wouldn't it be
a good idea? Wouldn't it be fair if one of them could say, "Wait
a minute, fellows, let me think that over."

A page of the Mercier notes fluttered to the floor. He bent to
retrieve it and when he straightened Lee was standing in the
doorway.

"Mr. Secretary, I hope you will forgive my returning and not
regard it as an intrusion. I wished to speak to you alone and thus
spare the President further worry."

"Please proceed, General."

Lee advanced into the room. The shadows were thickening and
in the dimness he stood so arresting and impressive that he
seemed not human but a marble figure one might admire in
a park.

"I am disturbed, Mr. Secretary, that I have not your support
for the Pennsylvania campaign."

"You will have the President's."

"I respectfully request to know why I have not yours."

"Respectfully request nothing from me, General Lee. I am
not in a mood worthy of such elegant address."

"Are you asking me to leave, sir?"

"I am asking you to rest the matter of the Pennsylvania campaign. I am not a military man. Discussion of it—between you
and me—can lead to no conclusion of value."

"And yet I ask the reasons why—"

"I doubt that you would understand my reasons."

"You judge me inadequate for the undertaking?"

"I would judge Napoleon Bonaparte inadequate. No, no, I
take that back. It is an evasion." He peered through the blue
shadows of the cabinet room at General Lee. "The truth is that

there is no question involved of one general performing more
brilliantly than another. There is only you and the Pennslvania
campaign inseparably linked. No other general, in my opinion,
would consider the invasion. It is a compulsion of yours and
yours alone."

"I do not understand."

"I warned you that you would not."

Lee said, "I fear that you are unable to clarify your remarks
because you are attempting to spare my feelings. Please feel
free to speak."

"Very well, General. I will speak. I will quote, as a matter of
fact. I will quote Robert E. Lee. 'Trusting in Almighty God,
an approving conscience and the aid of my fellow citizens, I
dedicate myself to the service of my native state in whose behalf
alone will I ever again draw my sword.' Did you not say those
words?"

"I did indeed."

"And you meant them. By God, you meant them, General.
You have never championed a plan that was not likely to serve
Virginia. You have never breathed a warning that did not speak
her name. President Davis values your military judgment above
that of any man alive, yet you never told him that General
Pemberton was not competent for the command given him at
Vicksburg. You have not said that General Bragg is a tragic
failure in the field. Why have you never—"

"I am the commander of the Army of Northern Virginia.
Only that. It is not my place to criticize other officers."

"It is your place by reason of the influence you exert upon the
President. It is indeed well-mannered of you to refrain from
disparaging brother officers but it is a piece of courtliness the
Confederacy cannot afford. However, General, I have seen no
evidence that the Confederacy's needs move you very deeply.
You are a Virginian, not a Confederate."

"And *you* are a Confederate, Mr. Secretary? Permit me to say
that such is not generally believed. The people think of you as
a man who is as much at home in New York as in New Orleans,
as comfortable in Paris or Washington as in Charleston or
Richmond."

The lamplighter had passed and fastened a fitful, yellow flame outside the window. The glow of it played upon Lee's face and there was a curious sense of unreality about him as he stood there in the flickering light.

"The people think of me as a traitorous Jew, General Lee. I will say for you the thing you are too well-bred and too kind to say."

"Sir, I am certain that—"

"You need consider my feelings no more than I have considered yours. Here in the gathering darkness where we can scarcely see each other the talk can be frank. Such a moment will never come again. Let us make the most of it. Let us assume, for instance, that you sustain crushing defeat on Northern soil. Have you realized that it will mean a twin debacle from which we might not recover?"

"Naturally I have considered the possibility of defeat."

"I spoke of *twin* defeat. Once again you are not thinking of Vicksburg. General, back in the days before you and Jackson fought the battles around Richmond there was consideration of sacrificing this city. I remember that the suggestion made you weep."

"It did. I am not ashamed."

"Of course not. Why should you be? I only ask did you weep for New Orleans or Nashville? No, I am certain that you did not, and that is rather unfortunate because if you can weep only for Virginia, one day there will be only Virginia for which to weep."

"I do not follow you, sir."

"It is not a complicated route. You can follow me. If Virginia is protected at the expense of the rest of the country all around her, there will be loss, despair, and surrender. The enemy will creep closer and closer and at last we will stand on a piece of ground that has become a lonely, threatened fortress."

"I go north to guarantee the safety of that fortress."

Judah nodded. "Of course you do, General. And I know that you do it believing it is all there is to do. No man may escape from the way he is and the way he thinks. And duty and right, as you see it, will always serve Virginia. And yet I must warn you—you cannot draw a sword for Virginia. Before it is too late you must come to know that the sword is useless unless it is drawn for places you have never been and for people you have never seen. General, you must draw your sword for the protection of people who are not Virginians, and when you have done so you will have at last guaranteed Virginia's safety. Only that way can you do it. Only that way."

The room was dark now save for the flickering, yellow light on the face of General Lee. Judah looking at him saw no anger in the eyes, no sullenness or resentment.

There is not another general in the Confederacy who would have taken what he has taken from me. By now any other would have resigned, but he does not have to prove anything. He is not touchy or sensitive about his honor. He has no need to advertise it, for it is recognized and accepted as completely as the morning sun. He has no doubt of it, nor has any other living person. Only, dear God, why does the greatest soldier in the Confederacy have to be R. E. Lee, the Virginian's Virginian?

Judah sat down, suddenly weary, suddenly spent. "I want to thank you, General," he said, "for listening to so much that must have been unpleasant."

Lee said, "Mr. Secretary, it was I who urged you to speak."

"It was admirable of you. It was even more admirable that you did not urge me to cease speaking."

"I am prepared to listen if there is more you wish to say."

"There is no more."

"Then I shall leave you, Mr. Secretary."

"God go with you, General."

And Judah sat alone and thought of Vicksburg. He thought of the people there who trusted poor Pemberton. What if Lee of Virginia had been born in Arkansas? Or Alabama?

Tell me, God. What of that? Would it have helped? Or am I only the old familiar figure—the civilian who can always tell the generals what they ought to do?

And the lads who had been entrusted with the test of the bells had evidently been alerted to watch for Lee's departure. Now the din began again. Loud, clear, insistently, the bells rang through Richmond. Judah sat tensely with the terrible, deafening clangor washing over him in nerve-racking oceans of noise. The yellow lamppost light fell palely upon the place where Lee had stood. Lee was gone. He was walking down Main Street and every step he took brought him closer to Pennsylvania. All his life every street he had ever trod had been the road to Pennsylvania.

And the bells continued to ring and to ask, "Can you hear me, war clerks? In case of emergency, can you hear me?"

And Judah thought that it was well that the bells should be carefully tested.

From the window of his office Judah saw a man carrying a small cedar tree. A child somewhere in the city was going to have a Christmas celebration but doubtless the tree would have to be the beginning and the end of the festivities. With candy at eight dollars a pound and a small cake selling for ten dollars what could one expect of a father whose shoes were ragged? Judah's eyes followed the man out of sight. Poor fellow, at his door he would have to find a way to cast off his dejection. He would have to straighten his shoulders, summon a light of triumph to his eyes, and walk into the house with the air of one who has never seen a happier holiday season. Perhaps he would even have to shout "Merry Christmas" to an anxious wife. Judah turned wearily from the window.

There were letters on his desk. Quite a few of them, though none looked interesting. One from Charleston. He recognized the handwriting of his sister Hannah. What were the other letters? Nothing of importance. Perhaps the day was gone when letters of importance would come to his desk. Now his mail was mostly filled with suggestions and requests from citizens. He realized his secretary spared him the sight of letters that were nothing but abuse.

The time was past for those communications from Mason and Slidell that in other days had brought encouragement. Long ago—had it been only September?—he had written his last coded instruction to Mason.

> *The British Government, my dear Mason, has no intention of receiving you, and your continued residence in London will be neither conducive to the interest nor consistent with the dignity of the Confederacy.*

There had been no need to inform Slidell that hope had vanished. Slidell's letter had arrived in August with the news that Louis Napoleon could no longer find time to bid him even a swift good morning.

Benjamin, the United States Ambassador in Paris is today even controlling the Emperor's choice of friends. I have found it very difficult to keep my temper amidst all this double-dealing. This is a rascally world and it is most hard to say who can be trusted.

Judah thought the letter should have been framed. Slidell's observation that deception was sometimes practiced on this sinful earth was amusing enough to brighten a dreary day. However, it was not cheering to remember that after July, Mr. Dayton, of the United States Embassy, had been placed in the position where he could fearlessly challenge Louis Napoleon to make a choice between friendship with himself or with Slidell. Judah sighed and turned to the letter from Hannah.

Dear brother Judah:

Though I write with love and pride in my heart this is not a family letter. A group of Charleston people have approached me with a request that I write and inform you how they and I feel regarding something that happened here last month. We do not know whether you will carry our complaint to President Davis or not. We do not even know whether it would be proper for you to do so, but in any case it was decided that I should tell you of something that angered the citizenry of Charleston.

Last month when Mr. Davis came here I was not among the crowd who went to the depot to greet him and cheer him but some of my friends were there. They were infuriated to see that General Beauregard, who received him, was given a brief military salute but no handshake, no smile, and no words from Davis.

In case you do not realize it, Judah, General Beauregard is Charleston's hero. The only reason Charleston is not oppressed by conquerors like his own New Orleans is because Beauregard has magnificently defended our city against awful odds.

Now this I witnessed myself: President Davis addressed us from the steps of City Hall. He mentioned everybody's achievements and triumphs—except Beauregard's. Our well-loved general stood right at Davis's elbow and never once was he mentioned or recognized. Not one word was spoken of the gallant

*defense of Charleston! We were resentful enough to hoot or hiss
but we controlled ourselves while the President praised every
general whose name entered his mind—except Beauregard. It
was obviously a calculated insult and we resent it! We resent it
for this splendid man who has had nothing but illness, sorrow,
and bad treatment. Charleston stands while all Davis's favorite
generals lose battles and cities and the faith of the people. I
don't know if there is any sense in telling you all this, Judah,
but my friends and I felt the letter should be written.*

God bless you and guide you through these dark days.

Hannah

Judah tore the letter into small pieces and tossed it into the
wastebasket.

No, Hannah, there is no sense in telling me all this. I cannot
make the President believe that Beauregard deserves a smile, a
handshake, or a word of praise. I will write to you and I will tell
you that President Davis is devoted to all his generals. I will tell
you that he is incapable of an unkind word or deed though sometimes thoughtless due to his headaches and the terrible pressure of
work and responsibility. And by the way, Hannah, did you know
that General Beauregard hates me so intensely that he cannot
stomach the sight of me? Oh, yes, my name was on the order that
relieved him of his command after he had whipped the Federals at
Manassas.

Judah walked to the window again. Was it going to rain? It
looked threatening, but perhaps he could reach the Presidential
Mansion before the storm broke. Davis was ill again. Yesterday
the rumor had spread throughout the city that he was dead. Davis
was only suffering one of his attacks of dyspepsia, but somehow the
word had flown from office to factory to hearthside that Stephens
was now president.

Mallory had said, "Funny thing about it, Benjamin. Did you
notice that nobody was crying?"

Judah thought of Mallory's remark as he was admitted to the
mansion. Mallory was right. Nobody had cried. Perhaps it was
because they knew that Stephens, who rarely came to Richmond,
had only union in his heart and that with Stephens there would
be peace.

The butler led him to the family parlor on the east side of the house and he was surprised to find Varina there alone. She had decked the cheerful little room with evergreens and crosses and as he entered she turned from the work of hanging tinsel stars in the windows.

"Forgive me, Mr. Benjamin, for having you brought here. The President is resting on the sofa in his office and I thought—Mr. Benjamin, I had to see you."

"I am delighted, Mrs. Davis."

"Please sit down." She seated herself upon a tufted settee and he chose a chair opposite. "Sir, you are always so kind and understanding. I must ask you what I am to do."

"About what, dear lady?"

She turned from him in anguish, her eyes tormented, her mouth twisted in despair. "Everyone hates me so. How can I change it? What am I doing that is wrong?"

"Mrs. Davis, if you are seeking company in your misery, you have it. If you are seeking advice you have come to the wrong man. Had I the power to turn the public's hatred into love I would have done it long ago."

"Mr. Benjamin, if I ride out in a carriage I am an arrogant nobody trying to play the part of a queen. If I walk I am a coarse western woman lacking a First Lady's dignity. If I entertain I am insensitive to the suffering of the army. If I do not entertain I am shirking my duties. If I go to the hospitals I am only trying to make myself seem compassionate. If I do not go I am without pity for the wounded. Mr. Benjamin, what am I to do?"

He looked at the cardboard boxes she had set aside for further use. He saw that one box still holding a few shreds of tinsel had come from Germany via Bermuda. The blockade runners couldn't be expected to carry ugly, useful things when Christmas spirit ran high and tinsel stars would fetch a pretty profit.

"Mr. Davis told me that you, sir, fearing yourself an embarrassment to him, have offered to resign." She managed a small smile. "This course is not open to me. What then can I do?"

"There is nothing you can do. I learned long ago that there is no defense against cruel accusations. You must maintain utter silence, for anything you say is wrong."

"Mr. Benjamin, it is not vanity or any such frivolous thing that

makes me pray for public approval. It is only that a hostile attitude toward me indicates a lessening respect for the Confederacy.
It frightens me and I feel there is something I can do. I will do
anything. Anything at all."

He was touched by the girlishness of a gesture in which she
checked a tear with the back of her hand. A girlish gesture from
Varina Davis, the sunburned First Lady whose hair was turning
gray. She was asking not for advice but for sympathy. Who would
seek advice on the subject of popularity from him? Did she not
know that Richmond had rejected the President's order for a day
of fasting and prayer simply because it had been signed by Benjamin, the Jew?

"Mrs. Davis, when people are unhappy they need scapegoats.
They single out certain personalities as targets for their antagonism. It is hard to bear but it must be borne, for there is no escap-
ing it. When I come to live in a new city I always ask myself 'What
will happen here?' When I first saw Richmond I heard the cheers
of excited men and women but even then I knew the answer to my
question was not 'You will know nothing but happiness in this
place.' There was war, and war is terrible. People suffer, and when
they suffer their tempers grow short."

"But what have I done to them?"

"You have done nothing to them. They are hungry and despondent. They must grumble or die."

She turned away from him. "I cry myself to sleep at night," she
said.

Do you, Mrs. Davis? Try crying at a desk in the middle of the
afternoon. In some ways it is more satisfactory. It sends one to bed
cried out and ready for rest.

"Mr. Benjamin, in June I am going to have another baby. I feel
like screaming when I think of it. Where will the child be born?
Into what? What will I have to offer him? What is to become
of us?"

He reached for her hand. "Your baby will be born upstairs as
little William was," he said. "He will be born into the Confederacy. You will have love to offer him and I will say that no
woman in the world who now carries a child knows any more than
you know what June will bring to her and hers."

"That is true, of course, but I have such doubts, such worries."

"Do not worry. Remember this, I beg of you: Men assigned you the task of being First Lady but God selected you to mother that baby. So which, Mrs. Davis, should you regard as the greater responsibility?"

She looked at him and smiled. "A talk with you does much for me, sir. I suppose I am soothed by that beautiful voice of yours that melts all those who hear it. Or perhaps my heart is lightened by the amusing thought that probably no other Secretary of State has been confronted with the problems of a pregnant First Lady who pities herself." She rose from the settee and came toward him. The smile was still there but her eyes were wet as she brushed his cheek with a kiss. "Mr. Benjamin," she said, "I think you are wonderful."

"The impossible has happened," he said. "Benjamin is at a loss for words."

She was as different from Louisianians as though she had come from another planet. When she was pregnant she said so and even appeared in public after her figure was no longer lovely to the eye. But there was a special magic about women like Varina Davis. Anywhere in the world you could buy a clinging red mouth. Where did you go to buy a kiss that felt like the handclasp of a trusted friend?

Jules said, "I see that Grant is now in supreme command of all the armies of the United States. Who is this Grant, Brother?"

Judah stared at him. "Of course you are fooling. You must know who Grant is."

"Oh, I remember Forts Henry and Donelson and the more recent Vicksburg but *who* is he really?"

"A man from Ohio, Jules."

"Is he any good?"

Judah shook his head. "Of course not. He only wins battles."

"But that is good, isn't it?"

"I was attempting irony. Grant is good, my boy. Every general North or South has a book on Napoleon's tactics hidden among his belongings, but Grant just keeps hammering away, never stopping to read about Napoleon. As a matter of fact he probably can't read."

"But he must be able to read. He is a West Pointer."

"Irony again, Jules. But whether he reads or not the war will change now that we have Grant at our throats. He is a man who likes to play the game but he is also very keen on getting to the end of it and hearing the winner's name announced."

Jules nodded. "I know what you mean. There are those who say our General Hood is just like him."

"Who says that? Hood's mother?"

"Don't bark at me, Brother. I did not say it. 'Those' said it. Some other 'those-who-say' report that Hood has the heart of a lion and the brain of an ox. But definitely he is reputed to be the bravest Texan of all the brave Texans."

"Hood is a Kentuckian, Jules."

"So is President Davis but is he not the bravest Mississippian of all the brave Mississippians?"

"So stipulated."

"Do you know what J. B. Jones told me?"

"No."

"He told me that Mr. Davis always confuses courage with ability and that he thinks the main requirement for leadership is a loud voice with which a man can bellow, 'Come on, men. Charge!'"

"Don't believe anything that Jones says."

"Oh, I do not, Brother. I only use him as an instrument through which I keep you informed of sayings in the lowly circles."

"You would be amazed, Jules, at how little they differ from sayings in the more rarefied atmosphere."

The truth of his statement was proved that afternoon when Mallory raised Hood's name. They had driven out to the country to breathe some fresh spring air. It had been an idea of Mallory's.

"I know it will sound foolish, Benjamin, but I think a look at the countryside would be good for both of us. What do you say we do it Sunday?" He had grinned, feeling a little silly and yet anxious for the outing. "The wild flowers are in bloom and—Christ Almighty, Benjamin, we may never see them again."

Judah, to whom the loss of wild flowers would have been one of the lesser blows of a cruel Fate, had agreed to accompany Mallory. Now they drove slowly through the spring greenness, the horse dreamily enjoying the fragrant air, the men pleasantly conscious of the clean, colorful world around them.

"Beautiful, isn't it, Benjamin?"

"Beautiful indeed." Judah glanced sidewise at Mallory. How odd that Mallory needed wild flowers and the little green hills. Anyone would have placed Mallory's choice of relaxation in an entirely different category.

"There's nothing like it. When a man is depressed he needs to get back to the simple things. There's something about a day in the country that makes you feel young and new again. I am so sick of Richmond and Davis and war and defeat and—"

"In other words you are a citizen of the Confederacy, my friend. Everyone has such periods of hopelessness. They come and they go."

"Mine don't go. I'm concerned about a lot of things. One of them is Hood."

"Hood, Mallory? Why does he concern you? He is not an admiral."

"No, the son of a bitch is a general."

"And why is the general a son of a bitch?"

Mallory said, "I don't like him. All the time he was recovering from his latest wound in Richmond he was courting Davis, obviously playing up to him and—"

"Oh, I reject the notion that he was consciously angling for Davis's friendship."

"Listen, I heard him say, 'Take the field yourself, Mr. President, and I will follow you anywhere.' A man who says that to Davis isn't trying to get himself hated, you know."

Judah laughed. "Hood meant it. I'm sure he did. He's a thoroughly honest, openhearted young man, who would not know the first exercise in the art of deception. He admires Davis or he would not have spoken those words. Mallory, after all, it is not a crime to admire Davis."

Mallory said, "Conceding that Hood wasn't just laying it on, that he meant it, Benjamin, I'm scared. You know how Davis detests Joe Johnston."

"I have a vague idea."

"Well, now that Hood is with Johnston's army in Dalton, what happens if Johnston and Davis get squabbling again? You know as well as I do. Davis will relieve Johnston and give his command to Hood."

"Oh, no, Mallory. Hood is too young and inexperienced."

"Davis in a sudden, ugly mood, Benjamin, would give Johnston's command to your brother-in-law and, come to think of it, I would prefer Jules to Hood."

Judah said, "It is too nice a day to think of relieving Johnston. Mallory, you came to look at the wild flowers. Give them your full attention."

Mallory drove in silence for several minutes, holding the reins loosely in his hands, permitting the horse to amble at his own pace.

Judah fixed his eyes upon a small, white house in the distance. Who lived there? What was that family's heartache today? The loss of a son? The price of clothing? The lack of medicine?

"Benjamin, what am I going to do for shipping? I have no machine shops, no rolling mills, and no shipwrights."

Judah did not reply. He thought of the four cruisers and two ironclads that French shipyards had been building for the Confederacy. They were lost now to Mallory. Dayton of the United States had settled that.

"I am awfully downhearted about the situation, Benjamin. We're in trouble."

"There was never a moment when we were not. We were born into trouble. You knew that when you quit Washington. Why are you downhearted now?"

"Because I need shipping."

"You needed it then."

"But in those days foreign nations allowed their concerns to build for us. I got the *Florida* and the *Alabama*—" Remembering brought a sudden light of joy to Mallory's face. Judah, looking at him, thought that when Mallory was a very old man the memory of the *Florida* and the *Alabama* would make his faded blue eyes gleam as they gleamed now. "Benjamin, I never prayed for intervention. I never expected it, but if recognition had come, England and France would be building for us. With enough ships we could win. If I only had enough ships."

Judah said, "I'm glad we drove out here today, Mallory. It does a man good to get away for a while from his office and his worries."

"All right. All right. Wait till you come to me sometime with tears in your eyes. Do you know what I'll say? I'll say, 'Benjamin, remember the day we drove in the country and you refused to listen to my troubles?'"

"And I will say, 'Yes, Mallory, I remember it well. It was the day we drove for hours and hours and I thought you'd never open the God-damned picnic basket.'"

Mallory laughed. "I forgot it. Honest to God, I did. Are you hungry, Benjamin?"

"Hungry? I'm starved."

They ate their lunch and for the remainder of the soft spring day they talked of other times and other places. Mallory's mood lightened and as they drove back to the city he was singing the parody on "Maryland, My Maryland" that meant fight in any bar-room where a Marylander drank.

> *"We're southern folks in Baltimo'*
> *But to secede takes grit you know*
> *We'll stay here safe and brag and blow*
> *Maryland, my Maryland."*

On the lawn of Judah's house Jules awaited them with a sorrowful face. "Go to Mr. Davis," he said. "A dreadful thing has happened."

Burton Harrison met them at the door of the mansion. The young man's eyes were red, his voice choked. He lived with the Davises and the children were very dear to him.

"He fell from the north piazza down to the brick pavement. Poor little Joe. So gentle, so affectionate. Will you go to the drawing room, gentlemen? Mr. and Mrs. Davis will be strengthened by the knowledge that you have come to them in their sorrow."

General and Mrs. Chesnut were in the drawing room as well as Mrs. Barksdale and Mrs. Semmes. The ladies were weeping, and through the house could be heard the piercing wail of Catherine, the Irish nursemaid. All the windows in the house had been opened to the beautiful spring day and no one had remembered to close them. The curtains blew wildly, the gaslights flickered, and those who sat in the drawing room could hear overhead the constant tread of the President as he paced his chamber in an agony of grief.

The drawing room filled as others came to weep. Mr. Harrison saw that food was set out but no one touched it. The heavy tread upstairs never ceased as the hours passed.

Judah inquired for Varina. The doctor was with her, alarmed, of course, considering her condition, but she seemed to be bearing up more stoically than the President.

"He is simply out of his mind, Mr. Benjamin," Harrison said. "He is suffering horribly. If there was only something I could do."

Judah and Mrs. Chesnut stayed all through the night. In the early hours of the morning they were led upstairs. Mrs. Chesnut to Varina. Judah to Davis.

The President sat stunned and haggard on the edge of a chair. As Judah entered the room he raised his head and said, "Little Joe always prayed with me. He was the one who came running to me. He was like an angel and God has taken him to Heaven." He fell to his knees weeping stormily. "God, help me to bear it. Make it clear to me that he was never mine, but always Yours." He knelt there sobbing for a time, then suddenly turned to Judah. "Why did it have to happen? Is there any reason for such a thing? Why was Little Joe not spared to us? Tell me that. What have my wife and I done?"

"Sir, it is God's will. No man can know His purpose."

And when Little Joe lay in the drawing room surrounded by flowers Judah wept with Davis and on the other side of the white casket stood General Wise.

"My heart aches for you, Mr. President," he said. "I, too, lost a son." And he looked at Davis with pity and understanding.

Judah suddenly felt a weakness sweep over him, a sickening dizziness.

"I will pray that some day I will see the murderer of my son mourning for his flesh and blood as today I mourn for mine." Wise had spoken those terrible words on the day his son was buried. Judah looked at Little Joe. This baby, could he, too, be a casualty of Roanoke Island?

Of course not. How could a man of sense believe or even think — But Judah was shivering as he stood beside the white casket listening to Davis's dreadful sobs and seeing across from him a man who had been careless with his curses.

Beloved:

We are in splendid health. I read in the papers that the Con-federacy's health is not of the best and if this letter is captured I believe it will not matter. I suppose it is no secret from the United States that Grant makes life no easier for you. I also read that Varina's new baby is a girl. That must have disap-pointed her, for if a boy she could have imagined him a re-placement for Little Joe who fell from the piazza. Though I suppose he could not in any way be replaced, poor little fellow.

Last night I went to the opera. It was my first evening out since the death of my mother. In New Orleans I would not have been seen entertaining myself for at least a year, as you well know, but Paris is different. I did not even wear deep mourning here. Papa was hurt and shocked, but the customs of New Or-leans are not the customs of Paris. To return to the opera, I en-countered there none other than Orleanians. The famous, im-portant, dazzling, enchanting Mr. and Mrs. John Slidell. They greeted me as though they had been searching for me for years. My escort was a friend of a sort of relative of mine. He owns a few French newspapers and I think Slidell knew who he was be-fore introductions were made. In any case Slidell was cordial and talkative. He did not mention that he is no longer a bosom friend of the Emperor's, though everyone knows he is not. He said that he and Mathilde will remain in France for evermore.

He said, 'My Royal Street house is inhabited by Yankee of-ficers. I would not live in that house again any more than I would use a towel that a filthy animal had rolled on.'

When I mentioned his country place he said, 'We used that only for vacations. I could not live in the country even if they restored the property to me. Paris is our home now.'

Mathilde said, 'Besides, our grandchildren will be French and they will be here. Why should we live in Louisiana?'

They seemed very happy and lighthearted and not at all like people who are thinking of General Grant. I am thinking of him. In the dark of the night when everyone is asleep I am thinking of General Grant—

So am I, Natalie, my darling. I am thinking of General Sher-man, too. Have you ever heard of him, Natalie?

Sherman operating in Georgia against the army that had been Johnston's. It was Hood's army now. Johnston had been relieved, and the Yankee soldiers had cheered at the news that they now faced Hood instead of Johnston.

But Grant. One could not sneer at him because he had underestimated the Army of Northern Virginia. One could not laugh at him because he had expected to take Richmond with relative ease. One found no comfort in the fact that Lee had given him the bloodiest thrashing a modern general had ever sustained and that Grant had been forced to settle for a dismal siege instead of a swift and sparkling victory. There was no encouragement in any of this, for in the end Grant with more men, more food, and more arms would dictate the peace terms.

Memminger had resigned and Trenholm was now Secretary of the Treasury. In the attorney general's office Watts had been replaced by George Davis of North Carolina. Seddon was growing despondent and anxious to leave the War Department.

Mallory asked, "You quitting, Benjamin?"

"How can I? Who would move the pins on my war maps if I left my office? You quitting, Mallory?"

"I should say not. I've contacted an Indian who's going to build me a fleet of ironclad canoes. What do you do to kill time, Mr. Secretary of State?"

"Why, I play games."

The games had begun with the bribing of Northern newspapers. Nine hundred thousand dollars had been distributed in likely sections in the hope that editorial writers could sway the November vote away from Lincoln. That was the way the games had begun. Now they had become a mad romp of men in false mustaches and foolish disguises who had followed the scent of the nine hundred thousand dollars to Richmond. It was astonishing how many there were who had been loyal to the federal cause until the discovery that treason was a business.

Clement Clay had been sent to Canada to organize from there the Confederate sympathizers in the United States. Clay was a sincere man, a trusting man who had faith in every adventurer who could whistle "Dixie." They came through the lines to Richmond, to Judah's office, and told of melodramatic achievements and escapes. They hinted of friends in the North so powerful and important that their names could not be breathed. They promised extraordinary developments and they asked for money. Trenholm dealt out the gold and the mysterious figures moved out of Richmond to gallop down the main street of St. Albans, Vermont, or set a wastebasket aflame in a New York hotel or hold a meeting in a Brooklyn basement.

Meanwhile General Grant besieged the Petersburg line and Sherman threatened Atlanta. And Judah, who had once thought he had something to give the Confederacy, sat in his office and looked with deep melancholy upon a wan little man who had positive information that Lincoln would be defeated in November.

"You must hold out, Mr. Secretary, because I have my contacts and they have never failed me. McClellan will be elected and he will give the South its independence. So hold out. Remember I told you."

"Oh, I will remember."

The wan little man raised his finger significantly. "Now there is this possibility: Lincoln could win—"

"I'd thought of that."

"But if he does then the Southern sympathizers in the North— and there are many, Mr. Secretary—will rise up in wrath and demand the cessation of hostilities."

"That will be nice," Judah said.

"And I will tell you this, Mr. Secretary—"

"No, no, dear sir, tell me no more. I am already so full of joy at our bright prospects that I could bear no further revelations."

Atlanta fell. Lincoln was re-elected. Grant sat grimly waiting for Richmond to starve to death. Fighting around the city became so steady that no one remarked on the rattle of windowpanes and the sights and smells of battle.

Desertions increased, and Lee wrote to Seddon stating that the numerous reprieves to deserters were wrecking discipline and reducing the army alarmingly. Seddon handed the letter to Davis, who answered that when a deserter's sentence was reviewed and remitted it was not a proper subject for criticism by a military commander.

It was reported that Lee's face purpled as he read the President's note but he said nothing. He had General Grant to think about, Grant and the holding of the Petersburg line that was Richmond's only hope of survival.

And Richmond listened to cannonading southeast of the city, the people trembled, and flour was five hundred dollars a barrel. Sherman's army captured Savannah and turned north.

"Will nothing stop him, Brother?" Jules asked.

"Nothing."

"You cannot really believe that. Why, you have just renewed the lease on this house."

Judah said, "I know, but neither Grant nor Sherman signed it. Are you going out tonight, Jules?"

"You must be mad. The weather is not fit for man or beast."

"That never deterred you in the past."

"Perhaps I am tired. Everybody is tired, Brother, except you. How is it that you never get that worn and weary look that has become such a familiar part of the landscape? What sustains you?"

"That is easy to answer, Jules. I am sustained by the delicate foods that the newspapers say I dine upon while the soldiers starve. Did you enjoy the glorious repast we wallowed in tonight?"

"Right down to the last tasty paragraph, Brother. What was it?"

"I don't know. I did not dare to ask." Judah looked at Jules anxiously. "Did you get enough to eat?"

"Of course."

"Sometimes I think you are hungry. Natalie would never forgive me if I let you starve."

"Nor would I." Jules examined his fingernails. "Brother, may I ask the question?"

"What question?"

"The question everybody wants to ask. What success will our peace commissioners have with Lincoln?"

Judah did not reply. He thought of Stephens and Hunter and Judge Campbell on their idiotic journey northward. They had been sent to say that the Confederacy still wanted everything she had wanted in '61 only now she would like it with peace.

Jules said, "I heard that as the peace train passed the lines our soldiers cheered, and then Grant's men saw it and cheered, too. Brother, will Lincoln cheer?"

"Not very loudly, Jules. He will wait for another day."

Jules sighed. "All of a sudden nothing is right with us. If we are not soon favored with a victory I believe President Davis will remove God to an inactive command."

Judah smiled and stared thoughtfully into the fire. A victory? How could such a thing ever again be hoped for? Lee was dealing in miracles by simply holding the federal army out of Richmond. Still people dreamed and spoke of future victories. And now the bells were ringing again. Why was it always on the coldest nights or in torrents of rain that the war clerks were called to defend the city?

Jules muttered his annoyance and rose from his comfortable chair. He went to the hall and came back with a heavy coat, his woolen cap, and gloves. He seated himself and began pulling on his boots. "I am looking forward to the warm weather. What a pleasure it will be to do my heroic work in a balmy breeze."

Judah watched him in silence. Last time the bells called him out Jules had slept on bare, frozen ground. What was the sense of it? Where was the reason? The boots were on now. Jules had the ridiculous cap pulled low about his ears. He had his rifle and he was ready.

"Good night, Brother."

"Jules—wait."

"I cannot. The bells are ringing. You hear them."

"Yes, I hear them. Jules, don't go."

"Don't go! Richmond is in danger."

"Of course it is, Jules. Richmond will fall. We cannot save it."

Jules said, "I have known that since Gettysburg. Haven't you?"

"It does not matter what I have known. Tonight I tell you, Jules, one small war clerk freezing out there will not avert or retard disaster."

"One small war clerk! Do you think all those bells are ringing just for me? There will be scores of us."

"Scores is a correct estimate indeed. The clerks have had their fill of war."

Jules walked toward the door. "We have a very select organization now," he said. "Only one's friends, you understand. Good night, Brother."

"Jules. Jules, listen. Never in all the time we have been to-

gether have I reminded you that you are not well. Tonight I ask
you to think why you are not in the army. Jules, you cannot with-
stand much hardship or fatigue. You must not—"

"Oh, but I must, Brother." Jules jauntily waved a thick woolen
glove and was gone.

Judah stared again into the fire. It would not be so bad if
only dignity had survived. But the Confederacy, like a drunken
bawd, no longer remembered the days when she had been gentle
and clean and well-mannered. Now congressmen brawled among
themselves and spit tobacco juice upon the floor of the Senate
chamber. They ate peanuts and tossed the shells carelessly aside.
In every state deserters skulked in the darkness, looting the homes
of defenseless people and praying for a Northern victory. The
newspapers openly jeered at the President and stooped to the
pettiness of calling his wife a heavy, middle-aged woman. Nothing
remained but the dogged persistence that still animated the brave
of heart. Actually that was all there had been in the beginning.
There had never been a nation.

And he sat alone listening to the ringing of the bells as he
had listened to them in the cabinet room before Lee's invasion
of Pennsylvania. The fire died but still he sat, and because he
had never been afraid to look upon the face of truth he looked
now. And he found himself still not afraid of that familiar face
but deeply saddened by the harsh angularity of its features.

Carefully, methodically he destroyed the personal letters and
memorandums that he had accumulated in his desk. This office
was not really his today. J. B. Jones was in command, directing
a squad of clerks as they filled packing cases with documents and
state papers. Judah realized that he was tolerated only because
occasionally they needed a word of advice from him.

Jones, one of those people who is at his sprightliest in disaster,
chattered ceaselessly.

"We could use the nice flat surface of Mr. Benjamin's desk
except that I suppose Mr. Benjamin needs it for something or
other. Well, no matter. The whole thing is ridiculous anyway.
All this effort! All this packing! If the government is forced
to fly, then what earthly use exists for preserving a record of
its ineptitude?"

Jones was hoping to be sharply reprimanded. He was longing for the opportunity to take insult. Judah smiled to himself.

Does he think me fool enough to rebuke him? Now when his job is almost at an end and he has no further use for humbleness? No, Jones, I will give you no excuse to walk out and escape the packing.

Judah watched him as he advanced to the solemn duty of taking the flag from the wall. It was a large flag and there was a time when Jones was almost enveloped in its folds. He teetered dangerously on the ladder and Judah ran to the rescue but Jones descended safely. Judah turned back to his desk and Varina Davis was standing there.

"Why, Mrs. Davis."

"Good morning, sir."

She was still in mourning for Little Joe and the dull, black garments were no more somber than her eyes. He cleared a chair for her and waved the clerks out of the room.

"Where is the President, Mr. Benjamin? He is not in his office."

"The President has ridden out to Camp Lee with Colonel Lubbock. He was not expecting you."

"No," she said, "he was not."

He observed a briskness about her, a calm determination. Her head was high and her lips set firmly.

"Friends of mine visited this morning and told me that General Sherman has entered North Carolina. Is that true, Mr. Benjamin?"

Jones had left the flag in a large, bulky mass upon the desk. Judah looked across it and said, "It is true, Madame."

She nodded. "I thought so. Of course his object is to unite with Grant here in Virginia."

Judah with eyes narrowed in puzzlement studied her. Not a friendly word, not a warming smile from this woman who had a dozen times asked for his understanding.

"Since my husband is absent and there seems to be some need for haste I suppose you will help me make arrangements."

"Arrangements for what, Mrs. Davis?"

She said, "I want my children moved out of Richmond. My

sister and a few servants will accompany them but the roads are full of rough men so soldiers will be needed."

He turned his eyes away from her but not before he had seen the firm lips grow white and had heard a high, choked note of misery in her voice.

Now it was clear. Now he understood. She was afraid of friendliness today, afraid of warmth. She had come here knowing that only by holding herself aloof could she bring herself to speak coolly of parting from her children. Only by convincing herself that she was a tough-minded woman, born for war and its sacrifices could she carry out the plan she had made.

"You are not going with your children, Mrs. Davis?"

"No. They do not need me."

"Not even the little one—the one you call Pie-Cake?"

She did not look at him, choosing instead to examine the stitching on her black-bordered handkerchief. "I have said that none of them need me."

"If they do not need you, Mrs. Davis, I am hard put to imagine—"

"Mr. Davis needs me," she said. "Is that difficult for you to imagine?"

He said, "Mrs. Davis, I will tell you something. Your husband loves you devotedly, but no man needs his wife at the expense of having his children feel lost and frightened."

"They will be safer anywhere than here. I am determined to have them leave Richmond."

"A splendid idea, but you must go with them."

"That is unthinkable. You perhaps do not value a woman's contribution to a man's strength of purpose. I assure you my husband has high regard for my opinion and takes new courage from knowing I am near."

He said, "No man would ask his wife to send her children from her."

"He did not ask and he would not ask."

"I am sure of that."

"But I know where my duty lies. It lies with the President. Anyone can take care of children."

"Can they really? I did not know. I supposed there were small things that children need from their mother. Her arms about

them at bedtime or perhaps her voice assuring them that all is
well in the dark hours of the night."

"Mr. Benjamin, these are small, sentimental things."

"Of course. I was only thinking that children in an unfamiliar
world cry for the woman who was their blessed link with security."

"Pray be still, sir. I am very tired of your persistent effort to
see me as nothing but a soft woman who is incapable of facing
reality. I am a strong woman, sir."

"I must ask a question. Do you like being a strong woman?"

"Of course I like it. I am accustomed to it. You are the only
one I ever met who refused to recognize me as a woman who
could face trouble without flinching."

"And I am the only one you ever met who will say to you:
Go ahead and flinch."

She raised her eyes to his. "You do not understand how much
the President needs me, how he leans on me."

"I understand but somehow I am unimpressed by his needs
when I weigh them against those of his children. Mrs. Davis, how
can you think of sending them away from you?"

She closed her eyes and tears glistened upon the dark lashes.

"I cannot bear to think of it," she whispered, "only it must
be done."

"No, it must not be done. My dear, have you a picture in your
mind of standing at Jefferson Davis's side as Richmond burns
around you? Long since he will have gone from here. He will be
riding like the wind toward safety."

"And I will ride with him," she said.

He took her hand and patted it gently. "And you are the
woman who faces reality? You would only impede your husband's progress. I beg of you, do not set your children adrift
simply because you have fashioned for yourself an idea of where
you should be and how you should behave if Richmond falls.
The children must be your main consideration. Do you not wish
to be with them, guarding them—"

"With all my heart, sir."

"Then go." He looked at her with a steady, unblinking gaze.
"I disappointed you because I was not the man to come to you
with the Confederacy's burdens and problems. And yet despite

your disappointment it pleased me to see that you would turn
to me when you were in trouble."

"I could not bother my husband with my small heartaches."

"Madame, the truth is you could not bring yourself to admit
to him that you had such. You wanted him to see you always as
a brave and smiling woman—a strong woman."

She said, "I wanted him always to see me as the woman with
whom he fell in love."

"And so he sees you but the view you have given him will be
your undoing. For, smiling bravely and strongly, you will say
to him: I have arranged to send the children away. I will stay
here with you. And he will have no way of knowing that within
you there is agony and terror and heartbreak. He will think you
have chosen as it is your nature to choose. Dear lady, he doesn't
know you as well as I. You have not let him see you weep."

She was weeping now and he went to her and put his arm
about her. Varina, the horsewoman who had taken the jumps
with such ease and grace that no one had guessed that she was
frightened. Varina, who had grown so tall and sturdy that even
in girlhood she had been expected to carry burdens. She had
tried. All her life she had invited the weak, the troubled, the
sickly to rest their cares upon her. And they had done so without
once discovering that in the mind of the strong, reliable woman
there was confusion and doubt.

"Mrs. Davis, I will make the arrangements for the wagons
and soldiers. But you must leave Richmond with your little
ones."

She wept silently into the black-bordered handkerchief.

"Come, that is enough now," he said. "There is one perfect
moment to cease weeping. It is achieved just at the point where
the heart is somewhat lightened and the eyes have not yet become
red." He smiled at her as she lifted her face from the handkerchief. "This I should say is that moment."

She rose from the chair. "Mr. Benjamin, I will go home now
and I will think about—"

"There is no time to think. With the other precious possessions of the Confederacy you must leave Richmond at once."

"Is it right for me to go?" she asked earnestly.

"There is no other right thing for you to do."

She said, "If you say so, Mr. Benjamin, I know I can believe it."

Davis returned from his trip to Camp Lee late in the afternoon. He poured himself a glass of water from the pitcher on Judah's desk and swallowed one of the large white pills that nowadays he carried with him.

Judah waited while Davis mopped the perspiration from his brow, then he asked, "Have you any late news concerning Sherman?"

"No. Have you?"

"None has come here. I have spoken to the cabinet members as you requested. In the event of flight—"

"Will Breckenridge accompany us?"

"He is eager to do so." Eager indeed. Breckenridge who had been vice-president of the United States and was now Confederate secretary of war was having nightmares in which a gallows figured largely.

"Who else will go with us?"

"I am not certain of Trenholm. Steve Mallory you can of course depend on, and our latest attorney general."

Davis hit at his dusty boots with his riding crop. "I trust that you did not suggest that flight was imminent. For all we know Richmond will still be resisting invasion a year from now."

"Did General Lee hold out that hope to you?"

Davis shook his head in annoyance. "No, and I am becoming rather impatient with General Lee. He has not the former fire that one admired so much in him. He is as full of dismal warnings and evil predictions as an old woman. He is fearful of holding Petersburg much longer. It is *I* who am forced to point out to *him* how far we are from surrender. It is a fantastic state of affairs."

How strange it was that only the President withheld praise of Lee's amazing stand against the federal forces. Only Davis failed to appreciate that Richmond had stood because of Lee's determination and the spirit he had instilled in his men.

"I cannot believe that warnings from Lee are just babblings, Mr. President. He is not that kind of general. And incidentally I would like to say that his soldiers are deserving of—"

Davis waved his riding crop in a careless gesture. "You need not call my attention to his soldiers. I have long known them to be superb. But then all our men are great fighters. You must remember that the South is the only place in the world where gentlemen go to a military academy who do not intend to follow the profession of arms."

Once again he had forgotten the farm boys, the salesmen, the carpenters. This was an army of aristocrats and West Pointers out there manning the defenses. With his dying breath Davis would maintain that the cavaliers were fighting the peasants. He was establishing a legend, an apology for defeat. The theme would be that gentlemen had been vanquished because they recognized rules and courtesies. He was creating a useful, comfortable fabric of myth to keep the cold out of his bones when the winds blew of a winter's night. Perhaps he would weave it so large and generous that all the South could huddle beneath it, and in the end it might prove more satisfying than victory. Under the warm blanket one could rest forever happy in a delusion that was sure to grow more beautiful, more indestructible with every passing year.

"It was not their prowess I was about to mention, Mr. President. It was their greatness of heart. Those ragged, starving boys gave up their scant rations today, asking that the flour and bacon be given instead to the hungry women and children of Richmond. It was that I wished to comment on. I believe they are deserving of some special notice. A word from you, sir, I think would be appreciated."

"I will send them a message," Davis said. "However, I do not believe the sacrifice was needed. People here are not actually in dire need."

"They are, Mr. President. Let us accept that as a truth, for it is nothing less."

Davis sighed. "I refuse to become discouraged," he said. "And it is fortunate that I am so constituted. What would happen if I succumbed to dismay? And it is a wonder that I do not, with Lee complaining on one side and Johnston on the other." He jumped to his feet irritably. "What ridiculous hysteria gripped people, making them think that Johnston must be returned to his command? Why did they think he could hold Sherman back?"

Judah said, "I do not know. After General Hood led that fine army to its death and returned only the skeleton to Johnston I cannot imagine what Johnston was expected to do."

Davis peered into one of the packing cases, reached in and drew out a pile of documents. Jones had tied them neatly together. Now Davis removed the string and examined the top pages with an interest that suggested he had found something long sought.

"What are these?"

"Coming from that particular packing case, sir, they must be copies of the Confederacy's correspondence with Mexico."

"Oh." Davis dropped the documents back into the box. After all they had not been what he was seeking. They were not the full directions on how to win a war.

"Because people are incredibly, dangerously stupid I now have Johnston again to confound me. They clamored for him to be restored to command. Even the soldiers. Mr. Benjamin, did you know that as I reviewed the troops in Macon the soldiers shouted at me as they passed? Such a thing is unheard of. On formal review before their president they shouted, 'Give us back Johnston.' What, in the name of God, did they think Johnston could do?"

"As I said before, sir, with what was left to Johnston I cannot guess."

Davis's mouth twisted. "Well, the people have Johnston now and they also have their adored Beauregard. Two quarrelsome men. Two power-hungry egotists."

Judah said, "These are our generals, Mr. President, our bulwark against disaster." He began folding the flag that still lay upon his desk and Davis crossed the room to assist him.

"At least Lee remains," Davis said taking two corners of the flag in his hands. "For all his wretched grumbling Lee will always act in the best interests of Richmond."

"You may be sure of that," Judah said.

They folded the flag and refolded it till at last it was a compact silken square. Then Judah carried it over and laid it gently beside the seal of the Confederacy which was also to be carefully prepared for shipment into oblivion.

The first stop was Danville. The people were dazzled by the sight of the President and his entire cabinet. Davis was offered a fine house in which to rest. From there he issued a proclamation. He informed the citizens that the military situation was grave but not hopeless. General Lee, with his army intact, had brilliantly chosen to relinquish Richmond. The war was very far from being lost. The people must have faith.

"Faith in what, Brother?" Jules asked.

"In God of course."

"Oh, that is all right then."

Reagan said, "Do you think we will make Danville the new capital and remain here?"

Breckenridge had been drinking. He laughed boisterously. "I wouldn't rent a house, Reagan. My guess is that we'll just wait here for Lee and his boys and see what happens then."

Judah sought Trenholm out. "The men at the arsenal have not been paid for months."

"Lots of people haven't been paid for months, Benjamin."

"You're speaking to a man well aware of that fact, but the men here—"

"I don't know what I should do."

"In that case keep the money, Trenholm. Keep it till the Federals take it away from you."

Trenholm wrinkled his brow. "That could happen, I suppose. I'd rather pay our soldiers of course."

"Not in Confederate bills, Trenholm. In gold."

They were still waiting for Lee and his army when the news came. Davis took it badly. His face whitened and he shook with rage.

"I will never understand it," he cried. "Never. How did Lee reach the conclusion that surrender was necessary?"

Judah said, "You can be sure he did not reach it without sober consideration, sir. He was trying to join you. You can see that from the location of Appomattox on the map. He did not willingly fail you. He was forced to bow to the inevitable."

Davis grimaced disagreeably. "For all your superior mind you have never grasped the fundamentals of military art. The truth as I see it now is that Lee's poor health undermined his resolution. I should have relieved him a year ago."

"As to that do not reprove yourself, Mr. President. Rest easy in the knowledge that Lee's admirers would have interfered with your taking such a step."

"Lee's admirers! I wonder how many he has today. Had I given the command to someone else I might have preserved Lee's fame for him. Now, like all defeated generals, he will be forgotten."

"Virginians have good memories."

"Then they can remember Richmond in flames—terror, looting, lawlessness rampant. If I had been Lee— But what is the use of reviewing his errors now? Without his army we cannot stay in Danville. We must press on to a union with our other forces."

Greensboro, North Carolina, next. Fifty miles southward. A terrible trip by night with the federal cavalry known to be haunting the countryside. Judah in a springless army wagon thought of the soldiers and marines who rode guard for the President's party. An impressive army of seasoned men, but they were hungry, unpaid, and sick of war. If Stoneman's cavalry should confront them—

The wagon shook and swayed, and Dr. Hoge, the Senate chaplain, prayed aloud. George Davis, Attorney General, whose home was in North Carolina spoke of his motherless children and wondered if the Federals would hang him.

Adjutant General Cooper, almost seventy, talked as a man making new acquaintances in the salon of an ocean liner. He recounted small anecdotes, explored the possibility of mutual friends, and sang the praises of his home town, which happened to be New York City.

"I remember the night Verdi's *Rigoletto* made its American debut," he said. "It was at the Academy of Music."

"Yes, yes, I was there," Judah said. "It was magnificent."

"Did you see *La Traviata* also?"

"I regret that I did not. Was it as fine?"

"It was glorious, sir. It was an evening I can still recall with joy. The enchanting voices of La Grange and Brignoli come to me at this moment in memory."

Jules said, "I am a coward. I can remember nobody's enchanting voice. I remember only that Stoneman's cavalry is near. I am shamed by the bravery of you opera lovers."

General Cooper spoke to Jules out of the darkness. "Son," he said, "we opera lovers are so God-damned frightened we're numb."

The Reverend Hoge could be heard to stir uneasily.

"I am sorry," the general said. "When we reach Greensboro I will wash my mouth out with soap."

Greensboro could not be said to have received the President and the cabinet. Greensboro only permitted them to enter. No one wished to offer hospitality. The federal forces were too close. The cabinet was obliged to apply for dinner to their army escort.

Mallory gloomily surveyed the rations of bread and bacon that had been unceremoniously stacked at the side of the road.

"Christ Almighty, what a gruesome spot for a picnic."

Judah said, "It doesn't figure to be a picnic, my friend."

It was drizzling and there was not a bed for any man of the wagon train save Mr. Davis himself. Coincidence had favored him. A nephew of his first wife had a home here and there was room in it for Davis.

The young man's landlord objected violently. "If the Feds come for you, Mr. Davis, will you give yourself up?"

"Certainly not. My escort and I will fight—"

"That's the point I'm making. What becomes of my property after the skirmish? Broken windows, bullet holes, grass ripped to hell. God damn it, I own this house. I think it's my right to keep you out of it."

Judah said, "A lawyer's opinion is that you have no jurisdiction over the guests entering this house. A gentleman's opinion is that you have addressed the President with unbelievable disrespect."

The man laughed. "President? What's he president of?"

Davis stared straight ahead of him into the gray mist that obscured the trees and even the houses across the street. He gave no sign that he had heard the landlord's remark. He took no notice of the gold pieces that were dropped into the landlord's hand.

The nephew of Knox Taylor Davis led him into the house and brought him a glass of wine.

Davis said, "Mr. Benjamin, I will have to confer with Johnston and Beauregard. I must know their plans and they must know mine." He clenched his fist and swallowed hard. "How ironic it is that in the Confederacy's most desperate moments I must treat with men who have never had my confidence."

"Ironic indeed," Judah said.

They walked into the room unsmiling, the generals who had never had his confidence. Their reserve was a warning that Davis chose to ignore. He was toying with a piece of paper, folding it into elaborate patterns, looking up from it to smile at them. To smile at Johnston and Beauregard. They saluted coldly and at his invitation they seated themselves.

"Of course you both know Mr. Benjamin."

They nodded.

Davis said, "I asked you here because I feel that I should do nothing, absolutely nothing, without the advice of my military chiefs."

Johnston smiled now but it was a bleak and bitter smile. He said, "It had never occurred to me that you could possibly regard advice from either of us as worth having."

Davis said, "Nonsense. Your advice is of the greatest value to me."

Beauregard, his sad, soft eyes resting on Davis thoughtfully, said, "Do you know there were times when I would not have believed that. I must have been mistaken."

Judah turned away and looked out the window at a small girl chasing a puppy. In the room there was nothing to see but the painful drama of a man drinking the bitter dregs of a potion he himself had brewed.

Davis said, "There is a great deal for us to discuss. Lee's surrender has, of course, created a desperate though not a hopeless situation. We must concentrate now upon putting new heart in the people."

"New heart?" Johnston asked. "Did you say new heart?"

"Yes. Of course your first task will be to see that your soldiers do not lay down their arms as Lee's have done. Their resolution to continue the struggle will be an inspiration to the fainthearted. Next we must have a victory in the field. It does not matter how small or obscure."

Johnston's voice dripped acid. "Have you any particular field in mind where you would like this victory to take place? We have twenty-five thousand men and the Federals number three hundred and fifty thousand!"

Davis made a neat triangle of the paper in his hand. He said, "Numbers never give a clear picture of military possibilities. Think of the times we were victorious though outnumbered."

Beauregard said, "Those were other days. Do you think this is the army of the Confederacy's high noon? These men are but gallant ghosts, dazed survivors of the army that was. They live with hunger and sickness and death and they do not sing as they sang in other days."

Beauregard's Creole style of speech Davis had always detested. Now he must be grateful that Beauregard spoke to him at all.

"A victory," Davis said, "would make them sing."

Johnston jumped from his chair in sudden fury. The chair fell backward and Davis's tautly stretched nerves caused him to wince at the unexpected crash.

"Mr. Davis, do not speak of my men as though they were green troops in need of seasoning. I knew them when they were the finest body of soldiers who ever trod this earth—yes, including the Army of Northern Virginia. They are heroes. Every one of them is a hero. If it were not so they would have deserted Hood when he threw them heedlessly, planlessly against Sherman. They are more than heroes. They must be something more or they would have killed Hood for what he did."

Judah said, "General Johnston, the President meant no insult to your men."

"Certainly not," Davis agreed heartily. The smile was becoming a ghastly, frozen ache upon his face. "My thought is that we must use their well-tested courage to the greatest advantage. It is for these boys who remain in arms to set an example of gallantry for the civilian population. Your men could be a nucleus for reinforcements, for—"

Beauregard asked, "From where would reinforcements come?"

Davis answered so swiftly that it was clear that he had pondered the question. "Deserters would return, sir. Men who had been cowards would suddenly feel shame, the old, the young—"

Johnston waved his hand in dismissal of Davis's words. "You are dreaming," he said. "The people consider the war at an end."

"And I say they do not. My people will never—"

Beauregard's eyes glinted with sudden, naked hatred. *"Your* people? At what point in this tragic, blood-drenched span of years did free Southerners become *your* people?"

"I used the word only—"

"Only because you have never felt otherwise," Beauregard said. "It may come as a surprise to you that we are not your people. None of us."

Judah said, "We serve nobody by wrangling. Let us return to the reason for this meeting."

Davis for a moment remained quiet, rubbing his face thoughtfully. A vein in his temple throbbed and his lips trembled, but he was smiling when he turned again to Johnston. The piece of paper had become a boat.

"General Johnston, what do you suggest? What should we do at this highly critical stage in our affairs?"

Johnston said, "We should contact Northern authorities."

"That I think would be futile. They would not agree to any terms at all."

"I did not mention terms," Johnston said stiffly.

The smile was suddenly gone. "You meant we should surrender!"

"That is exactly what I meant."

Davis stared at his two generals. "Surrender? You? You, the defenders of the South, are prepared to consent to her degradation?"

Beauregard said, "We, the defenders of the South, are opposed to setting guerrilla bands loose to terrorize and demoralize her— all in order that you may continue to hear yourself called Mr. President."

Davis lowered his eyes and said, "I will ignore anything you say that bears not on our common anxieties." He raised his head and looked squarely at Johnston. "So you advise surrender?" Johnston nodded. "You also, General Beauregard?"

"There is no alternative."

Davis sat back in his chair and regarded them with an expression that was familiar to Judah. One often saw it in the eyes of an inexperienced lawyer, that triumphant gleam that tele-graphed, "I have you now."

Judah shuddered. Davis was readying a trap and when he sprang it, God help him. Judah looked away from the light that had blazed again in Davis's eyes.

"You have both felt since Lee's surrender that you, too, must yield?" Their silence was their assent and Davis, his voice ring-ing with confidence, walked in for the kill. "This cannot be so," he said. "Something impels you and your men to continue. If it did not then how is it that you did not rush to surrender when the news came that Lee had done so?" He looked at them challengingly and when they did not speak he urged them. "Answer me that," he demanded. "Answer me that."

And Beauregard answered. He said, "We remained, sir, to guarantee your safety."

Davis leaped to his feet. "You did what?" He crumpled the paper into a ball and threw it from him. "What did you say you did?"

"We remained to see you out of North Carolina and on your way to safety."

"I asked no favors of you," Davis cried. "Never. Never."

"You had no need to," Johnston said. "We knew our duty." The generals walked to the door and Johnston opened it. "As soon as you have left here, as soon as I know you are well on your way, I will contact General Sherman."

Davis said, "One moment, please. I have given no word that this meeting is adjourned. I have still an order for you. Before you surrender you are to detach your cavalry and send it after me."

Johnston gave him a long, cold look. "You know better than that. I have dealt honorably with you and I will deal honorably with General Sherman—and with my men."

They did not salute. They walked away from him, Johnston and Beauregard, the generals he had hated, the generals who would hold till he was beyond the reach of Sherman's men.

Davis sat down heavily upon the bed. "They did not act like any generals I ever knew," he said dully.

Judah touched him encouragingly upon the shoulder. "I will return later, sir."

Outside Beauregard was mounting a lean and hungry horse.

"May I speak to you, General?"

Beauregard turned and faced him, his eyes showing the honest, unveiled detestation that he felt. "It will do you no good," he said shortly.

"I have not come to speak of matters already settled, sir," Judah said. "I have come to ask where you will go when Sherman has accepted the surrender."

Beauregard's eyes glistened moistly. "I am going to what is left of New Orleans," he said. "I am going there to place flowers upon the grave of my wife and to try to build for myself and my fellow Orleanians a world in which we can once more live."

"I thought you would want that, sir. You will take an army wagon no doubt and—"

"Have you objections?"

"No objections, General." Judah looked steadily into the dark, angry face. "Sir, I have come to you with a request."

"A request?" Beauregard asked incredulously. "I am Beauregard. Don't you recognize me? Or have you forgotten that you are not my friend?"

"I remember, but even so I have come to you trusting in your—"

"Trusting? Trusting in Beauregard? That is strange indeed." The general turned his gaze away from Judah and it was to the bony horse he spoke. "I was relieved from a command that was mine by every right. I was insulted in every possible manner. When I was ill I was accused of deception. I was less respected than an army mule. I was disbelieved and doubted and treated by the government so badly that I will never recover from the heartbreak." The brooding, grief-stricken eyes came to rest on Judah's face. "All that happened to me grew out of the order that sent me west, the order relieving me of the Virginia command that in all fairness was mine. Why did you do it to me?"

And Judah standing with Beauregard in the wet spring wind knew that he could not give an honest answer. For in the house behind him he had seen a man's pride beaten to death that day and some respect was due the corpse.

He said, "I did it because at the time it seemed a good idea. *I* did it, remember. Not my brother-in-law. I have come to ask you to give him room in the wagon, to take him home to New Orleans."

"He is Jules St. Martin, is he not?"

"He is, General."

Beauregard's smile was thin and contempuous. "I find your request astonishing. Do you think a St. Martin, a member of a Creole family, is yours to plead for? Of course I will take him home. I will take all I have room for of those who belong to Louisiana."

Beauregard turned his lean horse and rode away. Judah's eyes followed him out of sight. Beauregard, who had been superintendent of West Point in '61, Beauregard, who had been a respected man, happy in the security of his army career.

Judah shook his head sadly and went about the business of finding Jules and explaining to him that their journey together was over.

"I will do as you say, Brother. I will go with the lighthearted, merry Beauregard."

"Do not laugh at Beauregard. He is a fine man."

Jules said, "A fine man will be no novelty to me. I have lived with one for four years."

"I will always remember that you said that, Jules."

Jules grinned. "It was nothing. I am an emotional fellow. I say things like that to everybody."

Salisbury, where there was no place at all to live and plans had to be altered. Despite fatigue and roads deep in mud they had to continue on. It was a long way to Florida, to Florida and escape. Across the blue water there were the Indies and safety. Judah remembered the time long, long ago when he had pleaded a case that dealt with slaves who had thrown themselves upon a West Indian island and found rest. Rest. What a beautiful word. Florida. So far away. So many miles in the future.

Davis was ill and he rode in an ambulance with Trenholm, who believed himself to be dying. Everyone was slightly ill. The food had been horrible and there had been little sleep. Fear and dirt and weariness rode with them.

The wandering bands of deserters, the unruly mobs of civilians that robbed them of food and animals, were as disturbing as the constant threat of the Federals. The cabinet was uncertain of the President's guard, these soldiers who knew the war was over. The Confederate treasury. Half a million in gold had been sent to a secret destination. Thirty-five thousand dollars remained with the wagon train for the use of Davis and the cabinet, but only Davis himself, Judah, and Trenholm knew that it had been held back. In a belt around his waist Judah had five thousand dollars that Trenholm had given him.

"I may need it again, Benjamin. If I don't we owe it to you anyway."

Charlotte was the next stop. The town was sullen and inhospitable. No one would open a door to Jefferson Davis. Breckenridge, who had sallied forth to find the President a bed, returned to the ambulance triumphant and smelling like a barroom. He had found shelter for Davis.

"It's a bachelor ménage," Breckenridge explained. "A sort of devil-may-care fellow lives there. A fine chap and brave enough to offer a room to Mr. Davis."

Judah and Burton Harrison escorted Davis to the bachelor ménage. They arrived before expected. The devil-may-care fellow was very drunk when he admitted them to the parlor. From the sofa a frowzy-haired girl rose buttoning her bodice.

Burton Harrison said, "Mr. Benjamin, we can't permit the President to stay here. It is unthinkable."

It was indeed unthinkable but Davis dropped gratefully into a chair and said, "Thank the young man. I appreciate his invitation and will remain."

In the kitchen Judah found a Negro woman. He gave her a coin and she promised to bring Mr. Davis some food and clean sheets for his bed.

"This was a nice house before the old folks died," she said. "No place now for a real gentleman. If I were you I'd take that poor, tired man somewhere else."

"There is nowhere else," Judah said. "Will you do your best for him?"

"Yes, sir, my very best."

Outside, standing beyond the line of Davis's guard, a man

awaited Judah. "My name is Weil, Mr. Benjamin. I offer you what comforts my home affords. There is a bath and—"

"You are very kind, Mr. Weil." The man was a Jew and Judah was ashamed for him. In the presence of the equally homeless Burton Harrison to extend an invitation to a fellow Jew!

"Mrs. Davis and her little ones rested with us when they passed through Charlotte," he said. "I do not dare offer her husband the same hospitality. I have children and elderly parents and cannot risk a skirmish around my home. However, you and this gentleman are welcome."

It was at Weil's house that they heard the news of Lincoln's assassination.

"We must really make a run for it now," Judah said.

"Do you think we will be accused of hatching the plot?"

"That is a possibility."

Trenholm and George Davis decided that they would run no further. They left the party, and the wagons went on to Abbeville, South Carolina. The countryside through which they traveled was west of the burned and ravaged land that had intimately known the heavy hand of Sherman. The cavalry escort was tired of the assignment, bored with the slowness of the wagons, frankly disinterested in the honor that had been bestowed upon them.

Judah wondered why anyone believed that they would fight to save Davis and his cabinet. Why should they? He listened to their mutterings, looked upon their faces and knew they were not less realistic than he. They, too, saw no reason why young lives should be spent in protecting a handful of middle-aged men who had served them poorly.

When they grumbled aloud at the risk of an encounter with the Federals he questioned some of them and found deep resentment. They had expected a swift flight to Florida and a termination of the task assigned them. It had never occurred to them that Davis would linger along the road, calling conferences, resting for nights when he had a bed, and pausing for messages from his wife, who was forty miles ahead of them.

So now at Judah's suggestion Davis and the cabinet took to horseback and rode speedily through the fateful April days.

Georgia was not far. Then Florida, the sea and safety. Everyone spoke of Florida. Everyone but Davis. Judah looked at him and wondered. Why was Davis not speaking of Florida? And they came at last to Washington, Georgia. And still Davis was not speaking of Florida.

A hard-faced woman who had lost five sons in the war gave Davis a room. He smiled at her and offered his hand. She did not smile or let him take her hand in his.

"I am not sure how they would feel. I let you in because they may have been for it," she said and walked away.

Judah saw that the room was clean but without the smallest comfort. No pillow on the bed, no rug, no mirror. Not even a curtain.

He said, "Mr. President, I trust you will try to sleep at once. We are to be on the road again before sunrise."

Davis nodded. "Will you come to this room at four, sir?"

"To this room?" What whim was this now?

"Yes, in the morning before we ride forth I wish to speak to you."

"I will be here."

It was no hardship to arise before four in the morning for Judah had had no bed. The night had been spent in one of the wagons and his bones ached miserably. Mr. Davis's guard, already anxious to be off, passed him into the house where Davis waited.

"Good morning, Mr. Benjamin."

Judah looked closely at the President and saw that he had not slept. His face was pale and haggard but it was clear that he had been suddenly animated by a new burning hope.

"Mr. Benjamin, there has been something on my mind for days."

"I have been aware of that, sir." Judah leaned patiently against the wall and waited.

"At last I have decided to voice my thoughts. First I will reveal them to you. Later you may call the other members of the cabinet and we will have a general discussion."

"This morning?" Judah asked.

"Of course this morning."

"Sir, the guard will be seriously annoyed and we cannot afford—"

"The guard! I have ceased to call them by so military a title. I have never seen a more slovenly outfit of men than those surrounding this house."

Judah said, "I entreat you to be lenient and to criticize the men only beyond their range of hearing."

"Very well. Very well. But I will entreat you not to suppose that I am here to do their will. They must wait till I have completed business with my cabinet." He fell silent arranging his thoughts, and Judah, leaning against the wall, wondered if at the next stop there would be a place to bathe. Strange how a man went through life taking warm water and soap for granted.

"I have been thinking, Mr. Benjamin, that General Kirby Smith has not surrendered."

So that was what he had been thinking. He had been vexed by what he regarded as Lee's defection and had been busy making a new military hero for the Confederacy. Well, Kirby Smith in faraway Texas would probably serve adequately if a hero was really needed.

"No," he said, "Kirby Smith has not surrendered."

Davis nodded his satisfaction and began to pace excitedly. "And you can gamble that he will not. Not Kirby Smith! Mr. Benjamin, it will be an arduous trip but not an impossible one. With the help of God we will reach Kirby Smith and Texas and there we will make a stand such as the world has never before witnessed. There will be no talk of surrender and no peace till the North is ready to admit our invincibility. That, Mr. Benjamin, is what I have been thinking."

Judah said, "I must ask if you are serious."

"Serious? How can you ask that when you know that I am pledged to fight for Southern independence?"

"But the fight is lost, sir. You will not find an army in Texas to support you, nor citizens willing to prolong the bloodshed. And I must say I think the plan wicked as well as mad, for if you succeed in rallying a substantial force it could achieve nothing but a longer list of dead."

"And when were men not willing to die for freedom? You will see when we reach Texas."

Judah pulled himself away from the wall. "No," he said, "I will not see. I am not going to Texas."

Davis paused in his march up and down the little room. "Not going? Did you say you were not going?"

"That is what I said. I do not fancy the picture you have drawn. I have no heart for the business of prodding hungry soldiers into fighting on, nor for whipping up the patriotism of women so that they are willing to send their little boys out to die for us."

"You paint a tragic picture but I will admit war is horrible and this is war."

"You couldn't be farther from the truth, sir. War implies contest. There is no longer any contest. The South has been beaten."

Color flamed angrily in Davis's face. "I have not been beaten," he said hoarsely. "I will never be beaten. And I invite you to stand beside me, remaining steadfast to the cause, resolved to fight till breath is no more."

Judah shook his head. "I decline the invitation, sir. I am on my way to Florida and I hope you will also continue to ride in that—"

Davis said, "Florida is the destination of the coward, the deserter. I want no part of a plan that is dedicated to escape. You, I see, are no longer interested in the Confederacy. You want no part of sacrifice or hardship, do you, Mr. Benjamin?"

Judah said, "I want no part of your insane plan, sir."

Davis came close to him and spoke in a harsh whisper. "I was warned that all you wanted was ease and importance."

Judah looked steadily into Davis's flaming eyes. "Sir," he said, "before your name was known outside your own county I had ease and importance in such abundance that I could throw them to the winds. And in 1861 that is exactly what I did."

"Yes, in 1861 you deserted the United States of America and now you desert the Confederacy. You cannot remain faithful to anything, can you, Mr. Benjamin? It is true what they told me. I was a man without bigotry or prejudice and I rebuked those who warned me that it was not in the nature of a Jew to know constancy or honor."

Judah studied the bare boards of the clean, comfortless room. "So it has come at last," he said. "In the natural course of events we were long destined to reach this moment, were we not? It is but logical that as you stand here reaping the harvest of stupidity and arrogance that you can remember nothing—nothing except that I am a Jew." He raised his eyes to Davis's face. "I have served you well and I should feel within me a rising tide of rage but the rage does not come. The barb has been thrown so often that it has become blunted."

"I am aware that others damned you because you were a Jew. I never did. I never—"

"No, not till now. Not till the moment when you must face failure and explain it to yourself. Well, you have a satisfactory explanation at hand. Nurture it carefully, permit it to blossom. You will have no trouble convincing many a man that a Jew cannot be trusted."

"Words. Lawyer's words. The fact remains that you are abandoning the cause."

"I deny that the cause and Jefferson Davis are indivisible. The cause is dead and none of us dedicated our lives to you, though this you never understood."

Davis said, "Within a stone's throw of this house there are more than a thousand men whose lives are dedicated to me."

"Those men will never take you to Texas, sir. They will not die for you. If you hurry, their loyalty may last as far as Florida. For days I have been urging you to hurry. I have no wish to see you hanged, sir."

"I am not afraid. If I die, I will die with pride, for it will be in company with the finest men our land has ever produced."

"Do not deceive yourself. If you mean Lee, for instance, you will die lonely. No court will condemn men who fought the good fight on the battlefield. If you hang, sir, it will be with Mallory or Reagan."

"You have not mentioned Benjamin."

"No, I have not, for if they catch and hang you, you will be spared the indignity of dying with a Jew. The Jew they will never catch."

"You sound very certain of that."

"I am certain, for I have long been in league with the Federals. What kind of a Jew would I be if I had not betrayed you and the Confederacy from the very beginning?"

Davis sat down abruptly on the small, straight-backed chair and covered his face with his hands. "Do not ridicule me," he said. "I am not myself. Can't you see that? And I pray that you will not hold against me words that were spoken without thought or feeling."

Judah said, "The words have been spoken, sir, and it is too late to call them back. Neither of us could ever be unaware of what you have said to me this morning, and so my usefulness to you is at an end. Here and now I part company with you, for never again could I look at you without remembering."

"You cannot part company with me. You cannot travel alone."

"I can and will. In a moment I will leave you, but before I go I must tell you to consider well the guard out there. At every cowpath that wanders toward their land or the land of a kinsman the ranks have thinned. Do not think of Texas. Ride fast for Florida while there is still a chance."

"I have told you my plans, Mr. Benjamin."

"You have, and I say again that they are wild and wicked. Now I give you the last piece of advice you will ever have from me. The guard is dangerously ill-humored. Be on your way. In a moment I will not be here to urge you."

Davis did not answer. Judah turned from him, but at the door he paused and looked back and saw that Davis was weeping. And the sight of Davis's grief brought to Judah's mind the death of little Joe. A wave of pity engulfed him as the present struck a spark from the past and he realized that he was walking away from the door, away from freedom and back to stand with Jefferson Davis.

How can I be such a fool? Why don't I go? He is not a child who needs my guidance. If he makes haste he will escape and sit rocking quietly on a cool veranda, dreaming of the past and dictating his memoirs to Burton Harrison. He will live to collect Confederate relics and he will write letters to the newspapers, correcting errors as to the hour and location of events no longer important. He will argue about Gettysburg and defend forever the sacred names of the most incompetent generals. None of this for me. I will not write any memoirs or collect a single Confederate relic. I will always ask of life some-

thing more than a rocker on a cool veranda. When I walk
through that door I will no longer question why Gettysburg
was lost. And why do I not walk through that door now, this
very minute? How can I? Can I leave him weeping here alone
with the guard growing impatient and angry? Why not? What
is he but a man for whom I have already done too much?
And yet, God help him, he is a man who needs understanding
and kindness.

"Mr. President."

Davis raised his head high. "Leave me," he said. "You
made up your mind to desert so do it without further discussion. Go your way remembering, sir, that you have repaid me
poorly for befriending you. You were the last man I could
expect to fail me when one considers that I accepted you in my
cabinet and fought to keep you there though your career from
Yale to your last days in the United States Senate was one
long, filthy trail of dishonor."

Judah stood motionless for a moment looking into the eyes
of Jefferson Davis. Then he said, "Thank you, sir. Thank you
very sincerely."

This time he could walk out of the room without looking
back.

Eight

LONDON

It was a city of such awful antiquity that a man from the New World could but look upon it with reverence. Here was a city whose pride and independence had been so long established that William the Conqueror had treated with it separately, recognizing the necessity to accord London the dignity due a nation. Sections of wall built by the Romans, the Tower, the Abbey—one had heard, of course, but had not guessed the thrilling impact of seeing with one's own eyes these splendors of the past. To walk London's streets was to leave the nineteenth century behind and to remember that here one existed under a municipal government founded by Richard the First. This was the city of Spenser, Marlowe, and Shakespeare, and to converse with the residents was to find oneself listening to tales of the Great Fire as though it had taken place last Wednesday. To hear of the execution of Mary of Scotland one bent close to one's informant, for on this subject voices were discreetly lowered.

London was a city of magnificent architecture, of intellectual superiority, of horrifying squalor. It was a city that had sheltered more immortals than all the rest of the world combined, a city famous for its civilization and high morality, a city where a child could be jailed for stealing food. There was a withdrawn coolness about London. It was as evident in her manner as in her temperature. Even in summer her sunlight was only warm silver, the heat troublesome to none save those who had always

328

lived in a land where palm trees seemed fiction and the proper color of a sea was ice-cold green.

The room in which Judah lived was comfortable enough, even slightly luxurious if one did not look closely. The chairs had been strategically placed to conceal threadbare sections of the carpet and the draperies were not too badly faded. The bed was soft and it was clean so it was not really important that what the landlady called an easy chair had no comfort to offer. It was as good a room and as good an address as he could afford. Escape was an expensive business.

He sat at a small writing table and reread the letter he would mail to his brother Joseph.

Dear Joseph:

I know you will share this letter with Rebecca and Penina and then send it on to Charleston for Hannah, Solomon, and Judith to read. The letter is meant for the entire family but I chose to address it to you, Joseph, for of us all you are most like Papa. Of us all—including any who might be considered to have some gift for persuasive argument—you are the one who will earnestly and tirelessly keep repeating that which you believe. And I would like you to believe and repeat some of the matters in this letter.

I would like you to be in a position to refute any ridiculous stories which arise concerning my escape from America. I will tell you exactly how it was accomplished. I think you must know, Joseph, that I am not overly sensitive about what newspapers say of me, but they have had their fun. I am in London now, the Confederacy is dead, and it is time for them to find a new target. Incidentally, I was shocked and sickened by their statements that Jefferson Davis was captured while masquerading in the clothes of a woman. As you know I was not with him at the time of his capture and I have had no communication from him, but I know this to be a monstrous lie. Mr. Davis has been charged with many failings by many men, but I knew him well and I will stake my life on the fact that he is no coward and has never behaved as one. But perhaps by this time only idiots believe the story anyway.

As for myself, Joseph—I left Mr. Davis in Washington,

Georgia. *I bought a horse and some rough clothes, and, making it a point to avoid heavily populated areas, I made for Florida's west coast. I reasoned that I would be expected on the east coast by federal authorities, therefore I unsociably chose the west. It was a good choice, I suppose, but the business of getting a boat out of there delayed me for a month and I can tell you it was a month of chilling suspense. At any moment I expected to be apprehended, but fortunately my nerves are not of the jumpy variety and I survived the ordeal. Someone once told me that all good lawyers are good actors. Modesty forbids me appraising my legal ability but as regards my acting, dear Joseph, I have no foolish compunctions about stating very clearly that I am superb. And in the end I got a boat. Here I should really close the letter and let you wait for the next installment with the breathless impatience that Rebecca used to wait for Mr. Dickens's next, but I shall continue.*

On the 23rd of June I finally got out of Florida in a regular thimble of a boat. It wasn't at all like traveling on a Cunard liner. Six hundred miles of sunburn and terrible storms. Have you ever seen a waterspout, Joseph? I have. In fact I have seen two of them. The performance opened with a great black cloud and terrible wind. Instantly these twin devils were born and began their murderous journey toward our small boat. The roar was deafening and disaster seemed inevitible, but God was with us and the waterspouts miraculously veered away and we were saved. A quarter of an hour later all was as peaceful as paradise, with our boat sweetly dreaming on the breast of the Bahama Sea. The only flaw was that there was also a federal vessel sweetly dreaming not far away from ours. For a moment I wished the waterspouts back but the Yankee boys proved far less dangerous. The two men who sailed our little boat explained that I spoke only Spanish and that after an unsuccessful attempt at farming in Florida was returning to the Indies. I felt horribly guilty, so sympathetic were the Yankee lads at hearing of my farm's failure. One of them shook his head and said, "Poor feller and he ain't too young either. Hope he can make a fresh start." Somehow I treasure his words.

We arrived July 10th at Bimini and of course that ended
the risk of my being captured. It did not, however, give me
any guarantee that I would not be drowned. The sloop I took
passage on for Nassau promptly sank. Well, not promptly.
It waited till we were too far from land to swim safely back.
Three Negro boys and I jumped into a small skiff and had
a splendid view of our sloop as it sank beneath the waves. We
had one oar. It was eight o'clock in the morning and we were
all mightily depressed. For three hours we saw nothing but
sun and water. The boys were praying for a vessel to come to
our rescue. My prayers were more specific. I wanted a vessel,
too, but it had to be French or British to satisfy me. And at
last a British rescuer came and landed us back in Bimini.

Do you think that was the end of my adventures? Oh, no.
There is more to come. Another sloop out of Bimini bound for
Nassau. This one did not sink but it was so beset by storms,
calms, and self-doubt that it consumed six days in the process
of covering one hundred miles! But at last Nassau was achieved.
I had begun to think it as inaccessible as an island upon the
moon, but despite my joy in arriving at Nassau I did not
linger there. I went at once to Havana where I bought some
clothes that would prove acceptable apparel for a transat-
lantic crossing on a decent ship. The clothes are not, I may
say, the smartest I have ever owned, but I couldn't wear my
Georgia farmer's clothes aboard an ocean liner.

From Havana I went to the Island of St. Thomas. That will
mean nothing to you, Joseph, but to Solomon and Rebecca
and me it is that foolish, sentimental thing—the birthplace.
You Charlestonians can skip the next few lines. St. Thomas
is beautiful with a strange pure beauty that one never sees
in a city. Cities live only to grow larger and more important.
St. Thomas is like a flower that wants nothing but to be enjoyed for its sweetness. Of course our aunts and uncles are
dead. Their plantations belong to strangers but, ghostlike,
I drove past and paused, remembering the gold necklaces and
cool smiles of those queenly women who were somehow, and
quite remarkably, our aunts.

Charlestonians may now read on.

I left for Southampton on the 13th of August. It was a lovely *afternoon and everything seemed just right for a charming voyage. Everything continued to seem just right till half-past nine that night, when the ship caught fire! We started back at once for St. Thomas with part of the ship burning and all of us standing, so to speak, with one foot in a lifeboat. It was three A.M. when we accomplished—or rather the captain accomplished—the feat of landing at St. Thomas with every soul aboard safe. His ship, however, will be out of service for some time, I fear. Her deck had but an eigth of an inch of its original thickness and seven feet of water had been pumped into her hold.*

Two days later I was off again—this time with understandable misgivings, but to my amazement nothing at all happened. Not even in jest will I say that I found the uneventful voyage a bore. It was delightful and I arrived at Southampton on August 30th. That is the story of my escape, Joseph. If there is anything sinister about it, then wind and water are sinister. If there is deep intrigue, then fire is a subtle conspirator in league with persons of high station. I had money and I paid my way. I did not steal the money and you will observe that I "paid" my way. No bribery was involved. I never encountered a single person on my adventure that could have been bribed. I had no unusual assistance from any source. No federal soldier or sailor was corrupted by my vast stolen wealth. No Confederate sympathizer, posing as a loyal Unionist shielded my movements. In short, Joseph, my escape completely lacks the Dumas touch. There were no heroes and no villains and no thrilling dark encounters in deserted houses or on lonely moonlit beaches. No bloodstained gold. What a pity for those who like their news sensational.

In passing through Georgia I sent Rebecca nine hundred dollars in the care of an acquaintance of mine. I trust she received it. I suppose it is unnecessary to explain why I did not deliver it in person or pause for a visit. It is, I know, also unnecessary to add that I would have been happy to send her more but just could not manage to do so. In recent years the amounts I have been able to send Rebecca always represented the best I could do at the time but were never as lavish as I wished them to be. However, if God continues to bless me with good health I will see that she is comfortable again and lacks nothing.

I have not yet been to Paris to see my darling wife and daughter. I am looking forward, as you can imagine, to a wonderful reunion. It is five years since I have seen them, the longest five years of my life.

Well, Joseph, I now have you fully informed on the Life and Adventures of your older brother, former senator from Louisiana. Do tell anyone who will listen to you the facts as here presented. And if you are really as much like Papa as I think you are then you will tell them even to people who do not care to listen.

With deepest affection, dear brother, I will now end this letter.

Judah

It occurred to him that they would read with amazement that he had not yet been to Paris. The family would wonder if he had changed beyond belief or if always his ardent pursuit of Natalie had been a somewhat romantic pose. It was unlikely that any of them would guess the truth. And perhaps the truth was ridiculous, but nevertheless he could not go to Paris till the tailor had finished his two new suits. After five years Natalie, the elegant Natalie, must not be confronted with a husband garbed in cheap Havana clothes, a husband who would be a disturbing note in her exquisite little house.

He sat quietly at the writing table and thought of the shirt-maker and the bootmaker. He hoped they would fill his order as swiftly as the tailor had promised. Every stitch they sewed brought him nearer to Natalie. She was not across an ocean now but only a channel, and yet he could not rush to her, he could not still his longing till the tailor, the shirtmaker, and the boot-maker were ready. A humorous situation, material perhaps for a Parisian comedy. Still, if written as a comedy the playwright must never permit the audience to feel that the husband was a rather pathetic character, terribly uncertain as to whether or not he was really wanted in the exquisite little house. The element of humor might be lost entirely if the audience began to pity the husband.

The matter of money was never far from his thoughts these days. Again in his mind he added up the bills he must pay, his weekly expenses, the amount he must allow himself for his visit to Paris. Even with excursions into the cheapest sections of London in search of those restaurants where no one disdained a man who dined only on bread and cheese, the money dwindled appallingly. He would have to find some way of earning a few dollars—or rather a few pounds—while he was building his new life.

He got up from the writing table and walked to the window. London. He had inherited another city. And he remembered the long-lost day that he had stood upon the steps of St. Louis Cathedral and had vowed to make New Orleans his. He smiled. At seventeen nothing seems impossible. He was no longer seventeen. And yet—

I am not tired. I am not dejected and, by God, I am not frightened. Let us consider each other, London. You have much to offer. Is there anything of mine that you could use? Does the question seem presumptuous in view of all you have? Forgive me if it does. I am your humble servant, London. What will happen here? What will happen?

His daughter was a tall, grave girl, who strongly resembled the Mendes women. She sat on a hassock and looked up at him with eagerness and affection and he took pleasure from the warm acceptance he found in her eyes. After dinner she disappeared, leaving him alone with Natalie, and for the first time they dared to stare. Half-smiling, half-tearful they shamelessly looked at each other, seeking for change, for sameness.

"Well?" he asked.

She said, "Still the fascinating Benjamin. A little heavier perhaps but it is not unbecoming. At last you have ceased to look like a boy. At my age I am delighted that you are not quite so youthful as you were."

"At your age, my dear? Are you more than thirty-five?"

"Beloved," she said, "you are a flatterer, but it is so good to have you here. There were times I thought that never again—the newspapers said such terrifying things. You have no idea what they said."

"About what?" he asked absently.

"About what! About the war and what the United States would do if—"

"Were your eyelashes always so long, my darling?"

"Of course they were, silly."

"Natalie, I love you so."

"It is charming to hear, but I have said to myself, 'When Judah comes you must not be frivolous, Natalie. You must talk to him about the war and all those serious things that have been his life these long years.' So do proceed, Judah. Tell me whatever it is a husband wishes to tell his wife when he has returned from a terrible ordeal."

"I love you, Natalie. That is all I wish to tell you."

There was laughter in her eyes and upon her red mouth. "To tell the truth, beloved, it is all I wish to hear. I am not a woman who appreciates the cleverness of generals or delights in the harrowing details of slaughter and starvation. I am very happy that you do not feel the need to dwell upon unpleasant memories. You are here. Nothing else matters. Tell me that you missed me."

"I cannot say how much I missed you. There are not the words to describe my longing."

"Poor Judah." She brought a bottle of wine from the sideboard and poured with the sure and graceful movement of white hands that he remembered so well. She did not return to her chair but perched on the arm of his and bent close to him offering her mouth. He took the kiss cautiously. This was the drawing room of a house inhabited by four servants and Ninette.

"You kissed me that warmly at the railway station," she said.

"Indeed and I feel this room to be no more secluded than—"

"It will do for a while," she whispered. "It will do till you have kissed me as I have dreamed—"

He drew her upon his lap and held her tightly and found her lips even softer than he remembered them. And after a time she rose and took his hand and quietly led the way upstairs. Once, in another house, she had led the way upstairs. She was still as he had known her long ago in New Orleans. And it was not yet time to live again with Natalie. He was not prepared to face another ordeal of lies and deceits that his constant presence forced upon her. Perhaps he had dreamed, perhaps he had hoped, but the time had not yet come. His home would be London, and within himself he had known that all along.

She said to him, "It would have killed me if, after this long separation, we had gone to bed like any dull married couple and had desire creep upon us simply as a result of proximity. I want always to be exciting to you."

"You always have been, Natalie."

"Because I am not really a wife, beloved. I am your mistress."

He drew her closer to him. "Will you marry me?"

She sighed. "The mere mention of marriage makes a different personality of me. Suddenly I am a wife engrossed in the deadly concerns that befit such a creature. Tomorrow night the Slidells are coming for dinner."

"The Slidells?"

"Yes. I wrote Mathilde a note as soon as I knew the date you would arrive. She probably will develop a fearful headache as the dinner hour approaches but he will certainly come."

"Mathilde also, my dear."

"I am not sure her admiration for you will tempt her when she considers spending an evening with me."

"She will come, Natalie."

"If she does she will wear the most elaborate gown you can imagine. She has about a dozen, the dressmaker tells me, that were designed for wear at Eugénie's entertainments just around the time the Emperor discovered he could live without Slidell. Let me see, she has a pink, a yellow, a blue, a red—"

Mathilde wore the pink and she looked enchanting. She flew into Judah's arms and hugged him. "Does anyone mind?" she asked.

Slidell said, "I do. Step aside, woman, so I can hug Benjamin myself." Slidell, an imposing figure of a man, carrying the authority that goes with a handsome, vigorous old age. "How are you, Benjamin, my boy?"

And Judah looking up at Slidell felt only a surge of joy and exhilaration at the sight of the old familiar face. Slidell had come to France not to serve the Confederacy but to marry off his daughters in style. He had promoted the Erlanger loan, not for the Confederacy but for Baron Erlanger. In short, Slidell had acted like Slidell and it was hard to hate him for being the man he was. Especially when one considered that the reason for loving him was because he was consistently and unfailingly Slidell.

At the table the war was discussed of course. It could not, Judah realized, be any other way, but the surprising thing to him was the interest Ninette had taken.

"Oh, yes," she said in answer to his question, "I read every word I could find concerning the war, even those absurd little pamphlets circulated here to acquaint the French with the blessings of slavery."

"Absurd little pamphlets!" Slidell snorted. "Young lady, I will have you know they were extremely clever."

"Really?" Ninette asked. "What did they accomplish?"

Slidell grinned. "Here in my old age I have another Benjamin to cope with."

Ninette smiled shyly. "A very feminine Benjamin," she said. "I confess to being mostly intrigued by the dashing figures of the Confederacy. I was very sad when Jeb Stuart was killed." She turned suddenly to Judah. "What was he really like?"

Slidell said, "Your hero did not carry enough rank to do business with your papa."

"Didn't you know him, Papa?"

"Oh, I encountered him at many social gatherings. He was like everything you read about him, Ninette. Brave, gentle, humorous. He really did have a banjoist riding with him to lighten the grim hours."

"I am glad he was like that."

"He did not chew tobacco and he never took a drink and his religion meant so much to him that he did not live it on the front pages of the newspapers."

Mathilde said, "He sounds wonderful."

Slidell glowered at her. "Two moon-eyed ladies are more than I can stand, especially when one is my wife. Madame, look at me. Am I not as appealing as a dead hero?"

"Certainly not," Mathilde said. "And speaking of heroes— before you left America, Mr. Benjamin, did you see my brother-in-law—Beauregard?"

"I did indeed. We had some conversation regarding *my* brother-in-law and an assortment of Louisianians bound for New Orleans. By the way, Natalie, have you heard from Jules?"

"My father has. Jules does not write to me. I don't know why, but he does not. Only once have I heard from him in years. It was when Mama died. He wrote that he had a mass said in the Richmond church."

Judah nodded. "I remember that he did. Poor boy, he was heartbroken. I trust he is well and that all—"

"What do you think they'll do about Davis, Benjamin?"

"Keep him in jail for a while."

"You don't think they'll hang him?"

"No. Tempers are cooling. The danger is past, but if they'd caught him or any of us when the grief of Mr. Lincoln's death was fresh— Of course Davis will have a miserable time."

"I am sorry for his wife," Ninette said. "She seems so sweet and helpless."

Mathilde and Natalie looked at each other and laughed.

"What did I say that was funny, Mama?"

"We are thinking of Varina Davis, darling. We know her well. You knew her, too, but of course you don't remember. She is a tall, strong woman. Rather an Amazon really."

Mathilde said, "Sweet and helpless are simply not words that describe Varina Davis. She wouldn't be afraid of a cottonmouth, the Yankee army, or the devil himself. Sweet and helpless!"

Slidell said, "I guess you and Breckenridge were the only cabinet members who got away, Benjamin. Is that right?"

"Yes. I hope Mallory does not serve a long term. He is a good fellow, and poor little Reagan is all right, too."

"You do not care about the others?" Slidell asked.

"I do, of course, but Mallory was my friend and Reagan was rather pathetic."

Ninette said, "It is all very strange. It is like having read a book and then being confronted with the realization that the characters are real, living people. Papa, did you actually know Robert E. Lee?"

"Slightly, Daughter, slightly."

"Was he as handsome as they say?"

"I do not believe a handsomer man ever lived."

Ninette sighed contentedly. "It is all just as it was in the book," she said.

Slidell's mouth twisted in a wry smile. "Not quite, young lady. In books the heroes don't lose wars."

"In my book they didn't," Ninette said. "I have not mentioned that I also fancied Phil Sheridan and William Sherman."

When dinner was over Natalie announced the plan for the evening. "Mathilde and I know how you two want to talk together. Therefore we will make you a present of the drawing room complete with cognac and cigars. We will repair to my boudoir and a discussion of fashion."

When they were gone Slidell spread his long legs comfortably out before him and gazed at Judah. "Well, Benjamin," he said, "what can I do for you?"

Judah smiled. "If you had not asked I would have been disappointed, old friend, but there is nothing you can do. Nothing."

Slidell lighted a cigar and stared thoughtfully through the cloud of smoke at Judah. "You cannot mean that. Remember, I know you well. You never saved a dollar in your life and for four years you've earned practically nothing. So certain am I of your financial condition, Benjamin, that I have worried about your future."

"Very kind of you, Slidell."

"Well, what are friends for? I come to you tonight with three propositions. Any one of which will give you a new start." He narrowed his eyes and considered Judah. "Will you listen or are you going to get all huffy and proud?"

"Huffy and proud with you, Slidell? At this late date? I will lean back contentedly while you plan my future. Begin, I beg of you."

Slidell said, "Proposition one concerns an elegant office, an important position, and a salary of fifteen thousand dollars."

"Delightful. Do I sell my soul outright to the devil or does he simply hire it by the year?"

"He hires it by the year."

"Splendid. Splendid." Judah nodded and sipped his cognac. "Half-day on Saturdays?"

Slidell said, "You think I'm joking, don't you? This is a very solid deal, boy. I spent all last night threshing it out."

"With whom, Slidell?"

"With Baron Erlanger of course. It would be a great thing for you, Benjamin. He has a huge staff of lawyers and you wouldn't have to do a damn thing except give your personal opinion to the old man and let the others do the work. You would sit in on important meetings and advise the banking house how to—"

"What's proposition two, Slidell?"

Slidell went to the sideboard and poured himself a drink. "Benjamin, you're a fool. That could be a sweet deal." He looked around the drawing room with its fine furnishings and satin draperies. "If I know you—and I think I do—you bought this house outright for Natalie. It's small but it's beautiful and in a smart section of town. You'll never need or want anything better than this. All right then. Think how magnificently, how free of worry you could live here on fifteen thousand a year."

"I am thinking, Slidell, and the thought bores me to distraction. Did you ever know me to pine for security? Was my goal ever freedom from worry?"

"Well, it's about time it was."

"Really? Have you prudently retired to a small—but beautiful—house? Is your income neatly arranged in a cozy but permanent bracket? Are you—"

"God damn it, Benjamin, I saved my money. You didn't, and I'm worried sick about you."

"Sit down and calm yourself, Slidell. Proceed to proposition two."

"It's not as good as number one. As a matter of fact I thought you might take on both." Slidell studied the cognac within the small, crystal shell. "A publisher I know will pay a whopping sum for your reminiscences. I didn't get the terms settled but I know you can wangle a good price from him."

"My reminiscences? Now who would have thought the public could be induced to care about the cases I fought in California or the one in Ecuador or my triumph in the *Mussina* versus *Cavazos* matter?"

Slidell said, "Quit fooling, Benjamin. You know what they'll buy. They'll buy your four years in the Confederacy."

"Yes, I know. I know what they'll buy." Judah shook his head sadly. "It's a hell of a thing when you come to think of it, Slidell. I was a success for almost thirty years of my life, yet my four years of failure is what the man wishes me to write about."

"Well, it was a mighty interesting four years."

"Was it, Slidell? Perhaps you would like to write about it then. Personally I think I would like to forget it. I have not the temperament for dwelling in the past."

"The past! Christ Almighty, Mallory's in jail but the *Shenandoah* hasn't yet surrendered. They're still cleaning up Richmond and I heard only yesterday—"

"It's today now, Slidell, so let's talk about today. What is proposition three?"

"Well, proposition three goes back a little way, too. Could you possibly beat that up-to-the-minute mind of yours into recalling a plantation house that was named Belle Chasse?"

"It comes to me in a vague sort of way."

"All right then. There was a day when you and your Belle Chasse were in a bit of trouble and I, noble friend of your youth, offered you one hundred thousand dollars to get straightened out."

"*That* I have never forgotten."

"You refused the offer, Benjamin, and I took my little hundred thousand dollars and folded it into a small square and stuck it in my vest pocket. And do you know what? Just tonight when I was dressing I discovered it all safe and sound just where I had absent-mindedly put it that day. So I brought it along with me. Will you take it this time, Benjamin?"

Judah looked away from Slidell. Slidell, who couldn't help being a good friend any more than he could help being a bad lot.

"That's proposition three, Slidell? It's the nicest of them all but I have to say no to that one as well as the others."

"Why? Why, in God's name do you always have to refuse assistance?"

"I don't always refuse it but somehow I— Please Slidell, let me say that I am grateful and that I believe that no man has ever had a more generous friend than you have been to me but—"

"Listen to me. Take my advice, Benjamin. Grab all three propositions. They're all good and they're all yours. Not another man alive could have any one of them. I must say that for a fellow who has no plans you're—"

"I have plans. I'm going to be a lawyer."

"A lawyer! You're going to start all over again here?"

"No, not here. Not in Paris. In London."

"London! Why London? My God, here I could be of some help to you. Benjamin, you've picked out a rough road. London is boiling with good lawyers."

So was New Orleans, my friend. It had you and Roselius and Soulé and Mazureau and—"

"London has Atherly-Jones and Hedderwick and Spratt and Pollock, and, believe me, London doesn't need any Americans. What's wrong with settling down here at a comfortable fifteen thousand dollars a year?"

"I'm not the man for the job, Slidell."

"Would you be the man at seventy-five thousand?"

"Probably."

"That's what I thought."

"Have I made a disgraceful admission? My God, Slidell, I see no virtue in working for fifteen thousand if one knows one is worth more. And I see no shame in loving the things that money can buy. I have bought a lot of happiness for myself and others with cold cash. If God helps me, I shall do it again."

"*If* God helps you."

"Yes, if. Money is not contemptible. I have never seen a mean, unpleasant rich man in my life who would have been a kind and charming poor man. Money blunts no one's taste for culture and when it brings unhappiness it is only because it was poorly used. To me it has never been a villain. I suspect its most ardent detractors are those who do not know it well—though of course such reasoning would not apply to you."

"All right. All right. I only wanted to help. Go try to earn a million if you think you can, but, Benjamin, for Christ's sake, if you're going to bat your head against a wall at least do it in Paris where you have me."

"It has to be London, Slidell."

"You know you cannot just open an office and proceed to

accept cases, my friend. The English are rather fussy about English training for their barristers."

"I can learn what Englishmen have learned, Slidell."

Slidell poured himself another drink. With his back to Judah he sighed heavily. "You know what, you bastard? If you don't practice British law blindfolded and with stones in your mouth you're a God-damned coward."

There were a hundred and fifty students of law that term, many of them up from Oxford and Cambridge. Eager youths intent upon becoming lawyers. It startled them to find in their midst a man old enough to be the father of any one of them. Their glances politely wandered away, then furtively came back again and again.

Judah smiled at the lad beside him. "Good morning."

"Good morning to you, sir." Blue eyes, pleasant but puzzled. "Er—are you—"

"Studying law? Oh, definitely."

"I expect you always wanted to make it your career."

"All my life it is what I wanted."

"Splendid, sir. And now you have your chance? Is that it?"

"Yes, now I have my chance."

"Good luck to you, sir."

"I am glad you said that."

Judah wished he could tell Slidell something of the quaintness, the strangeness of his new life, but to do so would be to invite another lecture on the futility of the effort. Still, it would be amusing to hear Slidell's comments on the dinners. He would fail, as Judah himself failed, to perceive the connection between dining and studying law but it was very clear to the British. Every student was pledged to pay for a certain number of meals per term.

Judah wondered why the authorities did not simply tack a few extra shillings on the tuition and omit the dinners. But that, he realized, was strictly an American line of thought. Tradition was still efficiency's master in England. And who was to say that their positions should be reversed? Perhaps the young men at the lowly students' table received inspiration and encouragement from this custom. Perhaps it was a spur to young ambition to gaze upon successful barristers at the very next table to theirs and to see the great old leaders of the bar dining at the head table in splendid isolation.

When I get to that head table I will make it a point to nod cordially toward the students. Of course that is not the truth. I will not nod even frostily to them, for when I reach that head table I will be thinking as an Englishman thinks or I will not reach that table at all.

After the early months of study there would be examinations and students would be chosen to enter law offices as pupils and thus augment their classwork with practical observation. It occurred to Judah that once the examinations were finished he and the other students would be rather like young ladies at a ball wondering if they would be asked to dance.

He was spared the suspense. He was not to be a wallflower. During the first month of study he had a heart-warming message.

Dear Mr. Benjamin:

All London knows you are here and admires you greatly for your pluck and determination. Therefore I do not think I am behaving badly in anticipating the many invitations you will receive. It is simply absurd to await the examination papers before extending an invitation to you. Do come and study in my office.

My father is Sir Frederick Pollock, lord chief baron of the exchequer, and I, myself, have a rather substantial practice specializing mostly in mercantile cases. It is only proper that you make inquiries concerning us, thus assuring yourself of getting off on the right foot.

Respectfully yours,
Charles Pollock

And life formed itself into a neat pattern of hard work. In the morning he attended classes with other law students and in the afternoon he learned the methods, whims, and traditions of an Englishman's law office. In the evening he studied the books which Pollock said were indispensable to a barrister. And at midnight he turned to the business of earning a living. The London

Daily Telegraph was paying him about twenty-five dollars for every article on international affairs that he brought to them.

"Can you not find time for more than two a week, Mr. Benjamin? We could use four."

"No, I cannot find time. I am sorry. Could you, by any chance, pay me a few extra shillings if I wrote more fully, more—"

"Regrettably we cannot, sir. However if you would join our staff as an assistant editor we could guarantee an excellent salary."

"That is out of the question but I do thank you."

In the Pollock office Charles handed Judah a sheaf of papers. "Did I mention that I am counsel for the London Metropolitan Police? Here is something for you to stew over, Mr. Benjamin. Write me an opinion involving the right of police to search persons before they have been convicted of any crime. I am going to court. This will keep you busy in my absence."

"If you hurry," Judah said.

Pollock, a stiff, rather pompous man, gazed down his nose at his extraordinary pupil. Impudent fellow, the pale eyes remarked. Still, how did one chastise a pupil who had been a United States senator and a leader of the American bar?

Judah spent an hour with the police papers and regretted when the work was finished. Pollock, looking them over upon his return, read carefully and placed the papers in the "Finished Business" basket on his desk.

"There was no need to go back to first principles in justification of your reasoning," he said. "The report is for the London Police. It was not intended to be carved on Justinian's monument. I would prefer that you had given it less elaboration and used your additional time to write your comments on French maritime law as opposed to British."

Judah said, "I was also able to fit that in somehow, sir."

"Oh, really? Good boy." Pollock flushed violently and turned away. "I didn't quite mean 'good boy,' Mr. Benjamin, but it is difficult to—"

Judah said, "Sir, I am your pupil. When you wish to reprove me please do so. On the other hand, I beg of you, never withhold your praise fearing it will sound patronizing. I glow at a word of praise from you, sir. There is much I have to learn."

Pollock fiddled with the inkwell and did not look at his pupil. "Yes, yes. Of course. Of course," he said. "Er—why don't you come down to our country place over the week end? Hatton, you know. Rather nice house really."

Judah met Charles's father there. Old Baron Pollock, sharp-eyed, firm-voiced at eighty-three.

"I have known of you for years, Mr. Benjamin. Always considered you the world's greatest lawyer, with the exception of some of our English lads. It disturbed me that you might be captured. Dreadful thing to hang a good lawyer. I would have been very annoyed. Always wanted to hear those mellifluous tones of yours. How are you getting on in my son's office?"

Judah said, "I am happy there, sir."

"Good. Good."

"I am very thankful to Mr. Pollock for—"

The old man shook with quiet laughter. "Mr. Pollock? Charles? *I* wrote you that letter. Charles was furious. He said you would try to run his office." Baron Pollock bent close and peered into Judah's face. "You haven't tried, have you?"

"No, I don't think so, sir."

"Splendid. Take yourself off now if you choose. Have a look at our place. Rather proud of it, you know. The lake and all that. By the way, have you met Gladstone and Disraeli yet?"

Judah smiled. "No. Do apprentice lawyers usually meet Gladstone and Disraeli?"

Baron Pollock looked at him thoughtfully. "Ah, that's what disturbs Charles, is it? American humor. He has never understood it. It has a quality of underlying bitterness, has it not? Rather amused by it myself. Always fancied I would like America. I once thought—" Abruptly he fell silent and stared at Judah with deep concern in his eyes. "Good heavens, man. You're an American!"

Judah made no answer to this astonishing comment. Had it not already been established that he was an American?

"Mr. Benjamin, it has just occurred to me that you will never be called to the bar. It is an old practice of the Inns of Court to choose none but a subject of the crown. Did you not know that?"

"Yes, sir. It is my intention to become a British subject as soon as possible."

Baron Pollock's sharp black eyes met Judah's. "You are a

patient man, Mr. Benjamin. I will tell you truthfully that I had planned to inform the authorities that in my opinion it would be sheer stupidity to insist upon Judah Benjamin's taking three years of law courses. Now I see no purpose in shortening your studies. Until you are a subject, sir, you cannot be a barrister. A pity. A great pity. But at least we can see that you meet everyone worth knowing so you will be no stranger here."

So Judah met the great Gladstone and the fabulous Disraeli. He dined with Tennyson and had no need to hesitate at the poet's question "What words of mine, Mr. Benjamin, do you favor above others?"

" 'Man is man and master of his fate.' "

The poet was satisfied. "I like that, too," he said.

Judah visited the palatial country seat of Sir Joseph Hawley but could not remain for the entire week end. The *Telegraph* had promised an extra pound if his next article was in time for the Sunday edition.

Baron Pollock roared with laughter when Judah explained why he left before the arrival of the Prince of Wales. "I shall have to tell that to Hawley one day. What excuse did you give him for not remaining?"

"Excuse, sir? I told him the truth. Surely he can understand that a pound is too formidable an amount for a man to sacrifice for mere pleasure."

"Yes, yes. You are right. Hawley would understand. You have, however, refreshing notions, I must say. Is everyone in Louisiana so forthright?"

"Regrettably I cannot claim the characteristics of Louisiana, sir. I represented the state in the Senate but—"

"Ah, yes, I remember you were born in South Carolina."

"As a matter of fact I was not. I was born on St. Thomas in the Virgin Islands."

The old man gasped and his hand shook as he reached out to Judah. "What year, sir? Were you born while the British held the islands? Were you, Mr. Benjamin? Were you?"

"Why, yes, of course, but my father's naturalization while I was still under age made me an American citizen, sir—"

"Only in the eyes of Americans, Mr. Benjamin. You were born of British parents, under the British flag, and, by God, there are no words your father could say that will rob you of your rights on British soil. Tomorrow I shall go up to London and fight like a veritable dragoon and when I am finished fighting, sir, you will be a British barrister."

It seemed to Judah that there should be a view of New Orleans from his office window. He had sat like this before on another day, in another world, alone in an office, straining his ears for the sound of a client's footsteps. Always in the beginning there was the waiting, the hoping, the wondering. Well, a man could not sit idle. He must find something to occupy his mind, and so, as in the long ago, Judah was writing a book. It would be entitled "Treatise on the Law of Sale of Personal Property with Reference to American Decisions, French Code and Civil Law."

"A catchy title," Baron Pollock had said looking very pleased with himself. "There, Mr. Benjamin, that remark of mine has the ring of American humor, has it not?"

On Judah's desk along with his notes and references there was a small, neatly tied bundle of papers. They had been brought that morning by a clerk of a well-known legal firm. There was an envelope attached. It contained five pounds and the request that Mr. Benjamin read the papers and give an opinion. Mr. Benjamin had not even glanced at the papers. Five pounds? Good heavens, that wouldn't buy two good dinners.

Benjamin, you are alone in the office. Drop your guard. Be honest. It would buy two dozen dinners at today's standards. Pocket the five pounds.

He did not touch the papers. They were still unopened when the clerk returned for them.

"Tell your employers I have not read them. My fee is forty pounds for examining papers."

The clerk was back in a twinkling and Judah had his forty pounds. It was a triumph and he treasured it tenderly, for triumphs were few that year. He rounded out a full twelve months in his own office with records showing earnings of little more than two thousand dollars.

Sometimes in the night he thought about Natalie's annual income. In another few years that would be at an end. What then?

The position at Erlanger's, if Erlanger would still have him? Suppose he had been wrong? Suppose he failed at law in London? How was Natalie to live as she had always lived? Good God, you didn't bring a woman like Natalie to a room with worn carpet and faded draperies. Women had survived such catastrophes of course, but not Natalie—oh, please, dear God, not Natalie.

Slidell visited London and looked at Judah's office and at Judah's room.

He said, "Christ Almighty, Benjamin, quit breaking your heart. This is ridiculous."

"Not really, old friend. I will do better when my book comes out. It is nearly finished but the closer I get to the end the more fastidious I become about correcting, amending, and improving it. Also I am getting some notice for a little matter I handled last week."

"What are you doing handling little matters?"

"A figure of speech, Slidell. I revised the rules of a marine insurance company."

Slidell shrugged. "I am not completely stunned," he said. "I suppose any lawyer could revise the rules of a marine insurance company."

"In twelve hours, Slidell?"

"Twelve hours! *Now* I'm stunned. Couldn't do a job like that myself in less than thirteen. Did you take time off for dinner?"

"To tell the truth I did not. I worked straight through but it was worth it. I hear the job was expected to take two weeks. People are talking."

"But are they paying?"

"They will, Slidell. They will."

Slidell shook his head. "Hate to admit it but I guess you're a fair-to-middlin' legal brain. By the way, did you know anyone in the Confederacy named J. B. Jones? He says he was a war clerk."

"He *says?* My God, is the man here?"

"No. He has a book out. I just read it. You do know him?"

"Oh, yes. He worked for the firm before it went bankrupt."

Slidell said, "I found out all about you, Mr. Benjamin. It seems you are a very dishonest fellow, a very calculating man with nothing in mind but your own well-being. Moreover, it seems you are a Jew, and if you don't know how the war was lost I will tell you. It was lost because Yankees, Marylanders, and Jews became powerful and influential in the Confederacy. Oh, that's a broad-minded boy, that Jones."

"I had a feeling I was not his hero."

Slidell grinned. "You ought to read the book, friend. You'll froth at the mouth if you do, but it's damned interesting reading. It gives a picture of the Confederacy that—"

"It so happens, Slidell, that I don't need Jones's picture of the Confederacy. I had a better view of the scene than he had."

Slidell nodded. "I was hoping you'd say something like that. It gives me a chance to tell you that my publisher friend still wants your reminiscences. Benjamin, you could get a fine price and a chance to reply to some of the outrageous things Jones has said of you."

Judah stared. "Are you mad? Do you actually think I would argue with that dismal little war clerk? My God, Slidell, he's just praying that a controversy will make the book famous."

"No reminiscences, Benjamin?"

"No, Slidell. Never."

"You and Robert E. Lee are two of a kind."

Judah laughed. "If I were you I wouldn't say that to Lee."

"You're both tight-lipped, uncommunicative clams. He, too, has turned down a chunk of money for his memoirs." Slidell blinked his eyes speculatively. "You know what I think, Benjamin? I think an awful lot of things went on in the Confederacy that fellows like you and Lee are too damn decent to blabber about."

"Lee is probably too decent, my friend. I'm just bored with the whole subject."

"Are you bored with the idea of twenty-five thousand dollars? I think I can get that much for you."

"Slidell, I yawn at the notion of writing about what I said to Christopher Memminger and what Christopher Memminger said to Robert Toombs."

"But twenty-five thousand, Benjamin!"

Judah's next year in British law showed only a thousand dollars improvement over the first but his law book was still not ready. Remembering New Orleans and another law book, he had almost a superstitious feeling about the work. It was all very well to be that fellow from America with the flashing argument and the numbing sarcasm, but he had not proved to anyone that he deserved a place of importance at the British bar. The book must help him prove it. If it did not—

What shall I do about Natalie if I am not able to earn a living that will give her all I want to give her?

Feverishly he threw himself into another reading of his law book, weighing each word, each phrase for clarity and perfection. He was aware that this book must reveal intellectual power and a clear perception of essential rules in their practical application. Consciously he leveled upon the business of impressing the legal profession.

I am writing an advertisement for myself. In this book I must convince the world of law that it cannot struggle on without consulting me. I must make it plain that my opinion is of importance. I will have only this chance to tell the British bar that I am sorely needed. It will listen only once. This book must be as nothing before it has been or I am finished. This book with the tedious, ponderous title must be so profound that it will forever keep Natalie frivolous and without a care.

Day and night he bent above his work with burning eyes, writing, rewriting, deleting. The time for sleep was signaled by a headache so intense that he could no longer see clearly. By morning he was well again and ready to rewrite, anxious to rephrase a thought that he had written the night before, a thought that had seemed succinctly stated but now displeased him.

And at last, at long last, the book was ready for publication.

Slidell said, "I am glad to see you, Benjamin. It gets tiresome just lying here. What are you doing in France?"

"Oh, I needed a small holiday with Natalie and Ninette so I just dropped everything."

He had done just that. He had dropped everything and gone to Paris the day he had received the note from Mathilde.

Please, if you can, dear Mr. Benjamin. He knows he is dying. I can tell by the sad way he speaks and often he mentions you and there is such loneliness in his voice—

Slidell propped up on the pillows, his face sharp and bloodless, the eyes darkly circled.

"This reminds me of the day I first visited you, Slidell, in New Orleans. Remember? You were getting over an illness then, too."

"I remember." Slidell sighed. "That was a long time ago, Benjamin. Andrew Jackson was president."

Judah smiled. It was so like Slidell to figure time by the White House tenant rather than the calendar.

"Jesus, Benjamin, where do the years go? Mine went so fast. I can't believe it. It seems the war just ended, but it's six years since Appomattox."

"I know."

Slidell stared down at the silken coverlet. "It's been a big six years for you, Benjamin. Forgive me, old friend."

"For what?"

"For not having faith in you, for trying to talk you into being Erlanger's number-one office boy. Honest to God, Benjamin, I thought it would be a good thing for you. I didn't know how much courage, how God-damned much courage you had."

Judah said, "Oh, please, Slidell, let us have none of that. I am heartily sick of having the word courage applied to myself and to others who have acted only in the interest of self-preservation. People who work like mad to keep themselves from sinking are not, in my eyes, heroes, dear friend. I fail to see the glorious courage required to act in one's own behalf."

"You have plenty of courage," Slidell said doggedly.

"No. I will tell you what I have. I have a nature that rebels against distrust of the future. I have been complimented on my pluck but it was only elasticity of natural temperament, the inability to believe in failure. Despondency and brooding over adverse circumstances are simply foreign to my nature, so to compliment me on pluck is as foolish as to say that it is clever of me not to get rheumatism in my eleventh finger."

"Perhaps, but I crawl with shame, boy, when I think that I tried to convince you that the Erlanger office would be a nice, comfortable shelter. I'm a stupid old son of a bitch."

"Oh, I've known that for years. But let us not assume that I'm England's leading barrister just yet. I may still come begging for that job at Erlanger's."

"The defender of forlorn hopes," Slidell murmured.

Judah was startled. "What was that?"

"Oh, I hear things. That's what they're calling you in England, isn't it?"

"Yes, I guess so."

"Have you moved out of that rat hole you were living in?"

Judah nodded.

"And you have friends, Benjamin?"

"None like you, Slidell."

Slidell closed his eyes and tears fell weakly upon the hollow cheeks. "Benjamin, do you know I'm dying?"

Judah said, "I will not believe it. It must not be true. I have loved two men in my life above my father and brothers. One is you. The other was my poor brother-in-law, Jules. I am only beginning now to reconcile myself to his death. Slidell, you must not leave me, too."

"Write to August Belmont, Benjamin. Tell him that I—" Slidell paused, thought, then spoke again. "Do not bother about August. After all, he will see a mention in the newspaper that I am dead. He will say, 'Poor Slidell,' and he could do no more than that if he were here in Paris. Besides he is very busy. He has that ballroom of his to keep filled with celebrities, you know."

Judah nodded. "Nothing changes for August, does it?"

"Oh, I don't know. Last year he entertained Victoria's seventh son—and retinue of course. This year he has had nothing nearly that flashy. God, Benjamin, remember August's ballroom? Remember the day we picked out a necklace for Natalie? Does she still have it?"

"She does, Slidell."

"Mathilde, too, has every piece of jewelry I ever bought for her. Creoles are very sentimental. Mathilde will be all right financially. You must not concern yourself about her when I am gone. If she ever asks your opinion about remarrying, tell her to do so, providing he is not younger than she. I want no money-hungry rascal preying upon the girl I treated so tenderly and—I did treat her tenderly, Benjamin. Maybe you think I wasn't that kind of man, but I loved Mathilde."

"No one will ever victimize Mathilde, old friend. Do not worry."

"You will see to it? You will keep her from marrying a scoundrel?"

"Yes, *this* time I will."

Slidell smiled a slow, contented smile and turned his head drowsily upon the pillow. "You bastard," he said.

Mathilde beckoned to Judah from the hallway. "Before you came he was given something to still the pain so that he could talk to you. It has relaxed him so much that now he will sleep." Her face was haggard, her eyes stricken. "Oh, Mr. Benjamin, my heart is broken. They say he cannot last the week. Why does he have to die? Mr. Benjamin, he is such a good man."

A good man? Slidell? Of course. If Mathilde said he was not she would be lying. There was no good, no bad. It only depended upon who rendered the verdict. Was Mathilde to condemn Slidell for his activities in Louisiana politics? Were the people of Louisiana to forgive him because he had been a fine husband?

And I, who saw Slidell in his home reading to his children and loving them well, I, who knew him better than any other knew him, what verdict must I render? For I am aware that he controlled a state with thugs and threats. I saw him create a president, using every trick that had ever been devised, and I have not forgotten the Erlanger loan—but I could have turned to him for anything on God's earth. So what do I say of Slidell?

And in the end no soul searching was needed, for Slidell was neither good nor bad. He was only a man who had been Judah's friend, and Judah, standing in the drawing room of Slidell's residence, looking down upon the body of John Slidell, could only weep. He could remember only that if Slidell were to see his tears he would turn to him now, anxiously, eagerly, and he would say, "What can I do for you, Benjamin?"

There were no other friends. There never would be. If he had not known it before, he knew it well that first night back in London. Lord James stopped by for a glass of wine with Judah. Lord James of Hereford, who had opposed Judah in one of his earliest cases. A tall man of great learning and gentle humor. Judah remembered well how Lord James had waited for him that day as they left the courtroom after the first session. He had never met the man before and had been surprised by the question.

"May I have a word with you, Mr. Benjamin?"

"I am at your service, sir."

"Thank you. What I wish to say is this: For all I know you are the most brilliant legal mind in the world, Mr. Benjamin. I wouldn't care to dispute the point. However, in England we never explain the law to a judge. We never let him know that we consider his knowledge quite unequal to our own. We pretend that judges are at least as bright as ourselves."

Judah had bridled. "You criticize my manners, sir?"

"Oh, it isn't a matter of one's manners. It is simply that we've discovered that the old boys get fretful and rather antagonistic toward barristers who very obviously know more than they do. We smart fellows let the judges think they are far wiser than ourselves."

Lord James had left him then without another word, disappearing into a drab antique of a building in which he had his office. Now he was sitting here in Judah's flat, sipping wine and bringing Judah up to date on the week's important events in London courtrooms. Judah looked at him and thought of that day when with a few words Lord James had changed Judah's style of address to the British bench. Perhaps, despite the impression the weighty law book had made, the career would have gone glimmering, without a small warning from a big man. This, then, was also a friend, so perhaps he could talk to him of the grief, the emptiness within him.

"I am afraid I am not good company. You must forgive me. My mind keeps returning to the funeral of John Slidell."

"Would you like me to leave?"

"Oh, no. I would like you to remain if it is not asking too much. I would rather like to speak of him. Did you by any chance ever meet John Slidell?"

"What was the name? John Slidell?" Lord James looked puzzled and thoughtful. "Oh, of course. John Slidell, the Confederate commissioner to France. No." Was it imagination or had Lord James's eyes and tone suddenly become distantly polite? "I never met the man."

"He was my friend," Judah said quietly.

"Dreadful thing to lose a friend, Mr. Benjamin. I do sympa-

thize with you. I lost a cousin only last autumn who had been
rather close to me since boyhood. A splendid fellow. A bishop."

"Slidell was not a bishop," Judah said.

"No, no, of course not, but I daresay he was very dear to you.
These things are painful."

Judah looked long and hard into the gray eyes of Lord James
of Hereford. Here was a man who would do the sporting thing
for a stranger within London's gates. Here was a man of lofty
principles and ideals, and no doubt it was to his credit that his
eyes grew cool and his manner remote when Slidell was mentioned. He would not have consented to a meeting with Slidell.
He would not have taken his hand in cordial greeting. And all
this was understandable, but the acceptance of it was saddening,
for it only proved beyond a shadow of a doubt that there was
between himself and Lord James a difference that never could
be overlooked or forgotten.

So there would always be someone with whom to talk, someone with whom to share a bottle of wine, but there would be no
friends. There would never be a friend now that Slidell was gone.

Dear Hannah:

*In this same mail I am getting off a letter to Joseph which
is intended to raise his spirits, but you must help in this
endeavor. Good heavens, he mustn't take it so to heart that
the business failed. I will not pretend that $25,000 is only
pennies. It is a large sum of course, but the loss of it has not
injured me and, in giving it to him originally, I recognized
the hazard entailed. I am troubled by nothing but Joseph's feeling of guilt and inadequacy. From all I have heard he applied
his mind and time industriously to the project and should not
find fault with himself at all. Sometimes a man is not suited
to the world of business, and I believe this charge could be
brought against some of the grestest men who ever lived.*

*I am glad that he joined you in Charleston at this unhappy
period in his life. You will be good for him, Hannah dear.
Incidentally I will increase the amount of your monthly
check to ease the financial burden of his being with you. Also
I imagine that his grief at the loss of the business is rather*

*well known throughout the family and perhaps it has raised
a worrisome question in the minds of my young female relatives. Hannah, please let them all know that the loss will not
erase my earlier promises. The customary $1,000 for trousseau
expenses will continue as in the past so please assure all our
unmarried little chicks that Joseph has not ruined their lives.*

*My news is all good except that I am having trouble again
with my eyes as I had in New Orleans years ago. The headaches are the same as they were then but I am not doctoring.
I am far too busy in my pretty white wig and fetching knee
breeches. I am assured that this is the proper costume for
Queen's Counsel but I keep thinking that someone is playing
a great big prank and that I am making myself pretty ridiculous. One of these days I shall send you a picture of myself wearing silk stockings and a lovely silk gown. Show it to
no one! I warn you, you will not succeed in convincing anybody that you are proud of a brother who would attire himself
in this manner. I even wore this outfit into the Queen's presence, dear sister. My mission was to thank her for her kindness
to me and I assure you that I do thank her from the depths of
a grateful heart, but I kept wishing I was wearing a good
sensible broadcloth suit.*

*Three months from today I must appear at a breakfast in
my dear little buckled shoes and of course the gown and white
wig! Annually the Lord Chancellor gives a breakfast to the
leaders of the bar, and I'm sure it's very nice of him but, oh,
that white wig at breakfast. Wait till you see the picture of me
wearing it—*

The years. Nine of them had slipped away since he had asked
London if there was anything of his which she could use. He
had a new window now from which to gaze upon his city. The
new window looked upon a fashionable street near Buckingham
Palace.

Sometimes Natalie crossed the channel to spend a week or
two with him and he knew the joy of her presence at his table,
saw the admiration in the eyes of his guests. Even an English
house responded to the graceful touch of a Creole hostess, even

English servants felt that there might be something left to learn of elegance and perfection. But Natalie viewed London with nothing more than a kind tolerance.

"It is a fine, big city, beloved. That is all I can say for it."

So he visited Paris more times than Natalie visited London. Ninette had a suitor. His name was Henri de Bousignac and he was a captain in the French army.

Natalie said, "Is he not the youngest bore you ever met?"

"He does not bore me, darling. He is very well informed, very—"

"But, Judah, certainly girls do not marry because they are enchanted by a man's knowledge of what was in the morning paper."

"Perhaps Ninette does," he said thoughtfully. "She is not an ordinary girl."

"Neither was I but you were romantic."

"I knew what was in the morning paper."

"But you didn't talk about it. He does. As I say, you were romantic."

"My dear, army officers rank very high on the sentimental listings."

"This one is no Jeb Stuart," she said. "This one is a bore."

"Still if she loves him—"

"Loves him! Beloved, they walk in our little garden and do not kiss. They sit on the bench in full view of the windows. Never does he place his arm about her. Never does she reach for his hand."

Judah smiled. "When we first saw each other, darling, we were very young. They are not. The captain is thirty-two and Ninette is—"

"Don't say it."

"Very well, darling, but Ninette is not much younger than her captain."

"I know," Natalie said sadly. "I know. My mirror brings the news."

In the blackness of her hair two bright wings of silver gleamed, slanting back from her temples, accentuating the sweep of her eyebrows and giving an illusion of uplifted corners to the yellow eyes. The years had traced a delicate network of tiny lines across her eyelids and the smooth, white forehead had not been spared. And it gave him pleasure that she had not dyed her hair and that her pride was so great that she would not stoop to the cheap, obvious tricks of cosmeticians.

"My darling, throw your mirror away. I will tell you that you are beautiful."

She said, "It is easy for you to take the business of aging without protest, beloved. No one says of me that I look forty."

"And who says of me that—"

"The New York *Times*. Ninette has every paper that mentions you sent to her. She was so happy that Papa, according to the papers, looks and acts forty. Mama was not so happy, I will tell you. The correspondent who interviewed you must have thought I kidnaped and married you the day you were born."

"He was trying to be kind, Natalie. Surely I look my age."

"Surely you do not. I believe time has forgotten you and has ceased to mark the passing years upon you."

"A pleasant thought."

"Not to me. Age, beloved, just a little. Please."

He looked at Natalie, at the silver streaks in her hair, at the well-loved face that could never be less than beautiful. And he knew that he could plan now, could dream without fear.

"We will build a house," he said.

"A house! Who was talking about houses?"

"I am thinking aloud, Natalie. Would you not like a fine, new house?"

"Of course. Are we to have one?"

"Yes, darling. A house more beautiful than Belle Chasse, more elegant than the one in Washington."

"In London?" she asked and he saw disappointment in her eyes.

She must not be disappointed. Never. He shook his head. "No, darling, it will not be in London. We will build it in Paris. I will settle here. We will divide our time between our new house and small journeys to the Mediterranean. Would you like that, Natalie?"

"Beloved, I cannot wait."

"Only a little while yet, my darling."

Ninette was married in September from the Cathedral de Chaillot, and the De Bousignacs went at once to Orléans where the captain had been assigned.

"Curious, is it not, beloved? We began our life in New Orleans and they, the young ones, begin in what may be called Old Orleans." Natalie shook her head wonderingly. "It is a foolish observation of course, but somehow it seems to me that New Orleans would be too frivolous for that staid couple. They are quite amazing to me. They are not gay. They are not even light-hearted."

"In their way, Natalie, they are happy."

"In no way are they happy. They are only comfortable. Thank God, they do not know the difference. The capacity for delight exists in neither of them. All the way to Orléans he will be adding her dowry to the money my poor Papa left her and she will be reading Horace and Plato and—"

Judah laughed. "Somehow I do not believe that. Even a man who is very cautious about money and a girl who is an intellectual have been known to engage in emotional experiences."

"You know these De Bousignacs little, beloved. They are chilly people. But I shall miss Ninette. She was, after all, my baby."

"She will bring you a new baby some day soon, my darling."

Natalie sighed. "I will say again, beloved, you do not know the De Bousignacs. You do not know our daughter. She only thinks. She does not feel. Still, what shall I do without her? Who will explain to me the meaning of political occurrences or see that I am informed as to the latest volumes on matters I could not possibly understand?"

"The architects, the builders, and the decorators will keep you occupied, Natalie."

He purchased his land on Avenue d'Jena and the house was begun at once. He came monthly now to Paris to watch with growing excitement as the dream became reality. There were times, however, when the undertaking seemed full of disappointment and frustration. His sister Judith was building a house and her outcries against paid Negro labor amused him. She envied, she said, the reliable co-operation he would be receiving from sturdy, sensible white men.

> *My dear Judith:*
>
> *Oh, those sturdy, sensible white men. They are, as you say, so industrious, so dependable. Their industry in instituting strikes is the most remarkable I have ever seen and they can certainly be depended upon not to do a bit of work on my house. The plumbers, the carpenters, the gas-fitters, and the plasterers are all engaged in a devil's dance of wild confusion. I am seriously considering throwing away all the plans, retaining only the stables and coachman's quarters. The Benjamins would live with the horses and turn the rest of the grounds into one large rose garden. There is a danger however. The gardners might hear of my intentions. If so, they will certainly go on strike and ruin my rose garden—*

But in time it was completed. 41 Avenue d'Jena. A three-story stone house with marble stairways and shining banks of windows. He sat in his office in London and figured the cost. Eighty thousand dollars. And he could not remain seated, not when he had a house for which he had paid eighty thousand dollars. A man must give thanks where thanks were due and he went to his window and had a word with the city of London. Fourteen years ago he had come to her without a decent suit of clothes, and, considering the circumstances, a man could not be silent. London pressed a soft, moist hand against the pane. He raised the window and let her enter. And as she breathed upon his upturned face he spoke to her.

"Thank you," he said. "From the bottom of my heart, thank you." And after a moment he spoke again. "I know," he said. "I love you, too."

Joseph had sent him a copy of the New Orleans *Democrat* with an article outlined in red crayon. Judah read it with honest pleasure. Certain lines were starred for special attention. He read those first of course.

> *Always accustomed to do well and completely everything he undertook, Mr. Benjamin has been forced to reduce the*

amount of his labor within the compass of his wonderful ca-
pacity and industry. We doubt if these have ever been equaled
by any other aspirant for distinction and success at the English
or American bar. The briefs which he declines would make
another lawyer prosperous and famous. He is the recognized
head of the most exclusive and difficult institution in which
to attain prominence and success—the bar of England.

His chief clerk entered the room very quietly and stood waiting for attention. Judah raised his eyes from the New Orleans
newspaper and was not surprised that he did not see the trim
young man very clearly. It happened so frequently now that he
felt no alarm at the sudden stab of pain through his temples
and at the failure of vision.

"Are you still refusing all appointments for the day, sir?"

"Yes. Make none for tomorrow either. The medical profession
is never satisfied with one visit. I am quite certain that Sir James's
physician will seek to make a career of me."

"May I suggest, sir, that you speak to him of other matters
that do not seem to pertain to your eyes or the headaches?"

"What other matters?"

The young man said nothing for a moment, then spoke out
boldly. "Surely, sir, you have not forgotten that only last week
when you climbed the stairs too rapidly you reeled and—"

"An exaggeration. Reeled, indeed!"

"Your heart pounded. You could not breathe. I was terrified."

"Oh, I am sorry. My apologies."

"Sir, do tell these things to the doctor."

Judah had been right. Sir James's physician was not satisfied
with one visit. Only after half a dozen was he ready to reveal his
findings.

"There is no surgery, no medication that will assist in the
slightest, Mr. Benjamin. Only absolute rest will prolong your
life. The condition of your heart is—"

"Well, for the heart, of course, I can lie abed and still do a
great deal of work."

"No, sir. Your eyes will take no further abuse. If you persist
in using them they will give up the fight before your heart does."

Judah saw the physician waveringly and he stirred with impatience upon the hard chair which had been offered him.

"Very well. I shall rest. How long? A year? Two years?"

"Mr. Benjamin, I make it a point to speak the truth to patients who are strong-minded enough to accept the truth. I take it for granted that you would like to know exactly—"

Judah rose to his feet. "Sir," he said, "next week I appear in the House of Lords in the case of *Neill* versus *The Duke of Devonshire*. This case has been carried up from the Irish Court of Appeals. It is extremely interesting to me and has my attention to the exclusion of all other things."

He won the case. *Neill* versus *The Duke of Devonshire*. It was a good case to win. He smiled sadly thinking how good a case to win it had been. When it was over he went back to his office and called his chief clerk to him. There were final arrangements to make. Retainers to the amount of a hundred thousand dollars that must be returned. Announcements made. Farewells said. Oh, God, what a lot of nuisance accompanied the business of retiring.

He said, "Will you attend to it all for me, please? Just say that we are making no more appointments, taking no more briefs. Say that we are going out of business. Make it very clear that I have decided to retire."

The young man was weeping in a very well-bred English way. "Mr. Benjamin, sir, is there anything I can do?"

"Of course. I have just given you a whole list of things."

"I meant something more—more personal. Would I be of any use to you if I were to accompany you to the seashore or the Pyrenees or—"

"I appreciate your offer but I have decided to go to my home in Paris. My wife is there, you know."

His wife. Natalie, who detested illness. Natalie, to whom he had never turned for strength or sympathy. Natalie, the sundial who recorded only hours of brightness and warmth. It had been his mission to see that only the happy moments of life were hers to share.

He had thought of hotels and hospitals. In his mind he had fought a battle against cowardice and selfishness and he had lost. He could not face death alone. If Natalie were at his side, if he could see again the face that he had loved so long, so well, if he could once again feel her hand in his—

The bar of England honored him with a farewell dinner. Two hundred leaders of the legal world came to wish him happiness in his retirement. From his place of honor Judah gazed out at the faces of these men and suddenly they were not Britishers and this was not the Inner Temple. It was the St. Charles Hotel and tomorrow he would go to Washington as junior senator from Louisiana. And the speeches were full of praise and he waited for Slidell to speak.

Slidell, the road ahead leads only into the sunset and it is growing very late. Say something, Slidell.

But it was Charles Pollock speaking.

"I thought it a ridiculously detailed opinion to turn over to the London Metropolitan Police. 'Those chaps,' I thought, 'won't even see the point, he has hidden it so cleverly.' And I told my pupil that he had rather overshot the mark, but I had underestimated the London Metropolitan Police. To this day the opinion my pupil wrote is held in high esteem and referred to constantly—"

The Lord Advocate for Scotland spoke next. Then the Attorney General for Ireland followed by the Lord Chief Justice and the Earl of Shelbourne, Lord Chancellor.

The picture had changed again. Now it was the house on Condé Street and these men were Roselius, Slidell, Mazureau, Soulé, and Grymes.

God knows why they came. I am nobody but they do not seem aware of that.

He was filled with gratitude and amazement that none had refused an invitation to this first dinner that he and Natalie had given together. She looked so lovely in the deep-red velvet—

"The years are few since Mr. Benjamin was a stranger to us all and in those few years he has accomplished more than most can ever hope in a lifetime to achieve. Gentlemen, the health of Mr. Benjamin!"

And there were cheers and applause and he rose when they called for a word. He spoke his thanks and his farewell but he never remembered what he said to the men of the Inner Temple.

Oh, Natalie, my darling, I never meant to grow old and weak. Forgive me for coming to you now with burdens and sorrow. I cannot crawl away and die alone. Only smile at me and hold my hand, my darling. I have forgotten how to fight. Please, Natalie—

There was more applause and handshakes, tears, kind words. Someone had an arm about his shoulder. Slidell? No, no, of course not. Slidell was dead.

Everyone was leaving. A dozen of Britain's most distinguished men escorted him to his carriage.

"Home, Mr. Benjamin?" the coachman asked.

"Yes, home," he said. "I am afraid the festivities are over."

Nine

PARIS

❦

She was an old acquaintance, Paris. Different from the day
Judah had first seen her, more spectacular, more breath-taking.
The world had never known such boulevards and parks as those
which Louis Napoleon had bought for his city. They were his
monuments. Louis Napoleon. Dead for many a year now, the
man who had worn Napoleon's name with the comical effect of
any small nephew trying on his uncle's hat. He was gone. This
was the Third Republic and Paris lay cool and indifferent to the
deeds of monarchs or presidents.

Judah, gazing from his carriage window, thought of the many
times he had come to this city as a visitor. Paris, the brilliant
center of legend and dream. Strange how he had never given her
his full attention, had never responded to the spell she cast on
others. Paris to him had been only the city in which Natalie
lived. A village anywhere in the world would have been as
appealing if it had numbered Natalie among its residents. She
was here and he was on his way to her once more. He was going
home to 41 Avenue d'Jena. Paris was his city now and there
was no need to ask of her: What will happen here? No need at
all to ask the question.

Natalie had been watching for him from her window. When he
entered the foyer she was halfway down the marble stairs.

"Judah." She came to him, her arms outstretched in glad
greeting. "Welcome home once more, beloved."

The coachman carried his valise upstairs. Judah followed unhurriedly, remembering that stairs were enemies, haste, an agent of death. Natalie held his hand, artfully slowing her pace to his.

"Was your journey pleasant?"

"The channel was rough as usual but I have gotten accustomed to its playfulness. It does not bother me."

"I am not sure I believe you," she said and turned to gaze searchingly at him. "You do not look as fit as you might, beloved. Are you sure the channel did not—"

"Well, maybe it did a little," he said.

She laughed. "You experienced travelers are always ashamed to admit that you have even noticed the channel. I can't think why." She led the way to her sitting room. "What would you like, beloved? Wine? Coffee?"

"Nothing now, Natalie. I will just sit here and look at you, if you don't mind. What were you doing?"

"I was embroidering." She reached for her work and displayed it a little self-consciously. "The refuge of a woman who never had a mind for books and has lost interest in her mirror."

"What is it? A table cover?"

"Yes. It is intended for use beneath a vase of roses. One is supposed to work the pattern so realistically that it will be supposed a rose has dropped from the vase." She bent above the embroidery frowning critically. "I do not think my effort will deceive anyone."

"You remind me of Madame," he said. "Always I think of her with embroidery in her hands."

"I, too, remember her that way." Natalie sighed. "She seemed so old to me, so finished with life. Do you realize that when you first saw her busy with embroidery she was only thirty-three years old?"

"And she was not at all finished with life. Jules was yet to be born."

Natalie nodded. "Yes, poor, darling Jules." With a sudden, quick gesture she tossed the embroidery aside. "What a dreary conversation and you on holiday, beloved. Tell me some London gossip. Tell me anything that is bright and amusing. You know how I detest being dreary."

"Yes, I know well, my darling."

And he knew now he would use none of the little speeches he had planned. He had phrased them gravely, matter-of-factly, and there was even one with a slight touch of ironic humor about it. Carefully he had gone over each of them, trying to make a choice. Which would be the best to offer Natalie? What approach would prepare her for widowhood with the least pain, the smallest bruise upon a spirit that had no experience with heartache? But now, looking into that calm, untroubled face, he knew there were no words that would be right to offer her. Why must she be invited to meet sorrow halfway? It would come soon enough. Surely the tears could wait.

He said, "I know one piece of London gossip."

"Good. Do tell me."

"A certain lawyer of some prominence has retired from the bar. He intends to live for the rest of his life in Paris with his adored wife."

Her eyes opened wide. "Judah! Truly? You? Oh, beloved." She flung her arms around him and hugged him wildly. "Such exciting news. Let us plan to do nothing but marvelous things. Let us be the most frivolous old people alive, living for nothing but music and ballet and travel and—" She paused to laugh like a delighted child. "I know I sound like an idiot but you took me by surprise and I am a little mad with happiness."

On his second night in Paris he took Natalie to the theater. It would be, she said, step one in their new and wonderful life together. He dressed with especial attention to detail, staring solemnly into his jewel box, choosing studs and links as though a momentous decision were in the making. He chose the star sapphires Natalie had given him one birthday. No, he remembered now they could not be worn. One of the cuff links had come apart. It would have to be repaired. Repaired? Why? Well, perhaps Henri de Bousignac would some day leave the army. Tonight he would wear the pearls.

Natalie in cream-colored satin that suited her well. In her hair a diamond coronet he had brought her once from Washington and around her throat the necklace that had been selected in August Belmont's ballroom. She had kept her slimness, and he thought as he looked at her that she had not been lovelier at twenty. And he knew that this was the truth, for she was Natalie and the enchantment was forever, unchanging and unchangeable.

At this late date I will not try to analyze her charms, but those long gloves which are intended to create an air of elegance for their wearer are outshone by the grace with which she moves her arms. The gown is distinguished by the way she wears it, and surely there cannot be another woman to whom a diamond coronet must be grateful for its fine appearance.

And he thought of Madame, who had never been drab even in deepest mourning, and of Jules, who could transform a clerk's alpaca coat into a stylish garment simply by slipping into it.

In the theater he observed that people still stared at Natalie. More women now then men. She was aware of the glances and wryly amused by them.

"For years I was so pleased that I was still admired. I said to myself, 'You see, Natalie, you are as young and gorgeous as ever.' Then I happened to overhear a remark one evening that did little for my vanity. I heard a young girl say to her escort, 'Mrs. Benjamin is such a beautiful old lady.' "

He reached for her hand and held it within his own as the theater darkened and the curtain rose. His head had begun to ache and he could not see the actors very clearly but he could feel the fragrant warmth of Natalie beside him.

The evening was a success. She loved the play and he had managed to sit through the late supper, to eat a little, to drink a little, to act like a man who had no pain. There would not be another theater for them or another late supper. She would have to remember this for all the rest of time.

In the morning he did not arise but had his breakfast brought to him, and when Natalie came to his bedroom and gazed in curiosity at this phenomenon he smiled at her reassuringly.

"Perhaps it is still the channel which I was reluctant to admit upset me or perhaps I am just tired."

She said, "You look tired, beloved. You really do."

"Then I shall remain in bed. Possibly for the entire day."

"Oh, do. I will read to you. Would you like that?"

"Yes, indeed."

She brought a book, the newspapers, and her fancy work, and settled down comfortably for a quiet day of entertaining him.

"Oh," she said opening the newspaper, "here is something that

will interest you. Robert Toombs is very ill. He is not expected
to recover. The Confederacy's first secretary of state, it says. He
was, of course. I had forgotten. I hope the news does not sadden
you, beloved."

He shook his head. "It is as though I had not known him,
Natalie. It was another Benjamin, in another world who knew
Robert Toombs."

Another world indeed, and so many of its inhabitants dead
now. Little Vice-President Stephens. Clement Clay, the earnest
Alabaman who always did his duty the moment his wife told
him what it was. Randolph, Seddon, Breckenridge—my successors
in the War Department. Davis's favorite generals, the blunderers,
Bragg and Hood. Lee, the great Virginian. Poor Mallory, who
liked wild flowers. The famous duo that for a little moment in
history caused England to tremble on the brink of war, Mason
and Slidell. Slidell.

"You know, beloved, I was just thinking of Mr. Davis—how
ill he was so many years ago, how dreadfully Varina worried
about his health."

Judah smiled. "Yes, I remember well how precarious was the
health of Mr. Davis, but somehow he has managed to outlive
everyone who was feeling fine."

"Yes, even with serving two terrible years in prison. Have you
read his book on the Confederacy, beloved?"

"No." He stared in wonderment at Natalie. "How did you
happen to hear of it? Certainly you did not read it."

She smiled. "Not likely. I was told of it by Ninette. Incidentally, she was furious at his offhand treatment of her father."

"I am sorry she was disappointed."

"I did not say she was disappointed. I said she was furious. It
seemed odd indeed to her, considering the distinguished positions
you had held, that you drew no more notice from Davis than
Postmaster General Reagan."

Judah said, "It does not matter."

"No, I suppose not. Shall I read the article on Toombs to
you?"

"Read the news of Paris, Natalie. We are here and it is today."

She did not go downstairs for dinner. A table was set in the alcove of his bedroom, and she took a childish delight in the preparations.

"It is fun, is it not, beloved? Rather like a tea party. When I was a child I would sometimes be served upstairs and I always considered it rather an occasion. But did you say you wanted only a chop? What has become of your appetite, beloved?"

"It will return when I am rested."

"You need a good rest. You have worked so hard for so many years. If I were you I would not stir tomorrow either."

In the morning he reminded her of what she had said. "You have convinced me that meals upstairs are exciting and I have completely swallowed the notion that I need a good rest, so today—"

"Good. I shall read to you again."

"Perhaps for a time. But today will differ from yesterday in two minor matters. One, I shall lie on the sofa instead of the bed. Two, you will go for a ride or a walk or a visit. You cannot remain closed away from the spring sunshine for another full day."

"I am to be driven from your side? Oh, no. Tomorrow I shall bask in the sunshine if you will permit me to remain indoors today."

It was a week before he saw the yellow eyes begin to cloud with anxiety. He had spent most of his time on the sofa, assuring her that he was but yieldng to a long-hidden streak of laziness.

"It is wonderful to lie here and look at you and have nothing in the world that needs my attention."

Her head was low over her embroidery. He could not see her eyes. "It is a good thing for you to rest," she said, "but I am not pleased about your lack of appetite. You need a tonic and I shall see that you get one."

"Something that tastes horrible, I suppose. A mess of dreadful herbs, half-poison, half-magic such as Madame used to—"

"I would doubt that," she said. "The doctor is not from Louisiana. He is a Parisian."

"The doctor! No, Natalie, no. I do not need a doctor. You have not sent for him, have you? I will not see him."

She looked up from her embroidery. "Beloved, when a man

like you wants only to lie upon a sofa and to eat no more than you have eaten then it is time to see a doctor."

"I am fatigued, Natalie. Nothing more."

"In all probability," she said, "but in that case a tonic will help."

"I do not need a tonic. Tomorrow I will be up and about. As a matter of fact I was going to suggest that we take a short drive this afternoon."

"Not this afternoon," she said. "The doctor is coming."

Send word that we do not want him, my darling. There is still time. Still a little time. Perhaps there is another week or two in which we can continue to play that all is well. Once you are told—once you know— And is it for you I want the secrecy preserved? Or am I afraid that you cannot live with the realization of death, that you will disappear from this room, coming back only occasionally to bid me the time of day? Who am I protecting, Natalie? You or myself?

In the late afternoon the doctor was brought upstairs to him and Natalie left them alone. The doctor was no more than forty. A very young man. He used a British tailor, Judah observed, and his speech was peppered with English words which he tossed off airily. One could not expect understanding from so young a man or for that matter from a Frenchman who would rather be English.

"Now what is the main complaint, Mr. Benjamin?"

Judah said, "I am dying."

The doctor smiled. "I would doubt that, but I know what you mean—you feel continually tired? Disinterested in food? Generally weak and listless?"

"Exactly, doctor. As I say, I am dying."

The doctor looked up from the black leather bag and paused in the routine of withdrawing articles that he thought might prove useful.

"You say that very strangely, Mr. Benjamin."

"Sit down, please. I hope you will not think me disrespectful of your opinion if I tell you that no examination is necessary. My case has been under very thorough consideration in London and there I received the news that I cannot hope for recovery."

"I am very sorry, sir. Your wife—"

"She does not know. She is not to know till deception is no longer possible. Will you assist me in keeping her ignorant of the true facts?"

The doctor tilted his head to the side and pursed his lips thoughtfully. "I am ignorant of the true facts myself, Mr. Benjamin. Physicians are not in the habit of taking a patient's word as the ultimate and—"

"Give me a tonic, will you? Something simple and evil-smelling that will assure her that—"

"I can give you nothing, sir. I do not know your condition."

"I have told you I am dying."

"This might be the regrettable truth, Mr. Benjamin, but I do not know it of my own knowledge."

Judah sighed and took off his dressing gown. "Proceed, sir. Make the examination."

It was not possible that her hair was whiter than it had been only a month ago. Yet it seemed whiter. She moved so quietly through the room, her perfume drifting faintly, delightfully to him as he lay upon the sofa.

"It is time for your tonic, beloved."

He raised himself slightly and she smiled at him. He swallowed the medicine and grimaced.

"I guess it was not the channel," he said, "or plain fatigue. I probably contracted some illness on the boat. I mention it because I am now willing to admit that I am a great nuisance."

"You, beloved?" Natalie patted his cheek lightly. "You could not be a nuisance."

"Natalie, I think I shall be weaker before I am stronger again. You must hire someone to—"

"Hire someone? Am I then discharged? Good heavens, beloved, I thought I was doing such a magnificent job of nursing. I was telling myself that Florence Nightingale couldn't have done better."

"Natalie, darling, when I rise from this sofa I can scarcely reach the bed."

She knelt beside him and put her arms around him. "Judah, three of our servants are men and they will be glad to help you. One of them will be kept upstairs all the time, right outside your

door. You will have him to lean on. For all else I will, I think,
be adequate. Do not ask for, do not wish for me to let a stranger
take my place." She raised her head from his shoulder and
smiled. "I am a jealous woman, beloved, and you are mine."

He closed his eyes and lay still and he was not sure whether
or not he dozed. It was often difficult to know sleep from reality.
She was across the room from him now, sitting silently in the
white velvet chair, her pink frock pale in the dim room. She
never seemed to leave. She was always there. Natalie, my darling,
will you still be there when you know the truth? You who are
repelled by all that is somber and grievous, will you be there
when it is impossible for you to be further deceived? Will you
smile at me then, my darling? No, it is too much to hope that
you who served no apprenticeship in the school of heartache will
know how to smile. But she was there now and he must make
the most of it.

"Natalie."

"Yes, beloved?"

"I am awake and I will seize upon the occasion to say that I
love you."

"You took the words right out of my mouth, Judah. I was
just thinking how much I love you and that I have some delightful news."

"Tell me."

"Do you remember that couple we used to know? I think their
name was De Bousignac—well, they are coming to visit us.
Isn't that lovely?"

Thank You, dear God. I have so wanted to see my daughter
again. How could I ask for her without alarming Natalie? Now
You are sending her to me and I am grateful. Thank You,
thank You.

"It is ages since Henri has had a vacation—I don't suppose one
calls it a vacation from the army—but whatever it is he has finally
gotten it. They will probably be able to stay quite a while."

"That will be splendid."

And so he held her in his arms again, his daughter, who had
the look of the Mendes women. And he clasped the hand of her
husband and felt within himself the knowledge that all was
well with them. They talked in their quiet, serious way about

the army and about the future of France, and Natalie said, "You are boring me. I want to show you the garden."

And she whisked them away and Judah smiled a little to himself. The army and the future of France had not completely caught his interest either. He could no longer imagine next year or next month. Not even tomorrow. Fortunate that Natalie had so boldly stated her boredom. He might have fallen asleep as Henri spoke to him—still, Henri was no guest. He was one of the family.

And he thought about his family in America. Many of its members no longer lived. Many of its members he had never seen, but the last promises had been kept. He had educated all whose fathers could not afford the luxury of education. None of his blood had been neglected, none had known the humiliating experience of turning to a stranger for assistance.

Natalie? That was different. There was no way to part from a wife. There was no clean-cut conclusion such as one found in the successful marriage of a daughter. Consolation must be found in the knowledge that she would have the means to travel, to entertain, to buy whatever it was one bought when time has made all things valueless.

We should have had five years together. They would have been such wonderful years. Even three years. Or one. I should have given myself the chance to sit watching her as she embroidered, to smile remembering that the "beautiful old lady" is the girl who told me the story of Bouki and the macaques. We should have laughed together, and I would have felt great happiness sitting here with her in the sweet calm of the quiet years. I stayed too long in London. Too long. And now there is nothing.

Nothing? There was the nearness of the only woman who had ever had his love. There was her smile and the touch of her cool hand upon his forehead. And that would last yet for a day or two. It would last till the gay Louisianian who still lived behind those yellow eyes removed herself from the dreary process of what was happening in this room.

Don't go, Natalie. Don't leave me, Natalie!

And she was there. "You called, beloved?"

"I do not think so."

She came to his side and smiled down at him and he saw that though she smiled her eyes were wet. He saw that it was true, her hair was whiter and the lines in her face more deeply etched. And he saw that she had not been deceived.

"Oh, Natalie, my darling. My poor darling."

Her arms were about him, holding him tenderly to her heart. "Beloved, are you in pain?"

"Not now, Natalie."

She kissed him gently and she said, "I will always be near. You never need call again. I will be within a whisper of you."

"I love you, my darling. I love you."

"Think then, Judah, how much I must love you, for after many years love strikes a perfect balance with that which one has received and I have received everything."

And to assume that she meant jewels or houses would be to deny the sorrow that he had seen in her eyes.

"I am always proud when I hear people say you have the greatest mind of your time, beloved. I know it to be the truth, but I know something else, something they do not know. I know you to have the most understanding heart."

And his mind went back many years to a night when he had stood in a small room in New Orleans and had told his God that he would marry Natalie St. Martin. And he had prayed that night for the strength to accept her as she was and never to expect her to be that which she was not. And his prayers had been answered. Nothing that he had asked had been forgotten, for on that night he had also prayed that he would love Natalie always as he loved her then.

"Beloved, I have not the words to say how much, how very much I love you."

It was true. It had always been true. She loved him. In the small room in New Orleans he had not dared to ask for this. But it had been granted to him. Natalie's love. And he knew that it had been given to no other man, and those who thought that love and her hungry sister were interchangeable or even bore a resemblance knew little indeed and were pitiful fools.

"Do not weep, Natalie."

"Was I weeping?"

"Yes, my darling. Dry your tears. I cannot bear to see you sad, for I think I am happier tonight than I have ever been."

He went no more to lie upon the sofa. The need for pretense

had passed. Natalie sat beside him reading aloud when he wished to listen. Mostly she remained silent but ready for conversation when he desired it. Ninette and Henri were never far away. They visited his room and he was aware of the signal that Natalie gave just a split second before he tired of them. The doctor came, too. The young man in the British-tailored clothes. He came with medicines that made it possible to return Natalie's smile, to know moments when the newspaper interested him, to even laugh a little, occasionally.

And there was a morning when he heard Natalie astir in the room, felt her presence, and breathed the fragrance of her perfume. He knew he was awake and it seemed that a heaviness had left him, that here at last was a day in which he could say quite truthfully that he felt better. Still, there was a strangeness. His eyes had no wish to open. His limbs were content to rest where they were.

Natalie kissed him and spoke in her low, sweet voice to him.

Why do I not answer? I have the words but not the wish to utter them. She will understand. She will know that I am speaking to her in my mind. Later I will tell her what I thought as I lay here.

And it was a day on which Ninette and Henri came to the room. The doctor as well. And after a while he heard Natalie speak and an unfamiliar voice replied to her. To whom did that voice belong? It was a cultured voice. Beautiful French. Who was it? And why had a stranger come? It would be simple, he supposed, to open his eyes, to sit up, to discover for himself the identity of his visitor, but he had not that much curiosity. To lie quietly was such comfort, such joy. Who would have guessed at so profound a truth, that life offers nothing better than rest when one is weary?

The conversation continued in subdued tones and he took pleasure in hearing the gentle, cultured voice of the visitor. It did not matter what was being said. He had not even searched for significance in the words that reached his ears. But now suddenly there was meaning and he understood.

"But, daughter, I have no reason to believe your husband is a Catholic."

"You must take my word, Father. He attended the St. Louis Cathedral with me in New Orleans. Also St. Aloysius's in Wash-

ington. It was in New Orleans that he became a convert. It was
there that—"

"I have known of Judah Benjamin for many years but never
did I hear that he was of the church."

"Why should you hear it? It is a thing not generally discussed.
Why—why, his religion meant so much to him that he did not
live it on the front pages of newspapers."

Natalie, it was Jeb Stuart of whom I said that. And, darling,
do not lie to the priest. You know I am not a Catholic.

"He did not attend mass. I never saw him at church. Daughter, tell me truthfully why you are pretending that your poor
husband is a Catholic."

"I am not pretending. You must believe me. You must, Father."

Now you are crying, my darling. Don't, please, don't. The
priest is right and you are wrong. Admit it and he will forgive
you for lying to him.

"Do you wish to pray with me, daughter?"

"Later. Now I wish you to administer to my dear husband.
Please, in the name of the Virgin, Father, don't go until you
have—"

"I am perplexed. Never before have I—"

"Never before have you been called by a sorrowing wife?
Father, I beg of you, do not go from this room without—"

"He is unconscious, but all the same do you not think that a
rabbi should be summoned?"

"A rabbi? Father, you do not know what you say. He was a
Jew. Yes, my husband was a Jew, but when he married me he
was not forgiven. I was not worth his sacrifice. Never, Father, never
was I worth it. He married me knowing full well that he would
not rest with his people. I have read that he must die without
a prayer—he must lie in ground that is sacred to no one."

"It is sad. Very sad. But the excommunication of your husband
from his church does not inevitably make him a Catholic."

"No. No, of course not. Don't you understand? He studied
Catholicism and embraced it wholeheartedly. It was his wish
and of course mine, too, for we must be buried side by side. In
life we were often separated. In death it must not be so. Father,
let him lie where men will pray for him. Let him wait for me
with my parents at the Cemetery of Père Lachaise. Let him rest
where I can go to him when a world without him is more than

I can bear. Do not send him away without a prayer, I beg of you. Please, Father. Please."

And there was a silence in the room, and Judah suddenly felt upon his eyelids a light touch and he heard words spoken in Latin by the cultured voice. And in his mind Judah translated what he heard.

"Through this holy unction, and of His most tender mercy, may the Lord pardon thee whatsoever sins thou hast committed by sight."

His ears, nostrils, lips, and hands anointed and prayed for. His feet, too, the feet that remembered King Street in Charleston, the warmth of Louisiana's sugar land, the floors of the United States Senate, and the carpet upon which one stood to bow to Queen Victoria.

"Through this holy unction, and of His most tender mercy, may the Lord pardon thee whatsoever sins thou hast committed by thy footsteps. Amen."

Natalie, my darling, may the Lord pardon thee if it was a mortal sin to deceive the good father and to falsely secure intercession for me. But surely He will understand what you have done and why you did it. And now I will lie where men will pray for me. Because you love me I will not go without a prayer, and so the last fear, the last doubt has been removed, my darling, and there is nothing left to dread. For in the end there is but one God and Beth-Hiam can be no different to Him than the Cemetery of Père Lachaise.

Natalie was weeping. For what reason? Soulé and Mazureau and Grymes and Roselius had all accepted the invitations. No one had refused. Slidell would be there, too. The dinner was going magnificently. Who would have guessed that Natalie could be depended upon? He had expected nothing from her—nothing. Natalie in deep-red velvet— No, she could not wear that gown for he was dying and he would be buried from the Cathedral de Chaillot. It was a pity that Natalie must wear black. But a widow in deep-red velvet would look very odd on the steps of the Cathedral—the steps of the Cathedral—

AKNOWLEDGMENTS

In assembling this material the works of many people known to Mr. Benjamin were consulted, and those that proved useful were: *My Diary North and South* by W. H. Russell; *Jefferson Davis, a Memoir* by his wife; *A Belle of the Fifties* by Mrs. Virginia Clay-Clopton; *A Diary from Dixie* by Mary Boykin Chesnut; *Recollections Grave and Gay* by Mrs. Burton Harrison (Connie Cary); *Rise and Fall of the Confederate Government* by Jefferson Davis; *A Rebel War Clerk's Diary* by J. B. Jones.

Additional sources of the period were: *Richmond during the War* by a Richmond Lady; *Life of Jefferson Davis with a Secret History of the Confederacy* by E. A. Pollard and Mr. Pollard's *The Lost Cause: A Southern Girl in '61* by Mrs. D. Giraud Wright; *The Tribute Book* by Frank Goodrich.

Military information was furnished by *Stonewall Jackson and the American Civil War* by G. F. R. Henderson; *R. E. Lee* by Douglas Southall Freeman; *Lee's Lieutenants* by Douglas Southall Freeman.

Among the books that provided the background of Mr. Benjamin's New Orleans years were: *New Orleans: The Place and the People* by Grace King; *New Orleans: Its Old Houses, Shops and Public Buildings* by Nathaniel Courtland Curtis; *La Fitte the Pirate* by Lyle Saxon; *Creole City* by E. L. Tinker; *The Romantic New Orleanians* by Robert Tallant; and those wonderful books *New Orleans City Guide* and *Louisiana* of the American Guide Series.

The Jews of Charleston by Charles Reznikoff and Uriah Z. Engelman was in frequent use while compiling the Charleston sequence. And *The Diary of George Templeton Strong*, edited by Nevins and Thomas, was very helpful in reference to the New York visits of Mr. Benjamin.

Help came from many authors and their works. The ones that cannot be omitted are: *The Confederate States of America* by E. Merton Coulter; *Beauregard: The Great Creole* by Hamilton Basso; *The Story of the Confederacy* by Robert Selph Henry; *Dan Sickles* by E. Pinchon; *Conflict* by G. F. Melton; *Disloyalty in the Confederacy* by Georgia Lee Tatum; *Jeb Stuart* by John Thomason.

It has been left to the last to acknowledge four books that were indispensable in the writing of this novel. *Statesmen of the Lost Cause* by B. J. Hendrick, and *Experiment in Rebellion* by Clifford Dowdey are two of these. The others are the fine biographies *Judah P. Benjamin, Confederate Statesman* by Robert Douthat Meade, and *Judah P. Benjamin* by Pierce Butler.

much had been accomplished because he had done his best and had recognized the unimportant things for what they were. Here he must do the same.

He worked even harder at Yale than at Fayetteville. A fourteen-year-old freshman held a position that was painfully peculiar. To be an average student was insufficient. One must constantly, unfalteringly demonstrate for faculty and student body alike the quality of one's mind.

The Reverend Jeremiah Day, president of Yale, invited Judah to the study of his red brick house.

"I wanted to see you, young man. I've heard fine things of you."

President Day was a heavy-set, gray-haired man garbed in faultlessly-fitted black broadcloth. His voice boomed richly with pulpit inflections. His commanding manner was such that Judah thought President Day could easily found a new religion and garner a million converts if the fancy seized him.

"So you are from Charleston? A magnificent city. It is years since I have had the pleasure of visiting it but I still remember its beauty and charm. Tell me, young man, what are you learning from us here in New Haven?"

Judah swallowed nervously. "Sir, I am taking—"

"Oh, I know your courses. It has, however, been my sad observation that Latin and logarithms fade from one's mind when college days are done. What are we teaching you that will prevail through later life? What are we giving you that will assist in building your character, that will accompany you through long, weary years, giving you strength and courage?"

Judah raised his eyes to the comfortably rounded face of President Day. "Sir, I am learning how to bear my burdens."

"Good. Good. Excellent."

The major burden was the young man with the buck teeth. Three times a day Judah sat at table with him and never without wondering if the ordeal could be avoided.

Could I live without coming to the dining room? Could I feed myself on bread and cake upstairs? What a difference it would make to me if I never had to see him. The others, the ones who laughed at his jokes could be endured. In themselves they were nothing, only garden variety sycophants. Alone they would have been harmless nonentities, but they had been enlisted and drilled by the young man with the buck teeth.

"Over the summer," Bucktooth said, "I'm going to train a monkey to enter Yale next semester." He had finished his dinner and was in a mood for banter.

"A monkey?" someone prompted.

"Why not? It will not be hard on the little fellow. He will be so thick-skinned that he won't object to being where he is obviously not wanted. Certainly Yale will have no objections. They take everything. They take children and they take—" He leaned across the table and peered at Judah. "Do you know you ate pork tonight?"

"Very kind of you to have noticed."

"I always notice you, Benjamin. You interest me."

There was laughter, the perfunctory laughter of people who anticipate the great amusement to come.

"Why did you choose Yale, Benjamin?"

"It was recommended to me by one who admired the institution so greatly that he advised me to overlook the type of person that might be encountered here."

The young man with the buck teeth jumped to his feet. "You're asking for a thrashing, you know. I can't punch a baby but I can spank one. How would you like to have your backside turned up for a strapping?"

Judah felt a sickening wave of fear rise within him. For a moment he did not recognize the sensation. It was new and it was awful, the dryness of the mouth, the icy prickling of his skin, the desire to run.

Why did I answer him so impudently? Why did I not ignore him or give him a soft answer? But if I had done so, would I now be happy? No, I would be ashamed instead of frightened, and that is misery, too.

The dining room was swimming before him and he was trembling, but he rose from the table.

"If you wish to thrash me, come do it—if you can."

They stared at him, all six of them, and there was silence in the room. He could hear the rapid thud of his heart and the sickening fear within him had not abated. There would be pain when the strap fell upon his bare bottom and he prayed that he would not cry out for mercy.

It was as clean as any room in his mother's house. His trunk and his possessions were here, a good fireplace in the corner of the room, a chair, a table, a chest of drawers, a lamp. What more did he need?

There was a sharp rap upon his door and there stood Bacon with a pleasant smile.

"May I come in? My name is Francis Bacon."

"Oh, do come in, please. Yes, I know your name. I caught it in conversation. I am Judah Benjamin. Sit down. Take the chair. I will sit upon the bed."

They seated themselves but words did not come in a brisk interchange. There was a reticence, a slight discomfort evident in Bacon's manner.

When he spoke it was hesitatingly. "I—I would not make a point of this matter, Benjamin, except that it was raised at the dinner table. I was able to control it then but it will be mentioned again and if you know about it—well, you may be saved embarrassment.

Judah was puzzled. "I don't understand."

"Here in New England there has been a recent upsurge of—I mean to say there are organizations being formed. They are new but quite popular and most of our well-known people are putting money into—Benjamin, it's a cause which will work for abolition."

"Abolition of what?"

Bacon stared in wide-eyed disbelief. "Abolition of slaves, Benjamin."

"Oh." Judah considered the matter. "I never heard of such a thing. How does the organization function? What does it intend? Abolition means to do away with, to destroy. Your father wouldn't kill the poor creatures, would he?"

Bacon's eyes flashed but his voice was steady. "I said abolition of slaves, Benjamin, not of Negroes."

"Your pardon. I see you thought me facetious. Truly I did not understand. This is a new idea to me and one that seems as practical as abolishing horses—your pardon again—I mean as practical as abolishing the necessity for horses to work."

"People are not horses, Benjamin."

"This is incontestable. Actually I own no horses and no slaves."

Bacon smiled his pleasure. "I congratulate you on having your conscience clear of such a weight. Of course my principles would permit you a horse."

They laughed together, Bacon sobering to remark, "I would not have you insulted in case you or yours were slaveholders."

"You are very kind, Bacon." There now, that was better. They had laughed together. Oh, it would take time but New England reserve would yield eventually and there would be conversation and cordiality. Already a pattern was beginning to form. Bacon would be his friend and gradually the others would accept him, too. It required only patience. Even now he felt comfortable enough with his visitor to inquire into the strange incident that had occurred in the dining room.

"That young man whose father and brother are both Yale graduates—" he began.

Bacon said, "The same is true of myself, by the way."

"Really? I wanted to ask—what dissatisfied him at table? What was he scolding the landlady for?"

Bacon flushed hotly. "Benjamin, I entreat you to put the matter from your mind. He is immature and overtalkative. A good chap who has not yet come to terms with his deeper self."

Judah averted his eyes from Bacon's unhappy, red face. "This is more distressing to you than to me, I know, but since I have so awkwardly blundered into this we must complete it. His displeasure was caused by my presence, I see. Is it that I am not a Christian?"

"He will forget by tomorrow that he has even mentioned it."

"Will he?" Judah considered. "Tell me, Bacon, have you ever known a minister well enough to ask a question of him?"

"My brother is a minister."

"Then ask why it is that the men closest to God can accept and even respect those of another faith while the ordinary churchgoer, who professes to esteem the beliefs of his minister, will often be a narrow-minded bigot?"

"My brother cannot answer that question," Bacon said. "He has often asked it of himself and of my father."

After Bacon had gone Judah stretched out upon the bed and determinedly kept his mind upon the fact that after all he was where he had wanted to be. For four long years every deed, every thought had been directed toward this day. He was at Yale. That